Blood Moon

Blood Moon
The Bad Moon Rising Series

Johnny Bryan Ward

Beyond Thought Productions

Blood Moon
©Copyright 2015 by Johnny Bryan Ward

Acknowledgments

This book is dedicated to my granddaughter Adelyn.

I would like to thank my husband and best friend, Clay, for his tireless support and effort in helping to keep me focused and inspired on this writing journey. He lets me bounce ideas off him and edits my work with a most critical eye. Thank you babe for helping to make me a better, more detail oriented author. I love you.

Thanks to the beta readers David Edkins, Nataya Bostic, Lupe Ortiz-Tovar and Clay Finck. Your input and insight into this world I am creating is invaluable and your honesty is refreshing.

To Lori, thank you for copy editing not only Blood Moon, but Blue Moon as well. Your critical eye is extremely appreciated and your professionalism is top-notch.

A special thank you to Nate L. and Jennifer Renee' Spangler of Blanc Kanvas Art Productions for the beautiful and creative character artwork. You can view the artwork on www.JohnnyBryanWard.com.

Thanks to Brandy Walker, of Sister Sparrow Graphic Design for another amazing book cover.

To continue following me and my journey, please visit **www.JohnnyBryanWard.com** and sign up for news and updates. You can also follow me on Facebook, Twitter, Instagram and Pinterest.

Prologue

Luke 8:30
And Jesus asked him, "What is your name?" and he said, "Legion"; for many demons had entered him.

Ephesians 6:12
For our struggle is not against flesh and blood, but against the rulers, against the powers, against the world forces of this darkness, against the spiritual forces of wickedness in the heavenly places.

Job 24:17
For the morning is the same to him as thick darkness, for he is familiar with the terrors of thick darkness.

Revelation 6:12
I looked when He broke the sixth seal, and there was a great earthquake; and the sun became black as sackcloth made of hair, and the whole moon became like blood;

Acts 2:20
The sun will be turned into darkness and the moon into blood, before the Lord shall come.

Chapter One

Victor was doing as the master ordered, although he wasn't happy to be leaving his side. What did salvage his ego was the master entrusting him with this secret, one that had ramifications beyond this evenings' events. The master trusted him, but told only him what his next move was. He knew he would fulfill the master's wishes down to the smallest of details.

Gina was still unconcsious. Victor wasn't sure what the master did to her to make her sleep but he was glad he didn't have to deal with her struggling and trying to use magic on him. This gave him time to think about the best way to get her out of the house.

The Balashon had a private jet in the hanger at the Richard Lloyd Jones Riverside Airport near Jenks. If Victor could get her to the airport and into the jet, he would be able to get them out of the country and to one of the European estates. According to the master, Gina was the ultimate insurance plan. The fact the master sensed this in her astounded him. He was going to be a just and benevolent leader to those loyal to the Balashon, but will strike a deadly blow when needed. This was a gift laid in their hands and the master was taking advantage of it.

There was risk that came with Victor leaving the master to fight the male witch Demetri and the vampire

Aldrik, but he felt confident the master would smite them both down with little effort.

Victor didn't think he needed to grab anything other than some paperwork and scrolls that were essential to the sacrificial rituals. He had an ancient Balashon grimoire, used by witches employed many years ago to come up with these rituals that Victor wanted to take. A few clothes were chosen and some essential weapons he might need to get out of Tulsa. He was getting excited about leaving, but not about leaving the master behind. The master had told him of two locations to seek out in Europe. He would be checking both extensively to ensure they had the required seclusion. He told Victor when the time was right he would join him and the female witch, but that it had to be completely safe before he would do so.

If the master was not able to join, it would mean he had been vanquished, but Victor had been given instruction for what to do in that situation. In just a few short minutes, the master came up with such an elaborate plan that could involve months to execute.

With his bag packed, Victor grabbed Gina and put her over his shoulder. He made his way down the hallway to the reading room. Pushing on the King James Version of the Bible, the bookcase moved to the side exposing a dark tunnel with a flight of stone stairs leading down further into the basement.

As Victor moved down the stairs slowly, one step at a time, he found the lighting was set on a sensor system, activated by body movement. It gave just enough light to see the steps below his feet, which allowed him to move deeper into the stairwell.

Moving past the first floor, he quickly, but safely, made his way into the basement. Victor walked to the wall directly across from the stairwell. He was looking for a button, that when pushed, would expose another tunnel. Looking carefully at the wall he noticed Balashonian symbols. Seeing something a little out of place, Victor walked to the wall and pressed the symbol that represented the third eye, the mind's eye. It was representative of the opening of the wall of the brain, exposing a new path, a new journey.

He was correct in his assessment. When he pushed the button, the stone wall gave way making a loud creaking sound as dust blew outward. The tunnel had not been used in years.

Eyeing a wooden torch on the wall across from him, he walked over, took out the torch and dipped it into the clay jar containing fuel. Using the lighter from his pocket, Victor lit the torch and as it burned brighter, he wasted no time in making his way into the narrow tunnel. Protecting Gina's head, he quickly made his way down the path hoping it was going to come to an end soon. Gina was still sleeping soundly and if Victor were to guess, he expected her to sleep for a while.

Victor made a mental list of all the things he would need to procure once they arrived at their final destination. He needed rope to secure Gina with before she woke up. He would have to come up with some type of monitoring system to make sure she wasn't using her powers to get out of the bindings.

Damn, Victor thought to himself, *this tunnel was longer than I had imagined it would be.* Just when he was thinking it wasn't going to end, it did. He came to another room that had symbols all over the walls. It was one of the Balashon's tests to make sure you were worthy of passing through. If you were someone who happened to escape and got lucky with the symbols in the first room, the complexity of this one would trap you.

He bent down, gently laying Gina down on the floor as he looked at the ancient symbols trying to figure out the meaning. He could tell by the writing on the walls that he didn't want to guess wrong.

Victor expected this one to be a more complicated sequence. As he was going over each symbol on the wall, he was growing more and more frustrated. He had to get Gina out of this room and to the airport as quickly as possible. He didn't think for a minute that Demetri or the vampire would get past his master, but stranger things have happened.

Just as his frustration started to get the better of him, he heard something from behind. Turning around and finding the room empty except for Gina and himself, he heard it again and this time realized it was a voice inside his head, but it wasn't his voice. It was the voice of his master.

"You must choose the symbol of the Balashon, then the third eye and then the symbol that represents me, Bastiquil. They have to be in order or you will both be killed. Don't fail me Victor. I have entrusted you with a most special treasure and I need you to see her safely delivered to the final destination," Bastiquil said, but only in Victor's head. No one around would have heard a thing.

Victor spoke to him, as if he were standing next to him, "I will not fail you master. Your will shall be done."

Victor found the symbols the master referred to and they were each a good ways apart on the wall, but pushing them one by one in the exact manner in which the master told him, Victor smiled as an opening in the wall revealed another stairwell, this time leading upward.

Grabbing Gina and putting her over his shoulder, he reached down for his bag and shot up the stairs, which led to another door. This time it was an average looking door. As he opened it, he realized he was in a garage housing two black SUV's, much like the one he had been driving since he arrived in Tulsa. Opening the door to the passenger's seat, Victor set Gina in the seat and buckled her in. Clutching his bag, he raced to the driver's side and opened the door. Throwing the bag into the back seat, he jumped in the driver's seat and pulled the keys down from the visor.

Victor put the key in the ignition and started the vehicle. Pushing the garage door button, he slowly pulled out once the door opened. He realized this was an ordinary house, with a two-car garage, down the street from the Balashon mansion, where his master currently fought the vampire and the male witch.

Victor pulled onto the street and made his way down Lewis Avenue. He was driving within the speed limit, but he was feeling the urgency of getting to the jet and into the air. As he passed 41st street, he suddenly realized he was coming to a dead end due to construction. He had forgotten they were doing road construction on the interstate and the bridge that crossed over it. He maneuvered some side streets until he was able to work his way back to Lewis.

Heading south on Lewis passing 71st, he was almost there, but had to see it one more time, just one more time before he left. *It was meant to be a symbol of hope for people. It was a reminder in times of joy, fear or tragedy all you had to do was put your hands together and pray. Pray to the God in the heavens and he would send forth his wrath upon those who would seek to do you injustice.* Victor laughed to himself. He didn't laugh because people would pray, but that they thought there would be an intervention, someone who would save them from themselves, him or his master. Well, they would need a lot more praying hands than this large statute if they wanted to be saved. The world had been occupied by demons and creatures of the night since the dawn of time and there has been no divine intervention. "Keep praying Tulsa," he said, "you are going to need it before my master is finished."

Victor finally navigated his way to the Arkansas River bridge, to Elwood Drive where the small airport was located. He felt relief knowing they were almost there. He was charged and excited. He would do everything the master had asked. He was to tell no one but the pilot where they were going.

Victor called ahead for the pilot to meet them at the airport, to have the jet fueled and the pre-flight check completed before their arrival. The pilot had made arrangements for the SUV to be let through the gate so he could pull right into the hanger where the jet had been kept. Pulling into the hanger, the aircraft was just outside and ready for takeoff.

Jumping out of the vehicle, he snatched his bag from the back seat, and ran around to the passenger side where he unbuckled Gina. Grabbing her, he headed to the jet. The pilot already had clearance to take off so all Victor needed to do was get them both inside the cabin of the jet. Reaching the airstairs of the plane, he climbed up and gently got Gina through the small plane door to the cabin. He buckled her in a seat, laying it back so she could continue her sleep through this journey of the trip. Victor shut and locked the door to the jet.

Victor gave the pilot a thumbs up, as he closed the door to the cockpit. Victor took a seat beside Gina, buckled in and smiled to himself when he felt the jet start to move. In a matter of minutes they were racing down the runway. As Victor felt the tires lift off the ground, he was satisfied knowing he and the witch were safely in the air headed to a destination only known by he, the pilot, and Bastiquil.

Chapter Two

Demetri awoke, disoriented, not realizing where he was. It took moments for everything to sink in but when it did he jumped to defend himself, quickly realizing he was chained in the exact spot where Brandy had been sacrificed. Pulling on the chains, he winced in pain as they constricted. *Where are Gina and Aldrik*, kept going through his mind. The bodies of Brandy and Ella had been taken away. The thought of not making it in time to keep them from being killed and not stopping the demon from possessing Alex ate away at him.

His guilt turned to anger as he sat bound to the chains, in the blood of Brandy and Ella. *The blood, it's everywhere; the smell, oh my god, the smell. Why go to all this trouble if it was not in time to stop the ritual from happening?* As he knelt there on his knees, mind racing, thoughts stomping through his head, his emotions started to intensify, his anger reaching new heights.

Before he knew it, a visible static electricity started shooting back and forth between his fingers, tickling the palm of his hands. It wasn't like a shock from touching a charged hand to a receptive pair of pants. These were tiny visible lightning bolt charges firing back and forth within his hands. The charges formed balls of contained electricity. These were new to Demetri; energy balls were Gina's thing.

He was used to being able to form invisible balls of energy, but he hadn't been able to pull this one off, until now.

Closing his eyes, he focused on the energy being conducted from his hands. He focused on nothing else and as he focused harder, the more intense the energy became. The tingling sensations were growing in strength. It was a new sensation, a powerful one, but it felt so damn good to feel something other than guilt.

He focused on his senses, his third eye, and the environment around him, trying to find a way that he might free himself. He concentrated on his hearing, his smell, and as he listened in, he could hear the sounds of people in what seemed to be a celebratory mood, one of happiness and arrogance. The smell was intense, foul, and he wasn't sure what it was. He realized it was the smell of human blood, the blood of Brandy and Ella he was kneeling in.

He became enraged and let out a yell. He heard footsteps as they came running into the room to check on him. It was two members of the Balashon and as he focused on the sounds of the nearing footsteps, he didn't bother to open his eyes. He just listened and waited, his anger growing more intense. Shocked, they saw Demetri on his knees, lightening balls in both hands. One let out a gasp. That was enough for Demetri to pinpoint their location and as he did, he sent forth the balls of electricity with such speed and force that when it struck the men's chests it burned a hole right through them killing them where they stood. Both men fell to the ground.

Demetri felt more powerful now as the thoughts and memories started flooding back to him. The memories were loud, deafening, intense and sharp. Some felt like knives working their way through his brain as he knelt on the blood drenched floor of the sacrificial room.

Demetri could feel panic, loss of control, and claustrophobia setting in from being bound while these intense feelings, visions, and memories did a stomp dance in

10

his brain. He knew if he did not get a handle on this soon there was no telling what he would do, to himself or others.

Remembering the feeling of calmness and serenity he felt when he was meditating at Gina's before she had come home to find everything in her home and store floating, including Demetri, he wanted to return to that place, if only for a minute. Getting arranged carefully on the floor, legs in a lotus position, although his arms were limited due to the chains, he knew if he focused long enough he could calm himself and figure out a way to break these chains. It wouldn't be an impossible feat for his newfound powers. The problem was focusing those powers and making them work for him and not against him.

He continued to focus, like he had a few minutes ago when he was able to zero in on those two Balashon members. He wanted to understand his powers; he wanted to become one with them. He wished he had more time to work with them, practice with them before he had been put in the situation of having to prematurely do battle with Bastiquil, but the timing of it he couldn't change, no more than he could change the outcome for those who were lost. *I will avenge you. I will make sure your deaths at the hands of that devil worshipping scum are avenged. I will stop them no matter what the cost; I will kill every last one of them.*

He knew he needed to quiet his brain, still his thoughts, or he was not going to be able to do anything. *Focus on one thing.* And even though some would think of concentrating on sound, he decided not to do that, because to hear those in the other room celebrating death, celebrating the resurrection of a demon, was more than he could bear. So he concentrated on the smell of the blood. His only thought was of it. He decided to think about what it smelled like, the intricacies of the odor, the decay of it. This brought him around to thinking about where it came from and then he found himself concentrating on his heart, the pumping and beating of it as it pushed blood through his own body.

The heart had a unique beat to it, a way of making one feel at ease. It could speed up at the thought of something exciting, scary, and anxious, or it could slow down at the thought of relaxing, the peaceful serenity of nature or when one was asleep. *The heart was an amazing organ and an integral part of survival, of existence. Would it be too much to say that the heart fed the soul, or the soul fed off of the heart? One without the other didn't seem possible. Were the two joined hand in hand, the heart being the key to the soul? Once the heart is removed from the equation, the soul was free once more to move on from the current body it inhabited.*

These questions seemed to calm Demetri, making him relax and fall into a meditative trance. He was searching for something, a light, a door; one that would open up the power within his body that he so desperately needed to access. He searched through his mind, his body, and his own soul. He was watching a light, in which he created in his mind as the guide or transporter for this meditation and sent it forth within himself in search of an answer. He wanted to know how to combine these powers into one. He wanted to know how to control them without having to separate one personality to the next. *It had to be possible, didn't it?*

As the light moved onward, searching his mind, his thoughts, his visions, he was once again reminded of the past life meditational journey he took and all of the visions he saw along the way. He thought of Aldrik and of them being on the ship together when they were younger. He thought of all the other visions he had seen and he wanted them all to merge into one. *Let it be so, let it be so, let it be so*, he kept chanting to himself internally. Demetri had never really considered himself a witch. He didn't know what he was. He thought maybe more of a psychic, but he began to realize that he was all of those things; he was everything his past lives were. Most people don't typically get a chance to see their past lives played out like he did and he attributed his own

12

powers and Gina's to this new ability to see back as far as he did. One day, if he got the chance, he would love to see just how far back they could go. *Did the memories go back further than Bastiquil?*

As he relaxed, he began to feel himself rising off the ground. He wasn't sure why he noticed it this time when he hadn't before, but he felt himself rising. He could hear the chains rising along with him as the steel clanked with the rise. He was moving slowly so he didn't think anyone in the other room could hear over their own noise.

As he rose, he kept thinking back on what was the one thing to link it all together; what was the key to opening this treasure box of memories? He could feel himself stop in mid-air as the chains reached their limit, but the body still wanted to rise. He might have gotten himself into a predicament here. As he felt his arms being stretched as the body rose and the chains fought back, he was almost at a point where the pain threatened to bring him out of his meditative state. Just then, something remarkable happened. The chains from the tension of being pulled started to slide, painfully, but slide none-the-less off of his hands. The blood on them allowed it to be used as lubrication. All at once the chains were loose and falling to the ground as he kept rising.

As he was floating, his thoughts started to become clearer. He started to think about the brain, how it was one of the most untapped organs, but was it really just an organ or was it a key waiting to unlock all the mysteries and magic that the past held within it. *The basic elements of one's survival, the survival of the brain relied heavily on water, air, food, and minerals from the earth, that were created by fire. The four basic elements for a witch, water, air, earth and fire; could it be that simple? We only use ten percent of our brain or at least that's what studies show. Could it be that the other ninety percent is holding untold secrets and magical mysteries that if tapped into, could change a person and the world forever?*

13

Just as Demetri felt he was getting it all figured out he was interrupted. "Help, he's loose. He killed Matthew and Rick," a guard was yelling at the others in the other room.

Demetri opened his eyes and extended his legs, but found he was still not touching the floor. He was floating and in control of his powers.

Ten men came running into the room with weapons of various types; some had guns, others swords, but they all came with something. As one took aim at Demetri, another grabbed his arm and said, "The master told us not to kill him. He wanted him alive, but he didn't say that we couldn't shoot him in the legs or arms."

"You should have shot when you had the chance," Demetri said, as he started to disarm them one by one with his mind. He was pulling swords out of their hands, as the weapons floated up into the air just out of their reach. One man took aim at him and fired his gun, but as the bullet rushed at him, it stopped short of his leg, within inches, and the bullet then turned, took aim, and went hurling towards him at the man who pulled the trigger. The last thing Demetri saw from him before the bullet entered his forehead, destroying his brain, was wide-eyed disbelief, which was ironic since they had just raised a demon a few hours ago. Demetri one by one disarmed the men and as their weapons rose in the air, the weapons turning on the men who just held them. He smiled at the men as the swords went flying at them, sinking into their chest and the guns fired, hitting each in the forehead like the one before. *Ten men, ten dead.* It gave Demetri considerable pleasure to send them all back to the hell they were so intent on unleashing on this earth. He hoped they'd burn in fire for eternity.

Demetri lowered himself to the ground and once his feet felt the floor beneath, he took off running through the house looking for any signs of Gina or Aldrik; he would even settle for Bastiquil at this point. The house seemed deserted; Bastiquil must have left with the other men taking Aldrik and

Gina with them. Before he took off in search, he closed his eyes and tried to focus one more time, this time on noise, on anything that might trigger his sense of hearing. He focused intently, listening carefully and what he heard at first, took him off guard, a faint beating of a heart. *I must not have killed all of the men in the sacrificial room; well, I will rectify that. I'm not going to have any of them walking out of here alive!*

Making his way back into the room, he listened and found he did not hear a heartbeat from any of these men. *They are all dead, nothing alive at all in them. There must be someone else in the house hurt,* because the heartbeat he heard was distant, almost gone. He prayed that it wasn't Gina. He knew it wasn't Aldrik because it would take a major act to kill him, due to his age, his strength, and his healing ability. It could easily be one of the Balashon members, but he had to find whoever it was just in case it was Gina.

As he closed his eyes and listened again for the heartbeat, he could hear it, but it was fading. He willed himself to the sound of the heartbeat; he told his body to take him to it. He was thinking of only one thing, to be taken to the beating heart. As he concentrated on the sound, he failed to notice he was sailing through the air or that when his body was approaching a closed door, the door opened on its own, right before he would have crashed through it. The only thing he was thinking about was the beating heart.

As his floating body went downward in the house, he did feel coolness, the temperature shift in the air as he entered the basement. As he got closer to the heart, the beat got louder and louder. His eyes were still closed as he came to a stop.

Demetri opened his eyes and saw the dead bodies of Ella and Brandy. He knelt down and felt Ella and found no pulse. When he felt for Brandy's pulse, she jumped at the touch of his hand and started to panic. Ella had been placed on top of her, trapping her, but she was so weak and drained she was on the verge of being delirious.

"Get off me, get off me; leave me alone," Brandy screamed, with what could have been considered a whisper to some. She was so weak, but the will to live still kicked in.

"It's Demetri; I'm not going to hurt you. I am here to help," he said, trying to calm her down. He lifted the dead body of Ella off of Brandy and discarded it to the side.

"Alex, what happened to Alex?" Brandy asked in a weakened voice.

"I am sorry. I wasn't able to stop the demon before he entered Alex; I'm afraid we may have lost the Alex we know," Demetri said, with a sad look in his eyes.

Brandy was crying now, from the pain and from the news of Alex. "Alex is still in there, Demetri, Alex is alive. We have to help him. Promise me you will help him."

"I will do what I can but I have to get you some help," Demetri said, as he started to lift her.

Wincing in pain, Brandy stopped him. "No, leave me. I am dying anyway. You must go help Alex."

"Well, I am sorry to be so stubborn, Miss Brandy, but right now, I am getting you to a hospital so you can be there to greet Alex when I bring him home," Demetri said. "Is that okay with you?"

Brandy cried as she looked up at Demetri. "You know, I'm sorry. You are not as bad as I thought you to be. You just might be a good guy," Brandy said, before passing out.

"Don't let that get out to anyone. It could be bad for business," he said, to the already sleeping Brandy. As he lifted her up, he ran for the stairs leading out of the basement. Reaching the top, he ran through the house and out the front door where he found a black SUV parked in the circular driveway. Putting Brandy in the passenger seat and buckling her in, he ran around to the driver's side and jumped inside behind the wheel. Reaching down to turn the key, he found that it wasn't there; it wasn't anywhere.

"You have got to be fucking kidding me," Demetri said loudly. *I don't have time for this*, he thought. Placing his hand over the ignition, he sent a burst of energy and the vehicle started. *Yes, finally something went right.* Putting it into drive, Demetri peeled out, heading down the hill towards the closed gates. Before he got to them, he reached up and waved his hand, as they burst outward, clearing a path. He kept reaching over and checking Brandy's pulse as he made his way to the hospital's emergency room.

He pulled in and put the SUV in park. He ran around to the passenger side, opened the door, unbuckled Brandy, and pulled her out of the car and into his arms. As he ran through the ER doors, the hospital staff were running to meet him with a gurney. Placing her down on the gurney, he shouted to them what he knew of her wound and turned to make his way out. The nurses were calling after him but he kept running until he reached the SUV and took off in search of Gina, Aldrik, and Bastiquil.

Chapter Three

Bastiquil was delighted to see the array of people standing in line to get into the club called The Other Side. He loved that name and remembered it from the recollection of memories he was getting from within Alex's head. This would be the perfect place to start his conversions, to gather his forces. He knew he had a full army of men from the Balashon that would gladly step up and fight on his behalf. He still needed some to stay exactly where they were, in positions of great power in this earthly world. He might need them later, if and when the world decided it would fight back. But for now, he was going to enjoy his time here.

He approached the door to the unmarked building with Aldrik and numerous other Balashon guards. He was met at the door by the two men working security.

"The line is back there," the bigger of the two said, pointing to the back of the crowded line. Alex had been here before, but he wasn't considered a regular like Demetri.

Bastiquil just laughed at the men. The people standing in the line looked at him like he was crazy, but then they joined in with this laughter.

"Look mister; get to the back of the line. Better yet, why don't you just leave?" The security guard proceeded to stand his ground.

"You will let me in," Bastiquil said, looking at the man intensely.

"Is that so? Why do you think you deserve to be let in over these other folks?"

"Because, I said so," Bastiquil said, as he leaned in and whispered something to the two guards. As he did, they moved to the side letting Bastiquil and his party pass through.

This did not sit well with the crowd who started to yell and raise a stink. "Hey you wanna be star-crossed fucker! Get to the back of the fucking line," yelled a random voice, as the crowd cheered in approval.

Bastiquil turned, looking back at them with the most grotesque gaze, his eyes becoming black. "Silence, before I kill you all," Bastiquil yelled back to the crowd, causing some to turn and run and others to just stand there in silent horror.

Walking through the doors of the club, he was overcome with the lights and sounds coming from the large black boxes. His ears tingled from the vibrations of voices and music. Able to see things others were not, the colorful strands of wavelengths fascinated him. The display was amazing. The music hurt and delighted his ears at the same time. *What a magical place.*

As he made his way further into the club, he noticed people were gathered in a section of the floor and were moving in unison like the dancing of the days of old. This was a much different type of dancing than he was used to seeing. It looked more like one would see and feel while having sex. Intrigued by it all, he wanted to delight in everything this world had to offer.

Making his way to the dance floor he placed himself in the center and began to mimic their movements. He loved it. The touching. The feeling. He found himself with people all around. They would reach in and touch his face, arms, and chest. One was on the ground rubbing his leg. He had not felt anything like this since the orgy he had had before Zamaranum vanquished him back to his own hell almost three thousand years ago. He could feel his excitement growing. The anticipation showed in his movements, his head, and even his cock.

He was mesmerizing everyone with his dancing, his charm, and his looks. He sent out an aura that was intoxicating. It was hypnotic and was putting a spell on the crowd. They took his robe off of him and he was standing nude and erect in the middle of the dance floor. The only one that seemed to not care about this display was Aldrik, who seemed to be immune from his charms.

People all around started making out with each other. The people on the floor with Bastiquil were all over him. They were kissing him, pleasuring him, taking him to ultimate heights of intimacy and feeling. This quickly turned into a club-wide orgy. The essence of Bastiquil, his powers, were leaking out into the room. His sexual desires were overloading everyone; they were all out of control.

Bastiquil was taking one girl on the dance floor while others held her up like they were a makeshift human sling. She moaned in ecstasy. As Aldrik watched this happen, he saw the strangest thing. He could have sworn he saw Bastiquil's, well Alex's, tattoo's move on his body. It was as if the tattoos were joining in. Aldrik was in shock. He couldn't believe what he was seeing. Then one of the tattoos reached out from his flesh and grabbed a hold of one of the men standing next to him and brought him around so he could join Bastiquil in his pleasuring of the female. There was a huge smile on Bastiquil's face. The music kept blaring on.

Aldrik was able to hear the rustling of the humans and the creatures downstairs that had gotten word of something wild and strange happening upstairs. They started to make their way upstairs, at least the ones who were not tied down, clamped down, or already dead. Everyone wanted to see the wildness, this unbridled orgy taking place. Even the people on the second floor were coming down to see. As they came near, they succumbed to the spell Bastiquil was casting and grabbed at the person next to them, ripping their clothing off.

Aldrik was at a loss as to what he should do. He wasn't joining in on this club-wide rape Bastiquil was causing. However, he did have the opportunity to escape while Bastiquil was occupied. He could leave, quickly, without opposition and go find Demetri. He was the only one who was going to be able to stop him.

Deciding that was what he would do, he made use of his vampire speed and was out the door before anyone could stop him. It was so fast, no human would have noticed.

As the creatures from the basement came forth, the vampires immune to the spell being cast on the humans were going to have a field day. This was open-hunting season for some; for others it was a moment to join the orgy and have their way with many different types of people.

As for the werewolves, they were affected differently because they were part human. They were supernatural given their ability to transform into a wolf, but as for the human side of them, they were succumbing to Bastiquil's spell. They were joining in on the action just as the others were.

The vampires out to feed on prey made the mistake of their lives when they showed their true nature and started to feed on the unsuspecting patrons of the orgy. The people they were foraging on thought it part of the pleasure of the orgy and did not fight them. This blood lust did, however, catch the attention of the tattoo on Bastiquil's back. It alerted its master. As Bastiquil continued what he was doing, the large tattoo started to stretch outward from the flesh of Bastiquil. Almost as if ripping itself from being forever confined by the ink it was created with, the creature stepped his foot down on the ground for the first time. Pulling the rest of itself free, it stood up, stretched and walked over to the feeding vampires.

Grabbing one by the arm, the tattoo creature pulled the vampire off the victim who was almost drained. Ripping the arm off the vampire and tossing it across the room, the vampire screamed out in agony and pain. The only ones who even cared about this were the other vampires in the room who were not under the spell of Bastiquil. They all came charging at the creature with speed, might, and in numbers. The creature was unimpressed by this and continued to tear the vampires limb from limb. When able, he would rip the head off of a vampire before moving on to the next.

The vampires did not know what they were up against as they fought it, clawed at it, bit at it, but found nothing seemed to phase it. The creature would grab one by the throat with one hand and the other by whatever it could wrap its hand around. He would squeeze down on them crushing and ripping out the throat of the vampires and breaking whatever else it grasped. It wasn't but a few minutes until the vampires were destroyed and the creature returned to its master, joining ink and flesh once more until it was absorbed back into the master's flesh. The blood of the vampires that was on the form of the tattooed creature burst into flames as the creature became flesh-art once again.

Chapter Four

Demetri was driving around looking for any sign of Bastiquil. He was sure if he found Bastiquil he would find Aldrik and Gina. He'd been all around the area surrounding the mansion and turned up nothing.

"Think outside of the box," Demetri said aloud, speaking only to himself. "What if there were still some of Alex's memories in there that Bastiquil could access? What if he knew some of Alex's favorite spots?"

He decided to run by the bookstore. It would make sense that Alex's memories would take Bastiquil there especially if they had Gina with them. But once he got there, he was relieved but still sadly disappointed to find that Gina was not there, nor did it appear that anyone had been there since they had left earlier. He started out the door and was once again startled to find Aldrik standing outside. Demetri fell into his arms and hugged him.

"I was so worried about you and Gina. I didn't know what happened. I must have blacked out after being knocked into the wall," Demetri said, as he hugged him.

"You were thrown through two walls, Demetri. He almost killed you," Aldrik said, unable to cry, but desperately wanting to.

"Well, he didn't kill me and we need to stop him before he hurts anyone else. Where's Gina? Is she not with you," Demetri said, with panic hitting his voice.

"I am not sure where Gina is. I have not seen her or the main guy wearing the leather loin cloth with tattoos since we were locked out of the room," Aldrik said.

If he had Gina, then they must be planning on using her as bait to control Demetri somehow. "We must find them."

"I don't know where she is, but I do know where Bastiquil is," Aldrik said to Demetri, who was looking at him with eyes wide. "He is at a club called The Other Side."

"Of course," Demetri said, hitting himself on the forehead. "That should have been one of the most current, emotional memories Alex experienced. Of course, he went there."

"Well, there is something else you should know," Aldrik said, stopping Demetri in his tracks. "Bastiquil seems to have all of the people there under some kind of trance. The whole club is engaged in an orgy with Bastiquil leading the entire thing."

"Are you fucking with me, Aldrik?" Demetri asked him. "That is some sick shit."

"I am not messing with you, Demetri. I am not sure why I seemed to be immune to it. I wasn't immune to his powers, but I was immune to this. I am not sure how much help I can be to you though, with him being able to control my movements," Aldrik explained.

"Well, there is an entrance up a ramp that leads to the upstairs area. It's accessible from the east side of the building. If you could make it up there and just be ready to act, if and when I need you, that would be great help," Demetri said.

"Demetri, you must be careful. If he is able to control that room like that, he will be able to make them attack you. Not only would that be a massive number of people, but they are innocent people," Aldrik pleaded.

"I'm aware of that. But if this is the only way I can stop him, then I must try. It is not my intention to hurt anyone, as it was not my intention to even allow this possession to take place, but it did. The only redeeming factor right now is that Brandy is still alive, or she was when I left her at the hospital emergency room," Demetri said.

"Well, that is a bit of good news then," Aldrik said. "I am just asking you to be careful. He has a ton of tricks up his sleeve and he will not go without a huge fight."

"Well, if he wants a huge fight, that is what he is going to get," Demetri said, as he walked past Aldrik, closing the door behind him.

"I am begging you to reconsider this attack on him at the club. There is too much risk. Too many innocent people could be killed if you attack him in such a public arena," Aldrik chased after him.

"I don't have much of a choice. I can't allow Bastiquil to keep up the abuse on those people. I also can't risk losing Bastiquil, which would mean losing any information where they might have taken Gina. I am going to try my damnedest for no one innocent to get hurt, but there are casualties in any war," Demetri explained.

Aldrik didn't like what he heard from Demetri and for an undead creature to be bothered by this, disturbed him even more. He would give his life for Demetri, and he felt that Demetri would do the same. But we are talking about a powerful demon. He had moved Aldrik and Demetri around like they were marionettes. This was going to take a lot of focus and energy on Demetri's part. He knew if Demetri could just focus his powers, tap into the primal side, the survival mode, he just might have a shot at beating this thing.

They climbed into the SUV and headed toward The Other Side. They had to hope that Bastiquil would still be there.

"I'm sure Bastiquil has noticed my abandonment and betrayal by now. He will not hesitate to kill me on sight." Aldrik was speaking as Demetri drove. "He's not through taunting you. He wants to make sure it's Zamaranum he's killing, not you. He will make sure Zamaranum has control before he tries to destroy you.

"Tell me what is really on your mind. You are holding back what you want to say to me." Demetri called him out, knowing he was correct when Aldrik looked out the window.

"I wonder if you and Zamaranum are two separate personalities or joined into one. I suspect you are one. This means that you just need to tap into Zamaranum's memories to gain access to his powers. The power has been in you all along, even before the past life journey mediation. It has always been in you, hidden behind the walls the brain puts up, barriers that keep people average and typical. But you are far from average and typical, Demetri. You are one of the truly great and talented ones, blessed with the ability to knock down some of the barriers and gain access to more knowledge and power. That's what makes you a great witch. You have already been tapping into that unused ninety percent of the brain," Aldrik paused, thinking about what stood before them. "This will be a battle to the death, Demetri. One of you will not be coming back from this. You know this and so do I. I don't know if Bastiquil knows this or if his arrogance and cockiness has him feeling all powerful?"

Aldrik placed his hand on Demetri's as the SUV sped down the streets of Tulsa. The silence was deafening. Both were stuck in their own thoughts, their own plotting, and their own concern for the other. They had not gotten to spend as much time with each other as they wanted to. Demetri was the only one taking the knowledge with him that their lives were joined. They were destined to be in each other's lives, for he had seen their past and he was living the present. The future was uncertain, but if he didn't survive this and was reborn, he felt confident he would once again find Aldrik. Their paths would cross again. This gave him comfort. He tightened his grasp on Aldrik's hand.

He drove to the east side of the club, showing Aldrik the entrance ramp to the second story. Jumping out of the SUV before it stopped moving, Aldrik headed to the ramp. Demetri drove to the front of the club and parked the SUV. No point in hiding now. Bastiquil should and would know that he was here. There was no one standing in line and there were no bouncers waiting outside. This was not a good sign. He got out and walked to the front door. He tried to focus his breathing and his thoughts so when he entered the building he would be ready for anything. But what he didn't expect was anything was waiting for him as well.

Chapter Five

Opening the doors to the club, he walked inside. He was calm, collected, and ready to die if it would save the ones he loved. This made him a dangerous man. For one to have such conviction in something that they were willing to die for it, well, this is the stuff that heroes are made of, but sometimes one has to die to become a hero.

Walking in, he was met by a club full of nude people all standing in unison, looking at Demetri. Aldrik had been correct. Bastiquil had these people under his control and Demetri was public enemy number one. He didn't want to hurt them, but he was not willing to let Bastiquil walk out of this place, intact. He was sending him back to wherever he came from or he would die trying.

"I always admired men who were willing to die for what they believed in," a voice said, from behind the wall of people.

"What is it that you believe in Bastiquil," Demetri asked him, not fooled by the cloak and dagger of his charade. "Where is Gina?"

"Well, that is easy, Demetri. I am assuming that I am talking to Demetri? Zamaranum is too cowardly to come out and fight me face to face," Bastiquil said, trying to provoke Zamaranum. "I believe in me, a world where darkness rules and I sit on the throne. As for your Gina, well she is somewhere you will never find her."

"Those are powerful words, but there is cowardice behind them. You stand behind a wall of innocent people instead of facing me head on. And oh, by the way, I will find Gina," Demetri said, not fazed at all by his words.

Just as Demetri had expected, the wall of people parted, as the demon came forward. He was wearing the black linen robe again, which was partly opened down to his abdomen, like in the dream. Demetri hoped this didn't go down like the dream had. He could not think such defeating thoughts. His focus needed to be on Bastiquil.

"Do you even know what you are capable of, boy? Do you know the power that resides within you? You were one of the greatest witches of all time. You stood next to the most powerful entity to walk this earth, me. Then you betrayed me. You let greed and envy take over and you stamped out both of our lives in one day. Well, today that will not happen and it doesn't have to happen if you join me. Join me and let me teach you what true power is. Let me help you tap into the raw power flowing through your veins. I am asking this of you, but only once. It would be a shame to see such power and talent turned to dust, but I will kill you, make no mistake about it," Bastiquil said, as he walked toward him smiling.

The arrogance on Bastiquil's face was more than Demetri could bear. "Well, it sounds to me like you need to stop talking so much and get to doing," Demetri said, while sending a energy ball that knocked Bastiquil backward into the arms of one of the naked onlookers.

"How dare you disrespect me," Bastiquil said, with fury leaking off his tongue. Bastiquil raised his hand and two of the nude onlookers went flying through the air at Demetri. Before they made contact with him, he rolled out of the way as they crashed into the wall. Demetri was sad for them but didn't have time to think about that right now.

Jumping up, he started firing energy balls at Bastiquil one after the other. As they came towards him, Bastiquil just knocked them away, causing the balls to hit the person standing nearest him on each side, killing them instantly. "I can keep this up all day boy, can you?" Bastiquil asked, laughing at him. "How many more people have to die before you realize you were never strong enough to defeat me. You had one chance at that and all you did was delay me by a few thousand years, but hey, who's counting?" Bastiquil raised a hand and two humans morphed into werewolves and charged Demetri.

Demetri managed to knock down one of the werewolves with an electric ball but missed the other as he crashed into his body sending Demetri flying backward and into the barstools lined up against the bar. As Demetri struggled to get his wits about him, he realized the same werewolf was charging again. This time he used his telepathic powers to send him crashing into the opposite wall. As he did, the other wolf was back on its feet and coming at him again. Demetri made another electric ball and flung it at the wolf's head causing it to explode sending fur, blood, and brains in all directions.

"What's it going to take for you to give up, Demetri? When are you just going to give me Zamaranum and let this all be done?" Bastiquil asked.

"Why? So you can get your ass kicked again by Zamaranum? I mean come on, who is the masochist here?" Demetri mocked him.

This sent Bastiquil into a rage. He came stomping across the floor until he was standing over Demetri. Reaching down he picked Demetri up by his neck and flung him across the room. Then he did something familiar to Demetri. Bastiquil held out his hands to his sides and lifted them slightly, which caused Demetri to begin to rise off the floor.

This was not good. He had provoked him too much and Demetri remembered how this ended for the female witch in his vision. He had to do something quick. Closing his eyes, he began to try and relax himself, to clear his mind of all thoughts, even the one of Bastiquil trying to blow up his body from the inside out. He went back to the time when Zamaranum lived and fought Bastiquil. He spoke inside his head to the memories of long ago. *I need you, I need you now,* Demetri pleaded to those memories of Zamaranum. *Come forth and avenge your death. Use my body as a portal and a weapon. Don't let this beast win. Don't let him rule one minute longer in this world.*

Bastiquil was amused by the young witches who chose to close their eyes while they were being torn apart. Bringing his hands together as one would to pray, he brought them towards his face and chanting a few words, he waited just a few seconds longer, savoring the moment. Then when he had enough, he let his hands fly outwards so that the body of the young witch would implode on itself. But to his surprise, it didn't. It just floated there with eyes still closed.

"What is this?" Bastiquil asked.

"What? You think you are the only one who has learned a thing or two in three thousand years," Demetri said, but it was not Demetri's voice. His eyes opened with a hot fiery power exuding from them.

"Zamaranum?"

"Hello, old friend. I bet you thought you would never lay eyes on me again," Zamaranum said to Bastiquil.

"Oh, I was counting on it!" Bastiquil shot back at him. With a force that was greater than anything he had ever summoned before, Bastiquil sent Zamaranum flying across the room and down the stairs into the basement. Bastiquil was seething at the thought of him.

But before he even had a chance to think, a great wind burst up from the basement into the room where Bastiquil and his followers stood. Upon that wind rode Zamaranum, floating up the stairwell and into the room. He hit Bastiquil with a lightning energy ball the size of a baseball and as it hit him, Bastiquil let out a great cry as did the tattoos that it hit. The tattoos moved to where they were on each side of the burnt flesh. Zamaranum raised his eyes at this, impressed.

Bastiquil dropped his robe and held his hands out to his sides. The tattoos begin to stretch outward from his flesh, pulling free as they stepped away from Alex's host body. Standing in front of Bastiquil was a zombie, a giant troll, bats flying around him, snakes crawling around him and skeletons standing beside them. His army made from ink looked real. They had taken on a three-dimensional form and were ready for battle.

As Zamaranum hit the ground, the army of ink came charging at him. First the bats were flying at his face, then the snakes were crawling up his legs, wrapping around him tightly. As he lifted himself off the ground, he began spinning around and around until he sent the snakes flying off him and the bats were hit with energy balls as they scattered away from him. While he was still in the air, he felt something wrap a strong hand around his ankle and squeeze down with a deadly grip. Zamaranum screamed out in pain as the giant troll pulled him down from the air, securing him on the ground. The other creatures approached him as well and begin to grab ahold of him and squeeze tightly. The snakes had found their way back to him and secured themselves around his neck, wrapping tightly, squeezing his air until he was unable to breath.

Lying on the ground, unable to move, unable to breathe, all hope seemed to be fading from Zamaranum. He tried to fight his way back up but was unable to move. He was fading quickly. He had one chance left. He had to find a way to quickly meld all of these past lives together. *Secure the knowledge into this one life, so that they can all battle this demon as one force.* He closed his eyes again, knowing that he only had moments before these creatures would crush the life out of him. He tried to build a force field around himself but found he was expending a lot of power. He began to focus, to clear his mind except for one thought, one word, and that word was unity.

Aldrik was watching quietly from above and as he did he could no longer bear looking at this, his best friend, his lover being crushed, suffocated while he stood up here doing nothing. As he crept along the scaffolding until he was directly above Bastiquil, he dropped with lightning speed and knocked Bastiquil to the ground. As he did, he started ripping at him, clawing at him, pounding him with his supernatural strength.

As Bastiquil became enraged, the creatures that were attacking Zamaranum became distracted and looked over at Bastiquil. This gave Zamaranum the moment he needed to recite a spell, one that only he would know, and one that was so ancient that it had not been spoken for thousands of years. As he said it out loud, winded from the attack and lack of oxygen, Bastiquil froze as he heard the words being spoken.

"NO," Bastiquil screamed from the ground, throwing Aldrik off of him. Aldrik landed on his feet. The men from the Balashon attacked Aldrik, catching him off guard as he was concentrating on getting at Bastiquil. But the strength of Aldrik was no match for the men, at least the ones here at the club. Aldrik was snapping their necks and ripping their throats out, quickly laying them to waste.

As Zamaranum finished reciting the spell, the creatures that were holding him securely to the ground were sent flying off of him with just a whisper. A light so bright it almost blinded everyone in the room came from Zamaranum, who was now back to Demetri. The light sent the creatures fleeing to the safety of flesh. They each hit Bastiquil at once, sending him to the ground as they made themselves one again with Alex's body.

Bastiquil enraged at this tried to send them back out, but they were not moving. They were being blocked by someone or something. This time it was Demetri who was laughing at Bastiquil. "Did you lose your hold on your pets?" Demetri mocked him.

Bastiquil raising his arms out to his side trying to get Demetri in the air again began stomping around like a mad man when nothing happened.

"My turn," Demetri said, as he raised his arms out to his sides and Bastiquil was lifted into the air. Bastiquil's eyes told it all, he was in shock and appalled that he was not able to fight this witch that was attempting to use his own spell against him. Bringing the palms of his hands together, Demetri bowed his head toward his fingers and then opened his eyes and was peering up at Bastiquil.

Aldrik was talking to Demetri, trying to speak to him. "Demetri, listen to me. Alex is an innocent in this game of lies. He doesn't deserve to die, the demon does."

Squeezing one of his palms shut, Bastiquil let out a scream of pain, while Demetri pushing his other hand to the side of his body. By doing this, he was pulling the demon out of Alex's body. Demetri was speaking to Aldrik now but not saying anything out loud. It was only for Aldrik to hear and was said inside of Aldrik's mind, *"This is your only chance, get him now."*

Aldrik wasted no time at all, he flew at Alex's body, crashing into it as it was still floating in the air, sending Alex along with himself across the room and rolling onto the floor.

The demon in his true form was quite impressive. He was cursing at Demetri, swearing his revenge, swearing to rip him to shreds. Demetri held tight to him as he called upon the realms to open up, to open up and reclaim what was lost to them, what should never have come from them. As the floor begin to crack and a bright light shown through, Bastiquil was screaming at Demetri not to do this. But as Demetri slammed his hands together, the dark demon went flying back into the light of the cracked floor. The light vanished and the floor sealed back up. It was if he had never been.

As Demetri fell to the ground exhausted and hurting, the people around him begin to come out of the spell Bastiquil had over them. As their minds cleared, they scrambled for their clothes hoping to hide their nudity. This one was sure to be written off as a drug party gone bad. Demetri couldn't be bothered by it.

As he got to his feet, he rushed over to Aldrik and Alex, who both lay on the ground. Aldrik was okay, but Alex was out of it. He must have been knocked unconscious upon impact with Aldrik. Demetri knew Alex would feel like he had been hit by a truck tomorrow, if he woke up at all. There is no telling what kind of damage the demon did to him while residing inside.

Aldrik quickly jumped up, picking Alex up in his arms. He and Demetri had decided it best if they get out of there before the police were called. The less they had to lie, the better. Demetri didn't want to be in another interrogation with the police. As they walked out of the club, Demetri, still limping some from the grip of the troll, was happy to have survived the night. Quite frankly, he didn't think he was going to be able to pull it off.

As they got Alex laid out in the back seat, Demetri and Aldrik jumped in the front of the SUV and took off as it was getting dangerously close to dawn. Aldrik had to be safely behind dark walls before that happened. They would go back to Gina's. There was a basement Aldrik could sleep in while Demetri tried to get Alex awake and back with them so they could begin their search for Gina.

Chapter Six

The flight was a long and choppy one, but Victor was used to such flights. He had flown all over the world and experienced many rough flights. Some would have made weaker people mess their pants, but not Victor. He was always strong, in charge, and willing to do what was needed for the job.

As Victor sat in his chair contemplating the past few weeks, he was so glad the witch, Gina, was still out. He didn't feel like dealing with her questions, her struggling, and of course, the turbulence. This is some of the worst he had experienced to date. Not many people could handle such a rough flight. There would have been vomiting and people screaming "Oh God save me," or "Jesus, just get me through this." Nope, Victor, didn't need it, nor did he want to listen to it.

The pilot phoned earlier informing him they were going to be experiencing some "nasty chop in the air." Thinking back on it, he didn't seem to think it would be as big of a deal as it actually was. The plane was starting to feel like it could break in half at any moment. *That would really suck.*

Bored with this long flight, and having no one to talk to other than a sleeping witch, he got into the whiskey. He thought to himself *we will be fine. Everything will be okay.* Suddenly the door lit up with a bright light, followed by a crackling sound of thunder as it crashed all around the plane. This was madness. *If we live through this, I might just have to gut this pilot for his lack of judgment in taking us into such a fierce storm.* Victor guessed that the pilot didn't know what precious cargo they had on board.

When it seemed like the plane could not take anymore, the door to the cabin flew open sucking out the oxygen. Magazines and anything loose went flying right out the door. Victor, looking towards the door, saw a black, thick-clawed hand grab a hold of the inside of the door frame and pull itself into the plane. It was his master, Bastiquil. He had found them. *But why was he not in the vessel? Why was he standing here in demonic form?*

The door sealed behind him as he entered the cabin and the pressure seemed to start leveling off within. Victor wasn't sure what was going on, but it couldn't be good considering that the master was here, without the body of Alex.

Once the cabin stabilized, Victor unbuckled his seatbelt and made his way to Bastiquil, as the plane continued to bounce along in the choppy air.

"Master, what has happened to you? Why are you here without the host body?" Victor asked.

"Zamaranum has made his way to the surface of the male witch's memories and he was able to cast me out of the host body," Bastiquil explained, in a tone suggesting he was anything other than fine.

"What does this mean Master? What are you to do?" Victor pleaded. "I should have driven a dagger right through the heart of the witch, Demetri, when I had the chance."

"Well, all hope is not lost my young soldier. We still have the upper hand in this war. We may have lost this battle, but you can sure as hell believe we will win the war," Bastiquil said.

"What can I do for you Master? How can I help?" Victor begged.

"You are doing what you must for now. Taking the witch to safety, away from the filth she keeps as friends, is the best thing you can do for me now. She will be essential in our plan. No one will see this coming. No one...," Bastiquil laughed to himself.

"So what will you do Master? I didn't think you could stay in this realm without a host body," Victor asked.

"My time is limited and I must find a suitable body to hold me until I can get myself back into the vessel's body. He is being watched closely by Zamaranum, but I feel the male witch is struggling to hold on, to contain the information and power bestowed upon him. When he turns his head for a second, I will strike and reclaim what is mine. My life, my blood, my essence belongs in the vessel and it will be so," Bastiquil boasted, trying to sound in control.

"We can send the assassins master and kill the male witch. We can strike at him from all sides and he will falter, and fall to his death," Victor offered up to Bastiquil.

"I am afraid it is no longer that simple my devoted one. With the knowledge that came to him, especially Zamaranum's knowledge and power, the witch will not be easy to eradicate. But, if we can catch him off guard, the vessel can once again be procured and I will be able to join you," Bastiquil stated to Victor, who was feeling infuriated and disappointed in himself.

"Victor, fret not. Your brother in arms, John, had the perfect opportunity to eradicate this male witch, this filth, and he did not. To me, John is a dead man. He will soon feel what it is like to double-cross me, to not put the needs of the whole in front of his own," Bastiquil spewed. "These are trying times, but with persistence and hard work we will get through this."

"And what is to become of this witch; the one I am protecting?" Victor asked.

"You will continue to protect her with every ounce of your being. You will protect her as if she were me sitting next to you. She is a vital aspect of our end game and if she is hurt, it will hurt me," Bastiquil said, making sure his words were heard.

"I will protect her with my life, my lord," Victor said, bowing his head in respect.

Victor felt the jet being bumped around by the turbulence again. He had never had such a bad flight before in his life. He would be glad when this plane was safely on the ground. His master didn't seem fazed by it.

"Victor, what I am about to tell you is of the utmost importance. You must listen to me carefully," Bastiquil said, leaning in closer to Victor. "What is about to happen you will have no control over. You must do your best to make sure that you and the witch make it safely to the drop point. I wish I could help you through this one, but alas, I have no powers here."

"My lord, what is it? What has you so troubled about my mission?" Victor asked, confused and a little panicked that he might have upset his master.

"Victor, you must wake up, you must open your eyes. This plane is going to crash and I need you awake so you can secure the safety of the witch," Bastiquil said to a confused Victor.

"It's just a little turbulence Master," Victor said, with a curious look on his face.

"Victor, you fell asleep. That was the only way I could communicate with you, when I am not in the vessel's body. You have to be in a dream state. I need you to wake up Victor. The plane is going down," Bastiquil said to Victor.

"Wake the fuck up....NOW," Gina screamed at Victor, who opened his eyes and immediately went into panic mode. He had been caught off guard falling asleep, but he had also been able to communicate with his master.

Victor looked at Gina, who was still tied up and buckled into her seat.

"Do something Victor or we are going to die," Gina screamed. "The captain has been calling for you."

Victor quickly unbuckled his seatbelt and ran up the aisle to the cockpit door. Knocking on it, Victor waited until the captain opened the door. Entering the cockpit, he was taken aback by the chaos he witnessed. There were alerts going off, gauges swirling round and round, and a panicked captain trying his best to keep the plane in the air.

"Captain, what the hell is going on?" Victor barked.

"We are going down," the captain yelled back. "There are no ifs, ands, or buts about it. The time to salvage this has come and gone, we are going down over Iceland. You need to go brace yourself and make sure the girl is securely fastened in. I will try and give you a heads up right before we crash, but you need to be ready for anything. The gauges are not working accurately and I am flying solo here."

"How did this happen?" Victor asked.

"The storm was too much. The turbulence caused excessive damage and we were struck by lightning," the captain answered Victor's question, perturbed he wasn't doing as asked of him. "Now go, secure yourself. We have little time; maybe a minute at most."

Victor turned and made his way back into the cabin where a scared and anxious Gina awaited. Gina could barely handle the suspense of what was happening.

"We are going to crash land," Victor said, in a low, calm voice. "You need to brace yourself and be thankful we are crashing on land and not water."

"What do you mean water? Where the hell are we?" Gina asked.

"According to our fine captain, we are somewhere over Iceland," Victor announced to a shocked Gina.

"What the fuck?" Gina said.

Gina started to yell at Victor, but the captain interrupted. "Brace yourselves; we're coming in for a crash landing."

"Put your head in your lap, between your knees," Victor screamed at Gina, who did as told.

Upon impact, the plane shook with such force and vibration as it bounced across the hard ground, like a rock tossed across the surface of the water. The plane continued its brutal onslaught against the dirt, with the dirt being the only thing to slow it down. Suddenly, the plane spun sideways. Making contact with a huge tree, the plane was quickly cut right through the middle, and sent flying in opposite directions. One held the captain, who was now dead, and the other carried Gina and Victor.

The plane tore through the ground as a screaming Gina had flashes of her life and of the things she wished she had done. There were so many things she and Demetri wanted to do, to see in the world. She had wanted to expand her business; make it more global with an internet website. That didn't seem like it was going to happen or that it was the most pressing thing going on right now.

The plane was still moving. It met with a few more impacts of unknown origin, which caused it to bounce around like a ball in a pinball machine, then started to slow down before coming to an abrupt stop.

The bruised and battered Gina ended up passing out from hitting her head on the side of the plane. Victor was up and quickly went into survival mode, even though he had taken a beating himself. He had to get the girl to safety as his master had asked of him. The only thing concerning him now was how he was going to do it.

Chapter Seven

The clean-up crew for The Other Side was busy scrubbing up the mess brought on by Demetri and Bastiquil. It had been a long time since they had to go to this degree of cover-up, but the world was not ready for the full blown story of supernatural beings and their nightly excursions. It was all good and fine as long as it was Hollywood, but as soon as it touched their world, it became a big problem. So the clean-up crew would always be there to take care of the things others were not ready to know about.

Surprisingly, there were not as many deaths as originally thought and most people were buying the story they were given, about a bar-wide, drug-induced prank. Of course, there were people hired to take the blame, well paid for the time they would spend behind bars. But, it was all the nature of the beast.

The club would close down for a few months to give time for the gossip to settle and then it would reopen and typically things would go back to business as usual. The owners and the leaders in the Tulsa underground hoped it would play out like that.

As soon as the battle stopped and before everyone regained their wits, a secret, metal door came sliding down and barricaded the entrance into the basement, the Underside. It was unfortunate, for what was left down there would stay, supernatural or human, until it was safe to open things back up. The casualties of the night in the basement would stay hidden away, never to be talked about again. Bodies would be disposed of as needed and stories would be concocted to throw blame and suspicion away from the club. Regardless of what people might think about it personally, the overall belief of the leaders of underground Tulsa find the club a necessary evil. If it were not for the club, and the ability to let off steam and find willing people to be fed upon in a somewhat controlled area, the death toll would be a lot higher in the metro area.

Situations like the rogue serial killer who allowed news reporters like Kathy Reed to get a story out about ritual killings was what made it dangerous for the underworld. Yes, a serial killer can be explained away as a deranged human, but when it gets ritual like it did, well, it draws attention to cults and the supernatural. Luckily, with the battle tonight and the way it ended, it was possible that they have seen the last of the ritual serial killer.

Only time will tell if the cleanup was successful or not. Deny, deny, deny was the name of the game on this one. A rogue team of pranksters caught in the act as a prank turned deadly. Once the supernatural evidence was taken care of, the police would be called and an investigation would ensue. Kathy Reed would be all over this one. But, the owners had weathered worse than this. They would survive this one too and, in a few months, they would start opening up to the public again, slowly letting the crowds build back up.

Just as the clean-up crew finished with their version of what would become the cover-up, the club started shaking and rumbling. The floor cracked open as it had earlier in the evening during the battle. A light shined brightly as a dark figure came flying out of the crack. The crew heard laughter as the dark figure flew up and out of the front door.

Chapter Eight

Demetri paced the floor thinking about everything that happened the night before. He was still in shock that he had been able to overcome the demon. He had never felt such power coursing through his veins, never felt such a high as the one last night. He had made himself levitate. He made himself fly up the stairs from the basement at the club. Well, it was Zamaranum who had taken over and made it happen, but he still held the memories from the experience. Demetri wanted so badly to talk to someone about this. Alex was still passed out ever since he had cast Bastiquil out of him and Aldrik also did some damage from knocking him down. He knew Aldrik was downstairs, agitated and not sleeping. He had already been down there a few times to talk to him, but both times it ended up in a lecture from him. He didn't feel like getting another lecture about everything that had happened.

Demetri decided it best to get some air. He needed to get out and clear his head. He had too many thoughts going at once and decided that he wanted to be alone. Demetri set out in his jeep; he didn't have an agenda of where he wanted to go so he just drove. To his surprise he found himself at the hospital. He had just been driving around and must have subconsciously been thinking about Brandy. He decided to park the jeep and slip into the hospital to check in on her. He hated leaving her so brusquely at the hospital emergency room, but at least she had been given a fighting chance before he went and took on Bastiquil.

Demetri had called earlier after they got back to Gina's to check on her and the nurse said she had been moved to St. John's Hospital, across from Utica Square. Walking into the massive hospital he was greeted by a little old lady sitting behind the information desk. She eyed him over pretty good and Demetri was thinking he must look like a bruised and battered mess. More like a patient than a guest.

The little old lady was hesitant to give him information. She didn't need to voice it, she made the mistake of looking it up while Demetri was standing there and he saw it in her mind. Thanking her for her time, Demetri quickly made his way back out the door he had entered and found another entrance to the hospital, one free from prying eyes.

Upon reaching the 6th floor, Demetri followed the signs on the walls which led him to Brandy's hospital room. He just wanted to see her; to make sure she was okay. He felt remorse for not being able to get inside the house sooner and stop all this from happening to Alex, Brandy, and Gina and even to Ella. But he actually hadn't seen that one coming. *Ella willingly sacrificed herself in front of her son so a demon could reenter this world? Man, that's going to be some seriously fucked up therapy session for Alex; if he ever comes out of this coma he is in.*

Maybe they should have brought him to the hospital, but Aldrik thought it best to heed to caution and bring him back to Gina's. If needed, Aldrik's blood could do more healing for him than any doctor in this hospital.

Demetri realizing he was lost in his own thoughts, quickly brought himself back to reality and found he was standing outside of Brandy's hospital room. He peered through the doorway to see if she was alone. All he could hear was the beeping of her heart monitor. She had oxygen hooked up to her nose, but it wasn't a life support machine.

As Demetri entered the room, and walked over to Brandy who looked as if she were sleeping soundly. He didn't want to wake her, he just wanted to make sure she was okay, but as he stood there he found himself overcome with joy when she opened her eyes and looked up at him.

"Brandy, hey, it's me, Demetri," he said, not knowing really what the proper thing to say to one in this situation. "How are you feeling?"

Brandy looked at Demetri as a tear began to roll down her cheek. "You saved my life. I was left to die, but you saved me."

Demetri looked at her, his face softening, as he realized they had never gotten a fair shot at getting to know each other. Brandy only knew him as the power-wielding witch who attacked her best friend at a club because of a dream. Well, hopefully, this was an opportunity for them to get on the right track. "Contrary to popular belief, I don't enjoy watching people die. I don't regret for a moment what I did; I would do it again. It was the right thing to do," he said, moving from foot to foot uncomfortably. "So, how are you feeling?"

"Like Alex's psycho mother just plunged a knife into my chest," Brandy said, with a dry, quiet voice. She started to cry again.

"Yes, I'm just as surprised as you. The Balashon played that one out beautifully," Demetri said, as she quickly darted her eyes his way with a look of pain and disgust.

"Well, I don't really see any beauty in the fact that my best friend's mother tried to kill me so her son could be possessed by a demon," Brandy said, with all the energy she could muster up. "Oh my god? What happened to Alex?"

"Alex is back at Gina's place, sleeping. I was able to get the demon out of his body but I think the demon was in there so long he may have done some damage, so we are just monitoring him until he wakes up. Look, I didn't mean anything by saying the actions by the Balashon were beautifully pulled off. Sometimes when I am nervous, I put my foot in my mouth. Actually I do that quite often," Demetri said.

"Who is we?" Brandy asked. "You and Gina?"

"Actually, no. It is me and Aldrik. He is a vampire, a close friend," Demetri said, as if it were something said every day. "I was hoping I would be able to talk to you when I arrived. You see, Gina is missing. She was taken by the man they called Victor and we have not been able to locate her since we were all at the Balashon mansion last night."

"You left my sleeping best friend with a vampire? Are you mental?" Brandy made a move as to try and get out of bed, but winced in pain and lay back down.

"Okay, please let me explain. Aldrik is an old vampire and in control of his actions. He isn't driven or controlled by blood lust, so Alex is safe with him. I promise," Demetri said, as he looked at her face, and then looked down at the floor. "Plus, he's kinda my boyfriend."

"Your boyfriend," Brandy looked at him through tired, blood-shot eyes. "I don't think I will ever get used to this world."

"I tell myself the same damned thing every day," Demetri said.

"So you saved me even at the expense of your best friend? I may have misjudged you," Brandy said, as she began to get emotional again.

Demetri just stood there in silence as he smiled down at her.

"I don't know where they might have taken her. They kept me locked in a room with very little interaction with anyone other than Victor. He is the one who took me there, then there was the person who brought me breakfast, and those who took me to bathe. That was it, as far as interaction. They were not forthcoming with any information, especially when it came to the demon or Alex," Brandy said, as she took in too deep a breath and started coughing. This triggered

47

a deep pain within her and also set her monitors into overdrive as the beeping started going off.

Demetri reached over and put his hand on her forehead and she instantly fell asleep. The monitors settled down and he also put his hand over her wound and sent forth some energy he hoped would aid in a quicker healing time than one would normally have to suffer through. She had been through enough as it was.

Chapter Nine

As the sun began its descent and darkness took hold of the city of Tulsa, Aldrik happily came up from the basement to rejoin a sleeping Alex and a preoccupied Demetri. It wasn't that he was opposed to Gina's basement accommodations because he had definitely stayed in much worse, but he was going stir crazy down there knowing so much was going on above him. Gina had been missing now for almost 24 hours and they were nowhere near finding her.

"I heard you leave earlier," Aldrik said. "Did you go and check on the girl?"

"Yes, I did go check on her. She is doing about as good as can be expected. Her whole world turned upside down last night and her best friend's mother tried to kill her. All in all, she is doing okay," he answered, with a little bit more distance than Aldrik liked to hear from him.

"We will find her Demetri, we will. It might take some time due to the Balashon's resources, but we will find her. They can't hide forever. They had to have taken her for a reason, some type of insurance. They may want to trade her for Alex," Aldrik tried to offer some comfort to Demetri.

"I just have this awful feeling something is wrong, that things will never be the same again. It has been bothering me all day. I can't put my fingers on it, but I know what went down last night was a game-changer for us all,"

Demetri said, letting his face and his voice tell Aldrik where his mind was.

"Demetri, you can't give up hope just yet. We have just started our journey to find Gina. We can't give up on her," Aldrik pleaded.

"I am not giving up hope; I am simply stating we have been dealt a major blow. The demon struck me right in the heart, right where he knew I would be the weakest. The Balashon gets some kind of sick, twisted fulfillment from watching others pain. Just like with Alex, making him watch his mother stab his best friend and then to turn the knife on herself. What kind of sick fucks are we dealing with?" Demetri asked, hoping to find some solace in the words, but finding none.

"We are dealing with a group of people who are highly intelligent, highly financed, and believe with certainty, almost more than some believe in christianity, they are right and just in their beliefs and actions. We are dealing with a highly organized cult, who has lived in the shadows for 3,000 years. They have lived and operated in the darkness much better than any vampire could ever hope to do. They were not detected, they stayed the course and they will continue to stay the course. We just have to get back in the game and find them," Aldrik said, finally getting his full attention.

"They have been ahead of us the entire time. They have beaten us at every turn. The only thing we have done right was sending their demon back to hell where he belongs," Demetri said.

"Well, I am afraid that has only pissed them off. Vanquishing Bastiquil has made them more determined than ever to inflict revenge. It is what I would do if I were them. We have to try and get them to reveal themselves, show their hand, and make a mistake. They are desperate now. Their entire life's mission was sent back into that fiery pit. You basically killed their parental figure Demetri," Aldrik said.

"Are you trying to make me feel better? If so, you are doing a fucking bang-up job of it Aldrik. I know every moment which passes by, we run the risk of not finding Gina. I know every second we are not out there looking is another second closer to her possible death. I know the odds of the game. I just don't like the collateral we are playing with. I dealt them a death blow, why wouldn't they deal one back?" Demetri asked, in a desperate voice.

"These are a highly intelligent group of men. They will be out for revenge, but they will make sure you feel it to your deepest core. They will parade Gina in front of you until you can't stand it anymore. What I am saying is they will present themselves to you, they will by their nature. It is the nature of revenge. One will get the biggest bang for their buck by killing her in front of you. So we just have to make sure we are ready when the time comes to take action," Aldrik explained.

"I will move every stone on this planet to find her. I promised her that I would take care of her and I will not fail her in her darkest hour. I will find Gina and I will eradicate every Balashon member doing so," Demetri said.

"What if every Balashon member isn't of this earth? What if we are dealing with some supernatural beings as well?" Aldrik offered up as food for thought.

Demetri looked at Aldrik with a crazed look in his eyes. "I know full well what we may be dealing with. I have no misunderstandings about it. I expect at least half of the Balashon to be somewhat demonically affiliated. I would fight the devil himself if it meant I had a chance to get Gina back," Demetri said.

"Well, you may have to. You may very well have to fight, outwit, and defeat the devil himself before all is said and done. I just don't want you to have any misconceptions going into this that it will be fast and easy. More likely, it will be long and drawn out. If you think it will be fast and furious, then you are mistaken," Aldrik said to a deep in thought Demetri.

"What about Alex? What do you think is happening to him?" Demetri asked.

"Well, the longer he is under, the worse the outlook. I was curious if you had any spells you could use to bring him out of it? If all else fails, we could use my blood and see what happens?" Aldrik posed the question to Demetri.

"I have tried to listen to his thoughts, to see if I could see where he is or if he is still there. I get nothing but silence. He isn't dreaming of anything, he isn't thinking about anyone or anything. It's almost as if there is a void there," Demetri told Aldrik.

"Well, something is going on within him for him to still be breathing on his own. Why don't we just try some of my blood to see what happens? By giving him just little doses at a time, we should be able to give him just enough that it would serve as a healing property," Aldrik suggested.

After giving it some thought, Demetri finally conceded to letting him give Alex some of his blood. Demetri was frustrated he had been given all of this power but it was almost like it was in a time warp of its own. It only worked when he was under extreme duress, or so it seemed. *What good is having all of this power if I can't access it when I need it?*

"Very well, just a little. We will see if there is a change in him after the first dose," Demetri said.

Aldrik walked over to where Alex lay sleeping and bit his own wrist. He brought blood to the surface and forced Alex's mouth open just enough for the blood to drop in. As the blood filled his mouth, there was no sign Alex was responding. "It might take some time for…"

Before Aldrik could get his sentence out, a light began to shine from the back of Alex's head, right where the tattooed symbol referencing Bastiquil was. Demetri ran over to Alex and lifted his head up just enough to see the symbol indeed light up just like the ones on the ground did right before the hellhounds crawled through the hole.

Then before either of them could react, one of the tattoos on Alex's body reached outward from his skin and grabbed a hold of Aldrik's arm and brought it down to Alex's mouth. He started sucking more and more of the blood. Aldrik, tried to get away from him, but was unable to break the hold the tattoo had on him. Even with his strength he was not able to break free.

Demetri and Aldrik watched in horror as the tattoos on Alex's body came to life again, and became animated. They were active and watching. The tattoos were feeding off of the blood. This brought back memories of the previous night's events and of the casualties they all suffered because of the demon. *What is causing this to happen now? Why are the tattoos taking on form when there is no detectable demon inside of Alex?* Demetri summoned his powers and hit the tattooed arm with a burst of energy that sent it fleeing back into the safety of Alex's skin.

Aldrik was free and his self-made gash to his wrist was already closing up, healing itself. "What the hell just happened?"

"Hell is the right word," Demetri said. "We forget this body was made specifically for the use of hell itself. It was created to host an extremely powerful demon. I am sure it reacted to the demon running through your veins."

Aldrik looked at Demetri with hurt in his eyes, but with the knowledge that what he was saying was most likely the truth. Bastiquil said the same thing to him just last night; vampires are walking the earth due to a demonic possession of their blood, a blood demon. As much as it hurt to believe such a thing deep inside, Aldrik knew it made perfect sense. But to hear it from the mouth of the man he loves was like someone taking a sharp metal rod and piercing his heart. He did his best to hide his hurt, but he knew they could keep no secrets from each other.

Demetri walked over to Aldrik and placed his arm around his neck and gave him a tight hug. "Forgive me Aldrik. I didn't mean it to come out like it did. I know you had no say in what happened to you and for me to throw it in your face was just downright wrong."

"No need for apologies, especially when it is the truth. As much as it hurts to hear, I am here now, fifteen-hundred years later due to a blood demon running through my veins. It is what it is and we must move on from it. We have got to find out what is going on with Alex so we can concentrate on finding Gina," Aldrik said, hoping he masked the pain he was feeling from Demetri's remarks.

"Well, let's hope the blood running through your veins is enough to bring Alex back to us. It is crucial we find out what he remembers, what he knows about Bastiquil's plans for Gina. If anyone is going to know, it has to be him. Bastiquil was in his body, used it for his doing and then used it to plot against us, against Gina. If there is any chance of getting information on where Gina is, then Alex is our best hope," Demetri said, with honesty and a profound sense of failure. He didn't really believe Alex would remember what took place when the demon possessed his body and made him do despicable things to people. *How could he?* He had a demon attached to his soul, eating away at it, eating the good right out of him. *Was I quick enough to save him? That was the big question, wasn't it?*

Chapter Ten

Lincoln Reed was busy cleaning up from his previous client, his mind still on his boss, Alex, and all of the time he had taken off recently. In all the years he worked for Alex at Blue Moon Tattoo, he had never known his boss to take extended time off. If, for some reason, he did, he always kept in touch just to make sure things were running smooth. Blue Moon was Alex's baby and he had worked hard, long hours to make sure they were the best in town. Hell, it could possibly be said they were the best in the state.

Lincoln grew up in Branson, Missouri, and assumed his life would take the route of an artist. He could draw and paint just about anything and had made good money selling his art at the local festivals Branson was well known for.

He also grew up spending the summers on Table Rock Lake, a beautiful, clear lake where you could see down to the bottom. It was a gorgeous lake. They would water ski, ride Jet Ski's, camp, and just basically live the summer life of the lake. It was heaven there.

It was at Table Rock Lake where Lincoln met a tattoo artist he thought was just the coolest ever. His name was Jett York and he was tattooed from head to toe. He was the coolest cat Lincoln had met to date and Lincoln had seen many a different type of people come through Branson. Branson was a big draw due to the eclectic type of activities and entertainment held there.

Jett took the summer off to spend it at Table Rock with his family. His mother had just gone through a long battle with breast cancer which claimed her life. As a tribute to her memory, the family all got together to spend time celebrating her life. Besides, they would probably never get the opportunity to do this type of thing again.

Jett and Lincoln hit it off the moment they met. Jett was drawn to Lincoln's art and Lincoln was drawn to Jett's unique ability to capture art in tattoo form. As they spent the summer learning about each other's different style of art, Lincoln began to realize that he loved the art of tattooing even more than the art he was creating. Jett had spent the summer showing Lincoln the ins and outs of tattooing and Lincoln had caught on quickly. He was doing professional looking tattoos before the season ended.

Jet and Lincoln became best friends that summer and had continued to stay that way even though they didn't live in the same state. Jett went back to his hometown of Chicago where he had a tattoo parlor and Lincoln moved to Tulsa to pursue his new occupation as a tattoo artist.

Lincoln met Alex when he moved to Tulsa. Lincoln visited all of the tattoo parlors in Tulsa, eventually ending up at Blue Moon Tattoo. Lincoln took an automatic liking to Alex and Alex pretty much did the same. Alex saw a good, honest, hardworking man in Lincoln and Lincoln never forgot the break Alex gave him. He worked hard and tried to make sure when Alex was gone the place ran the same way. Clients were treated in the same fashion as if Alex were there.

Lincoln began to worry about Alex. This was the longest time he'd gone without checking with the studio. Alex trusted Lincoln and his other employees, but Alex was just like that, he liked to make sure everyone was happy and everything was running smoothly. He called Alex's phone many times and had yet to receive a callback. He resorted to trying Brandy's phone as she typically knew where Alex might be at any given moment. He had been unable to get in touch with her. *Things just don't seem up to par.* He definitely had his worry face on.

It was almost time for his next appointment to arrive, so Lincoln decided he could take a quick smoke break out back. Alex didn't allow smoking even in the break room and smoking in the room with customers, well, it didn't happen. Alex's rules. They were good rules as people like to think you always have their best interests at heart.

Lincoln yelled over at Jerry Black, who was busy doing a body piercing on some girl. Jerry was Blue Moon Tattoo's resident body piercing expert. "Hey Jerry, I am stepping out back for a minute. Let me know if you need me." Everyone working there knew "stepping out back" was the code for a break.

"No problem Linc. I have it all under control in here," Jerry yelled back at him.

Grabbing his cigarettes and lighter, he headed out back. Putting a stopper in the door so that it wouldn't close behind him, Lincoln pulled out a cigarette and lit it up. It was a nasty habit he knew, but we all had a few of those nasty habits somewhere in our lives. Habit, fetish, call it what you want, but we all have something. Lincoln thought about the word fetish and why it got such a bad connotation to it. It was essentially the same thing as a habit, but when people think of fetish they envision people in leather, sex toys, and orgies. Yes, those are all true, but lots of those could be considered a habit of the person who it was referring to.

Damn it is hot out here, Lincoln thought to himself, as he paced around in the back alley.

Deep in thought and sweating his ass off, he had no idea he was being stalked. He wouldn't have known it, how could he, the demon stuck to the shadows, lurking in the dark.

As Lincoln opened his mouth to bring the cigarette up for another drag, Bastiquil lunged at him, spinning and changing form so he would fit as he entered through his mouth. His back arched as Bastiquil cleaned house and made room for himself inside Lincoln. His body was jerking back and forth until he fell to his knees. Bastiquil was now one with him and had already begun to eat at his life-force, his soul. It wasn't the vessel, but it would do for now.

Bastiquil smiled to himself, happy to be in a body again and as he smiled so did the body of Lincoln Reed. For Bastiquil and Lincoln were bound together. They were one. What Bastiquil did, Lincoln also would do.

Bastiquil knew that he didn't have much time in this body so he needed to get to work quickly. He needed a knife and bowl. Once acquired, the fun would begin. Ever since he found out the vessel was a tattoo artist who painted skin for a living, Bastiquil knew what he wanted to do. He just didn't get a chance to do it before Zamaranum exiled him from Alex's body.

Bastiquil wasn't concerned. He could still put his plan in motion and find his way back to the vessel's body. Once he did, there would be hell to pay.

Chapter Eleven

As Victor jumped up trying to assess the situation, he felt a sharp, searing pain in his leg. Looking down, he saw a jagged, pointed piece of metal sticking into his right thigh. It was bleeding badly, but he had been so worried about the girl he hadn't even thought about his own safety, his own body. How could he protect the girl if he was dead?

There wasn't much left of the plane, at least the front end of it, but as Victor looked around he was able to find a blanket. Ripping the end of it so it was about six inches in width and about three feet in length, Victor set it aside while he looked over the metal shrapnel and its location. Even though, it was bleeding it had missed a major artery so Victor grabbed the ripped piece of blanket, gripped the piece of metal and slowly pulled it out of his leg. Blood rushed out of the wound as he expected it would. Grabbing the ripped blanket he tied off the wound and secured it around his leg. The bleeding should stop shortly, but right now his concern was getting the girl to safety.

They crash landed somewhere in Iceland, but that wasn't as bad as it would sound to most people. You see, Iceland was still in its peak travel season, although it ended at the end of August. This was August 21st, so they still had a good week or so before any bad weather, or at least that's what the books tell you. What Victor had learned in all his years working as an assassin for the Balashon was to expect the unexpected and he lived by this motto. So taking stock, he knew they needed to get to cover quickly before the rainy season was upon them. It would be cold and wet which wasn't a good combination.

Victor's only plan thus far was to head south. His gut instinct told him they were not too far into Iceland when the plane went down and by heading south they should be able to reach the shore. The sun had not been up long, but Victor was able to use the position of the sun to ascertain which direction they needed to head. He started to walk over to Gina and as he took a step he winced in pain as the gash sent ripples of electricity like pain through his leg. *This was going to be an interesting day.*

Making his way over to Gina he decided it was in both their best interest if he kept her tied up as long as possible. He would test the waters for a bit and see what her mood was like when she woke. If she was good, then maybe he will think about untying the binds.

Victor knew Bastiquil's spell over Gina had long faded, but she must have hurt herself in the crash or maybe she passed out from the shock of it all. That would not have been unheard of. As he looked her over, he could tell that she had some blood pooled around the right side of her head indicating she had hit her head when the plane went down. This was why she had passed out. She was hurt, but a hurt witch could be even more dangerous. She was still passed out, but the gash on her head had stopped bleeding and her pulse was within reasonable readings. She would live. There had been so much commotion going they both most likely would suffer from muscle and joint pain for the next few weeks. She could even have a concussion. Victor also needed to watch out for infection in his wound. He had looked all over the plane, or what was left of it, and didn't find a first-aid kit.

What he was glad of though was his bag that contained the ancient Balashon artifacts was still intact. Had anything happened to those, well, let's just say it would not have been a good thing. The bag contained clothes, but most importantly money, multiple passports with different names, and it contained the Balashonion Grimoire. The small bag from the SUV, the one he had thrown the weapons into, was nowhere to be found.

Victor grabbed the bag and tried waking Gina up. She did not respond to his first attempts. He tried several times. Just when he was thinking about alternative ways of waking her up, he saw life come back to her face. Her eyes opened slightly searching for vision and trying to avoid the sun. It took a few seconds for Gina to get her wits about her, but when she did she begin to hit at Victor with her bound hands. To this Victor wasn't fazed at all. He merely grabbed her hands and gave her a stern look.

"I know you don't like me, but we are going to have to work together if we are going to get out of here alive," Victor said to Gina, who looked at him with disgust.

"Why would I help you with anything?" Gina questioned.

"It is in your best interest. Look around you. Do you see this broken fuselage of the plane? Do you see a pilot anywhere? Me either. He is most likely dead. You and I are all we have now and we are in the wilderness somewhere in Iceland and we have to head south to hit the shoreline before the seasonal weather starts up," Victor told Gina, who looked at him with anger in her eyes. But logic quickly took over.

Just as Gina was about to say something to Victor, they heard a great boom of thunder. Victor just turned and looked, but Gina jumped as if someone startled her. Looking into the background of the horizon Victor could see that a storm was brewing. He could see the visible display of lightening as it danced across clouds fighting to push the sun out of view.

"I'm going to undo your seatbelt Gina, but I will not have this back and forth fight with you all day. I am also not afraid to hurt you. I realize you are a powerful witch, but as you could probably tell by my battle with your boyfriend, Demetri, I can handle myself against magic. So don't try me. Got it?" Victor asked, as she looked at him with hatred in her eyes. He just stared at her until she finally relented and shook her head in agreement.

"Where the hell do you think I would run to anyway? I have never been to Iceland. I don't know where we are in relation to the shore and I am pretty sure with any wilderness, at least if it is like home, it comes with some hungry animals," she said to Victor, who nodded in agreement.

"I think our best bet for the time being is to stay here inside the plane while the storm passes over. It looks like it is going to be a bad one and neither of us is in any condition at the moment to weather a severe storm. Can I get you to agree with me on that one?" he asked.

As much as Gina hated to agree with him on anything, she did give in. "I would have to agree with you. What are we going to do about keeping warm? It's not like we were dressed for cold weather as you kidnaped me from Tulsa where temperatures were 100 degrees," Gina asked.

"We are just going to have to make do with what we have at the moment and be thankful that we have a somewhat intact fuselage we can use as shelter from the rain. As for the temperature, here is a partial piece of blanket if you find you need some warmth," he said, tossing the torn blanket at Gina and pointed out the roof of the fuselage as if she couldn't already see it.

As he unbuckled the seatbelt, he told her to sit tight while he looked over the crash site for anything that might be of help to them. Gina did not argue with him as she knew this was not the time to take a stand. Being stuck in the wilderness in a country one has never been before was intimidating and she wasn't sure if they truly were over Iceland or not. Hell, Gina didn't even know if they spoke English in Iceland. This was not one of the countries she had ever thought she would come to, but she did know one thing for sure, Victor, may the universe help her, was the one able to get her to the safety of a city.

So Gina sat quietly in her own thoughts, thankful to have survived the crash. Her head was pounding as she thought ahead of the time when she would be forced to take a stand against Victor. At some point, she would have to so she could at least try and get a call to Demetri. But what if Demetri hadn't survived the battle with Bastiquil? She had not allowed herself to think things like that yet. Her dear sweet Demetri; he had been fully downloaded with an amazing batch of past life information and powers, but had not been shown how to use them. He needed her now more than ever and she was stuck somewhere, possibly in Iceland, with this brute of a man, Victor. Yes, she was biding her time for the exact moment when she would make her move against him, but she wanted the safety and comfort of a city, not the wilderness to do it.

Victor scanned the immediate area of the crash site in hopes of finding anything of use. He wasn't sure what he would find, but anything was better than nothing. So he scanned and rummaged and as he did, the storm got closer and closer. This must have been the same storm that had done so much damage to them in the air, the one causing the crash. This told Victor it was going to be one badass storm moving through and they definitely needed to take cover and ride this one out. He didn't want to be exposed to the elements when this monster hit. It was bad enough their plane had been torn apart. Although, one part of it was exposed and open to the elements, it also was a place for them to seek shelter from the rain that would be falling soon. At least it wouldn't be falling on their heads. Victor was able to find shards of metal that could be fashioned into a weapon, as you can never have too many, and he also found a few more blankets scattered around and the first-aid kit.

The first-aid kit had been opened, he assumed upon hitting the earth, but there were still some things inside it that they could salvage and use. He was especially thankful since he sustained a significant leg injury. It would do neither of them any good if his leg got infected and he could not fight to defend them from whatever presented itself as an obstacle to their safe return to the shore cities.

As the storm lit up the sky with flashes of lightning, followed by loud booms of thunder, Victor guessed the rainstorm to be less than a mile out. He made his way back to what was left of the plane and found Gina still quietly sitting there in her seat, with the torn blanket wrapped around her shoulders. He threw the other two blankets he had found at her which she begrudgingly thanked him for. It wasn't a few minutes after Victor made it back to the plane that the rain started pounding itself onto the ground outside. The noise it made as it hit the fuselage amplified as they did not have the luxury of the engines and the speed of the plane masking the noise. Usually, Gina loved storms, this one, not so much.

The lightning and thunder kept up its display of power and each time the thunder cracked, Gina jumped as if it caught her off guard. The truth of the matter was, it did catch her off guard because her thoughts were with her best friend. She had been taken away before she could see anything. She remembered Bastiquil removing Demetri and Aldrik by force out of the room and shutting the doors behind them, but she didn't remember much after that. She knew if Demetri could focus his thoughts, focus his strength, that he had a good shot at defeating Bastiquil, but if he wavered at all, even one slight instance, Bastiquil would move in for the kill.

Gina was brought back from her thoughts by another crash of thunder and the sound of Victor's voice.

"Are you comfortable?" Victor asked.

"For now, yes," Gina answered back.

"We need to be ready to act at a moment's notice so please keep that in mind when you are drifting off into your dark thoughts of hatred toward me and my master," Victor said.

"Ready to act for what?" Gina asked.

"We don't know what this storm will bring. We are in the only metal container in a field of trees during a lightning storm. We could be sitting ducks out here. Let's not forget there are also hungry animals, which will be looking for food and shelter during this storm too. We don't want to be caught off guard," Victor told Gina.

Gina just nodded at him as he started trying to custom the metal scraps he found into some type of weapon. Gina decided it in her best interest to watch him as he did in case she found herself in a situation where she needed to defend herself.

The storm raged on bringing more lightning, thunder, cold rain, and wind. This was going to be a long road ahead of them and Gina wasn't looking forward to it one bit.

Chapter Twelve

Brandy Helmsworth lay in her hospital bed, hurting, but not able to feel the full effects of the pain due to the morphine drip the doctor had ordered. Brandy couldn't help but think back on the past week's events. *Who would have thought demons, vampires, werewolves, hell, even witches with tangible powers existed? You see it all the time in movies and read about it in books, but to experience it first hand, to almost die from it gives a whole new outlook on life.*

Brandy finally knew Demetri and Gina; she understood what they were all about. Demetri tried to help people in trouble. He was there for the ones who needed him. It didn't matter if you were human or supernatural, if you were willing to ask for help, to accept change for the better, then Demetri was there to help.

Brandy felt guilt over how she had judged Demetri and Gina. She had thought they were out to hurt Alex and all along they were trying to help him. Alex was an innocent party in the affairs that transpired, but Alex also caused a lot of the pain himself by taking those damned mind altering drugs he got from that bastard drug dealer Brandon. Brandy had more than a few choice words for him. If she could, she would have Brandon locked away for good. Anyone that would willingly help another person self-implode was as bad as the person doing the damned drugs themselves, even worse.

Brandy had been waking up from nightmares of Ella, Alex's mother, stabbing her in the chest. The look in Ella's eyes as she did it, made Brandy tremble with fear. There was something wrong there, a vacancy in them, a vast hole of emptiness. Alex had always known something was off with his mother. However, he thought it had to do with his father leaving and his mother feeling abandoned, not that she was in on this entire conspiracy with the Balashon to raise this demon from the depths of hell. Ella, however, had this look of sincere regret on her face, or at least that was what it appeared to Brandy right before she stabbed her.

Demetri told her about Ella turning the knife on herself. Ella would have allowed herself and Brandy to burn in hell for eternity, to have their souls fed on by this fucking demon Bastiquil. This made Brandy so angry she could scream. The heart monitor was telling the story of how upset it made her. At one point, the nurse had to increase her morphine drip to get it to slow down. For the most part the morphine did its job, but she still continued to have thoughts about the previous night, the morphine just made them more bearable, and a little distorted.

The days leading up to prior night's events had not been a truly horrible experience. The Balashon members had treated her like she was some honored guest. They fed her, bathed her, changed her sheets daily, gave her fresh clothes, but had she known they were fattening her up for slaughter, she would have fought harder and made their jobs a little more difficult.

She wanted to see Alex. She wanted to know that he was okay. *What must Alex be thinking about his own mother killing herself? It must be pure torture for him. The look on his face when he saw them bring me out*, Brandy thought to herself. *He knew what they were going to do to me. The look on his face said he knew. That must have been why he was screaming at Victor, telling him it wasn't part of the deal. Bless his heart, so much pain and loss.*

Brandy picked up the hospital phone and dialed Blue Moon Tattoo somewhat out of habit and somewhat to feel and hear something normal. A big part of her knew Alex wasn't there, but that part wasn't in control, the pain, the morphine, took control and she wanted to hear Alex's voice.

The phone rang twice and then Brandy heard a man's voice pick up. "Blue Moon Tattoo, how can I help you?"

"Alex?" she asked.

"Alex? No, he isn't available right now. Can I take a message?"

"No, no message," Brandy said. "Wait, yes, I do want to leave a message. Can you tell him Brandy called?"

"Brandy? Oh, I am surprised to hear from you. Really surprised," Lincoln said, as he was being prompted by the puppet master Bastiquil. He was extremely frustrated she was still alive.

"Did you say you were surprised? Why would you say that," she asked, thinking that maybe the morphine had her hearing things.

"Oh, no, I didn't mean it like that. I just meant you typically call Alex on his cell phone. That is all I meant," Bastiquil said, trying to cover up her curiosity. His total shock of hearing the girl wasn't dead may have triggered her suspicions. That wasn't a good thing. He was going to have to take care of this right away. "Where can he get in touch with you?"

"That's okay, just tell him I called. I am sure he is probably too busy with the witches to care anyway," she said, as she hung up the phone. She couldn't believe she had just said that to Lincoln, but she also knew she meant it. If truth be told, she was jealous. Alex had spent so much time with the witches he wasn't there to protect her. *Man, that morphine is some truth serum for fucking sure.*

68

As Brandy drifted off to sleep, her dreams were filled with nightmares of last night's events like they were on repeat and she had to see it over and over again.

Chapter Thirteen

Bastiquil hung up the phone and grumbled to himself as he had not found out where the girl was. He had to get to her. Victor had wanted to offer her soul as sacrifice and so she would be. But he had to be careful, he knew this body wasn't going to hold out for too much longer and he still had work to do.

Bastiquil grabbed the keys to Lincoln's car and headed towards the door.

"Hey Linc, where are you going? You are supposed to close today," Jerry said.

"Plans have changed. I got called into the hospital for a test. It can't wait. Sorry Jerry, you are going to have to close today," Bastiquil said, secretly happy to be messing with the boy's plans.

"Dude, that sucks royally," Jerry said.

"Sorry, shit happens. Medical situations come first," Bastiquil said, as he opened the door and walked out into the parking lot.

"What a fucking asshole," Jerry said, as he turned and walked back to what he was doing.

Outside, Bastiquil was laughing as he climbed into Lincoln's car, placed the keys into the ignition and fired up the car. Backing up, he peeled out of the parking lot and headed down the street looking for any medical facility. As he was driving north, he noticed a blue hospital sign that was pointing him in the direction he was already headed. May as well go and find out what's up. If they are big enough and have the supplies he needs, then he wouldn't have an issue getting what he needed from Lincoln's body.

He had the radio blasting as he drove, happy to be doing some human shit again. He could feel the thrill one must get when operating a heavy piece of machine like this at fast speeds. It was intoxicating, thrilling, and fun.

He followed the blue signs that said hospital until he drove past it on the north side of 21st street. Pulling into the parking lot he parked the car spot and quickly made his way inside.

"Excuse me miss, but could you tell me where I might be able to find the blood bank or lab where they draw blood?" Bastiquil asked.

"Certainly," the overzealous lady said. "You follow the yellow signs on the wall down and around until you make your way to the south side of the building. You will find signs all along the way that lead you to the lab."

"Thank you for your help," Bastiquil said, trying to be polite like the humans do.

"God bless," the lady volunteer said.

Bastiquil stopped and turned around to look at the lady and smiled coyly at her. "That is not likely to happen ma'am, so you can keep your god."

The lady, shell-shocked, had no reply for Bastiquil other than her mouth hanging wide open. *If I were in the vessel and had full use of my powers, I would have made a swarm of flies invade her mouth. How dare she try to bless him with her god?*

He followed the yellow signs and made his way to the lab. Walking in, it looked like he was the only person there. Just as he was getting excited at the prospect of having the lab all to himself, he heard a gentleman in the back. "I will be right with you."

Bastiquil reached behind him and locked the door, as he did so, he stepped up to the counter and waited for the man to come up and check him in. A big man, with white scrubs came walking over to him. "Hello there, my name is Joshua. How can I help you?"

"Joshua, I need for you to get me some needles to draw blood and some blood bags to fill them up with," Bastiquil said, looking at him with a smile on his face.

"Do you have your order form from your doctor for me to be able to do this test and a copy of your insurance card?" he asked.

"Well Joshua, I do have this," Bastiquil said, as he reached over and tapped him on the forehead causing him to fall to the ground unconscious.

He jumped over the counter top to the side of the lab where he had access to the supplies he needed. Stepping up to the cabinets he opened them one by one until he found what he was looking for. He quickly grabbed a bag that was lying off to the side of the cabinet and started filling it up with needles, hoses, and blood bags. He grabbed some alcohol and band-aids and headed out the door and down the hallway.

Walking out of the lobby doors, he made his way back to the vehicle. He drove back to Blue Moon Tattoo. The studio was the only place he would be safe doing what he needed to do. When he arrived back to the studio, he immediately told Jerry he could leave and Jerry never had to be told twice. Jerry grabbed his bag and headed out the front door. Bastiquil locked the door to the shop so he wouldn't be bothered by anyone.

Taking out the needles, tubes, and blood bags he began to pull the needle out of its plastic wrap, then the tubing. After he had those in place, he grabbed the blood bags and alcohol swabs. "You are supposed to sanitize your arms before injecting it with a needle," he said coyly.

Wiping his arm with the alcohol swab, he hooked the needle to the tubing attached to the blood bag. Taking the needle, he injected it into the bend of his arm. He must have been a natural because he hit the vein the first time. Clicking a switch on the needle head the blood started to flow nicely down the tube. He continued until he had four bags of blood. Any human would have been feeling nauseous and faint, but being a demon made this easy.

Getting up and placing the bags of blood into the refrigerator, he turned and as he did he found himself looking into a mirror. The image looking back was of Lincoln, not Bastiquil and Lincoln was looking pretty bad. His face was blotchy. He had dark circles under his eyes and an overall look of someone sick. Bastiquil knew he was burning up this body quickly as it was not meant to hold a demon like himself. He needed the vessel, and he needed the comfort of Alex. It wouldn't be long before he would be forced to leave Lincoln's body and find refuge in another. Taking the four bags of blood from Lincoln's body really took a toll on him, but this body was temporary.

His plan was in motion. Soon he would have what he needed and the first steps would be complete. It was just about time for him to pay a visit to Phillip Anthony Green III, aka John Berryman. Things needed to be set right, and John was just the man to do that. John owed it to him.

Chapter Fourteen

Night seemed to comfort Demetri. A time when the sun was not beating down on them at a hundred plus degrees and time when one of his best friends was able to sit beside him and help talk him through this madness. Gina was nowhere to be found. Alex was still unconscious. Brandy was getting better and should be able to come home soon. That was the only good news they had had thus far. As time marched on so did the likelihood of finding Gina.

Aldrik had asked him if he had thought about doing a location spell on Gina. Demetri's thoughts were so scattered that he actually had not thought of it. It seemed every other thought wasn't his own, but rather a random mix. He needed to calm down, to regain control, to figure out how to work these new gifts, these new powers. He couldn't wait until the next time he was deep in battle to be able to use them. That wasn't going to work. People were depending on him to get it together, to figure this out.

Demetri thought back on what had happened when they gave Alex some of Aldrik's blood. His tattoos came alive and were fighting for the blood. They were reaching outward from his skin wanting the blood and they did this without the demon inside of him. This had a brand new meaning for Demetri. Alex was more than just a vessel. Alex already had a predisposition for the supernatural. His bloodline was from a demon. This direct link to Bastiquil and the fact his tattoos were handpicked by the demon through dreams had made his body into something more than a vessel. Alex of course followed every command, not realizing he had been used, not realizing he followed the will of his grandfather.

It didn't take Demetri long to figure out which one of Alex's parents were the blood link to his demon grandfather. *Family ties are strong and widely revered by many cultures. Many people do things just because of family, even though they may have a moral or ethical issue with what is being done. Who knows what could happen when you add family loyalty with the mixture of demonic blood? Imagine the power that comes with that! It may have been more than Ella could handle. No wonder she ended up being put in an adult care facility at such a young age.*

Demetri wished he were able to connect with Ella's brain, collect some of her thoughts. To be better able to understand Ella and why she did what she did would help them to better know how to deal with Alex. Alex was their immediate concern, and of course finding Gina. Brandy would be getting out and with the Balashon still running around, the team would not allow her to go home where there was no safety. When Brandy was released, she would come to Gina's home. It had become ground zero for them and also had all the ingredients they needed if a spell were called for.

Demetri had embraced the inner witch inside of him. He no longer struggled with the idea of it but was using it to his advantage. He figured the sooner he embraced who he was, the sooner he would be able to accept all of his new powers and his new identity, which included all his past lives. The fact that he wasn't still in a fetal position in the corner is a pure miracle. If it were not for the necessity to act, he may well have been stuck in the corner for a long time. It had been Gina who brought him back. It had been Gina who helped him understand, to function in the here and now.

Demetri glanced at Alex and then over at Aldrik. "I don't really see any difference in him," Demetri said.

"I am afraid I can't argue with you on that," Aldrik replied.

"So, what now? How do we wake him up? Do we try feeding him again? Your blood had to have some healing aspect to his body other than just feeding those fucking demonic loving tattoos? It had to," he questioned.

"We can try again if you wish. I would have to agree it should have had some healing properties. I have not known it to fail me in the past, but fifteen-hundred years is a long time to remember," Aldrik said, suddenly realizing who he said it to. "But, you already know that."

"It's okay Aldrik. I will figure this past life thing out. I just want you to treat me as you always have. No need for kid gloves," he said.

"Well let's give it a try and see what happens. If things go badly again, then we know we have to find another avenue," Demetri stated. "I have also been thinking about your blood. I know how you feel about it, but I think that we need to consider using it on Brandy so we can get her back here with us quicker than tomorrow afternoon or evening. I don't trust the Balashon. They will not want any witnesses left to tell their story."

"I too have been thinking. Actually, I am not in opposition to that course of action. We need all of our allies around and near us. It isn't safe for her to be left there all by herself. The resources of the Balashon are surely great and we are lucky that they have not found her yet," Aldrik stated.

"Well, let's get on with this and see what happens. Hopefully, we will be able to wake him up," Demetri said.

As Aldrik walked closer to the table, you could see the tattoos start to become animated. They knew the blood of Aldrik was near and they were hoping to get some more of it. This time Demetri was prepared for them. He would stop them from rushing on the blood so hopefully it would allow Alex to be able to absorb what he needed to heal.

Demetri began to concentrate on the tattoos, to picture them in his mind. He thought about them, about their permanency and how they would stay in place. They would not move from the place on the skin they were created. As Demetri closed his eyes, he willed it to be so. He sent out energy to Alex's body so it would bind the tattoos.

When Demetri opened his eyes, he nodded at Aldrik, who quickly bit into his own wrist so that the flesh was torn and blood flowed. He opened Alex's mouth and let the blood drop into it. It only took a matter of seconds before Alex began sucking on Aldrik's wrist, sucking the free flowing blood. This flow of blood was short lived as Aldrik's wrist started to heal itself. Enough blood had entered Alex's body. If it was going to heal him, then it would. If not, they were back at square one.

Both Aldrik and Demetri stood watch over him as they could both feel and see the tattoos looking at them, hungry and angry. The binding spell Demetri did worked. The tattoos were stuck in their spot, at least for the time being. Minutes passed that felt like hours, and then out of nowhere, Alex sat up quickly making both men jump.

"Mom, no! Brandy, I'm so sorry," Alex screamed!

Grabbing Alex by the shoulders, Demetri stood beside him, looking at him. "You need to calm down. You are safe, here with us at Gina's. I am sorry about your mother, she could not be saved. Brandy, however, we were able to get her to the hospital and she is doing fine. She is expected to come home tomorrow."

Alex's tears were flowing down his cheeks as he remembered the image of his mother stabbing Brandy in the chest and then turning the knife on herself. *Why would she do that? Why would she allow a demon to enter her son's body?*

"What happened to me? What happened after the demon entered me? Did I hurt anyone?" he said, as he took a big gulp of air. "Did I kill anyone?"

"Alex, none of that matters because it wasn't you. It was Bastiquil. It was that son of a bitch demon that should have never been allowed back here," Demetri said, trying to bring him some comfort.

"It matters Demetri. If I had no link to this demon then I can see you saying "oh yeah, you were innocent in all this" but that isn't the case is it? I am a direct descendent of this demon. I was born to carry him inside my body. My body was created by design for and by Bastiquil himself," Alex said, with conviction and a heavy heart. "My mother must have known. Somehow she knew."

"Listen, you have been through a lot in the last few days. Maybe you should lay it aside, I am not saying never to pick back up, but lay aside all of the questions for a bit and get some rest, some real rest," Aldrik stepped in, trying to help the situation.

"Rest, how can I rest? My body is on fire, it feels more alive than ever. I feel invincible," he said.

"You had been out ever since the demon was knocked out of your body at The Other Side. We were worried about you so we fed you some of Aldrik's blood so it could heal some of the damage inflicted on your body by the demon," Demetri said, hoping he would not freak out on them. "It is giving you a false sense of being high right now."

"You did what? You fed me vampire blood," he said to them, as if he could not believe they would add another atrocity to his long list of evil deeds. "No offense, Aldrik."

"None taken, my friend. After 1,500 years, you get used to it," Aldrik said, as he sarcastically smiled at Alex. "You will be just fine, after all, it's not like you are a pureblood."

"Can I see Gina? Where is she? I'm surprised she isn't here now," Alex asked.

Aldrik and Demetri looked at each other not wanting to overload the guy yet wanting to be honest with him. Demetri took a deep breath before speaking. "We can't find Gina. She has been missing since the other night. We were kind of hoping you would remember something about it so we could piece together why and where she might have been taken. Victor, that piece of shit, is the one that took off with her."

"What? Gina is missing? That can't be. Other than you, she is strongest witch I know. What could they possibly want with her?" Alex whispered, as he tried to wrap his brain around all of this.

"Well, we are the only two witches you know, but anyway, we were hoping you would have retained some of Bastiquil's thoughts? We were hoping once you woke up you could give us some insight. Right now, we have nothing to go on," Demetri stated.

"I don't remember anything after the possession. Can you not probe my mind and find out if there are any latent memories there? Can you not do some spell, work some magic?" Alex said, pleading with Demetri.

"Listen, I want to find her just as much as you do, but we are thinking the way your body is covered with the tattoo's Bastiquil chose, it puts some sort of block on you so I cannot retrieve your memories or thoughts," Demetri said, looking at Alex, hoping he stayed calm.

Getting up, Alex started walking around, looking for anything, looking for nothing. "We have to find her. She believed in me, in a complete stranger and got you all to risk your lives for me, my mother, and for Brandy. She doesn't deserve to be the one to pay the price for me. She isn't going to be another tragedy in this demonic family reunion," Alex said, stomping around the room frustrated with everything.

"Look, we have an idea you are not going to like, but please hear us out," Demetri said to Alex, who stopped moving and looked at him. "We need to get everyone together, just for safety sake. We need to get Brandy out of that hospital and here with us so we can protect her. As long as the Balashon is out there, she is not safe. We want to use some of Aldrik's blood to heal her so we can get her out of there tonight," Demetri posed the question to Alex.

Alex thought about it for a second and then looked at them both. "This isn't going to make either of us a vampire is it?"

"Not at all, my friend. It is a little more complicated than that. It just speeds up the healing and you will have a little bit of a high from it," Aldrik advised.

"Then let's do it. If Brandy is willing, then let's get her out of there," Alex said, as he grabbed a hold of Demetri's arm and started dragging him towards the door.

Chapter Fifteen

The rain continued to pour down all around them like a tropical storm. The wind slapped them around, as it came swooping into the broken fuselage and sent chills down Gina's spine. Cold, wet, and hungry, Gina resolved herself to buck up and make the best of this horrible situation. She was stuck in what was left of their crashed plane with the man who kidnapped her, who was responsible for countless murders, with no remorse, and who helped a demon enter the body of a decent man. Yes, this situation could definitely get a lot worse, so she decided to make the best of it.

Gina knew she needed Victor, at least until they were shore side and in a city where she could call Demetri for help. She couldn't believe how this turned out. It was a nightmare within a nightmare. They had little food and water so decided it best to ration it out. They were going to need to get a move on soon if they were going to get to a city before they ran out. Victor didn't seem to be as concerned about that as she was, but she had to admit she didn't know what was going on inside his murderous brain. His kindness to her had taken her by surprise. She had expected a gruff and tough Victor, but he has been supportive and protective of her. This only led to extra suspicion on her part.

Victor had been out to kill her or at least harm her for days leading up to the full moon. As soon as Bastiquil took possession of Alex's body, Victor was all about being nice to her, helping her, protecting her. There were times that she felt the need, the want to hit his brain with a large energy ball and fry it, but then her guide would be incapacitated.

Victor, on the other hand, had been watching Gina with curious and protective eyes. The master wanted her guarded at all cost and he wanted her brought safely to one of their European compounds, but the plane going down didn't help the urgency of making it on time. He knew they needed to get on the journey towards the shore, but this rain would be a massive hindrance.

Victor also couldn't shake the nagging feeling they were being stalked, but he couldn't figure out by what. He could feel eyes on them, could sense something or someone watching their every move. This only led to his desire for them to be on their way as quickly as possible.

The rain started to let up so the time had come for them to head out. They packed what they needed and what they could safely carry and still be portable and speedy. Victor strapped on a utility belt he found and placed knives and other weapons inside. Gina wasn't sure what type of terrain or wildlife, including human wildlife, they would run into. From what Victor had told her they were not even sure how far inland they were, so for all they knew the shoreline could be miles away. But at least they were going to be moving towards something and not lingering back waiting for a rescue, which would not come.

They headed out in the misty rain with a new coolness in the air, which had not been there until the storm rolled through. Victor led the way and Gina did her best to keep up. He moved at a fast pace for someone with a leg injury which made her curious as to what he was moving to or moving away from. The terrain was absolutely breathtaking. Gina had never realized Iceland was such a gorgeous place. Thoughts of Iceland generally included ice, but it was so green and so beautiful. Gina could make out snow on the mountains in the distance and from what she gathered in the brief conversations she had with Victor there were glaciers here. Victor also warned her not to be fooled by the serene beauty of their locale. Iceland was not a place to be trifled with. He hoped they were on the south side of the mountains because if they had to cross them, the likelihood of them making it out alive dropped substantially.

Gina was not used to this type of hiking, it was fierce, fast, and the weather made it quite treacherous at times. Fast-flowing streams filled with the storm's run-off were a stunning view. Every so often you would catch a glimpse of a bird in the sky, a wild fox, and some rabbits. The nature here was breathtaking. Victor told Gina a majority of the island country of Iceland was mostly uninhabitable desert, impassible in the winter. The greatest majority of people who make up the population live near the shoreline.

"The greenery of this place in which we have crash landed gives me hope that we are not far from the shoreline. Had we been further inland, it would have meant most certain death," Victor told her.

Gina couldn't help but think Victor must be an expert on geography and terrain due to his line of work, but this area was like nothing Gina had seen or experienced before. "What about the pilot? Even if he didn't survive is there a chance that the radio still works? What about a beacon we can activate?"

"The answer to your many questions is no. No, there will not be any activating of beacons and the radio runs off of a battery that happens to be in our end of the plane. Besides, we will not be calling for help even if we had the opportunity. So if you want to make sure we make it to the shoreline alive keep your mouth shut and keep up with me," he said, with an authority that Gina took as offensive.

As they pressed onward, Gina was getting a vibe from Victor, nothing mental, just a feeling, maybe from his energy. He was intense, motivated, and on guard. His eyes were darting everywhere, watching everything, but his body was always in a stance, even in movement, of someone ready to attack.

The path they were on was taking them into a wooded, hilly area. Gina was already tired from the night's adventures, her body ached, her head hurt, and she was going on empty. Sleep came in short increments as the rain beat down on the fuselage of the plane. She couldn't help wonder how Victor kept going. He had a gash in his leg which had to be hurting like crazy and he had less sleep than she. Maybe that was why she was getting the vibe from him.

They came upon a brook. It was not as flooded as some had been on the trail. There were rocks to use as stepping stones, but the water flowed rapidly around those rocks. Easing their way across, Victor instructed her to take one step at a time, one foot in front of the other, and to not try and force her way across. *It was so kind of him to explain what I need to do if I happened to fall into the stream and get carried downstream. Actually, he had been a condescending prick about the whole thing.*

Gina had grown up in rural Oklahoma and figured she had a thing or two she could teach the master asshole. But, she kept her pace. She let well enough alone and started to plan how she would escape once they made it to one of the villages on the shoreline.

Reaching the other side of the stream, something felt off, really off. Gina could tell Victor felt it too. What could it be? Neither of them knew. But they quickly found out as they made their way into the wooded areas once more. It started out with a broken twig, actually multiple broken twigs. Something or someone was tracking them. It sounded like more than one person, but Gina couldn't be certain. Victor was on high alert, preparing himself for battle. He removed his knives that he previously strapped to his thighs.

As the sounds were getting closer to them, Gina's heart rate sped up. Thoughts were going through her mind as to what type of people these were and if they would be able to help her escape her captor. She also knew he would not let her go without a fight and Gina didn't want people dying on her behalf. She could tell Victor was ready to pounce on whoever was about to come walking up on them.

Then panic struck her heart as she heard deep breathing, guttural, primal breathing she instantly knew it could not be human. Fear entered her heart, as she remembered how heavy the footfalls were on the twigs and fallen branches in the forest behind them.

Then another sound escaped from the mouth of the stalker, a deep exhaling of breath. There was no mistaking it was a growl. Victor looked at Gina and gave her a signal to be quiet, to start easing herself behind him. Gina slowly obeyed his command, as she didn't think this was an opportune time to disobey.

Out of the tree line came the most beautiful, but deadly looking bear. Massive in size, it looked hungry and it looked as if it were staring at dinner. As the bear made its way towards them, slowly, in a dominate way, it was shaking its head back and forth as if it were already agitated with them. For what, she didn't know other than it probably was looking to eat them.

Nearly three feet from them, both Gina and Victor knew they would not be able to outrun the bear. If you learned anything from the television shows on National Geographic or Animal Planet, it was despite their heavy build, they are adept swimmers, runners, climbers, and possess an excellent sense of smell. Victor must have known all of this, because he still had a battle stance. *Can he seriously think he could take on this bear?*

The bear with its retractable claws swung its paw at Victor in an exploratory manner. Victor quickly stepped backward to avoid the blow, but by doing this Victor must have challenged the bear's dominance and it rose up on its hind legs. It stood at least eight or nine feet in height. It let out the loudest roar Gina had ever heard from a live animal.

It was pissed by Victor's blatant defiance of authority and it looked like it was going to charge.

Still on its hind legs it moved closer to them and swung its paw again, but this time Victor swung back with one of his knives and sliced the bear's skin directly behind his paw. This angered the bear even more. The bear came down on all fours and charged at Victor who pushed Gina out of the way, as he lunged to the opposite side barely missing the attack. The bear, now between the two of them looked back and forth as if trying to decide which the better option was. Gina knew this did not bode well for her as she did not hold two knives in her hand for defense and the bear had already felt the stinging cut of Victor's blade.

As the bear turned towards Gina, her heart sank as she remembered everything about bears said, *not to run*. But running was her first instinct. Gina did manage to put a tree between herself and the bear. It made a faux lunge at Gina to test her resolve. When she did nothing, the bear started to come at her. Out of nowhere the bear was pelted with rocks of considerable size which served as a distraction. Surely, the size of the rocks alone was hurting.

The bear stopped and turned back to look at Victor, who had another rock in his hand that he let fly at the bear, hitting it in the head. The bear let out another of its guttural roars. "Run Gina, now. Run," Victor screamed.

Gina turned to run and as she did her mind went to, *what happens when I get away from this bear? I don't know where I am. I have no weapons to protect me if another bear happens along.* She was defenseless in the man-made weapon sense. No, Gina wasn't going to run; as much as she hated Victor, she needed him to get her safely to the shoreline. She needed him to protect her. Just thinking those thoughts made her want to vomit. Gina did put a bit of distance between herself and the bear and as she stopped running, she turned to look back at the bear and Victor.

To Gina's shock and amazement, and probably to the bears, Victor made a running dash directly at the bear. Just as the bear swung its claws at him, Victor went airborne jumping free of the claws and over the bears head landing on its back. Victor wrapped his arms around the neck of the bear and squeezed it with a death grip, his legs wrapped around the bear's abdomen, or as much as they could considering its size was larger round than Victor's legs were long.

The bear writhed in frustration and pain, wanting to knock Victor off and away. It thrashed its head back and forth as Victor held tight to his grasp around the bear's neck. Gina looked on in disbelief. *What in the fuck is going on?* Never in a million years had she thought this would be anywhere in her memory bank of things she would recall one day. She was looking at a man, a trained assassin, who was wrestling a bear trying to eat them for dinner.

Victor grunted in pain and exhaustion as his grip on the bear waned. The bear, which she didn't see coming, took to the ground in an effort to knock Victor off. The pain from the weight of the bear on Victor's injured leg made him scream out in pain and Victor let go of the bear in an attempt to get the bear off of his leg. The bear wasted no time in getting up and regrouping. He turned and made a run at Victor, who happened to roll out of the way just in time to miss the full force of the bear's speed and velocity.

Gina was feeling a magical energy source nearby, but she couldn't put her finger on it. She had been feeling this way since they left the crash site but had just chalked it up to nerves. She had to focus on this attack happening now, that would ultimately end in either the bear's death or Victor's. If it was Victor's death, then it inevitably meant hers was coming quickly after. She decided to act. If there was energy around her, which there always was, that was pure science and physics, then she could pull some electricity out of the air. If she could tap into whatever magical energy source was lurking nearby she might be able to handle this bear or at least misdirect it.

Victor busied himself trying to stave off the bear's attack. He miscalculated the bear's reach and the bear's claw tore at his chest, ripping the cloth on his shirt and into the skin of his chest. The blow was enough to knock Victor off his feet and onto his ass. The bear charged at him and before Victor could get out of its path it pounced on him holding him down on the ground with its massive paw and weight of its body. The bear looked at him and just as it was bearing down at Victor with its mouth full of sharp teeth, Gina blasted the bear's brain with enough energy to knock three grown, human males unconcsious.

The problem with that, a bear wasn't a human male, an animal yes, but it still felt the sting and pain of Gina's attack on it. Screaming out, the bear, dazed and confused as to what had just happened, took off running back in the direction it had come from.

Gina stood in awe. *It worked.* She had not expected it too but felt inclined to do something as she still needed Victor to help her escape this wilderness. Looking down at Victor she saw blood, ripped clothing, and an anguished look on his face that must certainly be pain and ego mixed into one.

"You're welcome, by the way," Gina said.

"Welcome? If you were able to do that in the first place, then why the bloody hell didn't you do it and save us all a bunch of grief and pain?" Victor yelled out.

"It's a fucking bear, you asshole. I didn't know if it would work or not and quite frankly that seemed to be the only safe time to actually get close enough to do it. This may be everyday shit for you bear whisperer, but this is all new territory for me."

"We need to get the hell out of here before he decides he isn't as hurt as he is hungry and comes back. It is bad enough he can track our smells," he urged her.

"We need to do something about your cuts. If we don't, then you run the chance of getting infection," she said.

"Do you really care what happens to me?" When silence ensued, he said, "that is what I thought, so don't pretend to care about my well-being."

"Listen here, you don't get to do that. My entire life and the life of my friends have been turned upside down because of you and your murderous cult of a secret society. You tried to kill my friends. You kidnaped me. You don't get to play the misunderstood victim with me. That isn't going to fly this time," Gina blurted out, furious at his arrogance and accusation.

"What pray tell do you plan on putting on these wounds to keep infection from setting in? Are you planning on asking the elves for help in this matter," he asked, wincing in pain.

"Elves? What are you talking about?" Gina probed, curiosity peaked.

"The elves of the Icelandic forest. You did not know that over 80% of the population of Iceland believes in the existence of elves and their powerful magic. The people of this country go out of their way to avoid pissing any of them off. They are revered here," Victor explained.

So that was the magic I have been feeling all around me. The elfin magic. How flipping amazing is that? She wished that Demetri was here to share in this experience with her. But alas, she was stuck with this murdering idiot whom she will have to help save if she wants to get off this island.

"Well, I do not need the elves to tell me this is Ahillea Millefolium, derived from the Trojan War hero, Achilles. It's also known as Soldier's Woundwort, Bloodwort, Nosebleed, and many other names. It can be used to stop a person from bleeding to death." Gina gathered some up as Victor looked on at her in amazement.

"Why are you doing this for me?"

"I am not doing it for you. I am doing it for me. I want to live. I want to get back to my life and that is not possible if you sit here and die on me, so I do what I have to do to get what I need. What I need is for you to get me the hell out of these woods and to a city where there is food, warmth, and no bears," Gina said, as she crushed up some of the Yarrow, as it is also known as, and placed it on his wounds inflicted by the bear.

Taking part of the blanket and ripping it into strips, Gina placed the strips over the Yarrow to make sure they stayed in place. While she dressed his wounds, she decided it best to do the same with the wound on his leg. It did her no good to heal one wound just to have him die from another.

They were promptly up and on their way to what she hoped was shoreline.

Chapter Sixteen

Brandy lay in her hospital bed still on morphine, but being tapered off of it gradually. She had to admit she was feeling better. Glad to be alive, she felt so helpless laying here, doing nothing to help Alex or the others find Gina. One thing Brandy had plenty of time to reflect upon was the knowledge that can never be taken away from her. That knowledge was the existence of the supernatural.

Science had always been the solid ground Brandy held to. It had been a way to explain all of life's events that seemed convoluted in mystery, in magic. People who read the Bible, literally, and think there was a glorious resurrection of Christ after his being murdered on the cross had always been somewhat strange to Brandy. *Why do people take things literally? Why can't people just understand that sometimes things are written as metaphor and most certainly the Bible was written for the people of the time period it was referring to? It wasn't casting its historic meaning onto today's society, but yet they cling to it, they want it to be so. They use it to crucify others here in this day and age.*

But one thing stumping Brandy was the demon, Bastiquil. If she allowed herself to believe in the existence of a demon, does that mean that she was allowing herself to believe in hell? Brandy had never even thought for a second that a place like hell existed. Quite frankly, she still didn't. There had to be a scientific explanation for everything that has happened. *Maybe there is a rip in time, a break in the veil between worlds and something slipped through. That had to be it, but was that science?*

Just as Brandy thought she had figured it out, she let out a gasp of relief and started crying as she watched Alex come walking into her hospital room. She could not believe her eyes. Here he was, her best friend who she thought was going to be in a coma forever because of the demon she had been thinking about. With him came Demetri and another man who was striking to look at but who had a whiteness to his skin, much more than just being a caucasian man. It didn't take science to tell her that.

"Alex I am so glad to see you," she said, as tears rolled down her cheeks and she reached out her arms to hug him, even though it hurt to do so.

"Brandy, I'm so sorry I got you involved in this crazy ass shit and I am even sorrier you got hurt. I never dreamed they would involve you or mom in this," Alex said, leaning into her hug.

"Alex, I am sorry about your mother, but I don't think she was brought innocently into this. She had a look in her eye, knowledge of the event, and what was happening. I don't think this was her first exposure," Brandy said, feeling him out for his reaction.

"I have come to the conclusion she was more involved in this than any of us could have even dreamed of, pardon the pun Demetri." Demetri nodded he understood what he is referring to. "My mother, God bless her soul, was a confused lady who could not deal with the fact our family comes from a long, long, blood line of demonic decent. I so wish I had been able to talk to her before this all went down. I might have been able to reach her, to rationalize with her."

"Alex, I know you feel you could have changed this somehow. You need to realize this was a secret she had been carrying with her all of her life. If she didn't tell you about this, not even hinting at it, she never would have. Alex, she

92

kept this a secret to the end, she waited until she had stabbed me, until the deed was done. She left me for dead and then revealed herself to you. She was fully committed to what she was doing. She may have had last minute regret, but she went through with it. I'm sorry babe, but she knew what she was doing," Brandy said, voice cracking, tears flowing again at Alex's heartache.

Demetri wanted to lighten the mood and get Brandy out of here as soon as possible. The longer they waited, the more chance they stood of a Balashon surprise attack.

"Listen Brandy, we are here for moral support, but we also have another agenda," Demetri said, to a curious looking Brandy. "We want to get you out of here tonight and to do that we need to ask you to open your mind up to the possibility we are going to be presenting."

"Okay! What would that possibility be?"

"This is my friend Aldrik, and he is a vampire," Demetri said, as he looked at Brandy for reaction. Demetri looked at Alex and nodded he should move in now. Alex then approached Brandy and sit down on the bed beside her.

"We want you to drink some of his blood, not much, just enough to accelerate your healing. Then we can get you out of here and back to Gina's so we can ensure your protection. I did it earlier and it brought me out of my coma and allowed me to be able to come here and be with you."

To everyone's shock and amazement, Brandy looked at them all, one at a time. "What the fuck are you waiting for? Where is it and how do we go about this," Brandy said, to the three men. "Don't look at me like you are shocked I would agree to this. I am pissed off as hell and I need to get out of here so I can help you all find Gina and get some revenge on these assholes that did this to us. There is some payback in order. So if I have to drink some vampire blood to do it, then bring it on."

Aldrik stepped forward and stood by Brandy, who was still lying on the bed. He brought his wrist up and bit into it, which he then turned and held it to Brandy's mouth. "Just drink it," he said, as she reached up and pulled his wrist to her mouth. The taste was not what she had expected, but she continued to drink it nonetheless.

Brandy drank without abandon. She drank knowing if what they said was true, she would be walking out of this hospital in just a few minutes. No more needle pricks, no more blood pressure cuffs and beeping heart machines to keep you awake all day and night. Brandy would be joining the living again. And living was what she longed for. She had laid here and thought about the dead, her death way too long. The time had come to rejoin the living and she felt hell-bent on revenge.

As Brandy drank the blood, at first it felt normal, like a weird reality, *Aldrik's blood flows into my mouth.* But as she swallowed, as she let it slide down her throat, she felt a strange, intense feeling start to sweep over her body. It felt better than any morphine drip they put her on. She could feel her body reacting to it, absorbing its richness, its power, and its healing properties. Brandy was healing and she could feel it.

It seemed like a lifetime to Brandy, but it took only a few seconds, not even a full minute for her to receive the amount she needed to heal herself. When she pulled her mouth away, she watched as Aldrik's wrist closed up. No indication existed on his wrist this had even taken place.

Alex walked over to her with a warm wet napkin and wiped off the blood that remained on her mouth. "How do you feel?" he asked.

"I feel amazing, I feel healed, and I feel pissed off," Brandy said.

"Well, let's get you the hell out of here then," Demetri said. Demetri had grabbed Gina's jogging pants and t-shirt and gave them to Brandy to put on. He had assumed that the hospital would have cut the ceremonial robe off of her anyway when she was brought into the emergency room with the knife wound in her chest. They would have been also stained with blood.

Brandy started pulling off the strips of tape that held the needle to the IV drip in her arm and then pulled out the needle like attachment from her arm. The morphine drip was gone with it. Then she started pulling off the heart monitors which started flat lining. This definitely got the attention of the nursing staff. They came running into the room thinking Brandy was coding. What they found, a patient standing up out of bed, gown to the floor at her feet, and getting dressed.

"Miss Helmsworth, what are you doing? You shouldn't be out of bed." The nurses were genuinely worried about her.

"I am feeling much better, thank you. I will be leaving with these handsome men and I thank you for your assistance and for taking such good care of me." Brandy smiled at the nurses who were in shock to see her up and moving around with such ease.

"We really have to insist you return to your bed and let us get this IV back into your arm. We can't recommend you leave yet, you have not been released by the doctor," Brandy's regular nurse urged her.

"Look, I get it. You are looking out for me and for the hospital, but I will be walking out those doors just seconds from now. I appreciate all you have done. I have given you my insurance information and my billing address so you have all you need to be reimbursed for the medical attention you have given. Now if there isn't anything else, I want to thank you again and have a wonderful night," Brandy said, as she led the way out of the room with the three men following in tow.

The nurses looked on in shock and frustration as they knew there was nothing they could do to stop her. Brandy's regular nurse walked over to the heart machine and turned it off as she knew without a doubt Brandy was not flat lining. The nurses stood there as silence filled the room.

Chapter Seventeen

Bastiquil, aka Lincoln Reed, busied himself at The Blue Moon Tattoo parlor making sure his plans would be successful. He laughed to himself as he thought about the reality of the manipulation he inflicted upon Alex. He had been so young and ripe, ready for rebellion when he implanted the seeds of influence into his young dreams.

It's easier to reach an adolescent when they are sleeping. Their guard was down, they are vulnerable and you can do pretty much what you want to them because they would just wake up and think it all a dream. Which it had been, but there was some reality to it, Alex just didn't know it. The young were so easily duped. They want to believe, to be reckless, and to have meaning in their life. But, Alex was different than some he had contacted over the many years. Alex, his best creation, had his blood running through his veins. His bloodline had survived all of these years. It brought them here, to this moment in time when Alex had been born in an age of the ideal Blue Moon. The right ripple in time allowing him the power and opportunity to come through, to breach into this world once again.

Bastiquil had underestimated the witches of this time. He had not factored in the reach technology would play in their evolution of power. They had access to more information than any other witch in history and they were clever, insightful, and definitely a force to be reckoned with. He would not make this mistake again.

These witches I battled had real powers. They were not the fake, want-to-be witches. They were the real deal, which made them super dangerous. Demetri, he is a wise one, a clever one. He had somehow found the connection to his soul's memories. Not too many people would have thought of that. Not too many people would have had the courage to think of the past life connection, let alone take the risk of doing what's needed to make the connection. Very clever boy-witch indeed. That he inhabited the spirt of Zamaranum, born in the same time as Alex, his grandson, was no coincidence. It would seem the fates were against him too. But, Gina is the one who interests me the most. She is the one who will make all things possible. That one doesn't even know what she is capable of. She is ripe with powers that are just bubbling up, wanting to boil over, to spill into this world. She is the answer I have been waiting for. But, what is so perfect about it all is she doesn't even realize it yet. She doesn't even know she is the key. This was too perfect to believe.

It was an unfortunate turn of events though, their crash. That could not have been predicted. But, if anyone had the resources, strength, and determination to get her to the place Bastiquil had told him to take her, it would be Victor. Victor was a peculiar young man. He has impeccable taste and has a sexual appetite like none other. Bastiquil had played that one well. He had played Victor's parents and Victor too. He made Victor into exactly what he needed, a warrior, capable of taking on anything human or supernatural. He had so much strength coursing through his veins it was incredible. Bastiquil couldn't be prouder of Victor had he been his own son. Victor would make sure the witch was taken where he needed her to be. He would lay down his life to make it happen.

Speaking of sons, his had disappointed him greatly. Alex. What to do about Alex? Bastiquil needed inside his body badly, but as long as the male witch protected him, Bastiquil ran the risk of being expelled again. He would have to tread carefully with this one. He would rejoin his blood, his son, or great grandson as they say in this world, but he would have to make sure the boy didn't see it coming. He would have to find a way to separate him from the witch.

He smiled to himself as he formulated a plan. Yes, it could be this easy. Bastiquil laughed to himself as he continued mixing up his concoction. This is to be his backup plan. This would give him the edge he needed.

"What's so funny Linc," Jerry asked, as he came walking into the studio to find Lincoln laughing out loud to himself.

"What? Oh nothing. I was just thinking out loud," Bastiquil said. *What the fuck was he doing back here? He was supposed to be gone for the night.*

"What are you doing with all the ink out Linc?"

"Oh doing some quality control. It's something Alex and I talked about implementing but just hadn't gotten around to it. I had some down time so I thought I would get a jump start on it," Bastiquil lied.

"What is wrong with your face man," Jerry asked, looking at Lincoln with a most curious of faces.

"What do you mean?"

"Your face, it's all red and blotchy," Jerry said.

"Oh man, thanks for letting me know. I think I'm having a reaction to something," Bastiquil said, trying to act surprised but knowing he was burning up this body. He would have to find another one fast. Alex's body was made to contain a demon of Bastiquil's strength, power, and energy, but this one would burn up quickly, not being able to sustain the energy his demonic strength was putting out. Jerry just may be the next one that takes on his form. It depended heavily on how much Bastiquil is able to get done before the body gave out. "Why are you here?"

"I left my cell phone here and had to come back for it. You know my life is this cell phone, I'm lost without it, a chicken with my head cut off," he said.

"Those were the good ole days, a sacrifice of a goat, chicken, or cow," Bastiquil reminisced.

"No man, it is just a figure of speech; never mind. Have a good night man. Get some rest and get something to put on your face," Jerry said, as he walked out the door shaking his head at Lincoln, thinking he must be high or something.

Bastiquil continued on with his project mixing the ink with the blood he withdrew from his veins earlier. *This was going to be an exciting time to be in Tulsa. The people here would not have any idea what was coming and the rate of business for tattoos was steadily on the increase as more and more people became accustomed to them. I just have to make sure not to go through all of the employee's bodies before I am able to pull off this big plan.* He needed access to the studio though and this was the way it had to be. If he could get back into the vessel's body, the body he created, things would be good. Time was running out which was definitely not on his side.

Tomorrow the plan would go into full production. He laughed at the puppets who would willingly give themselves over after he invaded them. But, as he was laughing, he also started coughing, loudly and uncontrollably. *This body will not last much longer*, he thought to himself.

Chapter Eighteen

As they moved onward, the sky started to darken and storm clouds began to move in again. Night was near and they would be stuck out in the wilderness with no shelter from the rain or from the creatures that roamed the woods.

Victor was making it fairly well for having sustained some pretty significant injuries from the plane crash and the bear attack. His body was aching just from the impact of the crash. They were lucky to be alive and he would make sure that the girl stayed alive and as safe as he could possibly keep her. Victor had reached his limit on the bullshit he was going to take from anyone or anything else on this trip. He needed them to get to the shoreline so he could arrange transportation which would get them to their final destination.

He knew the girl needed time to rest and heal, but this was life and death out here, which in Victor's mind took precedence over what the body needed for rest. So they pressed onward, both in their own thoughts.

Gina couldn't believe they had survived a bear attack and a freaking plane crash, and they were still walking around in the wilderness hoping to find refuge in a town somewhere. Gina didn't know the layout of the country and she didn't know any of the names of the towns. She felt extremely tired and wanted so badly to just lie down for a few minutes.

Gina knew the danger they were in, she didn't need Victor to explain it to her. The crash, the bear, the other unknown creatures that were lurking in this forest, she understood this and could grasp the seriousness of their situation. Who knew what the night would bring, but whatever it ended up being, it was coming. The sun was gone and all that was left was the splash of red, orange, and purple lurking in the sky. A few minutes from now that would fade and they would be left with just the night. That did not give her any comfort.

They were coming up on the top edge of a hill and as they reached the peak, they looked over the terrain, down the hillside and became immediately disheartened they did not see shoreline. Gina looked at Victor who was busy scanning the area for anything that might give them shelter. Then she saw a look on his face. She didn't know for sure, but it looked like hope.

"Do you see something?"

"There," he pointed, "just inside the tree line at the bottom of the hill. There is a light and where there is light there is most likely shelter." Victor led the way as they started down the hillside.

Gina wondered if the people who had the light would be able to help her. She wondered if they would be able to take on Victor and win. He was injured, which worked in her favor. And, if she helped them take him out, then they would surely know where the next town was. Victor was like a wounded animal right now, he was an animal anyway, but add injury to it and he became unpredictable. She had to try though. This might be her only opportunity for a chance to escape him and get to a phone where she could call Demetri.

As they came down the hill following a path directly towards the light they were able to make out a small cabin placed directly inside a patch of trees which gave it some cover, but not from the light shining through a darkened forest. The closer they got to it, the more Gina began to feel anxious about what she planned to do. It had her on edge and a bit jumpy. She had never really planned a person's death before, but she knew death was the only way Victor would let her go. He had some insane attachment to her ever since they left Tulsa. What that attachment was, has yet to be revealed but she felt confident as time went on he would eventually divulge to her the big secret.

Victor cased the cabin like he would any other house. It was quick, but thorough and he made sure he knew exactly what he was dealing with. From the looks of it, they were only dealing with one man so he felt confident in his plan of action. Walking up to the door, Gina behind him, he knocked. Waiting patiently for the man to come to the door, Victor noticed him looking out of the curtains of the window to the left side of the door. Victor smiled at him and waved as did Gina. This prompted a friendly smile from the man inside the house who left the window and came to the door. Unlatching the door, he began to open it slowly and stepped forward smiling warmly at them.

"Halló," the man said, trying to show them a friendly welcome.

"Halló," Victor said back to the man, as he walked up to him, reaching up with lightning speed and snapped the man's neck. Gina was in shock, as the man fell dead to the ground, eyes still open. "Don't think I didn't know what you were planning," Victor said. "You can blame yourself just as much as you can blame him for being in the wrong place at the wrong time. Now get inside."

Victor picked up the man and carried him into the cabin where he found a closet to put his body. Gina, still shocked, had tears rolling down her face. *How could this have happened? This isn't what I had expected? How could he have known I planned on trying to get rid of him when we arrived?* So many questions ran through Gina's head until she just felt sick and ran to the kitchen sink to throw up. It was mostly dry heaves as they had not eaten all day, but she had drank some water. Victor looked over at her with a curious look, and then busied himself by looking through the cabin. She assumed he was looking for weapons, food, or anything of use.

The cabin, modest in size and décor, had a large open room containing a living area, dining room, and kitchen all in one. There was a bedroom and a bathroom separate from the main living area. That was it, nothing fancy, just a simple place for what looked like a simple man. But she would never know if the man who had lived here was simple or complex because Victor just walked right up to the man who opened his door to them and snapped his neck.

"You know something," she said with a glare, "you are a complete and utter asshole. You walk along killing anything that comes your way, not caring about the human existence. Not caring about the story or the life of that man. He did nothing but open his fucking door for us, to welcome us into his humble home and you fucking snap his neck. Who does that Victor? Tell me, who the fuck does that?"

"I do princess. Sometimes it is necessary to kill first rather than ask questions, when one is fighting a war," he shot back at her.

"A war? Are you fucking kidding me? A war? You raised your demon, you got what you wanted. There is no war. There wasn't a war between you and this man. You think everyone is against you, and it's of your own doing. You can't go around treating the human race like they are your own personal punching bag for your anger. If this keeps up Victor, you and I are going to have a major falling out, even more so than we already have. I will not allow you to keep doing this. I will not be a silent witness to your murderous and tyrant ways," she said, her face red with fury and hate.

"And what, pray tell, do you plan to do about it? I would really like to know. You think you know me? You think you know my heart? I can assure you it is pure and in line with my beliefs. I fight for what I believe in and I don't know if you can say the same. So before you pass judgment on me for fighting for what I have worked all my life, you need to take a look in the fucking mirror and see what skeletons are in your closet and just what you're fighting for," Victor said, with complete conviction.

"You are a fucking bastard," Gina shot at him.

"And you are a pretentious, spoiled little witch," Victor said, which just made her even more furious.

Gina stormed off into the bedroom and shut the door, locking it behind her. As soon as she walked away from the door, she heard a loud pounding on the door, and then another, until the door finally came flying open via Victor's undamaged leg. "Door stays open witch. Hate me all you want, but you need to get some rest. At first light, we are out of here."

"Fuck you," Gina screamed, as she lay down on the bed, tears rolling down her face. Not tears of sorrow, but tears of fury, which were not tears to be taken lightly.

"Red, you don't know how close you were to that very thing happening. But you were saved by the master, so count your blessings," he said.

"Rot in hell you fucking pig," she said, as she rolled away from his view.

Victor turned and walked out of the room and went back to looking for items that could be of use on their trek. He had found some food, a few knives, a gun, and some ammunition. But even more helpful was a map of the island country. With it he quickly ascertained that they were not too far from where he had hoped they would be. This made him happy. All he had to do now was get them safely to the shoreline, arrange transport to Scotland, which wasn't their final destination, but it was a safe haven for them as the Balashon had a safe house there where he could regroup.

Victor had to be careful. This trip was even more important than any of his missions in the past. Entrusted with the witch by the master, he had to get her to the place the master chose, without Balashon members knowing. Victor did not know why this particular detail was so important, but it wasn't for him to question the master. If the master doesn't want the Balashon to know he had the girl, then they wouldn't know. He knew he had to get her there, even though the dream he had on the plane told him Demetri had expelled the master from the vessel's body. What the male witch didn't know, he would have to do much more to get rid of the master.

When he was expelled three thousand years ago, the Balashon learned a valuable lesson. So they planned, they researched, they tortured witch after witch for information. They went through every ancient grimoire they could find looking for ways the master to stay in this world if anything like this were to happen again. So Victor knew the master was still in this world, in this realm, and he would make it back to them. But right now, it was Victor's job to get the girl to where the master wanted her to be. And this was just what he planned to do.

Chapter Nineteen

The bookstore had not been so alive with the sound of people for many days. Brandy, relieved to be back in the company of Alex and the other two men who helped to save her recounted to them all she knew, which ended up not being much. But they had her back, safe and sound under this roof and they could now busy themselves with the task of finding Gina.

They were going on 48 hours of no contact from Gina and Demetri knew the longer they went, the less likely they were going to find her. He truly hoped she was fine and still fighting, still holding out hope he would find her. He planned to, but they had no clue where to begin. When he had scryed for her before, it had been all over the upper regions of the Atlantic Ocean. Then he had to deal with Alex and then Brandy, but now his full attention could be focused on Gina. He knew she would have wanted him to help them first.

While the others were busy chatting, Demetri walked back to the world map he had laid out in the reading room and picked up the crystal he had been using to scry for Gina earlier. He held the crystal in his hand and then said an incantation to help charge the crystal. Blue light radiated from his palm as the crystal got a massive dose of energy.

Holding the crystal up and over the map by the chain it was affixed to, he begins to circle the crystal over the map, thinking about Gina, willing it to find her. It went round and

106

round and kept spinning until it suddenly stopped and landed in a perplexing and peculiar spot on the map. Demetri, stumped and amazed, didn't know what to make of it.

"Hey guys, come look at this. I have been trying to get a location on Gina and it landed on Iceland."

"Iceland? Why would he take her to Iceland?" Alex asked.

"There are many geographical reasons to take her there," Aldrik added, "but anonymity in a city isn't one of them. There are only about 300,000 inhabitants of Iceland, but if one wanted to make it difficult to find someone, the island has some treacherous areas that are hard to pass. How accurate are you feeling on the scrying?"

"Well I feel pretty secure in it. Gina always believed in it and for the most part, it worked. I have just started to embrace the fact I am a witch, but she has always loved the Wiccan ways. I will say, scrying is how we were able to locate Alex and Brandy," Demetri said to the group.

"This stuff is amazing to me. I am totally blown away by all this. The scientist in me wants to explain it all, but I am stumped," Brandy said, looking at them with a confounded looked on her face.

"Sometimes you just have to open yourself up to the fact anything is possible in this universe," Demetri told her. "The scientist in you has to feel it. You have to know energy from the brain can be manipulated and filtered through our bodies. You were not here for some of the most astounding things that we uncovered in our search for you guys, but we will have to get you up to speed quickly. We may very well need a scientist on this team of ours if we are going to save Gina and make sure the Balashon is not successful in anymore of their ventures. I do not put it past them to be working on bringing Bastiquil back and I fear what they are using Gina for."

"Are you with us Brandy," Alex asked, looking at her.

All eyes were on Brandy and there seemed no question in her mind as to what the answer was. "Hell yes! I'm in! I wouldn't miss getting revenge on these fuckers for anything in the world. I will make arrangements with my job for medical leave and I assume we are setting up shop here at Gina's," Brandy said, looking around at them.

"Absolutely," Demetri said. "Welcome to the team."

"Let me run the store, just so Gina doesn't miss out on all the hard work she has put into this place? Financially, I am fine. Plus, since I will be on medical leave I will still get a paycheck. I just think the more alive we keep this place, the better we will all feel," Brandy suggested to the group.

"Wow, I never thought of that and I am humbled by your offer. Do you not think it may be taking on more than you can handle at the moment," Demetri asked, hoping he didn't offend her.

"Not at all. Aldrik's blood has made me feel like a million bucks. I would so love to get my hands on a sample of your blood Aldrik, just for some scientific research," Brandy said in jest.

"You and every other scientist in the world," Aldrik said, smiling coyly.

"This may just work," Demetri said to the group. "For the first time in a few days I feel optimistic, I feel we might just find her."

"We will find her," Alex said.

"Let me make some calls and see how long it will take to get my jet here to pick us up. It will take us wherever we need to go," Aldrik said to the Demetri, as the other two looked on in shock.

"You have a private jet?" Alex asked. "Why would a vampire need a private jet?"

"Because I can afford one and it makes traveling much faster and easier, especially in the day time," Aldrik said, looking at them like they had asked the most ridiculous question.

108

Demetri was deep in thought over what the right move should be from here. After pondering for a few seconds, he looked up at the group and began to speak. "I think Aldrik and I should take the jet to Iceland and see if we can locate Gina before she is moved from there. As for Alex and Brandy, I think you two need to stay here. We need a network set up here at home base where we can check in and feed Intel back. Brandy, I assume, as a scientist, you are good with computers?"

"Yes, I'm pretty damned good actually. It will not be a problem setting one up. I will also make sure things run smoothly around here. Alex, you need to check in on your employees too. They have not heard or seen from you in days. I know they are worried about you, just as I have been."

"Yes, I know. I need to get things in order," Alex agreed.

"I don't like that we are leaving you two defenseless. I am not saying you can't take care of yourself, but the Balashon is still out there and their plans are still a mystery as to whether they will strike again or go back into hiding to lick their wounds," Demetri said to the two. "I may have an idea. It's a long shot, but it could work, at least temporarily," he said, pondering his thought further in his head. "I can try doing a protection spell on the store so that you are at least protected when you are here. I am afraid once you step outside these doors you will be on your own."

"Demetri, after all we have been through, besides death, I don't know what else they could possibly do to us they have not already tried," Alex said, as he looked at Brandy regretting it the moment it came from his lips.

Brandy, seeing his discomfort merely smiled at him. "Hey, they tried and they failed. The one thing they didn't expect was for me to live and for me to be as pissed off as I am. So let them fuck with me. Just let them try."

"Well, I have arranged for a friend of mine to drop in and keep an eye out on you anyway. It's not that I don't trust you and your determination Brandy, or the emotions from your loss Alex. I just want to offer you this gift because I can. He is unassuming to look at, but he packs a powerful punch. He will not get in your way. I promise," Aldrik said.

"That isn't necessary Aldrik. We appreciate the offer, but we don't want to put anyone out," Brandy stated.

"These people tried to kill you. They raised a demon from the depths of hell. You lived to tell about it. The Balashon will not like this at all. I wish we could take you with us, but alas, and I hope to not offend you, we will move faster without you. I have already called and made arrangements for my friend to come. I must insist on this, if only for my own peace of mind," Aldrik said to them both.

"We are not offended," Alex said, looking at Brandy to confirm his statement, which she did by shaking her head. "We know that you will be able to move faster without us and we have no power to speak of. It is no secret that we would just be in the way. So you need to go find Gina and bring her home safely. Every day she is gone is another day the Balashon wins. We can't and won't let that happen. So if what you need to be able to do your job is for us to have some man parked out here while you are gone, then by all means, let's do it."

"I appreciate your words and your willingness to help. You are truly a good man. I do want to stress the point, you are not powerless my friend. Your body has mystical blood running through it. It was created for a magical purpose. I would be willing to lay down odds you do have powers, but they have yet to be developed because they have not been triggered yet. I imagine the demon that used to lay inside you knocked open a few of those imaginary doors inside your brain. It is up to you to figure out how to activate them now that the demon is gone," Aldrik said, looking seriously at him.

Alex wasn't quite sure what to make of Aldrik's statement. He had always felt different but had he identified that feeling as a magical one, no. Hell no. How could he? Why would he? "What makes you think so?"

"Aldrik, no, not like this," Demetri pleaded with Aldrik, who gave him a soft smile and a hand in the air that was intended for Demetri to trust him.

"My young man. When I gave you my blood to help heal your body, the tattoos within your skin rushed up and were seeking access to the blood. They were hungry for it. The demon isn't inside your body anymore Alex, so how else are we to explain this other than to assume your body is a magical vessel. To what extent, we don't know yet. But, while we are gone, you might want to work on it a bit and see what you can find out. See if you can get your body to do any magic without supernatural blood being fed to you," Aldrik explained to the dumbfounded looking Alex.

Brandy was looking at both Alex and Aldrik with large eyes, taking in all that was being said. She felt determined to help these people who saved her. She knew she didn't have any magical abilities, but she did understand science. She did understand the elements they were working with. She felt maybe she and Alex working together might be able to figure this shit out.

"You men need to be preparing for your departure. We don't want to chance missing out on finding Gina or at least a clue as to if she was even there. We will be working here to keep things afloat and when you filter information back to us I might be able to run an analysis and hopefully come up with something," Brandy told them. She wasn't trying to hurry them along because she knew she felt safer with them here, but she also knew what it's like to sit captive for days wondering if anyone was going to come for you.

Demetri made sure to grab a few things he felt might be needed on the journey. A world map, a powerful and fully charged crystal for scrying, some weapons, cash, credit cards, passports, and such. He hoped it would be a short trip; find Gina and bring her home, end of trip. But Demetri feared it would not be that cut and dry. He assumed the Balashon must have contacts all over the world, an endless supply of money, and some powerful men both physically and politically in almost every major city.

Even if the demon was gone, the Balashon still pose a threat. They will not sink quietly into the shadows for another three thousand years. They will not let this small defeat in the battle of a global war go unpunished. They will strike with all they have, eradicate their enemies so next time there would not be any interference, any notions of stepping in. Prying eyes would be poked out, revenge would be key in this war for control of the underworld. But as long as he lived, Demetri was prepared to fight them, to go toe-to-toe with them, but he didn't want to have to lose his best friend to do it. He needed Gina by his side in this. He needed her home where she belonged.

Chapter Twenty

Growing up in small rural area outside of Joplin, Missouri, Mathias Jackson longed for a larger city, longed to be able to blend into a crowd and get lost within it. He didn't want for spotlight, he longed for seclusion, for the shadows.

His school years were not filled with fond memories. He was bullied, beaten, and spent most of his time alone trying to stay out of the way of the jocks, under the radar, and out of trouble. He felt that his isolation was penance for what he had done.

As the bullying intensified, so did Mathias' anger over it. Kids would poke fun at him for being too slim, his hair being too white. He was shorter than most. His voice wasn't quite at a man's pitch, but rather stuck between puberty and manhood, which made him more of a target.

When Mathias was 14-years-old, he found out about his powers. It started off small, like picking up a pencil with his mind and making it dance across his desk. One day he had escaped the chaos of high school and placed himself quietly under the bleachers by the baseball field. He enjoyed the solitude, the shade and most of all, the book he was reading. He liked to read because he could escape the hell that had become his life. He transported himself every time he opened the pages.

So enthralled with his book, he forgot his surroundings and did not see Toby Wayne Reed scoping him out from afar. Toby made his way to the bleachers and stood watching Mathias. He was the all-star jock at school and also in Mathias' view the number one bully. He had taken many a beating from him and today would be no exception.

The shadowed figure that appeared across his body was the first indication to Mathias that something was amiss. A silhouette stood in front of him and he froze when he heard the familiar voice.

"Whatcha up to, sissy boy? Lying here reading about other men?" Toby said taunting him.

Mathias stiffened, unsure of what to say or what to do. This was familiar to him, but always unpleasant. "Um, um, no, Toby."

"Whatcha um, um, umming about? You like reading about men, don't you, sissy boy?" Toby said as he climbed under the bleachers. "You like it a lot, don't you. Yep, you are a sissy boy, a queer, a fag."

"I am not, Toby. I am not," he said taking up for himself, but fearing the consequences that would come.

"What did you just say to me, sissy boy? What did you just say?" he said, moving in closer.

Mathias tried to crawl away from him, but Toby was fast, precise, an athlete. He had Mathias on the ground, with his back to the grass. "You like this don't you, sissy boy," he said, as he sat down on Mathias' chest.

"Stop it Toby, I mean it. Get off of me," he yelled, but Toby only laughed.

Slapping each side of Mathias' cheeks, one at a time, he kept mocking him. "What are you gonna do about it, sissy? I know you have been watching me, thinking about me. Haven't you, queer boy," he said, as he gestured to his crotch. "I think it is about time someone taught you a thing or two about being a man and what a man really looks like."

Toby easily jerked Mathias off the ground. Grabbing his neck, he forced him out from under the bleachers and headed off towards the wooded area behind the fence of the baseball field. Toby taunted and teased him the entire way. Mathias tried to pull free, but Toby just grabbed him by the hair and continued to pull him forward.

Tears rolled down Mathias' cheeks as he screamed out in pain, begging Toby to stop.

"You gonna be a bitch now and cry? Keep crying and I will give you something to cry about," he said.

As they came to a clearing, Toby pushed him to the ground. Climbing on top of him, he slapped him so hard his ears were ringing. "Quit crying or I will beat the shit out of you."

Mathias' brain was working overdrive, trying to figure a way out, but he knew that he couldn't overpower Toby. *Why is this happening to me? Why does everyone think I am gay?* He braced himself, gearing up for the worst.

"Let's see what you have going on down there, sissy boy," Toby said, holding him down with one hand and using the other to undo the button and zipper on Mathias' jeans.

"Stop it, Toby. Please don't do this. Please, Toby," he begged and pleaded with him, but he kept pulling at his jeans and underwear until he had exposed Mathias' cock and balls.

"Well, now I know why you didn't want me to look, sissy boy. No wonder you look at me during gym class. No wonder you look at us all. You want one like ours, don't you, you little fag boy," he said, laughing and taunting him. Toby reached down and slapped at Mathias' balls causing him to scream out in pain and more tears to stream down his face. "Well, at least you can feel something down there. I was beginning to wonder. You hardly even have any pubic hair, boy."

Turning his head away so that Toby couldn't look in his eyes as he continued to cry, Mathias just kept wishing it would end. He kept wishing that Toby would get off him and just leave him alone. "Please stop," he begged. Toby had done lots of things to him over the years, but so far this has been the vilest.

"Stop? Stop? We are just getting warmed up, sissy boy. You ready to see a real man? You ready queer boy," he said as he reached up and started to undo his own jeans, pulling down the zipper. Reaching inside his underwear, he pulled his own out. He had a look of surprise on his face. "Look what you gone and did, sissy boy. Look," he said, reaching down and grabbing Mathias by the chin as he forced his face to look up at him. "You done gone and made me hard, girly-boy."

Struggling to free his face from the grip that held it, Mathias felt a hard slap. Another followed. Each blow hit its mark sending a cry out of Mathias as Toby continued his reign of terror.

"You like what you see? You like seeing a real man? I know you do; you have been begging me to show you all year long. Now you are gonna look at it and show it some respect. Respect me, sissy boy." Toby yelled as he slapped Mathias once again up against his already red cheek. He looked up and saw a sly, evil grin on Toby's face. "Show me respect, girly-boy," he said as he forced him to look into his eyes. "Kiss my balls."

"No!"

"You will kiss them and you will do it now," Toby said, keeping a firm grip on his chin and holding Mathias' arms firmly with his legs, leaning forward and placing his balls on Mathias' mouth. "See, I knew you wanted to kiss them."

Opening his mouth, he saw a broad smile appear on Toby's face. Then Mathias bit down on one of his balls. Toby didn't see it coming. He let out a blood-curdling scream that even Mathias couldn't bear to hear.

He made his move and tried to knock Toby off of him. Toby's fist made contact with Mathias' nose and eye. Screaming out in pain as the blood rushed out of his nose, Mathias tried to grab his nose with his free arm, but Toby quickly pulled Mathias' arm back under his leg pinning him once again.

"You bitch! You little bitch! You are going to regret that," he yelled, as his voice cracked with the pain. "I tried to help you, girly boy. I tried to help you, to show you what a real man looked like. I took pity on you and you bite my f'ing balls? Well, let me show you something else. Let me show you what you taste like."

Grabbing a hand full of dirt, he forced Mathias to open his mouth and then shoved the dirt inside it. As he choked and tried to cough it out, Toby held his hand over Mathias' mouth. "That is what you taste like you shit for brains. You are the scum of the earth, the dirt under my shoes. Choke on yourself."

Reaching over and grabbing a stick that was near him, Toby kept one hand on Mathias' mouth. He proceeded to bring the stick down blow after blow against Mathias' balls. He kicked and writhed in pain, wanting to scream but unable to because of the dirt suffocating him. As the beating continued, he started to feel as though he were going to pass out. His body was telling him to fight, but his mind told him that he couldn't, not with this boy.

"Are you ready to take it like a sissy boy should?"

The thought of dying, the thought of this brute of a bully doing anything further to him pushed Mathias over the edge. He could feel something deep within his brain click, like a switch being turned on. He could feel the sensation coursing through his body. It felt odd, strange and wonderful at the same time. Something whispered inside him. *Move your fingers and the boy will move with them.* He willed them to move. He had no choice, either move them or die.

Mathias could tell by the look on Toby's face that something happened. His eyes were big, curious, and scared. His body went limp, his hand falling away from Mathias' mouth. Spitting out the dirt, Mathias let out a gasp of air and with it a yell of anger, hurt, and revenge. He let out a beast that had been hiding, locked away within his brain, just waiting to come out and play.

He stretched his fingers, straightening them fully. Just as the voice promised, Toby stood pants and underwear at his knees. Hearing the whisper again, *stand up, brush yourself off, pull up and button your jeans. You will no longer be a victim of any bully.*

As he looked at Toby's frightened face, a symphony started to play in his head. He suddenly knew what to do. With one hand held up in the air, he danced his fingers up and down watching in amazement as Toby started to dance at the same time. *What kind of magic is this?* He could feel the power within him and no longer felt fear, but rather control. When he raised his other hand, Toby's hand that held the stick rose upwards. Still commanding the dance, Mathias started to bring the opposite hand down and then up, down and then up and with each movement, the stick wreaked havoc on the boys crotch as he screamed out in pain until Mathias silenced him.

Walking up, Mathias, who stood a few feet shorter, looked up at Toby. When he spoke, he did so with authority and control.

"You will no longer look at me with anything other than a smile on your face. You will not have one bad thought about me. You will not tell anyone about this, nor will you even think about this again. You are a bad, bad boy, Toby. You call yourself a man? You are sick and deranged if you think this is normal. If I hear, even feel that you have told anyone, we will do this song and dance again. You will not have any balls left to kiss when we are done. Do you understand me?"

Mathias let Toby's head free long enough to shake it in agreement.

"Say it! Say you will never tell this to anyone."

"I promise, I promise Mathias. No one. I promise. Just let me go, please." Toby begged him, tears rolling down his face.

Mathias made one last grand gesture by raising his hand up in the air and as he did, the hand with the stick raised with it. Toby began to pee all over himself. When Mathias opened his raised hand, the stick fell to the ground, along with Toby, who cried still.

Mathias never had any more problems from Toby, but the one thing he wished was for Toby to hear the beautiful music playing inside his head while he took his lashing 'like a man.'

As he strolled along, R.E.M.'s "What's the Frequency Kenneth" played in his head and he hummed along to it. The young 22-year-old male walked down the street, not really looking at people, but taking in everything around him. He had a way of seeing things around him that others were not able to or did not care to see. Not even in a supernatural way, but rather an awareness of one's surroundings and the people within those surroundings. His head was mostly tilted down, looking at the ground, hands in his pockets as he strolled casually down the sidewalk along Peoria Avenue in the Brookside district.

He wore his standards, a pair of Levi 501s, a witty t-shirt that read 'Just In: Bitch You Didn't Make the Cut,' black Converse tennis shoes and a baseball hat covering his whitish blond crew cut hair. He wore glasses that were just your ordinary, 'buy one, get one' free from any major eyeglass company. He had been wearing them since he was little. He didn't try to be stylish and he didn't care whether he was in fashion or way out of bounds. He considered himself to be true to him and that is all that mattered.

Just as the R.E.M. song came to a close in his head, he looked up and saw the store, The Mind's Eye. *What an awesome name*. It made him think of what went on in his own head, much like another eye that could see and do things that he shouldn't be able to do. He didn't mind doing this, he owed Aldrik a favor anyway and he knew he could trust him. Aldrik had helped him out on more than one occasion when things got sticky. That is a tale for another time.

Aldrik had told him to knock on the door and tell them what his name is and that Aldrik had sent him. He had told him that he needed him to watch over the two with everything that he had in him, even if it meant killing. Aldrik had given him a summary of what went down here and it sounded like these were some bad ass dudes. You don't mess with people like that. He had much respect for a group that made themselves extinct for 3,000 years and then suddenly attacks. He couldn't say he liked what they did, but they did get his respect for theatrics.

Knocking, he didn't have to wait long. A girl came to the door and looked out the glass.

"Hi," he said. "My name is Mathias, Mathias Jackson; I am a friend of Aldrik's. I am here to help."

Recognizing the name, she unlocked the door. Opening it, she let him in and then quickly locked the door back. Reaching her hand outwards, she waited until he took her hand. "Hello, my name is Brandy. We are happy to have you here. Come on in."

So far, so good, Mathias thought to himself. "I hear you have a demon issue that needs to be addressed?"

Chapter Twenty-One

The morning started off just like any other morning at Blue Moon Tattoo. The employees arrived, the stations were set up, and the sterilized utensils were organized and ready for use. What he needed now was a client to come walking through the door. They had some of their regulars call wanting to be squeezed into the schedule and Lincoln had happily told them to come on in. He had also advised them today was a special day. Half price for any new tattoo and free touchups of existing tattoos.

The crew had told him Alex would have a fit. Giving things away for free would not pay the bills. Lincoln didn't want to pay the bills. He wanted to get tattoos on these people so he could test his theory. If he was correct in his assumptions, then all was not lost.

He didn't have to wait long. A young, beautiful girl, who after signing in and supplying her driver's license as proof of identity and consent of age, turned out to be 18-years-old. Aware of her beauty, but seemingly unaffected by it, she wanted to have angel wings tattooed on her back. Having just lost her mother to breast cancer, she wanted the comfort of having her guardian angel with her at all times.

Smiling, Lincoln advised the others he would take this one himself. He wanted to be able to provide the warmth and comfort of inking those wings on her. As he and the girl spent the next half hour sketching out what she wanted,

Lincoln then disappeared in the back to sketch out the details which would be then transferred by carbon laminate to the girls back. The entire time he hummed to himself, so prideful, so calculating. He would give this girl exactly what she wanted, wings to fly. When he finished, he took the copy out to the parlor and took the girl behind a curtained off changing room where he also supplied her with a towel to cover the front of her. She would need to have her entire back exposed for him to be able to complete the tattoo.

When she came out, he took her over to a private room where he proceeded to put her in a chair which looked backward, but actually it was designed for tattoos being placed on the backside of the body. As he cleaned off the girls back with disinfectant, Bastiquil surprised himself by how he could tap into Lincoln's memories and his talent. He could recall the entire procedure for doing this as if it were second nature. But, of course, Bastiquil prided himself on creating his best work of art in Alex.

"Are you okay to be doing this today," the girl asked timidly.

"What do you mean?"

"I don't want this to come across as disrespectful, but you look like you are ill," she said, matter-of-factly.

Confused, Bastiquil looked at the girl before he had his moment of clarity. "Oh, this," he said, pointing to his face. "No, I am fine, just an allergic reaction to the sun."

Looking at him, she decided he was telling her the truth and relaxed a bit. "Is this going to hurt?"

"Of course there will be pain, but with pain a beautiful memorial will be created for your loving mother. Bless her soul," he replied to her.

"She didn't like tattoos, but I feel that she would approve," she said, sounding a bit emotional.

"Of course she would approve. You are paying her great honor and respect," he said, smiling to himself, happy the girl was turned away from him.

As he transposed the outline of the wings to her back, he handed her a mirror in which he told her to check what the completed image would look like in the mirror behind them. As she did, she smiled brightly. "This is going to be beautiful, isn't it?"

"It most certainly will be," he said, taking the mirror away from her. He didn't need her trying to watch as he worked on her.

Removing the tattoo gun and filling it with his blood-ink, he turned it on and placed it to the girl's skin. She immediately began to squirm as the needle transferred the black ink into her flesh.

"You are going to have to be still, miss. I know it is uncomfortable, but just keep in mind why you are doing this."

As he proceeded to place the gun on her skin, the ink started to fill the skin with the most beautiful buzzing sound in the background. Bastiquil could feel the pleasure the sound brought to Lincoln's ears, he loved it and was drawn to it. He got such a sense of fulfillment from it, almost in a sexual way. Yes, that was what he was feeling, it was the same feeling one would get when being sexually gratified. *And people think I am sick and twisted,* he thought, as the waves of sensation trickled down his spine.

"Ouch, you are hurting me. It's fucking burning me. What the hell? Get it off me," she started to raise her voice in panic.

"Oh, for fucks sake," he said, reaching up touching her head and sending her into a deep sleep. "You people and your concept of hell are quite warped."

Laughing, he continued on with his project, moving at a faster pace since the girl was asleep. He wanted this to be perfect, to be the most beautiful set of wings imaginable, at least on a human. He worked on it for a couple of hours, during which time he had heard the door open and close many times while he was in there, meaning more works of art were being created with his blood-ink. *How perfect.* He turned, smiling at himself in the mirror, only to be confronted by the almost burnt up shell of a human body. His inhabiting of this body was coming to an end. It had been quite useful though. It had served its purpose and his soul was tasty. He had many skeletons in his closet, which would never be told, but they tasted delightful as Bastiquil continued to devour away at them. They were fuel for his existence.

The girl was still unconscious when he finished with her. She had wings spanning from the top of her shoulder blades, running all the way down to the top of her butt. The wings were pure beauty, pure magic. Within the design of the wings held the sign of Bastiquil. She was a sight to behold and he would soon find out if he was correct in his theory. He would use her and she would fly. She would soar high above in the sky and do his bidding.

When he had cleaned her up and bandaged her back, he touched her head softly waking her from her deep sleep.

"You did well," he said.

"I did? Is it already over with?"

"Yes, it is all bandaged up and you are ready to go. You fell asleep. Some people find it comforting and some don't. I'm glad you were comfortable," he said, smiling at her.

"Can I see it?"

"I'm afraid I have already bandaged it up. You were sleeping so soundly, I didn't want to wake you. Keep the bandage on for most of the day, then you can take it off. Don't use any antibiotic ointments or anything like that on it. It will itch while it is healing, but if you stop and get some non-scented lotion to put on it, you should be fine. It will take a few weeks to heal completely."

"It feels funny, almost numb in a way, but like there is something moving around in my back," she said, as she tried to turn her head and look at it in the mirror.

"You just had your entire back tattooed, it is to be expected. It will subside. You can go put your shirt back on now. Remember, no antibiotic ointments. It will just mess up the ink."

"Sure, okay," she yelled from behind the curtain, as she put her shirt back on. Coming out from behind it, she smiled at him, but the discomfort still danced across her face.

"I promise, it will be better quickly. You will feel as though you have wings within days."

She looked at him with curious eyes, mentally noting his blotchy skin again, then broke into a smile and walked out.

As soon as she closed the door behind her leaving him in the private room, Lincoln fell to the ground moaning in pain. "Dammit, this blasted body is all used up. I have to hurry if I am to get this done."

Picking himself up off the ground, Lincoln straightened himself and walked out of the room and into the parlor. He smiled to himself when he saw all the people filling the waiting room. *Yes, this is going to be a splendid day. And for you, my dear Lincoln, it will be a splendid day to die.*

"Linc, you look like shit," Jett said, as he pulled him to the side. "People are talking and don't feel real comfortable with you being around while you are looking sick. Why don't you take the day and maybe get some sleep or go to urgent care or something?"

"I think you are right. I need to get out of here. I have done what I came to do and now it's time to leave and get me a new body," he said to the bewildered Jett. "Please make sure you use up all of the ink or at least as much as you can. I have a new batch coming in soon and will want this batch gone by the time it gets here."

"Sure, no problem man. Just take care of yourself. You look like death is knocking on your door."

"If you only knew the half of it," he said, as he walked out the door.

Jett picked up the phone and proceeded to dial Alex's number. He smiled to himself when he heard the voice on the other end.

"Alex, is it really you?"

"Hey Jett, yes, it's me. I'm sorry I haven't been in touch, but I have been seriously ill. Just starting to feel better."

"Man, Linc must have what you do then. He is looking like death right now. I sent him home because he looked like he could drop any minute," Jett said, sounding concerned about Lincoln.

"Well, that isn't good. I will have to check in on him. How is the studio running?"

"Like a well-oiled machine, Alex. You know we have your back."

"I do know, my friend. I do."

"Well feel better soon, man. I was kind of hesitant about this special you told Linc to run today, but I have to say, it has got them coming in like droves. Word is spreading quickly. We have a waiting list hours long," Jett said proudly.

"What special are you talking about?"

"The half price on any new tattoo and free touchups on existing ones," Jett repeated to Alex, just as Linc had told him.

"What the hell are you talking about Jett," Alex said, furious at what he had just heard.

"Linc said that this sale was your idea, Alex."

"Well, it is not. Finish up the ones who have already come in for it and don't do anymore. Tell the others it was a limited time only and it expired at noon. Like I said, take the ones already in the door, but that's it," Alex said, hanging up the phone on a confused Jett. *When I get my hands on Linc I am going to strangle him,* Alex thought.

126

Chapter Twenty-Two

Another wave of storms was passing overhead and Victor couldn't be happier to have found this cabin for them to wait it out. He didn't know how long the storms would last, but at least he knew he and Gina were safe, for now. He had hoped to be shoreside, but that didn't seem to be in the plan for today.

The witch, in the other room, had finally drifted off to sleep and he, for one, couldn't have been happier. *If I have to listen to another one of her sanctimonious lectures again about how precious life is and it shouldn't be up to him to take another life in the pursuit of this quest of his...blah, blah, blah.*

He was proud of the weapons he had found during his search through the cabin. Looks like our dearly departed friend knew just how treacherous these parts were he lived in. Victor couldn't help but laugh, thinking he had probably expected to die of either old age or from a weather-related accident, not by getting his neck snapped for opening his front door to two helpless strangers in need. People were so gullible sometimes it made him sick to his stomach.

Victor knew he couldn't keep going on adrenaline forever, he would eventually have to get some sleep. His wounds needed to be attended to and he knew they would heal better if he got some rest. *The ambitious never had time to rest, we always have to be one step ahead. When you stop and take stock, that's when you get caught.* Victor knew that the chances of them being found out here, in the middle of who knows where, were slim, but even slim would not offer him comfort. He had made a promise to his master that he would get the girl to the castle safely, and he intended to do just that.

Having found some first-aid supplies in the bathroom, he decided it best to go ahead and clean the wounds again and put on new bandages. Removing the makeshift bandage of ripped blanket and taking out the herbal packing, he was pleasantly surprised that the wound looked as if it were already healing. *What do you know, this witch knows her herbal remedies,* he thought, shaking his head in amazement.

The wounds were clean, medication applied, and he had replaced the old bandages with fresh, clean ones from the kit. He had raided the closet and found some shirts that fit, a jacket, and a hat he could wear. He would have Gina do the same when she woke up or when he had to wake her up after the storm passed, whichever happened first. He kept the fire going and settled down in the rocking chair next to the fireplace. The warmth of the heat eased his aching muscles and made him sleepy. Rocking himself with the shotgun over his chest, he looked like an advertisement out of a gun magazine.

Pushing off with his foot as he rocked himself in the chair, he couldn't help but smile to himself. Relaxing was the only word that came to mind. He could totally fall asleep here with the heat massaging his aching body and the chair rocking him so comfortably.

"I'm glad you have decided to give yourself some time to rest, Victor."

He knew the voice, but he couldn't believe that he could hear it. The only time before had been when he was sleeping. Then it dawned on him, he was asleep. He heard laughing.

"My dear Victor, I get so much joy out of watching you. You are the man, the animal, the machine I have dreamed of having fight beside me. You have grown into a powerful man in your own right and I am so proud of you," Bastiquil said.

"What is happening, Master? I have not heard from you since before the plane crash. Are you safe," he asked his master, concerned for his well-being.

"I am where I need to be for the moment, as are you. I am glad to see that you are taking such good care of our guest. She is precious cargo."

"She is trying, at best. But, I will deliver her to you, to the castle just as instructed. This plane going down was a setback, but we will be back on schedule soon. I promise you, she will come to no harm under my watch," Victor reassured his master.

He could almost feel Bastiquil caressing his face and it felt so warm and caring. He wasn't used to being shown affection by anyone in the Balashon.

"I am not of the Balashon, Victor. The Balashon is of me. They are in existence to serve me, not the other way around. I show affection to the ones who deserve it and you my friend, my young apprentice, have served me well. Sleep, for you will need your strength and your wits about you. I fear we are not out of the clear yet."

"Do not fear Master, I will cut down anyone who tries to stand in our way. They will fall by my hands," Victor bolstered.

"I know they will. Rest, regenerate yourself. You are a powerful being, Victor. Never forget that. Never. I will come to you as soon as I can."

Victor slept well and dreamed of times when he and his master would be reunited.

Chapter Twenty-Three

The jet was flight checked, fueled, and waiting for them when Aldrik and Demetri arrived at the Tulsa International Airport. It had landed 30 minutes earlier. Aldrik moved around in the daylight as little as possible, but when he did he had to use a day suit. Lined with impenetrable, reinforced fabric of the highest quality, tailored to his stature, it allowed him to move in the daylight. The helmet had a tinted shield, which kept the sunlight out. He conveyed a resemblance of a svelte, futuristic military ops fighter.

He didn't know how Aldrik managed it, but they were able to drive out to the hanger where the plane was located. Once they boarded, they were immediately cleared for takeoff. As they taxied out onto the runway, Demetri was lost in thought of Gina. He had always been worried about her, but the guilt of not moving on this faster weighed heavily on him. He knew she would understand his decisions, but if anything happened to her before he found her, he would not forgive himself.

They waited in line for takeoff for only about five minutes, but it felt like five hours. Demetri needed to get into the air. He needed to feel like he would be moving towards Gina, towards rescuing her from her captor. Then the captain went full throttle with the plane and they were taxiing down the runway, Demetri breathed a sigh of relief. "Hang on

Gina," he said. Aldrik reached over and touched his hand to comfort him.

"We will do everything in our power to find her. Please don't fret, I know you are worried and rightfully so, but why would they take such measures to get her out of the country if they were just going to kill her? They could have just killed her at the mansion."

"Yes, I thought about that too. I don't know what they want with her. She is powerful, but she hasn't magically matured yet. So what's the angle?" Demetri placed his head into his hands as he felt the plane leave the ground. They were finally in the air. *She was a strong girl, a strong witch. She can protect herself, but if that brute of a man lays one hand on her I will rip him limb from limb.*

"I don't know yet, my love, but we will figure it out," Aldrik answered.

As the plane continued its upward climb soon to be reaching cruising altitude of thirty-five thousand feet, Aldrik leaned in closer to Demetri and put his arm around him. "Please tell me what is going on inside your beautiful head. I know there is something more than just worry for Gina. I have felt it since my arrival to Tulsa."

Turning his head to look into Aldrik's eyes, he smiled, and then turned away not knowing how to bring up what he wanted to talk to him about. He had been dying inside to tell him, to explain this, hoping that he would see this as a pure gift of fate, combined destinies. Looking away, he took a deep breath and dove in. "Do you believe that two souls can be destined to find each other no matter how many lifetimes it takes?"

"Yes, I guess anything in this universe is possible. I would not be one to dispute it due to the nature of what I am, a vampire. But why do I feel like you are not saying what you really mean? Please, Demetri, speak your truth."

"Well, as it turns out, when Gina and I did the past life meditation, to try to find out about Bastiquil and how we could defeat him, I found out much more than I bargained for," Demetri stated, biting his bottom lip.

"Again Demetri, you keep talking in circles. We have always been open and honest with each other. Why do you find it so hard to just tell me what this is all about?"

"Because what I found out is we knew each other while you were still alive, Aldrik, before you met death, only to be reborn a vampire."

Looking at him, Demetri knew that he was searching in his mind, in his memories trying to figure who and what he was referring to. Then he looked up at him with a look Demetri had never seen before on his face, a look of desperation and anxiety. "Floki? Can it be you?"

"I don't know, Aldrik. I only see images, feelings. I know I loved you, admired you, and looked up to you."

"I can't believe this. Words fail me right now," he said, as he looked into Demetri's eyes, searching, wanting to see something in them that harbored the past. It had been so long since he had heard Floki's name or thought about him. He was the closest friend that he had during that time of his life. He and Floki had become more than friends.

Demetri had a hard time gauging what Aldrik's thoughts were. He seemed lost in them, almost like a person who had taken too much valium. His face was stoic and unreadable.

"Please speak to me. Tell me what you are thinking."

"How am I to express fifteen hundred years of longing, wanting, wondering, of thinking I will never get the chance to be reunited in the afterlife with my beloved Floki. Whether there is a heaven or a hell, I am damned Demetri to be the walking dead that I am. I deserve a hell, if there is one, for what I have done."

"Don't talk like that, please. After all of these years you have lived, do you not believe in redemption? Do you not believe the good that you do will outweigh the bad? I have to think you know this, you have felt the connection, and you sense its strength, its pull on us. You know in your heart of hearts, Floki and I are connected, are sharing the same soul." Tears started to run down Demetri's face as he waited patiently for Aldrik to process this.

"Your memories deceive you, my love. They do not show you all of the truth, the monster living inside of me. They do not show you the wrongs I have inflicted, the lives snuffed out, way before their time because of me."

"I know you are a good man, Aldrik. I know you love me and you wouldn't do anything to hurt me. I see the many lives you help, the many souls that you have saved from being "snuffed out", to coin your term," Demetri said, trying to comfort him.

Maybe he had made a grave error in telling him. It wasn't like he had the full connection yet to Floki's memories, he could only see partial thoughts, partial truths of their life. Had he been selfish in his thinking it would give him comfort to know that Floki's essence still existed inside of Demetri's soul?

"Tell me then what memories you do recall? I would like to know," Aldrik asked.

"I know in each past life I was shown, it was me in some shape or fashion. It was pure and honest shock to find out that we had shared this life before. I don't have many memories of it yet, but I do remember that we were laughing and carrying on like two kids in love on your father's boat, during a fishing trip," he said, smiling.

"Yes, we had been friends since early childhood, but in our teenage years you helped your family by working with my father and myself on the fishing boat. This is what you are recalling, and yes, we had some wonderful times on that boat."

"I remember feeling happy, at peace, and much love towards you. I don't remember a whole lot after that, but I am piecing together the memories. They are like a puzzle which only have outside edges and the memories are the pieces in the middle. I have so many from so many lives. I find it hard to believe what is real and what isn't."

"Let me fill in some of the missing pieces for you. We were in love and we knew that from the moment we first met each other. As kids, we were inseparable and not much changed as the years passed. As teenagers, we shared our first sexual experience with each other and it continued on from there. Our parents were constantly trying to get us to marry this girl or that girl in hopes of our families merging with another so our families could prosper and carry on the bloodlines. But, it seemed we were not meant for that and our love could not be denied. We put them off as long as we could, but there came a time in our twenties when people started to talk, to whisper and make comments about the two young, healthy men who would not marry." Aldrik paused to look at him and there was obvious pain on his face when he saw Demetri's curious look of happiness as he waited patiently to hear more of the story.

"We had made a pact if our parents wouldn't stop with the pushing that we would run away together. But, in the end, the pressure was too much and your family, in desperate need of money, finally convinced you to marry a moderately, well-to-do family's daughter. I don't recall her name, it has been so long. Your mother was ill and your father got to where he couldn't work much so understandably you made the best decision for your family. Being hurt by all of this, I left town without any warning and made my way to the hills of Germany. I spent the better part of the three or four years there. I met a dashing man, one I felt safe with, confided and told everything. This ended up being one of the worst mistakes of my life."

"I can't believe I chose some girl over you," Demetri said, as his eyes welled up.

"You chose your family and that is the only choice you had, so don't be sad about that. My deciding to leave was on me. By the time I turned 29 years old, I had decided that I would make my way back to our hometown and see you again. I couldn't stand it anymore. Married or not, I wanted to make peace with it all. I told my mysterious friend, Lucius Von Adalwolf, what I had planned to do. He became enraged with me. He didn't want me even talking about it. Before I knew what had taken place, his face had become distorted, he had sharp, pointed teeth and when he grabbed me, he showed that he had supernatural strength. He had drained me of my blood before I realized what had even happened. But, I didn't expect him to turn around and feed it to me. He broke through the major artery in his neck with just the swipe of his fingernail and told me to drink. Feeling death coming on, I did as he instructed."

"I didn't realize. You never told me any of this before," Demetri said, shocked and in awe of the story.

"And I probably would not have told you if you had not been shown the past. I know it is cowardly of me, but it is a burden that I carry with me every second of this immortal life I walk through."

"Just tell me. It will be okay."

"When I woke up after being fed his blood, I found myself locked in a dark stone dungeon. There was no light, yet I could see. The door was made of steel and even with my newfound supernatural strength, I could not open it. I yelled for him, but he didn't come. Little did I know, he had planned a revenge, which would forever change me. At first, it was a faint sound. Thump, thump, and then I could make out that what sounded like beautiful music to my ears was a human heart. It beat with the most beautiful precision. I walked over to where I heard the beating coming from to find a man chained to the wall, scared, and confused. I had a thirst taking over me that just seemed to build and build until I thought I would burst. I didn't even know in the beginning what I thirsted for, but it soon became apparent to me."

"Holy shit," he said, after hearing this part of the story. "I cannot believe your maker, your killer, just left you there to discover on your own what and who you had become. To just chain a man up for you to feed on when you did figure it out is just cruel beyond measure."

"You have no idea my love just how cruel. I fought it at first, with all I had. Most vampires wake up thirsty and must have blood right away. I wasn't an exception to that. Lucius knew I would fight it. He knew I wouldn't want to feed on the man he had left me. By the second day I just about had lost all sense of reason, the only thing that made sense was the blood. I could hear it pumping in the veins, hear it thrust throughout the body with each push the heart gave. I lasted to day three. Aldrik, the man, no longer controlled me. The vampire nature took control. Even as I descended upon the man, I begged him to forgive me but didn't wait to hear his words. I feasted on him until no blood was left. When I realized what I had done, I cried, raged, beat on the door, begging for it to come off the hinges so I could get away from the death I had just inflicted."

"Aldrik, why do you still worry so about something you had no control over? Why are you so upset," Demetri caressed him, while he sat with his head in his hands, obviously distraught still after almost fifteen hundred years. This was one of the reasons that Demetri loved him so. Even though he was a vampire, he still showed the caring, mercy, compassion, and reflection of a human. He carried his sins with him, tortured by them. Demetri realized now what he must have been referring to when he talked about the wrongs he had inflicted.

"Because, it haunts me to this day. I know I will never get redemption, nor would I ask for it. I don't deserve it. He didn't deserve what I did to him."

"Who didn't deserve it," Demetri asked, curious about who could cause him to have such torment after so many years.

"Floki didn't deserve it. You, Demetri, didn't deserve it. My maker took the love of my life and tied him up for me to feast on as my first meal. I shall never forgive myself."

The look on Demetri's face told it all. He had no words.

Chapter Twenty-Four

As her anxiety gave way to her exhaustion, Gina drifted into a deep sleep. She felt safe in the cabin and, for some weird reason, she knew that Victor would not hurt her. Probably because if it had been his intent, he would have done it already. So in her frustration and pure hatred of him, she found refuge in her sleep.

She noticed a fluttering sound as if someone were trying to invade her dreams. She knew this wasn't uncommon, especially for witches. It seemed everyone wanted to invade a witch's dream, especially when they were in such a dreary state. But as you mature in your powers and abilities you learn they have no power over you other than what you give them. Sure there are some demons like Bastiquil who are powerful enough to invade your dreams and do damage, as Demetri and Alex found out, but for the most, it was ghosts and spirits hanging onto this realm instead of moving onto the next. These types of apparitions are the ones you learn to control. They can't get in unless you allow it.

But as Gina found herself falling deep into a dream, she transported herself to one of the most beautiful spots she had seen on this journey in Iceland. She sat overlooking a glorious mountain range of green, while purple, orange, and blue filled the sky as the sun sank lower, promising to disappear behind the mountains. There were gray and black clouds sparsely filling the sky, but the beauty of the sunset and the colors dancing from it hit her eyes with amazement. The land was a different matter unto itself.

As she watched the clouds pass by, she lost herself in the beauty of this land, this country, this island. Most people in the world probably didn't know the beauty it held, mostly because of its location, being extreme north, and its name. It was as if the people who named the two islands got them majorly mixed up. For Greenland was a land of ice with little greenery and Iceland, although it has glaciers, also held such green, lush, beautiful landscapes. Gina could easily fall in love with this land, if not for the fact she had been forced to be there.

"Why do you let such negative thoughts cloud your positive ones of beauty?"

Jumping, slightly startled, she looked over to see a small creature of a man. It had to be one of the elves Victor had mentioned. It was a glorious sight to behold. He stood there on a log next to where she sat on the grass. He wore simple, old world looking clothes, had blond hair, blue eyes and yes, he had pointed ears. He stood about six inches in height. If she weren't dreaming, it would all seem so real.

"What makes you come to the conclusion that what you see in your dreams has no real bearing in the waking world? You, of all people, should know better Gina."

"I, um, I know you are right, wait. How do you know my name?"

"We make it our business to know all people who grace our land. Especially those as gifted and powerful as yourself."

"I am blown away right now. This is truly one of the best things that I have been gifted to behold. What is your name, if you don't mind me asking? You know mine," Gina asked the elf.

"No, I don't mind at all. It is Thadius D. Funkenhelder, at your service madam," he said, as he mock bowed to her.

Smiling at his gentlemanly gestures, she still could not believe what she was seeing. And, of course, he was correct, she should know better than to instantly write something off as just a dream. My goodness, she just did battle with a demon, alongside a vampire. Nothing in this world should surprise her at this point, but she had to admit, she was extremely glad she can still find childlike awe in a world as strange and vicious as this one.

"You look so young Thadius. How old are you?"

He smiled at her, not blushing, but in a way that let her know that she had asked a not so simple question. "Time moves differently for us here in our world. I am 20 years old, but to the human lifespan, about eighty to a hundred years."

Not being able to hold back her surprise and enthusiasm, she laughed and threw her head back. Looking back at him she couldn't help but stare. "I am absolutely ecstatic to meet you Thadius. I am in awe. I hope you don't take my actions or laughter as rude. I just thought that you were of legend. Was it you I felt earlier in the woods?"

"Yes, it was I. I couldn't help but watch such an extreme battle as the one that took place. Never before had I seen such a display of strength and courage by a human. To take on a bear, that is amazing even to an elf."

"He isn't a nice man, Thadius. He has kidnaped me and is taking me somewhere that he has not yet revealed," she said, becoming solemn.

"I know," he leaned in and whispered to her, then laughed as if it were the funniest thing.

"If you know, can't you help me? Won't you help me escape him?" she pleaded with him.

"It is against our laws to interfere with human beings and their activities. The only time we would is if our way of life or homes were threatened. That is how we have survived

141

and lived so peacefully on this island as long as we have. Do you understand?" Thadius asked seriously.

"Yes, I understand," Gina said, as she bowed her head realizing that she truly had to do this on her own.

"Don't be sad; I am here with you now. Won't you tell me some stories of your life?" he asked, so cutely and innocently that she could not be mad or upset with him. This was a once in a lifetime event so she decided to do exactly what he had asked her to do, at least for now, and live in the positive, the here and the now.

Chapter Twenty-Five

As the body of Lincoln Reed quickly came to a gruesome end, the life force no longer able to keep up with the energy Bastiquil was burning up, the demon made a decision. The time had come for Phillip Anthony Green III, aka John Berryman, the roommate, to live up to his end of the deal. Bastiquil would find Phillip and would use him to make a stand against the witches, reclaim the vessel, and continue his reign of power.

With each step Bastiquil took, he could hear the crying out of pain from what was left of Lincoln's consciousness. This body was wasted and if not for Bastiquil inhabiting it, it would already be dead. By all rights, it should be laying on the ground right now.

Bastiquil did not want to draw attention to this death, this beloved staff member of the vessel, so he was taking it out away from the city to dispose of. If all went according to plan, no one will find it for some time. It wasn't hard to figure out a place to dispose of the body, all he had to do was look inward at Linc's memories and he found a spot perfect for what he needed.

It took Bastiquil about an hour to get to Lake Keystone, a favorite place of Lincoln's. Lincoln had spent many an hour since his move to Tulsa at Lake Keystone. There was a spot on the lake where the water was deep, the inlet narrow, with a swinging bridge connecting two sides.

Bastiquil expended most of the energy this body had left just getting there with the supplies he needed to make sure the body would not be discovered.

Stealing a car from an apartment complex near the tattoo studio, all Bastiquil had to do now was get to the lake and dispose of the body. He would then find his next host, wherever he may be, and get back on track with his plans.

He knew Lincoln would love being buried here and it wasn't in Bastiquil's nature to give a human what they wanted, but this one he would make an exception for. He needed to get this done and move on.

Bastiquil stood in the center of the bridge, hands bound with tightly gripped handcuffs, which were attached by a chain to a cinder block, ready for the plunge. He felt no fight coming from Linc and knew he had timed this one just right. Smiling big, Bastiquil mustered up enough energy to throw himself over the rope railing. As Lincoln's body fell to its watery grave, Bastiquil expunged himself from the body. Floating in the air, the black mass of demonic form, Bastiquil watched as the body hit the water with a tremendous splash, then sank deeper until it was no longer visible.

Bastiquil turned in the air, towards Tulsa, and headed back to the city, flying low over the water. It was time to find Phillip, or John as the vessel knew him, and try his plan out. Either this was going to work or Bastiquil would be no more in this world.

Chapter Twenty-Six

John Berryman had been laying low ever since the night all hell broke loose. When the male witch showed up and opened up an arsenal of Wiccan weapons on the Balashon and Bastiquil, the survivors scattered. Luckily, John was one of those survivors. He survived that night as he had survived many other things that life had thrown at him. The Balashon had taught him how to be strong, to deceive, to outwit, and to conquer.

John never ran from a fight, but this one felt different. He knew that he would need to get in touch with the Balashon soon, but they had all been given specific training on what to do if something like this happened. No one had ever thought it would happen again, but it had. No wonder it had felt different than most of their fights; this witch, Demetri had supernatural strength. But, John had been able to get the best of him at Alex's house; Demetri had not seen it coming. He felt safe with John because Alex felt safe with him. Of course, John was good at his job. Therefore, neither of them suspected him.

John busied himself in the restroom, grooming his face, after a long, hot shower. One of the many perks of belonging to an organization as large as the Balashon was you get multiple identities and plenty of money to back them up. John assumed most had either fled the country or like him, had taken up another persona just as they were trained to do. He liked this one a lot, Sebastian Von Leigerfeld. Having lived in Europe for most of his life, it was natural for him to take on a German accent. He spoke it fluently and most people seemed to be either intimidated or attracted to the accent.

As John finished up his grooming routine, still nude from his shower, he casually strolled into the living room area of the suite he had chosen at the Crown Plaza. Having ordered room service, he enjoyed a rare filet mignon with steamed asparagus and bottle of merlot. Sitting down on the sofa, he leaned back, with one leg hiked up on the cushion, with the other stretched out in front of him.

Satisfied with food, John began to have thoughts creep into his mind; sexual thoughts. With those thoughts, his already exposed cock begin to grow, become hard and long for more than just his hand this night. He longed for the touch of a woman, the feel of her wet lips brushing his, her kisses leading to other pleasures. As he began to picture this fantasy woman in his head, he let his hand slip down to his nipples were he ran his fingers over them, making them erect. He then let his hand slip down to his cock where he began to stroke it up and down as the images in his head played out. *Ah, you like that sweetheart, you like daddy's hard cock? Stroke it and show me how much you enjoy it.* John got closer and closer to shooting his load all over his bare chest, completely unaware he was being watched.

As John shot his load, Bastiquil came crashing through the penthouse balcony window. John didn't need to open his mouth in surprise as he had already had it open in self-ecstasy. With this opportunity, Bastiquil wasted no time in entering and securing John's body and soul. John could feel him taking over, but more than anything, John could feel the major disappointment his master felt for him at this moment. He felt the missed opportunities to take out the witch, the friend Brandy, and many others he had not even thought about until now. He deserved this death, but at least he would

146

be able to serve his master one last time, an attempt to make amends. Then his soul disappeared and Bastiquil took over.

Chapter Twenty-Seven

Gina's bookstore was about as ready as it was going to get for reopening. They were taking a chance by doing this, but they also knew Gina had worked hard to make the store what it was today and in some way it gave them all hope. It gave them hope things would be okay, order would be regained, and Gina would make it home safely. The chance of them being attacked here, in public was not as great as it was if they were still on their own.

Just the little time that Mathias had been there, Brandy felt safer, which seemed odd considering he wasn't a big guy like Demetri and she wasn't even sure what his power was. She thought it strange to even be using the word power in connection with a person outside of their human, physical strength. But, she had to admit, curiosity was getting the better of her and she almost felt safe asking him. Almost.

Brandy had spent most of the day going over Gina's inventory list, bank statements, ledgers, and the program Gina used online to order products. Brandy considered herself a smart woman and, in fact, she was; being a scientist was not an average lay man's job. Brandy already had ideas for improving Gina's existing system, little tweaks here and there, to make it more efficient and orderly. In a way, she didn't even mind if Gina came back mad at her for changing things around because it would mean she was alive and well enough to tell Brandy off.

Brandy eyed Mathias in the corner, sitting by the window, watching people as they walked by. Soon she would open the doors to the store again and hoped business would pick up as usual. For the time being, there was a sign on the door that read TEMPORARILY CLOSED FOR RENOVATIONS. She really wasn't sure what she would tell someone if they asked what renovations has been done since there hadn't been any. Brandy decided she didn't care one way or the other.

"Mathias, tell me something about yourself," Brandy inquired, hoping to spark a conversation with the mysterious kid.

"I like music," he answered, hoping it would end her desire to ask more questions.

"Any particular type of music?"

"The ones that have a beat to it," he answered.

"Doesn't most music have a beat?" Brandy shot back, not deterred by his lack of enthusiasm for her questions.

"I would suppose."

"I don't mind if you turn some music on," Brandy offered. "It would be a nice distraction."

"It is on."

"The music?" Brandy asked, looking puzzled.

"Yes, I hear it just fine."

"Mathias, I don't hear any music," Brandy said worried now.

"I wouldn't expect you would hear it," Mathias offered, "it only plays in my head."

Thinking he was being a smartass by this explanation, Brandy let it go, for now. She had enough to worry about right now than to tackle any of this boy's issues.

Chapter Twenty-Eight

In the reading room of the bookstore, Alex busied himself on the computer looking up all he could find on secret societies, demonic possession, tattoo possession, and mind control. It was not in his nature to just sit back and let fate have its way with him. There had to be a way to fight back. Gina had a great library of books to help his search.

His mind tried to soak in all the information it could on the topics, but it also kept wandering back to the scene where his mother tried to kill his best friend in front of him and then killed herself. The image of it racked his brain; the image of the hell hounds, or whatever they were, dragging his mother into that fiery pit, just as it had the others he dreamed about. *What could all this mean? My whole existence, or what existence I thought I had was a lie.*

He was the descendant of a demon. His mother and father had both betrayed him, left him for dead as far as he was concerned. It didn't hurt any less, but the not knowing was something he was just going to have to accept. He had to figure out a way to break the bond between himself and Bastiquil. There had to be a way. Just as Bastiquil had made the connection, it can be unmade. He just had to find the answer. If Gina were here right now, she would know and how to guide him through this.

How selfish, thinking of yourself, when she was out there fighting for her life, somewhere unknown, someplace far away if Demetri was correct. But the good news was if anyone can find her and bring her back safely, it would be Demetri. As he tried to bring himself back to the task at hand, his phone started to ring.

Reaching into his pocket, he pulled out his phone and saw the call from Blue Moon. He felt guilty for not being in attendance to help, but this was not a typical situation he found himself in.

"Hello, this is Alex."

"Alex, man I'm so happy to hear your voice. You have got to get down here right away. All hell is breaking loose." The voice on the other end stressed, obviously agitated and concerned.

"Jerry, what's wrong."

"We are having major malfunctions down here, man. There was a small fire, which ended up burning one of the clients. Then there is the issue with the ink supply, it's all gone, nothing left. The health inspector is here along with the fire chief and the police. They are saying if you don't come down here right now, they are shutting the place down, man. I can't lose my job, Alex," Jerry pleaded with him.

"Okay, okay, please tell them I will be there as quickly as I can," Alex reassured the panicked Jerry. "I'm on my way."

"Thanks, Alex, thank you so much. I will let them know."

As Alex hung up the phone he couldn't help but be suspicious as nothing like this had ever happened since he had owned the place, but in Jerry's defense, Alex had never disappeared like this before either.

"What's going on Alex?" Brandy asked, as she came into the room at the tail end of the phone conversation. "Where do you think you are going?"

Mathias also made his way into the room.

"There has been an accident at the studio. I have the authorities waiting for me to get there or they are shutting it down. I have worked too hard to make the studio a success not to go."

"Well, if you must go, you shouldn't go alone," Mathias stated.

"I can't ask this of you. You are here to protect Brandy, as well as me. I will be fine."

"The matter isn't up for discussion," Mathias stated, looking at him with a dare in his eyes, one which Alex knew he didn't want to call the bluff on.

"Fine, we will all go. Safety in numbers, right," Alex stated.

Now in the body of John, Bastiquil hung up Jerry's phone. Turning to Jerry, who was bound and gagged in the chair next to the piercing table, Bastiquil looked at him, smiling.

"This is where the fun begins my new friend, you played your part well, but now it's time for you to see what your boss is really made of," Bastiquil said, in Jerry's voice as Jerry stared at him, wide eyed and in shock.

Chapter Twenty-Nine

He just had this infectious way of getting you to do what he asked. Thadius was as cute, as he was funny. He would say something to Gina, then look at her with a serious face, then burst out laughing at himself.

"So come on, tell me a story. Tell me about how you came to be," he pleaded with her, with a look that she knew was his serious face, but also knew a laugh was sure to follow. She wasn't disappointed.

Gina began a tale which enthralled Thadius from the minute she spoke the first words until the last words spoken. She told the tale of her family, their migration to the United States from Romania and the subsequent years of living, loving, and raising their family in rural Oklahoma. It seemed like time stood still as she remembered her history. Retelling it brought out memories she had long since forgot, and some she had never told anyone. There were some she overheard as a child but had just thought them to be of legend, a myth. A story to scare little kids, but after seeing her mother's visible distress during the failed attempt at summoning her grandmother, Gina realized the stories must have been true. Her mother mentioned something was chasing her, even in the afterlife, it was coming for her, it knew she was talking to Gina and it wasn't at all happy about it.

Thadius reached over and touched the tear rolling down Gina's face.

"Why do you cry over things you have no control over?" he questioned, so innocently.

"Because people I love, people who have crossed over to the other side are hurting, scared, and being tortured by something evil."

"Do you not think this is of their own doing?"

Gina shot him a look of hurt and disgust which sent Thadius into his serious face, followed by nervous laughter.

"Pay me no attention, young one, I am merely speaking out of turn." Thadius tried to play it off, but Gina wasn't having any of it

"Thadius, what a hurtful thing to say. Explain yourself."

"I merely mean, we are in this life, this realm, for such a short time. We think we know what lies in the hearts and minds of loved ones, but do we truly know their plight, their struggles? Do we know the deals they have made, the songs their hearts have sung? We know what people want us to know, no less, no more," Thadius explained, in a way she could not be upset.

It makes sense unless you have Demetri's gift of seeing into the minds of others, how does one truly know what lies in the hearts of others? Gina thought.

"I should not be telling you this, but we have become such good friends." Thadius's disclaimer perked Gina's interest. "The path which lies ahead of you is wrought with such danger, such peril, it is hard for me to know the outcome. I see great power ahead, both from you and all around you. People want you, want the power within you for their own selfish gains. But, the dark will see no light until you have faced your demon and come out the victor."

Thadius shook his head as if he woke from a sleep, but Gina knew a vision when she saw one. He smiled at her as if he had just said nothing.

"Thadius, what do you mean?"

154

"Oh my, dear, look at the time. I must be on my way," he cackled, ignoring Gina's question.

"Thadius, please," she begged him. "Tell me what you mean?"

"I mean what I say and say more than I mean. This journey is yours, my friend. We shall meet again, I know it, I feel it, but for now I must bid you goodbye," Thadius declared, as he stood, bowed and with a smile on his face and a snap of his fingers, he disappeared.

Gina awoke, shaking off the fog which sleep had brought, still tired, but with a sense of awe and wonder about her. She knew enough to believe what she had just experienced was the real deal. Mr. Thadius had just honored her with a visit and now he was gone.

She thought back on all he had said, which wasn't a lot actually. She did most of the talking as he had asked her to do. He listened to her so intently and with such awe as if she were telling the most exciting and adventurous tale he had ever heard before. Maybe it was, but she doubted it.

Turning over in the bed, Gina could see the flickering of the candles burning in the other room, the room in which Victor awaited. Her bliss from the recent visit of the adorable elf suddenly turned to hatred as she remembered her current circumstances and immediately began to brood.

Thirsty, she got up and walked to the door's edge, leaning on the framework as she peered into the room to see Victor sitting in the rocking chair, head bowed downward, with a shotgun laid across his lap. Gina knew the shotgun wasn't for her in the sense of using it on her, but rather for protection from what lay out there, in the wilderness, in the dark. But she couldn't help but think to herself, seething inside, as she remembered the poor old man who had opened his door to offer them shelter from a cold storm.

She entered the room and walked over to the kitchen sink where she retrieved a glass that set upside down on the counter. Holding it under the sink, she filled it almost full of water and drank it down. She had been thirstier than she had thought. Filling the glass again, she turned to walk back to her room only to find that now the rocking chair in which Victor sat, was rocking back and forth. Through the darkness and flickering firelight, she noticed he no longer looked downward, but rather stared directly at her.

"Drink as much as you want princess, you will need it for the trip."

"Don't talk to me, you fucking murderer." Gina glared at him.

"Really, do we have to rehash this every time? Yes, I am the murderer, the boogeyman in your dreams. I protect you, yet I am evil. Seems like some people would be thankful to have someone watching over them," Victor commented, not hurt, but in a factual manner.

"I do have people watching out for me, I have Demetri."

"And where is your Demetri? Where is he now?" Victor stated, in a tone that dug to her very core.

Gina felt a sudden dizziness overcome her as she dropped the glass and a fog swept over her eyes and brain. She could feel herself dropping to the floor. It all felt slow motion to her, but it happened quickly.

Victor, leaping from his chair, caught Gina in his arms before she hit the ground.

When Gina finally came around, she slowly opened her eyes to find herself in Victor's arms, as he sat on the ground quietly holding her.

"What are you doing? What happened?" Gina questioned, confused and a little scared.

"Calm down, I am not going to hurt you. You fainted. I caught you before you hit the ground and thought it just as easy to sit here and wait it out as it was to pick you up and carry you to bed. I am here to protect you, not hurt you. I have pushed you hard since we left the wreckage site, but only for your protection. There aren't just bears and other wildlife we have to concern ourselves with, as you have witnessed in the past weeks, there are far more dangerous creatures out there," Victor explained, in a calming voice.

Gina felt the need to push away, to hit him, to run into the other room, but she was tired and weary and if truly honest with herself, the warmth from his body did comfort her.

Chapter Thirty

Aldrik sat in silence waiting for the cruel words of punishment to come, which he knew he deserved, but the silence continued from Demetri. All he heard were the engines of the plane which carried them closer and closer to their Icelandic destination.

When his bowed head felt the soft touch of Demetri's hand, he burst into tears. *How could this man he loves so much, his Demetri, show him so much love and compassion after hearing that he had killed him in a past life?* Demetri surprised him even more by leaning down and lifting his head slightly, so he could kiss his lips.

"The Aldrik I know and love would not do such a thing, maybe in the past, but not in this present moment. I know that Floki's memories are floating around inside me somewhere, but I feel no anger trying to make its way to the surface, so I am sure even Floki knew you had no choice in the matter. Forgive yourself Aldrik, because I do."

Aldrik had been so consumed with guilt and self-loathing for so long, he finally let it all wash over him. He sat in his chair and sobbed. Demetri sat down next to him, putting his arm around his shoulders, pulling him in close.

"Let it go, my love, don't hang onto this another second."

After what seemed like an hour, Aldrik turned to look at Demetri and, once again, became overwhelmed by the love and compassion he saw in his eyes.

"I have something I want to ask you and I don't want you to take it the wrong way," Demetri gazed at him, with a somber look on his face.

Aldrik mentally prepared himself for the onslaught he knew must be coming.

"Are you a member of the mile-high club?" Demetri asked, his face turning from its somber look, to smiling brightly and coyly.

Aldrik was caught off guard, which he knew was Demetri's intention to break the seriousness which had consumed them for a couple hours.

"Are you kidding me? I am fifteen hundred years old and have owned a plane longer than you have been alive."

"Well, I haven't joined the club yet," Demetri smiled, as he slid his shirt off. "You want to make me an honorary member or do you want me to work for it?"

Aldrik, recovered from his meltdown, but definitely not over the guilt he had been carrying around for a millennia and a half, grabbed Demetri by the waist and pulled him closer to him, until he straddled Aldrik's lap out of necessity.

Leaning into him, he kissed his lips with such passion and abandon they forgot the pilot was on board. Aldrik took Demetri's nipple into his mouth, carefully sucking and kissing so he did not bite into it. One thing he learned early on as a vampire, you can still have sex, but it takes a great deal of control and restraint not to get carried away and hurt someone. Actually, it took quite a while to learn this. When a vampire loses themselves in passion and lust, they sometimes lose lovers in the act of sex. Thus, the need for self-control and restraint.

Demetri, completely lost in the moment, savoring the sensations this beautiful man delivered to his body, felt like he could be like this forever. But, he also knew this was a feeling which doesn't last. Aldrik loved him, but he was also a loner, much like Demetri. As a couple, they made complete sense, at least in Demetri's mind, but to someone who has just been introduced to the concept of vampires, would think him suicidal and crazy.

But, none of this mattered right now, in this moment. This man, whom he loved so much, was showering his body with such tender kisses. Reaching over, he started to undo the safety suit which Aldrik had on, but with a nod of his head, he told Demetri no.

"This is about you my love, you and you alone. Let me cherish you, love you, and kiss on you. Let me give you the pleasure today. You give me so much, let me do this for you," Aldrik stated, in whisper of a voice.

Reaching around Demetri's waist and holding tightly to it, he turned them both, laying him gently down on the sofa seat in which they were sitting. The leather made a rustling sound when Demetri's back slid into it. He wasted no time in unbuttoning Demetri's pants, pulling them down as Demetri lifted his hips slightly, as they came to rest at mid-thigh.

"You are so beautiful Demetri," he said, gazing into his eyes, slowly letting the gaze drift down his chest until it came to rest on Demetri's hard cock.

Leaning down, he kissed the tip while gazing into Demetri's eyes, then closing his own, he slipped the hardness into his mouth.

"Oh yes," Demetri gasped, as he felt the pleasure overcome him. "You know exactly how I like it."

Needing no prompting, Aldrik continued to pleasure his cock, going faster, then slowing down a bit, letting his tongue work the tip until he heard the moans coming from Demetri's lips, then he would descend deeper onto it, taking it just a little further each time.

Loving every minute of this, Demetri reached up with both hands and taking his thumbs, he rubbed them over both of his nipples, heightening the intensity of the sensations he felt. The stress and worry of the last few days melted away for just a few minutes as the love of his life helped transport him into a sense of abandon.

Just as he didn't think he could take anymore without shooting his load, he placed his right hand on Aldrik's head, signaling to him the impending orgasm. Heeding this, Aldrik took his cock to the back of his throat before pulling out and licking on his balls, as Demetri shot his warm, milky manhood all over his own chest.

Aldrik straddled himself over him, hovering his mouth just over Demetri's, letting the hot, deep breaths send shivers of pleasure down his spine. Then bringing his lips to Demetri's, they locked in the most passionate kiss, one with centuries of memories guiding them, binding them.

A chime sounded, signaling they were starting their decent into Iceland, bringing them both back to the present and with it the reason for their journey. Demetri cleaned himself off and pulled his shirt back on.

"I fear we are too late," he said, as he sat back down on the sofa next to Aldrik.

Taking Demetri's hand into his own, Aldrik leaned over and kissed him on the cheek. "If we were too late my love, you would already know it. Your bond with Gina is too strong, too deep and spiritual in nature. I feel she is still alive, being used as leverage, but for what, I have yet to determine. But, rest assured, we will find her and her captor."

Chapter Thirty-One

The Blue Moon Tattoo Parlor seemed busier than ever, with a person in every seat being tattooed or going over books for another tattoo to be added. There was a steady rumble of conversation taking place over the buzzing sounds of the ink guns, some laughing and some grimacing from their own personal level of pain tolerance.

As Alex, Brandy, and Mathias entered the front door, Alex looked around the parlor confused and bewildered due to his prior phone call with Jerry. He quickly scanned the room but did not see Jerry or Linc anywhere. There were people doing tattoos on customers that Alex had never seen before. *What the fuck is going on here?* he thought. As his senses heightened, he began to fear what they had just walked into.

Making his way up into the center of the room, Brandy and Mathias in tow, Alex knew in his heart this was not right, something was amiss. Just when he had decided to leave quickly out the back door with Brandy and Mathias, something caught his attention out of the corner of his eye. He froze.

"What's wrong, Alex?" Brandy questioned, seeing his obvious apprehension.

Brandy's eyes followed Alex as he slowly turned to his right to find a girl whose back was turned to him, finishing a tattoo on the chest of a man. The girl had the most beautiful wings tattooed on her back. She slowly stepped away from the man laid back in a chair to reveal a bound Jerry, with duct tape across his mouth, tears flowing down his cheeks as his eyes, huge and begging, looked to Alex for help. Across his chest in large black ink was tattooed WELCOME HOME ALEX.

Brandy let out an audible gasp, as Alex stood there stunned, taking it all in. The girl with the wings turned her head slightly so Alex could see her face and grinned slyly at him. "Do you like my work, boss?" As soon as those words left her lips she quickly turned to Jerry, dagger in hand, slitting his throat from ear to ear as blood poured out of Jerry's neck, down his chest, and onto the floor.

"RUN," Mathias yelled at the two, as Brandy screamed at what she was witnessing and tears welled up in Alex's eyes as he knew exactly what was taking place here. This was his welcome home party from Bastiquil and the Balashon.

As they turned to run to the back of the room towards the back door, a group of five men stepped into the framework of the door blocking their path. The front door opened and then shut, hardly without notice, but the room fell silent as the dead bolt of the door turned making the loudest noise, or what seemed like it. The only other noise in the room was the heavy breathing coming from Alex.

"You have one thing wrong my son," Alex froze when he heard those words coming from the front door area, he turned and looked to find John, his old roommate, standing at the door. "This is your welcome home party from me, your father, Bastiquil, but the Balashon are not in attendance. These fine people you see before you now are your brothers and sisters in arms. They bear your blood, my blood, in their inked skin and will do whatever necessary to protect you."

Alex turned to Mathias. "Get Brandy out of here at whatever cost. Do not worry about me."

"No, Alex," Brandy cried, "I will not leave you again."

"Touching, truly touching," Bastiquil said, as he began to make his way into the room, moving closer and closer to them. "Do you really think your small friend here can get her past your brothers?" Bastiquil smiled at Alex's presumed innocence.

"These are not my brothers or sisters you sick, twisted bastard. These are cheap, knock off imitations of what you hoped I would be for you."

"Oh, I would agree with you one hundred percent my son, they are imitations of you, but they are not to take your place. You are still the vessel, you are still the one who will carry me into the future." Bastiquil smiled as Alex noticed not one person seemed fazed by his or Bastiquil's insults.

Brandy leaned into Mathias' ear, who had a firm grip on her arm and whispered softly into it. "Do you have a plan?"

"Oh, I have a sweet little Rolling Stones tune playing in my head right now. This demon is going to need all the sympathy he can get," he quietly stated back to Brandy.

Brandy bit her bottom lip at this and rolled her eyes thinking to herself, *we are truly fucked right now. This kid is supposed to protect us?*

Bastiquil turned to the girl with the winged back, who still held the dagger. "Show them my dear what you can do."

At hearing Bastiquil's command, the girl leaned forward, knees slightly bent. She had on a halter top which revealed her entire back. She looked as if she was in some kind of yoga stance, bent knees, back bent over, and chest and head running parallel with the floor. Looking up at the three, she smiled an evil smile, closed her eyes and began to make a noise, almost a grunting, pushing sound.

As all eyes were focused on the yoga grunting girl, you could have heard a pin drop when the wings inked on her back began to make a fluttering sound, almost a ripple effect

164

down the skin of her back. Then without hesitation, the wings jutted out from her back expanding outward to her sides almost four feet in each direction and began to flap them, slowly at first, then faster until she lifted herself a foot off the ground. Her point made, she let herself back down to the ground and looked over to Bastiquil, who beamed with pride.

"Well done my dear," he said, as she placed the wings back behind her, but ever ready for battle. "We shall call you Night Fury."

The girl smiled at this and bowed slightly to show her obedience and appreciation to her maker.

"Oh, and you my dear," he said, looking around Alex at Brandy. "You are quite resilient. I was extremely surprised to learn about your survival. When you called, I have to say, it caught me off guard."

"You leave her out of this you bastard. She has nothing to do with this," Alex shouted at him.

"Quite the contrary, she has plenty to do with this. She was to be sacrificed to me, but she just wouldn't die. But, I have much respect for the strong, Brandy; you will make a great addition to our family."

"You think I would ever help you with anything," she shot back at him in disgust.

"Not willingly, no. But, who said you had a choice in the matter," Bastiquil smiled at her, as the other people in the room began to rise, some taking off shirts, others not needing to as their tattoos were already revealed.

"We will all be one big, happy family. Even the runt, if he doesn't make me cross." Bastiquil grinned at Mathias, who just continued to move his head to the rhythm of the music playing inside his head, building up the strength needed to take on this crowd.

165

Chapter Thirty-Two

As morning broke and the dawn brought the sun, Gina awoke to find herself snuggled warmly next to the fireplace, wrapped in a blanket, pillow under her head and laying atop a bearskin rug. She could not tell if it was real or faux, but the comfort of it she was grateful for.

Nearby, she looked over to see Victor pouring two cups of coffee and she could smell the aroma of breakfast, but could not make out the smell.

"I hope you have an appetite? We have some toasted bread and some venison filets I grilled up on the stove. It should help with your energy and give us the push we need to make it to the shoreline today," Victor stated, holding the cup of coffee in the air and placing it down on the table next to an empty plate, letting her know it was time to get up.

"How long have you been awake? Did you get any rest?" Gina asked, as she got up and slowly walked to the table with the blanket still wrapped around her. She still felt a little awkward about last night but tried hard to play it off.

"I got enough, it doesn't take much to replenish me and, quite frankly, I never had much need or use for sleep."

"Well maybe that explains why you are a bit whacked in the head," Gina said with a brooding look, taking a sip of her coffee.

"Think what you will about me, but until you know my motives, my life, and my story you will never understand me, nor do I care if you ever do," Victor said, as he walked over to the table with skillet in hand, stuck a fork into the venison steak and placed it down onto the empty plate where Gina was sitting. Placing another steak onto his plate he then brought the toast and placed it down on the table.

"Eat up, you will need it," he prompted Gina.

Gina's thoughts were on last night's events. She had felt so strange, like a wave of nausea had swept over her, but it was so intense, so strong, she was unable to keep herself steady and knew she was going down. She knew it was probably a combination of stress, fatigue, and dehydration, but it also felt like something else, something she couldn't quite put her finger on.

"Listen, about last night," Victor started, as if reading her mind. "Please don't mistake my kindness for weakness. I will not have you thinking any more about your escape plans."

"I wouldn't dream of it, asshole."

"Well I am glad we are back to normal then and you are able to form such wonderful words with that extended vocabulary of yours," Victor looked at her, as he dug his knife into the venison.

"Fuck you, psycho. Don't presume to think you can lecture me about the path of the righteous tongue. Don't forget, I have seen your handy work up close and personal."

As they ate the rest of their breakfast in silence, Gina thought about her dream visitor, Thadius, and wondered if it was real or if she created him out of necessity for her own sanity. Either way, if it had been real, Thadius had told her he could not interfere in human affairs, so she was still on her own.

Victor had finished his meal before she did, so he busied himself with packing a backpack with the supplies they would need for the rest of the journey. There was food, water, a first-aid kit, clothing, and weapons in case they would need them.

Gina had to say, Victor was a strong man. She had seen him take on Demetri and last longer than she thought anyone could have. He also took on a bear to save her. *Who does that?* It's not something so far out of realm of possibility, but come on, they had just survived a plane crash too and he still had the energy to take on a bear. *What else was this man capable of?* Murder she knew was on his list.

As they gathered their things and readied themselves to leave, Gina stopped and looked over at the rolled up rug which contained the man. *I am so sorry we ever crossed your path. I don't even know your name. I hope you are somewhere peaceful. Please forgive me. Thadius, if you are out there, please watch over me.*

Walking out the door, Gina looked back to see Victor come out behind her, and stop in the doorway. Turning his head over his shoulder to look back at her, he flicked a lit match into the cabin. As the match hit the flooring, the rugs went up in flames, all to Gina's horror.

"What are you doing? It is bad enough you kill this man, but you have to burn down the house around him too? What if he has children who would want something of his? You are an evil man, Victor, pure evil." Gina ran out of things to scream at him, well, she had plenty to say, she just knew the words would fall on deaf ears.

"Come along miss bleeding heart. What is a dead man going to do with a house anyway?" Victor said, grabbing her arm and pulling her along.

Just as they hit the patch of trees, an electric jolt lit up beneath Victor's feet and sent him flying into the air, landing ten feet from where he had once been standing. Hitting his head on the tree where he landed, he immediately arched his back and then shot forward with the strength of his leg muscles, landing in battle stance. He scanned the area, looking for any oncoming attackers but found it was just the two of them.

"Is this your idea of a joke witch? A payback for the old man? Well, you will have to do better than this to take me down," Victor sneered.

"I wish I could take credit for it, but I cannot." Gina looked at him, shrugging her shoulders. Then she smiled inwardly as she heard the unmistakable laughter inside her head which could be none other than Thadius himself. Victor must have gotten too close to a protected patch of land. *Good for them for sticking up for themselves. Serves him right.*

Chapter Thirty-Three

They walked for hours, taking few breaks, except for the times Gina would insist out of pure exhaustion. He was a machine. A never-ending power supply of energy. Even wounded he had more stamina and energy than she.

As exhausted as she was though, she could not discount nor neglect the sheer beauty of this country. *It is stunning here, just stunning.*

As they came up towards the top of a peak, Gina decided to give it one more try.

"So are you going to tell me where you are taking me? It's not like I can tell anyone."

"Well, if you can't tell anyone, then why do you think you need to know? Let's just let it be a surprise. Besides, we are days away from reaching our destination, maybe even a week. It depends on how well you can keep your questions to a minimum and how quickly you can keep up." Victor turned and shot her a look.

"Listen, I have done a reasonably good job of keeping up with you and I even recall saving your life during and after the bear attack, so do not keep treating me as if I am a person you have to drag along on a fucking makeshift travois. I have pulled my weight at a time when you should have fucking died," Gina shot at him, disgusted and little hurt by the lack of acknowledgment from this barbarian.

"Actually, you are right. I am not used to people saving me. I do the saving. And yes, you could have let me die and I get why you didn't. I know it isn't out of love, kindness, or even liking me a little, I know you needed me to make it out of here in one piece, but it doesn't take away from the fact you did save me and for that, I thank you."

Gina had not expected this and was quite taken aback by it. There seemed to be so many layers to this man. She hated him one minute, confused by him the next, and then he was kind to her. But, she will not for one minute make the mistake of letting her guard down around him. He has shown her who he was, what he was capable of, even in his kind acts, it didn't take away from the fact he was a killer.

Whatever his agenda was, he was sticking to it. He was taking her to the place in which the demon ordered him to take her. She wished she had someone to talk this through with, Demetri, hell she would take Aldrik at this moment. But, it was only her and this man.

They had reached the top of the mountain and as she came to a stop, she gazed out on the most incredible sight. The ocean lay out before them, the city before it, and between them and it, a few more miles of terrain.

They just might make it out of this place in one piece.

Chapter Thirty-Four

The last reading Demetri had gotten on Gina from his scrying was not too far inland, but it was still going to take them some time to make it there. Aldrik had called ahead and had a helicopter waiting for them once they hit the tarmac and came to a stop.

Quickly deplaning with the weapons and supplies they needed, they rushed to the helicopter, Demetri with his hair flapping in the wind, and Aldrik unrecognizable due to the day suit he wore.

Once they were up in the air, Aldrik relayed the GPS coordinates from the map Demetri had been using. They were headed towards Gina or what they hoped would be Gina.

Demetri sat nervously, about to burst out of his skin. If he could have worked some magic and gotten this helicopter to speed up a few hundred miles per hour, he would have. His best friend was out there somewhere, hopefully not wounded and alive. He had never been a nail biter, but he felt so helpless in this moment he couldn't think of anything else to do.

As they passed over the terrain, Demetri's hopes of finding Gina alive began to fade. *If she had been dead though, why had the scrying located her. Why had it led them here to Iceland?*

It seemed like this was taking hours, but in actuality it had only been about fifteen minutes. In the distance, they begin to see signs of disruption in the landscape. A path of trees and dirt had been brutally removed. This was not good news. This was his worst fears coming to life. Their plane had gone down, crash landed in a beautiful, but deadly wilderness. Then the plane came into view, then more pieces scattered out. Wildlife moved about the area, instinctually being inquisitive, but this also meant the predators were probably doing the same.

Please be okay, please be okay. Demetri kept repeating over and over to himself as they came closer to the fuselage, into a clearing of trees. They started at the main fuselage of the plane, but there was still a path of destruction leading away from the fuselage which would have to be the front of the plane.

Before they even touched ground, Demetri had jumped out of the helicopter a few feet before landing, not listening to the pilot as he yelled at him to stay put. He ran quickly to the crash site with Aldrik behind him and began looking for Gina. He shouted her name several times before he had reached the plane, but once inside, he didn't know whether to be happy or fearful he did not find her. The animals he had seen around gave him more cause for worry.

A quick scan of the plane showed blood stains which had probably been sustained from the impact. It didn't go down smoothly for sure. Rummaging around he tried to find anything to show Gina had made it out. Then he heard Aldrik's yell outside of the fuselage.

"There, look," Aldrik pointed to two sets of footprints that led away from the plane. The ground was soaked from the rain, but it still allowed them to see two people had walked away.

Aldrik quickly ran at maximum speed which would be impossible for any human to keep up towards the wreckage site of the pilot's cabin. It only took about a minute before he stood next to Demetri again.

"The pilot is still in the cabin, or what is left of him. He did not survive and it appears he has become food for quite a few scavengers."

"Chances are it was only Gina and her kidnapper who were in the other part. If I'm right in my assumptions, then it would mean Gina walked away from this wreckage site." Demetri beamed with hope.

"I think you are safe in this assumption," Aldrik fed into his hope.

Please hold on Gina. Fight. Be the fighter I know you are. I will find you.

"We mustn't waste any time, Aldrik. We have to get moving now," Demetri pleaded, almost begged of him.

"I think the safest bet for us right now is for me to go on land, tracking their path, and you riding along with the pilot above," Aldrik offered, knowing Demetri was not going to like his plan.

"Who knows how long this will take and how far they have gotten. What if we don't have enough gas to just hover ahead, hoping you will find them before we run out and hoping we will even have a place to land when you do find them?"

Aldrik saw the desperation in his eyes and he felt for him, but he also knew this was the fastest, most efficient way for them to track her. Demetri simply could not keep up at his pace and he would force Aldrik to slow down and keep at his. Bad plan for helping Gina.

"Listen, Demetri, you know I love you. I would do anything on this earth to not see you hurt, so in this thought, I would not allow anything to happen to Gina if I can stop it. I can cover more ground without you. I know

174

you want to go, I know you want to be there, but it is a fact, I am faster than you. I would have to slow down just to make sure you were keeping up and you were not being followed or hurt by anything. So please, let me do this. Let me track them the best way I know how."

Demetri knew Aldrik was right. *He can move faster without me so I will have to put my pride aside and put Gina's safety first.*

Demetri nodded to Aldrik, who had already configured his helmet radio to the one with the pilot in the helicopter. Aldrik wasted no time and took off in the direction of the footprints. Demetri also made sure they were both hooked up with a tracking beacon in case they were separated, and as soon as he jumped back into the helicopter, he had the monitor out and the beacon activated. He heaved a heavy sigh of relief when the screen went active and Aldrik's beacon showed him moving at a high speed across the terrain.

It only took the helicopter a few minutes to be up and flying in the direction Aldrik had taken. Demetri knew if anyone could find her out here, it would be Aldrik. *Come on man, prove me right. Find her, please find her.*

The trees became dense and Aldrik was no longer visible by air, but he continued to move as a dot on the digital map. The helicopter traveled at a high speed to keep pace with him. He had always known Aldrik to be fast, but he had no idea just how fast he could move until today. Then it all stopped. The light on the display still lit up, but it had stopped moving.

"What's going on? Why did you stop? Are you okay? Did you find Gina?" The questions seemed to be endless as they kept skipping around in his mind.

"I am not quite sure what I have found. There seems to have been a battle here. There is blood. The ground is askew."

"What do you mean there is blood? Human blood?" Demetri asked, fearing the answer.

"Yes, it is human in nature, but not enough to have caused death. Although, it is quite a blood loss for any human being. But it appears to have been a bear attack. There are numerous bear tracks on the ground, and it appears the bear had been pushed and tossed around. Whoever this man is, he is strong. Are you sure he is human?" he quizzed Demetri, trying to take his focus off of the information he fed to him.

"I am almost certain. I got nothing supernatural from him except his immense strength."

"Well, I have to say, if Gina is out here with this man and he has every intention of keeping her safe, then she is probably okay. A man like this, one who can take on a bear, and live to tell about it, is a man who will do anything to protect Gina."

"You seem to have forgotten he is also the man who kidnaped her. So how is she safe with him?" Demetri asked, put out by his remarks.

"Demetri Marcus, she has already been taken, so all I am saying, is if she has to be out here with anyone, at least it is with someone who has the resources and skills to protect her. A man like this is a dangerous man, but if he wanted Gina dead, we would have already found her body."

Whether he liked this or not, Demetri did not give Aldrik the satisfaction of saying so. He still had plans for this man. The man who dared to take his family, his Gina. This man would die by his hands, one way or another.

Chapter Thirty-Five

The group of people began to form a circle around Alex, Brandy, and Mathias.

What a fucking stupid idea this had been. Why hadn't I listened to my gut? I knew this smelled like a trap.

"Why do you ask yourself these questions my son? You know we are destined for each other. You are a hollow being without my presence inside you. You have lived a solitary life, avoiding commitment, relationships, taking the pleasure as it came. I complete you Alex, not these earthly possessions. You love creating art because you are a piece of art. You make the decision Alex on whether these two live or die. You control this."

"If you mention one more time about laying a finger on her, I'm going to….." Alex's voice got so intense it almost sounded like a growl.

"You will do what?" Bastiquil interrupted. "You have no power over me, but you can't say the same, can you son?"

"I am not your fucking son, you fucking piece of shit," Alex yelled, as he ran at Bastiquil and hit him directly on the nose with his fist. Blood spilled from the broken nose of John, the host body, but no sound, cry, groan, nothing came from him. It was as if it didn't even faze him.

The group of people surrounding them took a step inward and Bastiquil raised his hand, advising them he did not need them.

Alex raised his hand again, hitting Bastiquil in the face. He used his other hand to pound on his chest. "You killed my mother. You tried to kill my best friend." Alex cried at this last statement as Bastiquil just stood, smiling, pleased by the anger and outrage that poured out of him.

"Alex, no," Brandy pleaded, as she placed her hand over her mouth, not knowing what to do for her friend.

"I think we are done here," Bastiquil smiled, as the head of John bent backwards, looking up towards the ceiling, preparing for the demon to emerge from his body to take its rightful place inside the vessel.

Just as Bastiquil was about to emerge, John's body was sent flying backward knocking down five people in the process.

The stunned crowd became enraged but wasn't sure how this had happened. Their anger turned to Brandy as they knew they were not allowed to touch the vessel. They could, however, detain him. Two of the men ran over and grabbed Alex by the arms, but as they did, they were immediately flung backward against the wall.

Brandy and Alex stood there speechless, not knowing what was going on.

Bastiquil rose from the floor without even having to bend his knees or use his arms. It was as if it were right out of an old black and white vampire film. When he had composed himself, he walked forward, only to be stopped mid-step.

"So boy, you think you have what it takes to defeat me," Bastiquil said, laughing.

Alex and Brandy turned and looked at Mathias, who had his arms in the air, and as he did, the people around the room were also frozen in place, unable to move. He began to move his fingers around and they began to dance. Alex didn't seem to be as surprised by this as Brandy was. She stood there, mouth open, speechless.

"My job isn't to defeat you demon, my job is to survive."

"Well, you picked the wrong profession this time," Bastiquil said, breaking free of the hold Mathias had on him. He began to walk forward, edging closer and closer to them, and then ran at Brandy. Just as he got within arm's reach of her, she screamed, ducking a bit, but Mathias flung her up in the air and back behind him where she landed safely on her feet.

"Impressive boy, but do you think you can hold all of us forever? Your powers are no match for mine." Bastiquil reached his hand outward, and as he did, Alex's body began to slide across the floor, slowly at first, then faster toward the demons outstretched hand. "You will not survive today, boy."

Mathias's hand flicked and a group of ten people went flying at Bastiquil, who held his other hand upward to stop them midair. He was using up an enormous amount of the host body's life source to be able to display such power, but he will not allow this scrawny boy to show him up. "See, even I know your tricks."

"You don't know all of them old man," Mathias said, as he sent one of the men frozen to his back, left side, flying across the floor at Bastiquil's feet. As he made impact, Bastiquil fell to the floor. The group of ten in the air fell to the ground. Alex also stumbled, but caught himself.

The demon, finding his footing, rose up, screaming at the top of his lungs. "Enough!"

"Ok guys, I think it is our exit time," Mathias said to the two, who did not need any more prompting.

Brandy and Alex ran to the door behind Mathias and as they did Bastiquil raised his hand in a gesture to stop them, but Mathias had already anticipated such a maneuver from the demon and hit him with everything he had, which sent the body flying backwards, crashing through the window at the front of the store and into the parking lot.

Mathias began to turn around and around, and as he did so, the group of people in the store began to move around too. He did this a few times before sending them flying toward the enraged Bastiquil.

Mathias turned and followed the other two out the back door as they ran down the alleyway. He had definitely used a ton of strength to take the demon on and, to his credit, he had done well. This was why Aldrik had chosen him. If he had to stay much longer and battle the demon, he knew he would not survive. To this, the demon was correct.

They ran towards Gina's shop, which was not too far away, and left the car behind they had driven to the studio.

Bastiquil still fuming, yelled out a command. "Night Fury, take flight and bring me the vessel."

With this, the girl flapped her wings until she was airborne, and flew off in the direction of the fleeing three.

Chapter Thirty-Six

Once Victor and Gina reached the city limits of Selfoss, he kept a close eye on her to ensure she stayed next to him and didn't cry out for help. They had a long talk on the walk to town, rather Victor talked while Gina listened, about how if she tried anything at all, he would pick random people next to them and start killing. He didn't care what age they were, he would just kill and their deaths would be on her hands. "You may as well be the one slitting their throats."

He is right in some aspect, but totally bat shit crazy in another. Gina knew what he was capable of and didn't want to put anyone else in harm's way, even if it meant her own death. She just could not handle any more killing.

This was not to say, if the opportunity presents itself, she will do what she can to take him out. *He is disposable, just like other's are to him. For everything this man has done, he deserves to die.* This thinking went against everything she believed in, but she felt no guilt about it whatsoever.

Victor busied himself on the public phone in a local park, while Gina sat on the ground in front of him. He had called someone and was speaking in what sounded like German, but she could not be certain.

From what Gina had gathered thus far, they were in a little town called Selfoss, in southern Iceland on the Ölfusá River, which led out to the sea.

Victor was yelling on the phone, his temper flared, but he seemed to have gotten what he wanted because he threw his hands in the air yelling, "Finally." Hanging up the phone, he looked down at Gina and smiled.

"Why are you smiling at me?"

"Because, we both get our wish," he said quite pompously.

"You are letting me go," Gina tested, knowing the answer.

"Even better, we are finally getting out of here. Get up, we will get you some food and be on our way to the docks," Victor said, grabbing her hand and helping her up.

As they made their way down the street, they passed a pub where a lively crowd of people inside were having an excellent time. They sang, drank beer, and were dining on langoustine, Icelandic version of lobster. Victor led Gina into the pub, pausing briefly to take in the crowd, and then finding a small corner table, they sat down. Victor went as far as to put his arm around Gina's shoulders pulling her in as if to kiss her, but instead he whispered softly into her ear. "You make one wrong move, and I will wipe out this entire bar. Now put your hand on my knee, laugh softly as if I had just told you something funny, then we will order our drink and food and be on our way."

Gina did as told, grabbing his knee, laughing softly, but could not miss out on the opportunity to let him know she is not some helpless creature. Instead, while grabbing his knee she sent a slight, yet shocking, energy into his leg, making him wince, but he never lost the smile on his face.

He ordered water and beer to go along with the langoustines, which was the house special for the day, but Gina pushed the beer aside wanting to keep her wits about her. He just grinned at her, pulling her beer next to his. Their food came with a basket of various forms of Icelandic breads such as Thunder bread, flatbread, black bread and baking powder bread, all of which hit the spot. They were famished from their adventure through the wilderness as Gina sit there, in a room of people, the wave of events over the past few days began to sink in. She remembered the ritual sacrifice in Tulsa, the kidnapping and evil grin of the demon who possessed poor Alex's body, the plane crash, the bear, the and dreadful killing of the man in the cabin. Then there was Thadius. She could never forget Thadius.

For Victor his experience was a different one, he sit there, plotting, calculating, making sure he was going to be one step ahead of the people he called for favors. Securing their passage out of this country wasn't easy, but he had done it. It would not be the most favorable form of travel, but it put them in the direction they needed to be headed. There was no trusting the men in which he had contacted, but they fit the bill for now. Bastiquil had specifically asked him to keep the Balashon in the dark, to not let them know he had the girl. He wasn't sure of his reasons, but it wasn't for him to question his master. He did as he was told.

"Are you going to tell me anything about your phone conversation," Gina blurted out, bringing Victor back from his thoughts.

"No," he told her bluntly.

"I am assuming you were arranging for our travel."

"Once again, you worry about things you have no control over," he said, turning to look at her as he shoved another piece of bread into his mouth.

"If I cannot control it, why not just tell me? Why keep it from me? Unless you think there is a chance I will break free from you," Gina probed, trying to get him to give her some clue as their destination. Hell, she would even take a clue at this point of their mode of transportation, although he had mentioned heading to the docks earlier.

"There are always chances for everything, I don't believe in dealing in those. I believe in dealing with certainties. But, if I were a man of chance, I do not believe we will be separated anytime soon. Eat up, time is running short," Victor told her with a stoic face.

He threw some money on the table for the tab and they were quickly on their way. She assumed he was upset with her, but that wasn't anything new. This had not been the most typical of kidnappings, especially by standard thought, or even Hollywood movie standards. She had not been blindfolded. No bag had been put over her head. Of course she was unconscious for the first part, so maybe she was assuming on this aspect, but it just felt different. She didn't feel like a person who was going to be put up for ransom. She felt like they had no intention of ever letting her leave, which did not make her feel any better about the situation.

If they had no intention of letting her go, then it meant their plan was long term, one which most likely included her death. But they also needed her for something or else she would already be dead, but for what she didn't know yet. She needed to keep asking, keep fishing for information from Victor, sooner or later he would give her something to help her figure this out.

Best case scenario, Demetri was looking for her. Worst case scenario, Demetri didn't make it out alive after his battle with the demon. Gina refused to believe the latter of the two, but she just had to keep faith and keep hoping.

Gina looked up to see they were walking down to the river's edge. There was a dock with many various shapes and sizes of boats. When they reached the dock, Victor held tightly to her arm, waiting, watching for someone or something.

A man, short, but stout looking in stature, approached them. He had on a hat, scruffy bearded face, and a mean looking scar across his left eye, and extremely calloused looking hands. He definitely looked like a man who had known hardship and tough work all his life. He was a scary looking man.

The man gave Gina a once over, smiling big to reveal missing and rotted teeth. He turned to Victor, pointing over to an area of boats as he spoke in the German tongue. *These fuckers are not going to give me anything to go on are they?*

Victor grabbed a wad of money out of his pocket and peeled off a few hundred American dollars, and gave it to the man. He looked down at it, spit on the ground, muttering "fucking American scum."

Gina knew the man was not going to be her knight in shining armor. He obviously had distaste for Americans and also gave her a sense he was not on the up and up. How could he be, working with Victor?

The man stepped aside or was forced aside as Victor made his way past him with Gina in tow. They walked down the pier in the direction in which the man had been pointing and came to a rather large boat, at least in comparison to the others docked here. As they climbed the ramp onto the boat, the men on board must have known about their arrangement with the man on the docks. They pointed in a direction and Victor led her along. Coming to a doorway, they passed through and headed down a flight of stairs.

Victor scanned the area which was obviously a supply or storage room. He found them a spot on the floor and led Gina over. Tossing their bag down on the floor, he looked at the floor and back up at Gina.

"Make yourself comfortable. This is going to be a long ride."

Chapter Thirty-Seven

The pilot found a small clearing in the trees to land. Demetri and Aldrik combed the remains of the burnt home in search of any clue leading them to Gina. Not much remained of the log cabin, which had been set ablaze. All that was left was rubble, and a body. There wasn't much of the body, other than torched skin and bones. But upon seeing it, Demetri immediately knew it wasn't Gina nor the man who took her. This person had been much shorter.

Some areas of the cabin were still quite hot, still smoldering from the fire.

Aldrik had been walking the edges of the cabin, out toward the entrance into the woods and believed he found their path once again. He had turned to Demetri to let him know he would continue on the path in search of them, but as he turned, he stopped in his tracks.

He found Demetri sitting on the ground behind him, in a traditional yoga position called lotus. His eyes were closed. "What are you doing? We have to get going."

"There is a great power here."

"Yes, I know, it is you, my love. We need to continue on before we lose them. He is obviously leading her to the shoreline."

"No, the power I am sensing is not my own. You go ahead, I will be along shortly. I just want a minute to try and connect with it," he said.

"Are you sure this is such a great idea? The last time you connected with great power, you transferred it into your own body, and I thought I was going to lose you," Aldrik pleaded, urging him to think twice about this.

"I am good. Keep going. I have my reasons for wanting to do this." His tone told Aldrik he would not change his mind, so he turned and was gone. He figured it best to save Gina if he could because he knew Demetri could take care of himself.

I can sense you all around me. Come out. Come into the light and let me talk with you.

He heard the gasps and awe. He also heard what he thought were giggles. They were all abuzz about how he knew they were there. They had been so careful.

I mean you no harm, great elven people of Iceland. I heard one of your kind mention my friends name when we were looking through the remains of the cabin. Please come forward and tell me what you know? I will not hurt you. Demetri communicated to them without speaking. All communication thus far had been with his mind.

"It is you great wizard who should be afraid. We do not fear you."

"I mean you no disrespect kind sir. I, honestly, want to speak with you," Demetri humbled himself, and his tone.

"My name is Thadius. I am the one whom you are looking for," the elf said, walking towards Demetri. "I am the one who spoke your friend's name."

"Hello Thadius, I am Demetri. What can you tell me about Gina? Is she okay?" Demetri refrained from sounding desperate because the last thing he wanted was to make them not want to speak with him.

"Your friend is alive, but she is not in the hands of a noble man. He has his own agenda or rather is working on behalf of someone else's agenda. But your friend is alive for the time being and was such a pleasure to talk to," Thadius boasted.

"So you and Gina were able to talk? Did she tell you what the man had planned? If I may, you are a great and powerful people, why did you not help her," Demetri inquired, curious to his answer.

"She told me no plans, as she did not know what the man had in store for her, but she is a feisty one with such a rich history. What a history she has. I loved hearing her talk about her past. But as for helping her, as I explained to her, we do not interfere with human affairs unless we have to. This rule has helped us survive too many millennia to count."

Demetri had to smile to himself. *Yes, she is feisty and, yes, she is still fighting because she had asked the one named Thadius to help her. This is all good news.* The fact she had told him her history did not surprise him in the least, she loved to talk and tell stories of the past.

"We did give him a little sendoff though, as he stepped too closely into our world as they were leaving. It didn't stop him, but it did get his attention," Thadius laughed as he remembered this.

"Well, I thank you for allowing me to speak with you and for telling me what you know about Gina. She is precious to me and I must be on my way in search of her." Demetri smiled at those who dared show themselves.

"Why do you work with the vampire? They are vile and evil creatures," Thadius asked of Demetri.

"Not all creatures of evil-origin remain evil. Aldrik is a good man. He is a loving man," he told the curious elf.

"You love this creature? Very curious," Thadius posed.

"I must be on my way. My friend Gina is going to need my help," he said loudly, so all of them who were listening could hear him. He would love to have stayed longer, but time didn't permit it.

"No, you must stay and tell us about your life, your history. We sense there is much you have to tell. You are full of magic and mystery at such a young age. We must hear your story," Thadius proposed.

He started to get the impression the elf was stalling.

"Another time, my friend. I will make every attempt to come back here and visit you again," he stated, starting to rise up from his sitting position so he could head out after Aldrik.

"We insist you stay young one and tell us your story," Thadius said, his voice firm, as Demetri found himself being pushed downward, back onto the ground. Then Thadius began to laugh as if it were the most natural thing in the world.

I'm not looking for a fight, but I have to be on my way. I would never want to harm another non-threatening magical creature, but I must insist you stop whatever it is you are attempting to do. Please! Demetri looked at the elf with longing, pleading eyes, not wanting to hurt them. But, he would not be held here against his will.

"There will be no fight, only story time," Thadius stated, skipping around in front of Demetri.

Demetri found himself with a growing anger inside. How dare they stop him from rushing to Gina's side? *So much for not interfering in human affairs. If they were able to hold him here, why had they not done the same for Gina?* As he sat there, stewing on all this, he noticed more and more elves coming out, making themselves visible, and skipping around with Thadius as he did his dance. He also felt more and more invisible energy, latching onto to him, holding him firmly to the ground.

As this began to have a claustrophobic feel to it, he started to get impatient and angrier.

The elves continued their dance.

"Okay, enough," Demetri yelled, in a loud, authoritative tone as he stood, breaking free from the elfin energy which held him down. As he did this, the elves went flying backward and disappeared from sight.

"I don't need to see you to hurt you," Demetri warned them. "Look inside me, feel the magic coursing through my veins. Try to stop me again and you will feel its full wrath."

Demetri walked towards the helicopter. As he did, he could hear whispers and whimpering behind him. They were all saying, "He is back. Oh no, he is back."

Demetri paid no attention to them as they had just broken any trust he had in them. Climbing into the helicopter, Demetri signaled the pilot that he was ready for lift off.

As they climbed higher into the air and headed off towards the beacon indicating Aldrik's whereabouts on the map, he allowed himself to feel it all, to feel what the elves had done to him, remember what they had said. *He is back.*

Chapter Thirty-Eight

They were all out of breath when they reached the bookstore. *What in the hell just happened?* Alex's mind went abuzz with thoughts. *Had Demetri not just vanquished the demon? How can this be?* He walked around in circles, trying to wrap his brain around how the demon was still here.

They all knew the Balashon were probably still around and pissed off, but Bastiquil, here again?

"Alex, talk to me. Tell me what's going on in your head," Brandy pleaded with him.

"Hey folks, shouldn't we be securing this place. I don't think the demon is going to let this slide. He seemed pretty hell bent on taking you as his door prize," Mathias stated, looking at Alex.

Brandy, annoyed at being interrupted, looked at Mathias with a glare that made him uncomfortable. "Listen, Demetri was kind enough to cast a spell on this place before he left. You see those symbols all over the walls? They are not an art exhibit. They are to keep demons out, so we should be fine from the demon. I just don't know about his lackeys. While I am at it, you could have shared what your power was. It would have been nice to know."

"Hey, I am here to protect you, not make social time with you."

"Well then, protect. Keep those sons-of-bitches out of here," Brandy said, then turned her attention back to Alex.

"He is using John's body as a vessel," Alex said loudly as he paced the room. Then he stopped as if something had hit him in the stomach, tears filled his eyes.

"Alex, talk to me, please," Brandy pleaded with him, as she grabbed him by the shoulders and forced him to look into her face.

"He killed Jerry, right there, in front of our eyes. Slit his throat, blood everywhere. And Lincoln, where is Linc?" Alex fell to his knees, his world imploding around him again. "Everyone is dying because of me. My mother, those poor people in the park, the guy at the river, Jerry, and he almost got you," he said, looking at Brandy who had already joined him on the floor.

Reaching over and wrapping her arms around his neck, she hugged him, letting his tears flow, letting his hurt and hate roll down his face. She held him until she felt the tension in his shoulders finally let go, and she could feel his body begin to relax.

"We will figure all this out, Alex, you know this, right," Brandy said, half believing what she was saying and half knowing it was utter and complete bullshit.

Leaning back from her arms, he looked at her, really looked in her eyes, scanning her face. "No, we won't, you know this and I know this. He will win, he will take me. He is right, ever since he left my body, I have felt hollow. I have felt like something is missing. I have felt something needs to be filled, replaced."

"Don't you do this? Don't you let him win by words alone? You are one of the bravest, most caring people I know Alex. How can you be what he claims you to be? How can you be just an empty, hollow shell of a man?" Tears rolled down Brandy's face as she said this to her apparently defeated best friend.

"I only see two ways out of this where innocent people, and people I love, don't have to die because of me."

"Alex, you are scaring me," Brandy said, as she waited in anticipation and dread of what he would say next.

"I either turn myself over to him so he doesn't hurt anyone else….or I kill myself so he doesn't have any option, other than to return to hell." Alex had a solemn, but serious face.

Mathias stopped pacing and turned to look at him with a shocked look.

Brandy's tears started to flow heavier, not able to handle such thoughts from her friend, nor defeat.

"You are giving up way too soon in this game, man. If you think I am going to let you do this on my watch, well, you have another thing coming. We will fight until we have no fight left and hope Aldrik and Demetri are back in time to help us," Mathias determinedly said to both of them.

"You can't stop this. You can't stop something destined to happen. If he wants me, he will take me. If I decide to end my life, you can't stop me," Alex eyed him, then turned his gaze to Brandy.

"You wanna bet? You have yet to see what I can do, so don't try me, Alex," Mathias buffed up his words, meaning every one of them.

"Why? Why would you allow more innocent people to die? How can you live with their deaths on your conscience? Those people in my studio, those are innocent people he has taken over. People whose lives are already destroyed because of me, because I won't give him what he wants," Alex argued.

"Those people are already dead. We can't help them, but we can change what happens next. We can stop him from getting you. How many people do you think will die when he gets inside of you? How much stronger will he be?" Mathias tried to refute his arguments, not seeing Brandy shaking her head at him to stop, to not go there.

But he had went there. He had said what he did and it was true. Bastiquil at full strength would tear this city apart, just for the hell of it. What he was capable of in just a regular human body was impressive. In a body made especially for him, he would be an unstoppable killing machine.

"You've proven my point better than I could, Mathias, and I know you don't mean to. The only way to save everyone is to end my life. He cannot take root inside me if there is no me left. He would have no choice than to return to where he came from." Alex looked calm, at peace. "I have made my decision."

"You have made nothing of the sorts. You will not do this to yourself, to me. You will be the Alex I know is in there, the fighter, the adventurous spirit. I won't let you do this, I won't," Brandy said, standing up, her resolve growing.

"How am I supposed to fight something supernatural, something demonic when I have no powers of my own? This fucking demon made me. He owns me." He slammed his fist down on the floor in frustration.

"But you do have powers. That is exactly what Demetri and Aldrik said before they left. They told you to learn to use them," Brandy said, feeling some hope.

"How do you learn to use a power when you don't even know what it is? It's not like I can flip a switch and BAM, instant powers," Alex's sarcasm and frustration were shining through.

The room fell silent as all were so lost in their own thoughts, they did not notice Night Fury stalking outside the windows, lurking, listening, and waiting for them.

The silence broke, when Mathias jumped into the air, clapping his hands together. "Actually you can just flip a switch. I did. Of course, it was tied to my emotions, my fight or flight response, but when it kicked in, it really kicked in. I kicked ass and took names."

"I have been in those fight or flight response modes. Actually, just a few minutes ago and nothing happened. I was putty in his demonic hands," Alex stated, feeling this entire

194

conversation was a complete waste of time. But what else did they have but time?

Brandy sat listening to them and decided to take action.

"We have an entire magical library here at our disposal. Let's stop talking defeat and get on the offensive. Let's make this work for us. We are safe here, for the time being, at least from the demon. I don't know about his subjects. We will just have to take it as it comes. But I can try and get in touch with Demetri and let him know Bastiquil is back. He would want to know this, right?" Brandy felt hope once again spring alive within her. This felt right, this felt like they were doing something proactive.

Night Fury took this all in. *The master will want to know this.* But going back to him without the vessel sounded dangerous. As she watched the girl walking over to the computer, pull up email and start typing, Night Fury assumed this email would be going to the male witch. *The master would not like this at all.*

Then Night Fury knew exactly what needed to be done. Smiling brightly, she spread her wings out to full span and began to flap them. Rising into the air, she lifted herself up and over to the back side of the building and found what she needed. Reaching out, she pulled with all her might, reaching inward and tapping into the demonic blood pumping within her veins until she heard the snap of the electrical wires which fed into the store. Satisfied with her success, she quickly flew back to her new master for whatever punishment he deemed fit.

Chapter Thirty-Nine

The boat had been out to sea for a couple of hours now. Gina felt the waves of the Atlantic Ocean and Icelandic sea hitting up against the ship. She wasn't feeling her best. Her stomach was queasy, but she hadn't been on a boat like this before and she wasn't taking well to the huge waves.

She looked over at Victor, who sat beside her, his face unmoving, his body rocking with the movement of the boat. *He is such an arrogant, unfeeling asshole. He just tramples through life, extinguishing another's life if they get in his way. Karma is a bitch, asshole, and you have a huge karma tsunami coming your way.*

Just as she was thinking her hateful thoughts about this man, a huge wave knocked the boat, sending her falling into Victor. Her head bounced off Victor and slammed against the metal of the boat, hitting extremely hard, knocking her into a daze. "What the hell..." Between being nauseous and hitting her head, Gina went out like a light being turned off.

Victor took her into his arms, making sure she was still breathing and her pulse rate steady, then held her tightly as the waves pummeled the sides of the boat, sending water over the decks and running down the stairs to the storage area they were sitting in. "This is going to be one hell of a ride witch. Best that you are sleeping while you can."

Gina found herself dreaming of times long ago, of ancient architecture, and lost languages. She dreamed of powerful witches, casting spells against the people of the land. As she walked along she couldn't help but think, *this is why witches have always had a bad connotation associated with them. Many have misused their gifts, going against nature, making it a dark and extremely dangerous power.*

But some have held to the tried and true method of using power for the good it was intended. But these ancient times have shown the true, dark nature of the witches here. Both male and female seemed to rule the land along with some much darker force. The people all ran scared and screaming, trying to find refuge and safe passage from this evil, infested land.

As she watched the scenes unfold, she saw what appeared to be a leader, decked out in full royal regalia, walking along, smiling, and laughing at the chaos which ensued in the city streets. He sauntered, taking it all in, not wanting to miss a second of the mass hysteria in which he had a heavy hand in creating.

But it didn't take long to realize she has seen this man before. Yes, he was the man she saw in Demetri's past life meditation. He was the man, the demon, in which she saw Zamaranum doing battle with before she pulled Demetri out of his meditative trance.

What am I doing here? Why? How am I seeing this? This has to be some residual leftover memories from the experience with Demetri. It doesn't feel like his memories though. How strange.

Then Gina recognized another person, a man, walking alongside the demon. It was Demetri, or rather, Zamaranum, speaking to him in a way to suggest they liked each other, trusted each other, and were actually friends. Gina also knew that in the end it was Zamaranum who stood up to Bastiquil and vanquished him.

Why was Zamaranum laughing at the turmoil and anguish the people were being put through? Wait, hold on and remember, this isn't Demetri. It may be his past life, his soul, but it isn't what makes up the Demetri she loves and knows in this life. But she couldn't shake the thought, *why am I seeing this?*

As they continued their walk, a young boy, distraught, afflicted with disease and malnourishment, threw himself at Zamaranum's feet.

"Please help me, please. I need your help sire. Please."

Gina's heart went out to the boy, who just wanted to feel better, wanted food and nourishment. Her heart broke with what she witnessed next.

Zamaranum stopped where he stood, looked down at the boy with disgust on his face. Looking up and over to Bastiquil, he quickly kicked the boy sending him flying into a nearby clay vase containing water, which burst upon the boy's impact as he cried out in pain, water spilling all around him onto the dry desert sand.

Bastiquil laughed and beamed with pride at this display of power and control and they continued on their walk.

Gina, even in dream state, fumed at this. She grew angry and longed to help the boy. She was angry at Zamaranum and Bastiquil. The fact they used such power on a human being, let alone a small child, disgusted and infuriated her.

As anger built inside of her, she knew it futile to scream at them as this was just a dream from a memory she had picked up helping navigate and retract Demetri from his past life meditation. But seeing them laughing at the boy, at his pain, at all the pain and destruction they have wrought in this time, she could stand it no longer.

Gina screamed at the top of her lungs, letting hatred spill out. It seemed to flood the entire dream world as everyone stopped and looked around for the source. To the people, it appeared to be coming from the heavens, but Bastiquil and Zamaranum knew they were being spied upon.

She didn't know what to do, she needed to wake up but felt trapped in this state, in this dream. *Oh shit*, she thought as Bastiquil looked in her direction.

Feeling like she was drawing back, trying to hide, in what, she didn't know. She was a spectator in this dream, but she desperately wanted to avoid the demon locating her. But it was to no avail.

Bastiquil, still looking in her direction, flew upwards at her, so fast it scared her even more than she was previously. "Spying on me witch?"

Gina could feel his hot breath on her face, his spit hitting her. Her dream quickly turned into a nightmare.

"Get away from me," she screamed, as she turned from him.

Reaching up and grabbing her cheeks between his fingers and thumb, he forced her head to turn until she looked directly into his eyes.

"Aren't you a powerful little witch, spying on me from the future? But do you really know who is spying on whom? I believe I have the upper hand on this one witch, you just don't know it yet. You give yourself away so easily, yet you know nothing. You will soon learn what true power is, you will know the taste of my blood," Bastiquil said, letting the last word roll off his tongue in a way which caused chills to run up and down her spine.

"You don't scare me, Bastiquil. Yes, I know your name. We have already defeated you once in this time. Maybe you don't have the upper hand at all," Gina said, with much disdain in her voice. "You make me sick."

"Oh, you will be sick alright, Gina. And yes, I know your name as well. As for defeating me...do you really think we would be having this conversation if you had?"

With this Bastiquil opened his mouth, bones cracking as he unhinged his jaw, his tongue forked on the end and licked her cheek, crossing her lips.

Disgusted, Gina began to choke while she struggled to free herself. His grip became tighter until she felt so panicked she screamed out. Her hands came up by his face as she summoned all known strength within and she hit his head with a burst of light so bright it lit up the evening sky, scaring all who saw it, even Zamaranum. Bastiquil had not expected such a display of power from Gina, who catapulted him at least three feet into the desert ground.

Victor still had a tight hold on Gina as she woke herself up screaming out. It wasn't surprising considering everything she had been through. He tried to calm her by reassuring her she was safe, even though cold water ran up and down the length of the cargo room they were in with each passing wave.

She struggled to free herself, still groggy from banging her head and still extremely aware of the dream. She struggled; Victor tried to calm her, easing his voice and words in such a manner to not agitate her more.

Gina stopped struggling, out of frustration, and began to cry. She sobbed for almost ten minutes until she was able to speak rationally.

"What has you so upset? You appeared to have been having a nightmare," Victor asked.

"He was after me," Gina whimpered, still in shock from the entire experience. "He talked to me, he touched me, and he even licked me," she shivered.

"Who did this?" Victor queried her, genuinely interested.

"Bastiquil, he tried to get to me in my dreams," Gina cried out.

Victor could not hide his excitement. He looked down at her, as she was still lying with her head against his chest. "The master contacted you? This is wonderful news. This means he is still with us, and things are going according to plan."

He beamed with joy as Gina's thoughts went back to what he had said to her. *But do you really know who is spying on whom...You will soon learn what true power is, you will know the taste of my blood.*

Chapter Forty

Darkness settled into the little coastal town of Selfoss. They had not been there long, but upon their arrival they began to search like crazy to find Gina or any sign of her. Having a fifteen-hundred-year-old vampire with extraordinarily heightened senses worked in their favor.

Aldrik was able to track them all the way to this town, but things became a bit more chaotic when you factor in other people, their scents, voices, and blood pumping through their bodies. In essence, Gina's scent began to fade and now they were stuck roaming streets, checking stores, pubs, restaurants, and any houses they could see into.

Demetri had his own powers at work and, even though it was a small town, he didn't have the speed of a vampire. He grew tired, weary, and hopeless as the search continued. No one's thoughts he scanned mentioned a strange couple, tourist couple, or anything. *This is like a fucking needle in a haystack,* he angrily thought.

Then he heard Aldrik's voice come over the head gear they were wearing for communication. "I think I have picked up her scent again. Start heading down to the pier next to the river."

Demetri took off running like a man on a mission, probably to some, more like a mad man. But this was his best friend since grade school they are trying to find. He really didn't care what other people thought about him at this moment.

Running through the streets, smelling the scent of the water from the river which fed into the ocean, he started to find hope again. *Could she be down there? Is she waiting for transport? What if they had already left and are in the Atlantic somewhere out of his reach?*

The wind blew through his hair, cooling the sweat flowing from his head down his body. His clothes were soaked. The sound of music coming from the local pub would have typically brought a smile to his face, but, tonight, the sound was just noise.

Some powerful witch I am. I can't even save my best friend. The life and magical knowledge and wisdom of more than forty lifetimes are stowed inside my brain and I can't even figure out how to unlock it. I know I can save her. I know I can. I just have to figure out how to tap into this power. These thoughts and many more were racing around inside his brain, so much so, he didn't even see the hole in the road until his foot landed inside it sending him tumbling and rolling across the pavement.

He screamed out in pain, scrapes with blood forming on his arms, but he got up and ran through the pain. He could see the lights of the piers which ran along the river just ahead. *Almost there, keep running, Demetri.*

About a hundred yards away, he saw the distinct outline of a man in which he knew to be Aldrik standing beneath a street light, just before the entrance to a pier. As he finally caught up to him, his breathing labored, his body drenched, and his arms covered with scrapes and bruises from his fall, he came to a stop. He stood there, bending over, hands on his knees trying to catch his breath.

"You are bleeding," Aldrik stated, smelling it in the air before he even looked down at his arms.

"I'm fine. Just tell me you have something on Gina," he said, the labored breathing making his words sound harsher than intended.

"Her scent definitely ends here, but the piers are shut down aside from some people who live on the boats and a few drunks passed out, lining the docks."

Demetri not hiding his frustration at this, moved forward into the entrance to the pier. "Well, I guess we are going to have to wake them up and talk to them." He broadened his shoulders, as he marched onward looking for the first person he would interrogate.

Aldrik proceeded to follow him, not sure of his intentions but having his back none-the-less.

Demetri boarded the first boat he came to in which he sensed a person on board. It wasn't a large ship, but rather a small- to medium-sized sailboat with a sleeper inside the cabin. Not bothering to knock on the door, he reached to open it, but found it locked. Aldrik began to move forward to open it for him, but before he could Demetri had just stared at the door and it flew open.

The man occupying the sleeper jumped up, scared, and hitting his head on the top side of the boat which covered his bed. Grabbing his head where the pain was inflicted, he turned, wide-eyed and surprised to find these two men standing before him. "What do you want?" the man yelled, reaching for a gun housed in one of the pockets along the wall of the bunk.

"This man knows nothing of use," Demetri stated, as he turned and walked up and out of the cabin.

With the gun in hand, the man brought it around to find Aldrik, standing before him, eyes glowing blue in the dark, teeth exposed, and razor sharp as he hissed at the man saying only one word. "Don't!"

The man, frozen with fear, laid the gun down on the covers, as Aldrik quickly fled the cabin and rejoined Demetri. Demetri had already picked the next boat to board, heading towards it with a vengeance. Just as they were nearing it, he stopped, almost as if he had hit a brick wall. He turned around, and, he found what he was looking for. He took off running towards the man passed out against the electrical pole at the end of the pier. Aldrik trailed behind him.

Demetri lifted the man with a scotch-induced stupor, onto wobbly feet.

"Wake up you piece of filth. Tell me what you know about the pretty redhead you were dreaming about?" Demetri shouted.

The short man had a beard and a hat on. He did not know what was happening to him or why, as Demetri pulled him in closer, bringing his face into the light. It was then the two of them noticed the huge scar which covered his left eye. The man turned his head bending over slightly as he threw up on the wooden deck beneath their feet.

"Tell me what you know about the woman you were just dreaming about, the red head with the mysterious man? I will not ask you again," Demetri said, as he pulled the man upright when he had finished vomiting his scotch dinner.

"Was will das amerikanische Schwein mit mir," the drunken man said, spitting his words at them with disgust.

"What the hell did this piece of shit say to me," Demetri asked of Aldrik.

"He wants to know what the American pig wants with him," Aldrik said, knowing the man would regret saying it, not really knowing the extent of what he has found himself involved in.

"Pig, huh, pig? You tell this bastard if he doesn't tell me what I want to know in the next minute, he will find himself fish food in this beautiful harbor," Demetri said, as he shoved the man up against the electrical pole.

"Beginnen Sie besser, sprechen über die roten Kopf. Er wird nicht zögern, Sie zu töten," Aldrik said to the man, not sure if it registered with him at first, but hearing the word kill seemed to spark a bit of recognition in his face. "Englisch sprechen. Ich weiß, dass du dich versiehst."

"I don't know about any red head," the man said stoically, preparing himself for a beating.

"You know, you piece of shit. Your mind gives you away. You arranged this for them. You acquired the boat for them," Demetri said to the drunken man, who seemed surprised he knew this. "What I don't know, is where you sent them. Start talking."

"I know nothing," the man stammered, right as Demetri brought his fist down on the man's jaw.

Dropping to his knees, he grunted as he placed his hand over his aching jaw. Shocked and unsure of how these men knew what they knew, he tried to think of a way out of this.

"You cannot get out of this. You will die in this situation if you do not start telling me what I need to know, NOW," Demetri screamed at the man, who hunkered down closer to the wood deck.

"I don't know where they went. I don't know." The man kept saying over and over.

Demetri at his wits end with this man, turned and took a few steps away from him before turning back around with the most ominous and dark look Aldrik had ever seen on his face before. It made Aldrik nervous as to what was about to happen.

Demetri focused in on the man still crouched on the deck and began to chant an ancient language in which Aldrik had not heard in a long time. Actually, it had just been spoken in his presence recently when Demetri and Bastiquil had done battle at The Other Side. Raising his hands out in front of his hips as he chanted, the man slowly began to rise in the air, eyes big and bulging.

"What are you doing? What's happening to me?" He began to scream and struggle, but to no avail, as his struggling was against air, not man.

206

Demetri continued his chanting, lifting his hands until the man levitated five feet off the deck. He combed through the man's thoughts and memories. His attention lay more on the man's thoughts than on the man himself. As he continued with his intense invasion, he paid no attention to the damage he inflicted. He really didn't care.

"Demetri, you need to stop this. You have stopped his heart. If you kill him, you will never find out what you need from him," Aldrik pleaded, not sure he was even being heard. Walking over to Demetri and grabbing him by the arm, he tried again to reach him. "Demetri, stop this."

Demetri blinked and looked over at Aldrik, as the man fell hard against the wood.

"Are you good," he asked Demetri, sincerely worried for him. Demetri just nodded his head.

Walking over to the man, Aldrik laid him on his back and kneeling beside him, he slammed his fist down against the man's chest right above his heart. A second later, he heard the heart start pumping again, although the man still lay unconscious.

Rising up, Aldrik turned to Demetri. "What did you find out?"

Demetri stood there, looking down at the man. He truly did not care if he lived or died because, in his eyes, the man was scum. But he refocused himself and looked over at Aldrik. "The man didn't know anything other than what he told us. But what the man didn't realize is he overheard something, something which didn't stick into his recall memory. They are headed for northern Scotland and they have a huge head start, more than ten hours lead time. They could be there already for all we know."

"This still gives us something to work with, so don't fall into despair yet my love. We will find her." He tried to comfort him as he took him into his arms and hugged him tightly. "We need to get to the helicopter and head back to the jet. We don't have any time to waste."

Agreeing with him, Demetri turned away from the man. Grabbing Demetri by the waist, Aldrik darted off at high speed taking them quickly in the direction of the helicopter. He also sent word to the helicopter to get refueled and to send word to the pilot to get the jet a flight plan for northern Scotland. They didn't know where they were headed, but they had come too far and been through too much to give up on Gina now. Besides, Demetri would rather die than give up on her.

Chapter Forty-One

Mathias came walking towards them with a lit candle in his hand. Ever since the power went out, they had been using candles and kerosene lanterns in order to conserve their flashlights in case they had to make a run for it. This was complete insanity. *We are sitting ducks, waiting for the fox to come sneaking up to devour us.*

They knew taking on Bastiquil even in human form was a risk but, for the moment, it paid off. They were alive and, for the most part, well. There were moments early on when Alex scared Brandy to the point she thought he was suicidal. But, for the time being at least, it seemed to have passed.

The first order of business was coming up with a plan of action. They could not hold out forever here and if Demetri didn't get back soon, they would run out of food, as well as options.

They sat quietly in the darkness with only flickering candles dancing eerily off every piece of furniture, bookcase, and walls of the store. At times, if you caught the light and shadows just right out of the corner of your eye, it seemed as if something or someone were sneaking up on you. It made for an edgy night and an even more daunting chance of getting any sleep.

Mathias made his way to the sofa, kicking his feet up on the coffee table, while music blared in his head. Brandy rolled her eyes at him, thinking him a foolish kid. But she couldn't discount him. This kid saved their lives today. He could have looked out for himself and gotten the hell out of there, but instead he stuck around, took on a demon and his army of tattoo toting mindless idiots, and got the three of them out alive. How he did it was still a mystery to her.

Alex sat on the upholstered chair next to the sofa, deep in thought. *What power could there possibly be within me. My free will? What good has free will ever done anyone who found themselves being possessed by a demon? There had to be a way to find out.*

As all were thinking their own thoughts, Brandy heard the cell phone ring. She ran over to the counter and picked it up and saw the display read UNKNOWN. She quickly thought about whether or not to answer, but decided it best in case it was Demetri or Aldrik calling on a secure line, or even Gina trying to reach them. Another second and her decision was made.

"Hello," she said, meekly into the phone.

"Brandy, is that you? Hello, Brandy." The voice on the other end repeated.

Brandy had never been so happy to hear Demetri's voice since she had first met him. "Oh my God, is it really you? Where are you? How are you? Is Gina with you?" The flood of questions just came flying out getting the attention of both Alex and Mathias who both were up and moving towards Brandy.

"Yes, it's me. We are still looking for Gina, but it is not looking good. It seems she is well hidden, maybe even dead," Demetri said.

"Oh no, don't say that, she has to be okay," Brandy said, with desperation in her voice.

"How are things there?"

"Well, I don't know how to tell you this, but Bastiquil is back and he led us into a trap today. If it weren't for

Mathias, he would have gotten Alex," Brandy relayed the information.

"Bastiquil? Back? How can this be? I thought I took care of him. I must not be the witch I thought I was," Demetri said, sounding wimpy and defeated.

Brandy, taken aback by this and his attitude, didn't know what to make of it. "What do you think we should do? We are running on fumes here and they have cut the electricity to the shop. Oh, did I mention, he has another army."

"This doesn't sound good at all, but I have a crazy idea that might work, but it will take a leap of faith on your part. Are you willing to hear me out?" Demetri asked of her.

"I am up for any advice at his moment," Brandy offered, thankful to have him on the phone, but cautious as something did not feel right about this. This didn't sound like bad ass Demetri she had come to know. Maybe the search for Gina was taking a toll on him.

"We are not able to come back just now because we have to keep looking for Gina. But, if you trust me on this, I think I can make things work for you until I get back," Demetri eased into this.

"What are you saying, Demetri. Please, just come out and say it," Brandy said, desperate to hear his plan.

"Let Bastiquil have Alex. This will buy you some time until I can get back."

"Are you out of your fucking mind? How dare you suggest such a thing to me, I just got him back," Brandy said, outraged at the thought and nerve of Demetri.

"What, what did he say," Alex asked her, moving in closer to the ear of the phone so he could listen in.

"Look, I know it sounds crazy, but Alex is made for this. It will not kill him and it will buy you time. It's your only option," Demetri said, actually starting to sound perturbed and irritated.

"Well, if this is the best the great Demetri can come up with then you can go fuck yourself. It won't happen like that," Brandy stated to him harshly.

Then all she heard on the other end was laughter. Soft at first, then building to a loud eruption of laughter. Brandy pulled the phone from her ear and held it up for the others to hear. Placing it back to her ear, she listened, confused and pissed off.

"I figured this would be your answer, but hey, you can't blame a guy for trying," Brandy immediately recognized the voice as John, Alex's old roommate.

"I'm coming for you all and I will get him back. You cannot stop me. I will rip you and the boy limb from limb and string your body parts up and down the street for birds to feed on. You will rue the day you ever....."

Brandy did not let him finish, she hung up the phone and threw it down on the counter.

"What is it? Who was it," Alex pushed, begging her to tell him.

"It was Bastiquil, pretending to be Demetri. He told me to give you to him and he would fix it when he got home from finding Gina," Brandy said quietly, staring down at the phone.

"What else did he say? Brandy, what the fuck? Talk to me."

Mathias stood there motionless, music-less, listening to the two of them. This demon was a bad ass mother. It took everything he had to hold him and his army off, but he had done it.

Walking up to Brandy, Mathias placed a hand on her back. She jumped slightly at the touch, but turned and smiled at him when she realized who it was. "Just tell us what he said, it will be okay."

"He said he is coming for all of us. He said he will get Alex and then he would rip you and me, limb from limb," Brandy winced, as she recalled the conversation.

"Like hell he will," Alex said, anger growing inside. He began to pace the room, to seethe at the thought of this demon threatening his friends, killing his mother, killing all of those innocent people. It became more than he could handle. Dropping to his knees he screamed out, hands to his head. As he did, the upholstered chair he was sitting in just moments ago exploded, sending debris in all directions.

On instinct, Mathias pulled Brandy out of the way just before a piece of the wooden foot from the chair went flying past her head.

"What the fuck was that Alex?" Brandy yelled at him, but Alex just sat there on the ground, looking at what was left of the chair.

"I think it is safe to say, you found your power, my friend," Mathias said, hoping internally he never pisses Alex off enough to turn his explosive power on him.

Chapter Forty-Two

Victor couldn't help himself, he liked the witch. He didn't consider himself a bad man, he thought of himself as a man who believed wholeheartedly in what he did, enough to kill or harm if needed. He couldn't say this about a lot of people though, many want to say they have strong enough convictions in their beliefs about something to stand up and fight for it, but would they do what was really necessary to make it a reality. He felt doubtful.

He sat on the floor, drenched from the water which still made its way down the stairwell at times, holding onto the witch. He could see why his master would want her. She was beautiful, strong, magical, and hard headed. Just what he could see the master breaking enough to mold her, create her into what he needed her to be.

Of course he was grasping at straws here, he didn't really know what the master wanted with her, but it didn't matter. The master had told him, she was of great importance to his work. She was to be guarded as if he were guarding the master.

He did just as he was told to do. Guard her with his life. Make sure she was provided for and make sure, above all else, she was taken to the stronghold they have in Europe. He would make good on his promise, just as he made good on getting the master back into this world.

It amazed him when he thought about it, an assignment of great importance took precedence over any other thought or fetish he might have. When he had time on his hands, he could indulge his fetishes, act upon them, but when he was focused on a task at hand, he was unstoppable. This was why the Balashon had picked him for the task of preparing the way for the master.

He didn't have many regrets in his life. Why look back on something you cannot change? You either grow from it and let it make you stronger, or you live in regret and let it eat away at your very existence until you are nothing but a starving little maggot on the ground, flopping around hoping to find some leftovers. Not Victor, accept what was done and move on. In his line of work, it didn't behoove him to dwell on the past anyway.

He was brought out of his thoughts by Gina moving around. She was beginning to rouse from her much-needed sleep. It had been an extremely long ride thus far and he had heard someone earlier state they were close to their destination.

She yawned and stretched a little and then turned closer to his chest, closer to his warmth. He knew what she thought about him, she had made this perfectly clear, but it didn't matter. The master needed her so he would take the best care of her he could. If anyone got in between them, they would not live long enough to even think about regrets.

There has to be something big coming for the master to take this much concern about this girl. There had to be something she and she alone could do for him. He smiled at the thought. The master had chosen him for this task.

He was looking down at her as she slowly opened her eyes, looking up, focusing on him. It didn't bother him when she rolled her eyes at him. He actually chuckled a bit.

"Please tell me we are close to land? I don't know how much more wave riding I can handle. This has made me sick to my stomach," Gina told him, not bothering to get off of him yet. She could feel the water moving back and forth across her feet.

"We are close, I have been advised. As we have gotten closer to land, the waves seemed to have gotten less abrasive. I trust you are feeling a bit better," Victor inquired, not sure of how she would respond.

"The nauseous feeling, it comes and goes," she said, looking up at him, then closing her eyes again. "Why have you been so nice to me? You didn't have to hold me, to keep me safe from the waves, to keep me out of the cold water. Why did you do it?"

He sat there for a moment, taking in the questions.

"Would you rather I am mean and nasty, cruel and insensitive? You really don't know me like you think you do. I do what I do because I have to. I don't want you harmed, nor do I want to harm you. I protect you because I am supposed to."

"So if it were not for Bastiquil telling you to protect me, you wouldn't? You would have let the bear get me, the cold water chill me all night," Gina asked, knowing the answer.

"If it were not for Bastiquil, we wouldn't even be having this conversation. The fact he wants you alive is why you are alive. You could have perished in the battle which took place at the mansion. You could have been slaughtered. Your reliable friend, you think he could take on the master, all of the Balashon, me, and still keep you safe? You have a warped sense of what went down Gina. The master saved your life," Victor said, in such a manner it felt almost sincere, almost genuine.

Gina still knew who she was dealing with, what he was capable of and what he was willing to do for his master and the Balashon.

"I haven't tried to escape you, I could have, but I haven't," Gina told him.

"You didn't try to escape me because you knew innocent people would have paid the consequences for your actions, and I can respect that. You took the noble path, putting others ahead of yourself. It is the making of a wise person," he said, as he smiled genuinely at her.

Laughing, she looked at him. "Did you just pay me a compliment? You called me wise."

"I said you are the making of a wise person, I didn't say you were there yet."

Gina laughed still as she sat up on his lap, stretched a bit and looked at him again. "Please tell me there is at least coffee on this boat? Maybe even some bread or crackers?"

"Are you kidding me, this is a boat. It wouldn't be sailing now if not for coffee. They live on it," Victor said, with a shocked look on his face, more to do with her naivety.

"Well, can we get some or are we stuck down here for the duration?" she asked.

"We are not stuck. Let's go topside and see what they are willing to give us," Victor offered, liking the fact they were not at each other's throats.

"What do you mean willing to give us? I thought you took what you wanted, when you wanted?"

"Getting between a sailor and his coffee is dangerous business, even for me," he smiled at her and winked. "Come on; let's see how generous these men can be." Grabbing her hand, he helped her across the slick metal flooring and to the stairs. He decided to go first, just in case there was any funny business going on up there. He also didn't need a wave hitting and knocking her off the stairwell.

Gina followed him up and out of the lower cargo hold they were in. The sun, although it hurt their eyes, was a welcome sight. It was early morning and they could see land up ahead. There were men running around all over the boat attending to their morning duties, or so Gina assumed.

Gina stood at the railing watching the sea churn and turn, seagulls flying about and dolphins swimming alongside.

217

It was an incredible sight and she wished she was seeing it under better circumstances. She would be in heaven if this was just a vacation.

Victor had walked over and was talking to the captain of the ship. She turned and saw the captain nodding at whatever Victor was telling him and then Victor stepped inside the galley.

Gina continued to watch the ocean, to see the land coming ever closer. She didn't know what land held for her, what the intent was, but she tried to take in the beauty of what she was seeing. She didn't notice until he was upon her. Victor stood beside her and handed over a steaming cup of coffee. She took it and thanked him. He then put his hand into his pocket and pulled out a piece of bread which looked like it had been broken off a loaf. Gina, starving, took it from him and began to eat it. He smiled at her.

Chapter Forty-Three

As the plane lifted off and the landing gear securely stowed itself, Demetri sat silently in his thoughts. *He missed her. They had been on foot ever since the plane crashed and now they were hours ahead of them headed for God knows where in Scotland.*

Aldrik was up in the cockpit talking to the pilot. As he sat alone, his thoughts would not stop tormenting him. *I should not have listened to Aldrik. He should have allowed the man with the scar across his eye to die, to become the same scum to the ocean that he was to the land. No matter, I did enough damage to the man that he will not be functioning properly for a long time, if at all.*

He looked up as the cockpit door opened and Aldrik came walking back to the sofa.

"Please, let this go. We did everything in our power to reach her before they escaped Iceland, now our search will continue in Scotland. We will find her, Demetri, I promise you." He leaned over and kissed him on the cheek, hoping to alleviate some of the stress he saw all over his face. It didn't work.

"What did the pilot say? Where are we heading?" he demanded of him.

"We are heading to the closest airport this side of northern Scotland. It's called Inverness Airport, which is 100 miles away from Lochinver. It's a small coastal town on the western side of Scotland."

"I have tried a locating spell, but so far it has turned up nothing. I can only take from this they are still on the move and it can't pinpoint her." He leaned over and put his head on his knees bringing his arms up and running his fingers into his hair. It was an act of frustration and it didn't go unnoticed by Aldrik.

Reaching over, he rubbed his hand up and down the length of his back, trying to give comfort even though he knew there would be none.

Letting out an exasperated grunt, he stood and started pacing around the plane. "Why can't we just find her? I have all of this power inside me and I can't do a damned thing to help her."

"I understand your frustration, Demetri. Let us not forget if it were not for your heightened powers, we would not have known to even come to Scotland, let alone Iceland. So don't keep holding onto this anger. You need to be clear headed and on top of things if we are going to find her. We had more to go on in Iceland, a spot, GPS coordinates, but in Scotland, we have nothing yet. So stop this sulking and get some rest so you can use those tremendous powers to find her," Aldrik abruptly stated, making him feel rightly chastised.

"I know you are right, but I just can't imagine a life without her in it. I have to find her, I just have to."

"And we will find her, I have told you this." Aldrik stood, stopping him from pacing around. "Look at me," he said, grabbing him by the shoulders. As he was forced to stop pacing and look into Aldrik's eyes, he began to cry. He was tired, stressed and going on empty. "You need to eat and then rest. We will be there before you know it. Now sit down, relax and let me get you something warm to eat and some water to help hydrate."

He helped him onto the sofa and walked over to the galley of the plane and began to prepare him something as promised. While he waited for the food to warm, he reached into the refrigerator and pulled out a bag of blood, which he kept stocked at all times. Putting the bag up to his mouth, he bit the tip off and quickly downed it, feeling refreshed and new. When he returned to where Demetri sat, he found him fast asleep.

Aldrik placed the plate of food back into the galley and walked over to where he lay sleeping and covered him with a blanket. *How is it, one so powerful, so beautiful, knows so little about himself. He must come into this knowledge and powers at his own pace or they will overtake him, maybe even destroy him.*

He looked down at him and smiled. He had never known such love for anyone in his life. Knowing he was the reincarnation of Floki made him love him even more, but it didn't detract from the love he had for Demetri, here and now. It was a love he could see lasting forever, but Demetri didn't have forever, did he? He had yet to take him up on his offer to turn him, but there was still hope, there was still time and there was still lots for them to do and see. He just wanted to cherish this time with him as long as possible.

Unbeknownst to Aldrik, Demetri dreamed of the sea. The water below them, raging and constantly moving in a never-ending pattern of turmoil and beauty, seemed to flow along with the movement of the plane. He saw the different colored hues of the water, bold and rich, dark and light. Depending on how you looked at it, it almost appeared soft and peaceful and in other places cold and dangerous.

He saw fish, dolphins, seagulls, and pelicans all dancing and twisting in a way only they knew how. But, as he watched them, he realized something more. He found himself close to the water, looking down at it. He felt the coolness of the ocean breeze caressing his hair as he glided across the water. But as he looked out, he saw land up ahead.

He soon felt the hard steel of a boat under his feet, and as he looked around he saw Gina, standing there, looking out across the sea watching the same land mass come closer, watching the same fish, dolphins, and seagulls at play. He smelled the coffee as she eased it up to her lips and sipped the hot brew out of the cup. Then he saw Victor, the man behind most of their misery. The man who helped this damned demon back into this world. The man, who was responsible for abducting Gina, stood next to her drinking coffee as well.

He felt as if he were right there with them. He actually walked closer to Gina and put his hand to her shoulder. She shivered as he did as if his hand were a cold northern wind chilling her to the bone. As she shivered, Victor stepped closer to her and put his arm around her, pulling her close. He knew Victor was keeping her warm, but, to see him even touch her sent intense rage up his spine, he thought he would explode.

He also knew Gina. She wasn't just cozying up to him for warmth. She was doing what she had to do to survive. His girl was alive, he could feel her. Just looking at her even in a dream brought so much energy and vigor back to him. He was going to find her and when he did, this man will die at his hands. He will make him suffer just like he had caused so much suffering.

Listening in on the scene playing out before him, he could hear them talking but, he also heard talking in the background. The crew on the boat was talking and readying the boat for landfall. He wasn't sure if he had heard right, but, when he thought about it, he remembered Aldrik saying this name.

One of the men on board shouted, "Lochinver ahead, ready the boat."

Demetri woke up from his dream in such a state Aldrik thought him crazed at first. Then as he calmed down and repeated the events of the dream, he realized this was one of the many gifts he had within him.

Aldrik immediately grabbed his satellite phone and called ahead, making plans for their arrival to Inverness and subsequent departure to Lochinver. Looking over at Demetri, it thrilled him greatly to see so much hope and joy return to his face. He was a talented witch, and when he tapped into the full power within him, he would be unstoppable. Aldrik could only hope this never came, such power was not meant to reside in one man. It can lead to obsession, torment, and possibly even self-destruction.

Chapter Forty-Four

The call from Bastiquil still had the group in a panic. The display of power which came from Alex had both Brandy and Mathias on edge, but the biggest surprise was to Alex himself. He could not believe something like this had been inside of him all along. He was grateful no one had ever gotten hurt from it.

Brandy's cell phone rang, making all of them jump and look at Alex. Then walking over to the phone, the three of them looked down at the screen and didn't know quite what to make of it when they saw Aldrik's name pop up.

"It's another trick," Mathias said.

"It's another game Bastiquil is playing," Alex threw in.

The voice of reason came from Brandy, who chimed into the conversation. "Let's not forget, when Bastiquil called earlier it came across as an unknown number. This is actually Aldrik's number and we need to answer it even if it might be Bastiquil. What if they are in trouble and need us?"

"Them in trouble, are you kidding? What about us here, trapped in this store, with no electricity and a demon army waiting to get us," Mathias blurted out.

"Enough," Brandy stated, as she picked up the phone, which felt like it had been ringing forever. "Hello."

"Brandy, is it you," the voice on the other line, which clearly sounded like Demetri, asked her.

"Yes, it's me, but how do I know it is you?" she cautiously asked back.

"What? I don't understand what you mean? Are you okay Brandy?" Demetri asked, worried about her.

"You called us earlier told us lots of things," Brandy proceeded with caution.

"I never called you Brandy...this is the first time I have attempted. What's going on?"

Something in his voice made Brandy realize it was Demetri. She knew in her gut, so she decided to dive in. "Bastiquil is back." The silence on the other end about drove Brandy mad. "Did you hear me?"

"How can this be? I defeated him, I sent him back to hell." Demetri could not believe what he was hearing and fear swept over him, a new fear for the people in Tulsa and for Gina too.

"I don't know how or why he is back, but he is. He is in Alex's roommate's body and he has created some kind of demonic army. One girl can even fly. She has fucking wings," Brandy told him, sure that she sounded like a crazy woman.

Demetri soaked all this in and felt guilt about having left them alone. But, they weren't alone were they? "What about the guy Aldrik sent over to protect you?"

"He kicked some major demonic ass, but we just barely made it out alive," Brandy told him.

"Made it out of where," Demetri asked, his head spinning from everything he was hearing.

Brandy swallowed, knowing she was about to get a lecture and knowing they all deserved it. "We got a call to go over to Alex's studio and when we got there we were ambushed."

"Oh my God, I can't believe you went there. Tell me everything, from the beginning," Demetri demanded.

Brandy spent the next fifteen minutes explaining to him everything that happened, realizing to anyone else it would sound like a far-fetched children's story. But she knew the man on the other end was taking it all in. When she finished, she waited to hear what he had to say.

"I am so sorry I left you all to fend for yourself. I thought it would just be the Balashon, which is bad enough, but I had no idea Bastiquil was still around," Demetri offered, his guilt shining through.

"It's not your fault, you know that don't you? None of this is your fault. You can't take the blame for every supernatural, demonic disaster that happens in the world. What is going on with Gina and your search for her?" Brandy tried to give him reassurance they were still holding strong, but in truth, she knew their time was limited.

Demetri gave her a run-down of everything that had happened thus far on their journey and even about the dream he had just had. He told her their plans once they arrive at the airport.

"At least you still have a lead on her. This is wonderful news," she actually smiled as she said it, though she feared for everyone's safety, Gina included.

"Brandy, you are safe from the demon as long as you stay in the store. As for his army, I don't know. I am not sure what he did to create them. But, the demon I know cannot cross into the building. How are the others holding up?"

"We are all shaken but haven't given up hope, at least not yet. We still have some fight in us," she stated, actually feeling better after talking with him.

"Well, this new power of Alex's ought to come in handy. He just needs to focus it on the target and let it go. Tell him to give it all he has in him. It's you or them. Let him feel guilty later. Right now it's time to fight. I will call some acquaintances who owe me favors and I will see if Aldrik has any other people in the area that can quickly come over and lend a hand," he told Brandy, with the hope he was giving her something to hold onto, to fight for.

"Thank you, Demetri. You just need to concentrate on finding Gina and bringing her home safely."

"We will do our best. Again, I am so sorry I'm not there to help you. But know I will do what I can. I will call the others as soon as I hang up," Demetri told her, as he glanced over at Aldrik, who was already on his phone calling in the troops.

"Thank you, Demetri, and may the universe be on all our sides." They both hung up. Brandy turned to both men and filled them in.

Just as she had finished explaining everything Demetri had told her, a rock came crashing into the side window of the store. Doors begin to shake as the handles were being turned. The three of them knew the battle they had feared was upon them. Brandy grabbed a handgun she had found while inventorying Gina's things and ran to the sofa for protection and cover. If they were going down, it wouldn't be without a fight.

Chapter Forty-Five

As the boat docked, it was evident this was a large fishing community, but not a large town. You could see the North West Highlands of Scotland from the boat. The only thing Gina could gather from overhearing the crew talk was that this town was called Lochinver. Looking out she could tell it was a traditional coastal town, with rows of white homes and small business lining the road which twists and winds along the waterway.

How beautiful and quaint. It wasn't until Victor grabbed her arm and told her it was time for them to get off the boat, when her situation came crashing back to her. She had been so overcome with the beauty of the place; she had almost forgotten she wasn't there to take in the local scenery.

"Where are we going?" Gina asked him.

"Just keep walking and smiling, just like you have been ever since you laid eyes on this town. Don't make a scene and I will tell you when we get off of this boat."

She did as asked, not wanting to rock what civility they seemed to have managed to build. Gina by no means trusted this man, nor did she like him, but she could not deny he had done some tremendous things to protect her. For what, she was still in the dark about. She hoped with this newfound tolerance, they would be better able to communicate with each other. She was also pretty certain he knew she would do what he asked because she did not want a repeat of what happened to the poor man back at the cabin in Iceland.

As they made their way from the dock to the road, they walked along, arm in arm as if they were a couple. No one thought any different and as far as she was concerned they shouldn't. Her guilty-conscious couldn't take any more killing because of her. The guilt was eating her alive.

Walking up the road, she could see the spectacular view of the town. It was a most lovely town, one you could get lost in. It was peaceful and serene. In the distance, she could make out the silhouettes of sheep roaming on the highlands. Along the beaches, Highland cows and hens roamed freely up the distant shoreline. *This is truly something you would not see in the states.* There wasn't much traffic to speak of. If she were to guess, there were probably five hundred or so people living in the town. She wished she had traveled more and hoped she would still have the chance to do so.

As they came around the corner, she could see the town of Lochinver on one side of her and rocks on the other which fed into the sea. She could see eagles flying around the cliffs of the shorelines. Spectacular was the only word which came to mind.

They kept walking until they came to a remarkable looking hotel, which had evidently been built to look like a castle. It was called The Culag Hotel. *Was he actually going to get them a room? Maybe even take a shower or, even better, a hot bath.*

Upon entering the front doorway, he instructed her to sit down near the sign-in desk. Gina did as told and picked up a brochure of the hotel. Gina read this beautiful hotel was originally built in 1873 as a shooting lodge for the Duke of Sutherland. It has twelve suites and has been run by the same family for the past thirteen years. It is a magnificent place, so stately and regal. She felt as if she were sitting inside a historical castle. They even offered deer stalking trips, sea angling, hiking trips, and even salmon fishing could be arranged by request.

She also noticed they offer a restaurant and a bar, named The Wayfarers' Bar, which is stocked with over one hundred single-malt Scotch whiskeys. *Damn, she could sure go for one of those now.*

When she had finished reading the brochure, she looked up at Victor standing over her, smiling brightly. She realized it wasn't for her, but for the people watching the attractive, but disheveled, couple who looked like they were on a romantic getaway. As she looked at him, she couldn't help but see what a remarkably handsome man he was. It just goes to show, you never know what was going on inside someone. She could only imagine the countless woman or men he had lured into his bed with his smile. But he also believed in what he was doing to a greater conviction than anyone she had ever met in her life. Even though she didn't agree with him, she would give him that one.

Taking his outstretched hand, she let him pull her up out of the chair and they headed to their suite. Once inside, Gina walked over to the bed and sat down on the edge. The entire trip had been torturous and she couldn't believe the last few weeks of her life. Never, would she have thought such a thing would ever happen, especially to her.

Magic had been a constant in her life, one she had not been hidden from. Her mother, grandmother, and great-grandmother had all been witches. But the existence of demons, she would never have thought real. Of course, books like the Bible and other literary work try to make one believe in their existence, but usually a rational mind can tell the true meaning of verse, as opposed to the fire and brimstone versions. It actually made her head ache.

Her stomach had been upset ever since the plane crash. She chalked it up to the impact, her nerves, and poor nutrition, but she hoped it would get easier. She felt more sluggish than usual. It actually surprised her that she was able to sleep as much as she has considering she was being held against her will by a serial killer.

"Why don't you go take a bath, soak in some hot water. It will make you feel better," he suggested to her.

"I feel fine," Gina lied.

"No, you don't. It shows all over your face. You are pale, lethargic, and are showing signs of getting ill. You need to rest for the night. We will grab some dinner and maybe you will feel more up for the task at hand tomorrow," he said, shocking her once again at his insight and thoughtfulness.

"Just what is the task at hand? Why won't you tell me? It's not like I can call anyone and tell them. You have already taken the cord for the phone and you watch me 24/7. So, what is the harm in letting me know where you are taking me?" Gina pleaded, getting emotional which she hated letting him see.

"Look, I will make a deal with you. I suggest you take it because I am not in the business of making deals with anyone other than my bosses or my master." He looked at her for acknowledgment.

Gina nodded to him, letting him know she understood him.

"You take a bath, I will take a shower and then we will get something to eat. If you do this without any fuss or disruption, then I will tell you where we are headed. Agreed?" He paused, waiting for her to answer.

"Agreed," she said as she got up and went into the bathroom to run some hot water for the bath.

"No locking the door either. I will bust it down if you even try." He smiled at her with a smile she knew did not hide any other meaning than what he had just said.

"The door will stay open. I am just thankful to get the chance to take a hot bath," Gina said, feeling grateful for this hotel and for not being stuck in some forest or boat cargo hold.

Gina reached down and felt the hot water which had filled the tub just over half full. Turning off the flow of water she placed a towel down on the edge of the tub to use when

231

she finished and began to take her clothes off. She didn't even care if he could see her. She just wanted to feel the warmth of the water as it surrounded her submerged body.

Victor watched her from the other room, admiring her body, its naked beauty, and her pale soft skin. He had wanted her so badly a week ago, but the master had his sights on her now and he will not do anything to interfere with that. He thought about some scenarios as to what the master had in mind, but eventually came to the conclusion that the master would tell him when he wanted him to know. Until then, it was business as usual.

As he watched her immerse herself into the steaming water, he began to take off his clothing until nothing remained but his bandages. He removed the bandages which covered his injury from the bear attack, yanking them off quickly, not even wincing at the pain. Walking into the bathroom he stood in front of the mirror placed above the sink and inspected the injury. It was healing up nicely thanks to the witch's quick thinking and resources.

"What are you doing?" Gina asked him, startling her when she opened her eyes to find him standing nude in the bathroom with her.

"I too need to shower. You are bathing, so shall I." He turned and walked over to the glass shower door, opened it to turn on the hot water.

"You could have waited till I finished," Gina said, perturbed at him and a bit embarrassed as she had found herself looking at his penis. Blushing, she silently chastised herself.

"Why? I am not trying to hurt you, nor do I have any sexual intentions towards you. You are a woman taking a bath and I am a man taking a shower. End of story," he said, as he placed his hand under the stream of water. When it reached his desired temperature, he stepped inside and closed the door.

Had either of them known what approached them from the outside, neither would have allowed themselves the comfort of relaxation, but there was no way to have known they were coming. They cloaked themselves with a power not even Gina could have recognized as a potential threat, so she continued to lose herself in the warmth of the water.

Chapter Forty-Six

He paced back and forth in the plane, thinking about every possibility to help them; including turning the plane around and heading back to Tulsa. The guilt of not being there to protect them weighed heavily. This blasted demon had been with Demetri for millennia now and he knew the dangers of not going back to take care of him.

In the end, his love for Gina won out. If anything were to happen to the group in Tulsa, he wouldn't be able to forgive himself, but his history and connection with Gina had to come first. It would cost him, for it was a decision that would eat away at him every day of his life. They are brave, but have already been through so much because of this demon. They also have heart, great powers, and a troop of strong backup headed their way. Between himself and Aldrik, they were able to reach a great number of friends and acquaintances who owed them. Now was the time to call in the IOU's.

Demetri made his decision and will stand by it, whatever the outcome. He knew everyone but Brandy had some kind of power and she would be his biggest regret if anything happens. Bastiquil had already put her through hell and back, but she survived. The thought of him doing anything else to her enraged him. He would make sure this blasted demon found his way back to the depths of hell if it was the last thing he did.

As they descended into Inverness International Airport, Demetri was beside himself. He wanted to get to Gina before anything happened to her. He wanted to get her home safely, and then deal with Bastiquil.

Aldrik reached over and put his hand on Demetri's. Without saying a word, Demetri felt the impact of the gesture. He felt so fortunate Aldrik was here with him. He didn't know what he would do without him. He had made this entire endeavor a possibility and he loved him for it.

As the plane's wheels met the tarmac, the adrenaline kicked in. When it came to a halt outside of one of the hangers, Aldrik quickly opened the door, exposing the sunlight into the cabin, but he already prepared by putting his day suit on.

They both ran to the helicopter waiting for them and as they got inside, it lifted off heading in the direction of Lochinver.

Demetri had conducted a locating spell using the map and crystal, scrying for Gina. It had landed at coordinates where, according to a local map, the Culag Hotel should be. He called ahead, but they would not give any information over the phone. Even if they would have, he was pretty certain they did not sign in under their real names, if Victor was even his real name.

As the helicopter propelled itself through the air, the landscape beneath was lost. Demetri's thoughts were everywhere. Aldrik busied himself with trying to reach the Tulsa crew and check on their status, but each time he tried no one answered. This did not bode well for them.

Had either of them been paying attention, they would have seen the giant, metal ax being thrown from the ground upwards at them. It wasn't until it struck the helicopter through the front window, impaling the pilot in the chest, that either of them was brought back from their current thoughts.

The helicopter began to spin out of control as they both struggled to get their wits about them. Sparks were flying around the inside as the control panel had also been severely damaged from the ax. Demetri tried to calm himself enough to make the helicopter levitate, at least enough to reach the ground safely. But they were going too fast and were too close to the ground for him to have enough of an effect to slow it down.

Within a few feet from the ground, Aldrik grabbed Demetri by the waist and used his strength and speed to push themselves outwards from the propellers reach, sending them both rolling to the ground.

Upon impact, the helicopter exploded sending shrapnel and pieces hurling at them before they themselves even stopped rolling. As a large piece of the propeller flew at Aldrik's body, Demetri hit it with a burst of energy knocking it off its course, just by inches, causing it to fly past Aldrik without harm.

Demetri smiled, knowing he was okay. As he tried to stand, he instantly fell to the ground, crying out in pain. Turning to look for the source of the pain, he saw a chunk of metal sticking out of the back of his left thigh. It took only a second for Aldrik to reach his side to inspect the injury.

"It appears to be isolated to the muscle only. I'm going to pull it out, but it is going to hurt like hell," he told Demetri, who began to prepare for the worst.

"Okay, on the count of three just pull it out..." Demetri tried to tell him, as Aldrik yanked out the shrapnel.

Crying out, Demetri's fist, hit the ground as a shock wave of pain rippled through his body. "What the fuck, Aldrik? What happened to on the count of three?"

"I never agreed to that. You are the one trying to come up with a distraction. I just gave you a better one," he said, looking down at Demetri.

Both men stopped talking as they heard vibrations ripple outward, as something heavy struck the ground. They both knew it wasn't from the helicopter, but more likely what helped to bring it down. Another vibration rippled and then another. They came like heavy footfalls of a giant and the sound of something dragging.

The two were scanning the ground in all directions, trying to locate the source of the sounds. Aldrik noticed first and reached over to tap Demetri to alert him. As they looked on, they saw what appeared to be a giant male, walking towards them. He stood at least seven feet tall with a full brown leather stitched skirt, which went all the way to the ground, a bare chest and a metal triangular mask with a pointed end coming almost all the way down to his navel.

They both looked on in awe as the man continued to move towards them. The most shocking aspect, at least to Demetri, was he carried with him a hatchet of sorts, with a two-foot handle and a five-foot blade made of steel. The blade and handle stood taller than the man himself, but just by a few inches. It was a killing machine, no doubt, but who sent it and why was the question.

When he was nearly three yards from them, he stopped, standing with the blade piercing the ground. Not saying a word, he just stared in their direction. They didn't move, not just yet, until they were sure it was there to kill them. But as the silence continued on, they began to realize it didn't have holes where eyes could look out, it didn't have a place for it to breathe. This could only mean one thing, it was already dead.

The two were sitting upright on the ground, looking and waiting. The man pulling the blade from the ground took a few quick steps forward and swung at their heads with such might it unnerved them both. Both instinctually laid back onto the ground allowing the blade to swing past, causing the air around them to disperse.

They both rolled to the right, getting up onto their feet. The first blow had been the helicopter, it was evident this thing had the strength to bring it down. The second was the attempt at beheading them. Whoever or whatever it was, had definitely brought the fight to them and they were not going to back down. They were too close. Both got into battle positions and began to fan out from each other. They had to dispose of it now so they could be on their way.

While Demetri formed in his mind the best plan of attack on this thing, Aldrik made a dash at him, running right into the line of fire.

Chapter Forty-Seven

Fight or flight? This was what went through Brandy's head as the first round of the demon's army came crashing through the windows. As she hunkered down behind the sofa for what was to come, she hoped they would all make it out alive. Bastiquil was strong, but the will to survive was stronger.

The first of the intruders, four men, all decent sized, came running towards Alex. They all knew Alex would be the target, the one they would want. Brandy and Mathias would be expendable.

Mathias, who had steadied himself against a wall with no windows, had already tuned into his favorite song for the moment and went to town on these brutes. Hands in the air, he stopped each one in their tracks, making them dance backward out of the window they had crashed through.

They all looked at each other, knowing this was just a test. The worst was coming. And they were not wrong.

Another group of ten, made up of men and woman, stormed through window opening and branched off in different directions. Some were hiding behind bookcases, in the shadows, and one even went for the door to unlock it, but Mathias stopped him in his tracks. But, as he concentrated on this one man, he was being stalked by two others who had been transformed into some kind of snake men. Out of their skin, snakes were hovering, hissing, and striking out. There were two snakes per arm, per man. It was one of the most disgusting things he had ever seen and one of the coolest all wrapped in one.

As he held the one man at the door, his concentration switched to the two snake-men who were closing in on him. He had them pinned on the floor, on their hands and knees. This was the way they were approaching him and he had just stopped them mid crawl. The snakes did not seem to be under his control as they still hissed and struck out at him. They had crawled out as far as the ink on the skin would allow, coming within inches of piercing his skin with their fangs.

Mathias quickly flung the men backward, knocking over a bookshelf in the process. Others began to advance, with five more jumping through the window. In the distance, Bastiquil could be heard telling them all to play their part. *This isn't going to end well*, Mathias thought.

Alex found himself cornered against a wall with two women and a man coming at him. He knew these people were innocent victims of a demonic maniac, but it also came down to survival. One of the women advanced on him and he flinched as he heard a boom ring out inside the store. Blood spattered from the side of the girl's head and hit the wall as she fell to the ground dead. Alex and the two others near him looked over to see a wide-eyed Brandy standing there with the pistol held out in front of her, both hands on it shaking.

Mathias turned up the volume a notch in his head as he smiled to himself at the sight of Brandy, such a sexy woman, who just went bad ass on this tattooed zombie, or whatever these things are now. He quickly dispatched another few out the window.

Alex turned his attention back to the two, one of which ran at Brandy. She did not hesitate to shoot the man right in the forehead dropping him to the ground. Alex could not believe what he was witnessing. He knew she was a strong woman but, for her to do this, took it to a whole new level.

The woman standing in front of Alex had barbed wire coming out of her arms. The wires lashed out at him, one nicking him on the cheek bringing fresh blood to the surface of the wound. The other arm came around for him, and trying to stop the barbed wire from hitting him, he focused on it and it exploded, sending the girl running till she knocked herself out by hitting her head on a wall.

The army kept coming. It seemed endless. *He truly is ready to battle to the end,* Alex thought. *He must have brought them all.*

"Alex, you need to get out of here, now," Brandy yelled at him.

"No, not without you," Alex screamed back.

Brandy was not watching from behind as she only expected the attack to come from the front. But, as she tried to keep her frustration at bay with Alex, she heard something behind her and quickly turned with the gun pointing outward.

"Hold up," screamed the young man. "Name is Ethan. Demetri sent me to help."

"You about got your fucking head blown off Ethan," Brandy screamed, nodding her head towards the attack taking place.

"I'm on it," Ethan grinned, grateful for a chance to rumble, to flex his supernatural muscles.

"So what is your..." Brandy tried to get out, but fell silent as she saw him morphing in front of her, clothes ripping, muscles expanding and pushing outward. His head started to contort, to change, to almost explode, but yet it didn't. His nails began to grow in length, to sharpen and thicken. He leaned forward as the transformation completed, then leaned back, front haunches outstretched as the remaining material of the shirt fell to the floor. He let out a howl from his now wolf-like face, which seemed to echo throughout the building.

The attackers in the building were still hiding, waiting for their opportunity to advance and take Alex to their master. They heard the howling of the werewolf in the building but didn't realize they had gone from the hunters to being the prey.

Ethan could smell them, he could smell them all. Not just the attackers, but the ones he had come to help. He could smell the blood running down Alex's face. He tried to focus on the attackers.

As he advanced, his front haunches were thrashing about with sharp claws ripping into flesh. They screamed in pain, but continued to fight back, fueled by the demon-blood tattooed on their skin. Ethan grabbed one and bit the man's neck, ripping the skin and his jugular as he did. The snake men, regaining their footing from the beating they had taken from Mathias, lunged at Ethan, grabbing hold of him as the snakes coiled around his arms and neck, striking at his skin, puncturing the surface with their sharp fangs.

The wolf within Ethan howled out with pain, but continued to fight. Another one jumped on top of Ethan as the weight of the many finally pushed him down to the floor. Mathias, busy with his own onslaught of attackers, was unable to help.

Alex was also being surrounded by more of Bastiquil's army which had jumped through the broken windows. He still visualized the blood from the arm which had blown up as he struggled to gain some control over his new-found powers, but knew he would have to use them.

Brandy, standing silently in the shadows, gun held outward could not help but feel they were in a hopeless situation. Without the help of Demetri, Aldrik, and Gina, all seemed doomed.

Chapter Forty-Eight

The winds blew hard around Urquhart Castle, which stood on the western banks of Loch Ness. The castle, remnants of a time long gone, was a sight for many historical enthusiasts and tourists, but none knew of the evil which lay beneath it, an evil which has for centuries been keeping its whereabouts unknown. This evil did not have to do with a giant cryptozoological Loch Ness Monster, although they were fond of it.

The twin witches had been in seclusion for centuries, living beneath the ruins of the castle, hidden away from man and his many evils. They had grown weary of this petty world of human versus human and longed for the days when wizards and demons ruled the land.

For the two to break their seclusion, it would be a rare day indeed. They could sense it, smell it, as it pulled up onto their shores. Its scent was in the air, seductive, luring, and rare. They wanted it badly and as they removed the barrier which kept them locked away from the outside world, they also unleashed their essence back into the land.

They were old, wrinkled, and graying, just as one would imagine of two female twins seven-hundred-fifty years old. They moved along, not in a sluggish way, but as if floating just inches off the ground. They moved with precision and intention. They would have it, it would bring them what they longed for, a world full of evil, of magical beings ruling once again.

The one in white, Arabella Cailleach Urguhart, had a veiled face, hiding the aging the witches had been unable to defy. The other, Athdara Dervorgilla Urguhart, dressed in black, carried with her a staff with a large diamond in it that wielded a heightened force of magic.

The sisters had foreseen the arrival of a new magical being. But this magical force was no match for the twins, who had also found a way to survive through the years. They had not yet been able to stop the advancement of time of their exterior form, but the magic within them was strong, vibrant and ready for battle. This new arrival, surely she would hold the key to unlocking their youth, along with the world they so strongly desired to see reborn.

They had felt the arrival of a great, ancient, evil power to this earth. He had awakened them from their slumber. He had crawled out of the depths of darkness to wreak havoc again on this world. A world where men and woman live their lives through a screen of electronics and signals, taking everything they have for granted. How do they think those signals were even discovered? If not for magic, none of their fineries would exist.

Soon, they would be thrown back into a world where humans cower at their feet. Other magical beings would also awaken. Sorcerers, dragons, and mighty beasts would run free.

The sister witches were approaching the town of Lochinver and the unsuspecting two who had finished their bathing and were both napping after having room service. Gina had for some reason been craving steak, which was peculiarly unlike her, but now she slept, dreaming of better days ahead.

Victor lay on the sofa just opposite the bed, lightly sleeping as he usually does, not wanting to give up control of his surroundings. But what was coming could not have been detected, unless one was looking out the window to see the misty fog slowly drifting into Lochinver, not from the sea, but from the land. It moved with the ease and beauty of a drifting cloud.

As the witches floated into town, hidden within the cover of the fog, no one was the wiser. It wasn't unusual for fog to envelop the coastal town, but today it came faster, and from a different direction than normal.

The witches descended upon the hotel where Gina and Victor lay sleeping.

The two were on a mission, one in which they did not intend to fail. They had long waited for this day, waited for the one who would bring back the days of old, where magic ruled the nation and wrought fear into the very heart of men.

The witches had earlier dispatched a weapon of great power to disable the two who had come to retrieve the girl. He was to destroy the vampire and to bring the magical one, the one who had transcended time and space, back to them. He would join their plight or die like the vampire.

The sisters had arrived at the hotel and could sense the one they were searching for in the room upstairs. She had a protector with her, but his protection would not be enough. They knew he was no match for their powers. He was not a magical being.

Arabel flicked her wrist and the balcony door which led into the room where Gina lay sleeping came flying open. Victor immediately awoke to find Gina still asleep but rising upward off the bed. He attempted to stand but found himself unable to. Athdara had him bound to the sofa in which he'd been laying.

Victor watched as Gina floated to the balcony door, turning until her feet led her onto the balcony. *It had to be Demetri*, Victor thought to himself. They had found them and now he would abscond with the witch if he did not do something to stop him.

Victor mustered all the strength he could between exhaustion and the injuries he sustained, and was able to break from the sofa and fight his way towards the balcony as the impressed Athdara realized she underestimated the human.

Gina floated out the door and had already crossed the balcony railings, hovering many feet off the ground. If she were to drop from this height, especially asleep, it could kill her.

Grabbing a hunting knife within reach, he bolted to the balcony just as Gina was lowered toward the ground. To his surprise, it wasn't Demetri who he would do battle with, but some female witch in a white cloak.

Not appearing to care about being on the second story, Victor ran towards the railing, jumping over the side and preparing himself to roll just as he hit the ground. He never made it that far. Athdara hit him with a lightning bolt coming from the diamond placed within the staff. The bolt sent him hurling up against the rock wall of the hotel, knocking the breath out of him.

As he lay there, trying to catch his breath, he looked up to see the two witches floating into a mist with Gina hovering waist high off the ground as the fog enveloped them. *Get up Victor, get up now*, he thought to himself. *If you don't get up now she will be lost and the master will never forgive you.*

Pushing himself up from the ground, Victor dug deep, grunting through the pain, and stood on unsteady feet. Looking around he spotted what he searched for. Taking off in a slight run, he bent over and scooped up the knife and took off in the direction of the witches.

Old crones, you don't know what forces you are dealing with here. As much as it hurt to run, he forced himself to pick up speed. It shouldn't be hard to track them, as the fog had retreated with them. *I will make you pay for this. If one hair on her head is harmed, you will die a horrific death.*

Victor knew the witches were powerful, so he knew they would not be easily ambushed. But he had to do whatever necessary to reach them. What awaited him, he did not know. He would save Gina or die trying, but not finding her wasn't an option.

Chapter Forty-Nine

Ethan struggled through the pain, pushing himself upward with his supernatural strength. The wolf within wanted to rip the throats out of these people attacking him. Even in his wolf state, Ethan could tell the numbers were against them.

More of Bastiquil's army came flooding into the store. The door was ripped out of the frame and came crashing inward from the onslaught of minions bearing down on it.

Ethan threw the attackers off him, sending them flying in all directions. He reared his head back and let out the most haunting howl. It sent tingles down Brandy's spine as she hunkered down behind the sofa, raising the gun to fire again. It didn't matter what she had seen through the last few weeks, looking at him was strange and eerie.

Just then, six more werewolves came jumping into the battle, a couple flying over Brandy's head. It all happened so quickly she didn't even know they were behind her. *Ethan's howl*, she thought, *he was calling for more help. There might still be hope.*

But even Brandy couldn't allow herself the indulgence of thinking anything good could come from this. She had just been introduced to the supernatural world, and her science-processing brain was being blown away by it. They were doing battle with a demon, one who would have seen her dead. He wanted her best friend and was willing to do whatever necessary.

Brandy was shaken back from her thoughts as the yells and screams raged on. She heard people screaming, wolves howling and yelping in pain. *How long could they hold out for? We are so out-numbered.* Brandy scanned the room again, looking for any sign of Mathias and Alex.

Seeing Alex, fighting Bastiquil's army as good as he was getting, made her both happy and sad. He didn't ask for this. He was born into this world an unwilling puppet, used by his mother, tossed aside by his father, and welcomed with open arms by his demonic grandfather. Her heart ached for him.

Then she caught sight of Mathias, out of the corner of her right eye. He was fighting a great many of the people the demon had sent in. Every time he would freeze some of them where they stood, another batch advanced. He was holding up, but for how long was anybody's guess.

Brandy let out a scream as she felt a hand wrap around the back of her neck. It gripped her tight and lifted her up from the floor onto her feet.

Her scream not only had drawn the attention of Alex but also the attention of Mathias and the wolves. Standing behind Brandy, holding her inches off the ground, was the newly formed and extremely powerful Night Fury. Her wings were spread at full mass, impressive in size, but terrifying in reality.

Alex turned towards her, blasting the few men who stood in his path. He focused on Night Fury, his anger uncontrollable.

"You let her go you fucking bitch," Alex screamed, stepping forward trying to concentrate on blasting out at the demon spawn without hurting Brandy.

"Don't even think about it," Night Fury spat out at him. "Do you honestly think you can dispense of me before I snap the neck of your loved one? You do love her, right? She is worth dying for, right?"

"Alex, you blast this fucking demon bitch. You kill her now. Don't worry about me. Just do it," Brandy pleaded with him.

"I am giving you one chance to let her go, then I am going to unleash hell upon you," Alex said in such a sinister tone, even Brandy was taken aback, but hopeful for his spunk.

"Quite the hero, aren't we. You couldn't save your mom and now you are willing to let your friend die for you too," Night Fury shot at him, knowing it would only fuel his rage even more.

"I will get a special thrill out of killing you," Alex said, eyeing the winged demon.

"You can try," she said, smiling back at him.

"Alex, stop holding back. Just kill the bitch," Brandy pleaded with him again.

"That will not be necessary," Bastiquil said, stepping outside the door frame of the shop, unable to enter due to Demetri's spell he cast on the place before leaving. "You will give yourself up willingly or you will be responsible for the death of your friends and the little doggies who came to your rescue."

All action stopped as the exchange of words took place. The demon in charge had finally showed himself, which could only mean he was ready to end this battle.

"Alex, why do you fight your destiny. You can feel the powers coursing through your body. You can feel me, my blood, and my strength fueling you on. Did you think these powers were good? That they were like your witch friends? They are demonic in nature, just as you are my son. You know I am right. You can feel it deep inside."

"Leave him alone," Brandy screamed out at Bastiquil, who just turned his head and laughed at her.

"I am nothing like you, grandfather." The last word rolled off Alex's tongue with disgust that would have made any human grandfather cringe. But to this, Bastiquil beamed with pride.

"You are more like me than you think, my son. You have a rage inside you right now that even I am proud of. Your hate for me has grown and I love you for it. Together we will rule as one, father and son," Bastiquil smiled again, pride showing on his face. He took a step closer to the store, moving closer to Alex.

"We will never be anything but enemies. You will die at my hands tonight, or I will die trying," Alex said, determination in his voice, all the while making eye contact with Mathias. At this, Mathias nodded his head.

"You my father, will know what pain you have caused me." Alex spewed his hate at Bastiquil, stepping closer to him, as the demon spawn stepped out of his way. "You will feel what it is like to have your life ripped out from underneath you and ridicule be your solace."

Bastiquil looked at Alex, smiling as Alex continued towards him.

"What are you doing? Get out of here Alex," Brandy screamed, only to have Night Fury tighten her grip.

"You have destroyed everything in my life I hold dear to me. You have ripped the innocence forever away from my eyes. I no longer see the world as a safe and harmonic place. I see the filth that lies in it, no longer under the surface, but on top, in plain sight. I see you everywhere. The evil fighting to rise, to extinguish everything good and right. You father will know what pain you have caused me. You will fear that pain."

"You make me proud my son. Yes, yes, embrace your anger. Turn it against me and make me suffer. Take your hatred and let it manifest and make you stronger. You will need your strength if you are to defeat me," Bastiquil said to Alex, who was somewhat taken aback by the encouragement being received by the demon. "What, do you not think I know you want me gone, that you want to destroy me? Well, get on with it, boy. Do your best. It will take all of your rage, hatred, and fear to do it, but you can do it. You can destroy me if you really want to."

Alex continued his walk towards Bastiquil, and as he did, Brandy felt like she was stuck in a mad house. *Why didn't Alex see it was all a trap? You are doing exactly what he wants you to do. He wants you to attack him outside of the store. He wants that.* Her thoughts were screaming inside her head and as they raged on, Bastiquil looked at her and smiled as if reading her thoughts.

Alex looked over at Mathias as if they had their own secret agenda. Mathias nodded at him again. Brandy watched the exchange but didn't quite know what they thought they were going to do. Brandy could see even a change in the demeanor of the werewolves. It was almost as if there was a plan unfolding she wasn't privy to.

Her heart sank as Alex made a running dash at Bastiquil, hatred and rage screaming from him as he crossed the room and lunged at the door where Bastiquil stood. As he tackled him to the ground, the action on the inside commenced as well.

Mathias sent the bulk of the demon spawned zombies all flying off their feet and slammed them into the wall across the room from where he stood. Ethan and the other wolves moved towards Brandy with a speed that took her breath away, literally, as Ethan grabbed Night Fury by the arm, pulling her backwards, freeing Brandy as she fell to the ground.

Before she could catch her breath, another one of the werewolves who had arrived after Ethan, grabbed Brandy and headed towards the back of the store.

"No, wait! We have to save Alex," Brandy screamed, as tears rolled down her cheeks. But, even as she said the words, she knew now what the looks being exchanged between Alex and Mathias had meant. Somehow, even the wolves had sensed it. Alex never meant to make it out. He wanted her safe and was going to do what he had to do to make sure that happened, even if it meant his own death.

The only thing playing in her head was Alex tackling Bastiquil and them both in the night air. Her best friend had sacrificed himself. As the wolf carried her out the back door, Brandy watched in a blur while the other wolves followed them. *We are just leaving him, leaving him to die. And Mathias, what about him?*

Night Fury came running out the back door and turned their direction. She extended her wings, flapping them, her feet off the ground, and headed their way. But as she started to clear the building, she was immediately stopped, mid-flap and began to descend rapidly towards the ground. Before even having a chance to fight it, she slammed into the asphalt of the back alley, cracking it upon impact.

Mathias stepped out into the alley, walking over to where Night Fury lay unconscious on the ground and kicked her several times in the side. Brandy could tell he was angry, but couldn't make out anything being said. It gave her some resolve to see him turn and start running in the same direction as the wolves were taking her.

So Alex is the only one, the only one to not make it out. My dear sweet Alex lost again to me. Fight him Alex, make him pay. Tears were rolling down her cheeks as they all retreated, trying to get a safe distance between them and Bastiquil.

Chapter Fifty

Alex Rogers had never considered himself to be a hero. He had gone most of his life as a loner, keeping himself at arm's length from most people. Yes, there were a select few who he had gotten to know over the years who he had let inside his circle, but, as it turns out, the joke was on him. They were put in his life to befriend him and keep him safe.

The only one real friend he had was Brandy. She had been his constant, his rock, from the first day he met her. He had never doubted her sincerity, and never doubted her love for him. He knew she would have gladly died for him back there in the store, had he allowed it. But he had made sure that would not happen. He had taken Mathias aside when they were alone and told him exactly where he stood on the situation. He had laid it all out for him.

"Look, let me just give it to you straight. I was born into this world, an unwilling participant, but a major piece of the game. I have come to accept my part in that, but Brandy, she is innocent in all of this. The only thing she is guilty of is befriending me. She doesn't deserve this and she didn't deserve what happened to her back at the Balashon mansion. When this goes south, and believe me, it will, you have to promise to keep her safe. You will do whatever you have to do to get her out in one piece, even if it means leaving me behind. I will do my part, I will fight, but we both know you barely got us out of the tattoo studio alive. Bastiquil will be prepared for us this time. He will know what he is up against. He will come at us guns blazing and he will kill anyone in his way. Don't let that someone be Brandy or yourself. I know that you made a promise to protect us, and you can honestly say you have fulfilled that duty. If I am to be damned to an eternity of living with that beast inside me, then I would rather die first and not allow him the satisfaction. But, what I will not allow, is for him to do any more harm to her. Do I make myself clear?"

"Extremely clear, and as much as I hate to sound unsympathetic to you, I couldn't agree with you more. I will do as you ask of me, but only if I can tell that we have exhausted all other measures first. Then and only then, will I abandon you with a clear heart," Mathias said, shaking his hand.

Alex knew he could trust Mathias, he couldn't tell you how, but he just knew. So when he looked over at him, and he shook his head in agreement with Alex, that was enough to fuel Alex for what he had to do. It broke his heart to know that Brandy would be witness to this, but she had already been witness to so much already. He could remember the look in her eyes and the brokenness as she saw it was his mother, his own mother, who was under the red robe. It was his mother who had agreed to murder his best friend. She had plunged the knife into Brandy's chest and she had in turn plunged it into herself, leaving Alex with questions that will never have an answer.

Everything he ever thought he knew about her was a lie. She had deceived him all of these years, his entire life. He couldn't even tell you if she had conceived him out of love with his father or if his birth was an act of loyalty to his demonic royal bloodline, the blood line protected all of these years by the Balashon. It didn't matter really, it was all a big lie.

Demetri and Gina had tried to help him. They had done their best. But in the end, even Gina had paid a price for his birth. She had been taken and he didn't know if she was alive or not. He hoped she would survive this, that she would live on. She deserved to have a long and happy life. She was truly a good person. He would miss her, but she would be better off without him around. If he were around, it would mean that the entire membership of the Balashon would be around.

It all led up to this one moment, this one act. Whether he was a hero or a fool, maybe both, it didn't matter. If his friends could live because of his death, then he would gladly do this. He owed them this.

It's funny what flashes through your mind in a moment of high stress, of high anxiety, when you are put into a fight or flight mode. It was less about the accumulation of his life's memories and more about the recent years, recent weeks.

As he made impact with Bastiquil and they both went rolling into the parking lot outside of Gina's store, he felt satisfaction. He had to admit the fact that Bastiquil resided in his roommate, John's body, also made him want some revenge. Revenge on both of them. He wanted this battle to happen. He wanted the father and son battle to end. He would also take a knife into his own heart if it appeared he would not be able to defeat him.

Bastiquil's laughter only fueled his desire to defeat his maker. He jumped to his feet and began kicking at Bastiquil, screaming at him. But as he did, the laughter just kept coming. Alex could feel it building inside him, the rage, and the anger. But something else was also at work within him. Something he couldn't explain, but he hoped would allow him an advantage against his demon grandfather.

"Get up, get on your feet you sorry piece of shit. You are nothing more than a reject from hell's gates."

Bastiquil was on his knees, bent over, picking himself up off the ground when he turned his head to Alex. "What, my dear boy, does that make you then? If I am all that you say I am, and you are on this earth because of me, then what are you, boy? You call me a piece of shit, but I didn't sit idle when my own mother drove a knife into my best friend's chest? I didn't allow my mother to drive a knife into her gut, time and time again until she fell dead to the ground and was carried away by hell's hounds. I didn't allow my two lovers to run off together. Where are they I wonder?"

"Shut your mouth, shut your fucking mouth!"

"How does it feel to know that the man you tried to seduce, the one you let jerk you off in the showers, is probably having sex with your precious witch right this minute?"

Alex could not stand the taunting any longer. The buildup he had felt before came flying out of him at Bastiquil. It came out as a scream, a guttural roar. The air between them became filled with waves of sound. Sound that carried with it a lethal force. Windows shattered as he released his anger, cars rocked back and forth where they were parked. But the most welcome sight was when he saw Bastiquil, in John's body, explode upon the force of power Alex hit him with.

All that could be heard over Alex's sobs as he hit the pavement was the car alarms going off which had been hit with the vibrations of the scream. He was sobbing for many reasons, but mostly because he was gone. He didn't have to listen to any more lies coming from his mouth. Even though some was truth, the bulk of what he had said was pure manipulation.

Even the sound of the alarms couldn't mask the laugh that hit Alex's ear like fingernails to a chalk board. He grabbed the knife in his pocket as he looked up at what was left of John's body.

"You thought you could destroy me? Me? The one who created you, who gave you those powers," Bastiquil's voice could be heard as a red mist came up from what could only have been the cellular remains of John. It swirled back

257

and forth until it was moving in a circular motion, with flashes of Bastiquil's demon form visible within the mist. "You can't kill me. I am forever. All you have done is what I have wanted you to do and that is clear a path for me. Create a way for me to come home to you."

As he heard the words being spoken, a calm overtook Alex. He opened up the knife, revealing a four-inch blade. Raising the knife upwards, he smiled at Bastiquil, who just looked at Alex with awe and admiration. "You will not have this body demon. You can go back to hell. No body, no demon."

Even before Alex started to move the blade down towards his heart, Bastiquil had already begun advancing on him, the red mist leading him to Alex. The mist hit Alex and went inside his mouth, nose, and ears, making its way inside him anyway it could. The black form of Bastiquil also hit him with such force that it knocked the blade right out of his hand as it was inches from his heart.

Alex seized back and forth as Bastiquil made his way inside him, back into the body he called home. As he did so, the army he had assembled, the ones that had survived, made their way towards him. They had a curious look about them but knew that this must be a good thing. As the body stopped seizing and came to rest, it looked upon them, eyes fully blackened. Falling to their knees, they all began chanting, "Hail Bastiquil!"

Chapter Fifty-One

The searing pain that was hitting Demetri's brain made him stop in his tracks. It was debilitating and hurt much worse than the shrapnel that had just been pulled from his leg. He tried to shake it, knowing that Aldrik had just charged the man and needed his help. But it would not leave.

Flashes were hitting his brain, images of something taking place, but he could not figure out what it was. Each time he tried to get to his feet, the pain brought him back down. Grabbing both sides of his head, he screamed and as he did a solid image appeared to him. The image was of John standing outside of Gina's store.

He was being given glimpses into what had just taken place back in Tulsa, back where the other half of their team was battling a demon while he and Aldrik battled something not of this world. He saw Alex use his powers to blow up the body of John, freeing the demon. *How can this be happening?*

"No!" Demetri screamed out, not being able to distinguish reality from the vision. "No Alex! You cannot kill yourself. That isn't the answer." The last thing he saw before the pain in his head subsided was the demon entering Alex's body, taking hold of the vessel again. He was thankful for the pain to subside, but the visions did not go away. He remained within the vision, the images still playing before him like a movie reel.

Demetri could hear the demon's army banding around him, chanting their accolades for his arrival. But as the eyes of Alex, blackened with the demon's power looked upwards, they appeared to be looking at Demetri.

"Zamaranum, you have chosen the wrong side. You thought you could send me back? Not this time, my friend. Such amateur play. I did not expect this from you. You have scattered memories, and even more scattered powers. You cannot defeat me and since you chose not to join me, you will die like the rest. Father and son are whole again. Their power linked again. You will regret the day you thought you could get the best of me, friend," Bastiquil spewed.

"What have you done to them? If you have harmed them in any way, I promise you, I will find a way to kill you. I won't just send you back to the depths of hell, I will demolish you, as if you never existed."

"Come now, Zamaranum. You dare threaten me? You know I cannot be destroyed. Look into yourself and you will find that I am telling the truth. I am as old as the earth, and yet, still a blink in the pendulum of time. You can do your worst if you wish, but I can assure you, I will still be standing when you are done," Bastiquil glared at him, walking closer as if he were walking into the movie watcher's line of sight.

"If you look past the huffing and puffing your ego is boasting right now, you will know that I believe within my entire being that I can eliminate you," Demetri glared back at him.

"Well, you cannot even defeat the creature in your midst right now, how do you expect to defeat me?" Bastiquil let out a laugh that was more like a roar.

Demetri was abruptly brought back from this vision by the screaming in the background. As he shook his head, feeling the dizziness of the vision and the lingering words of Bastiquil, Demetri could finally make out the struggle which was taking place just feet from where he sat in the grassy field.

260

He saw Aldrik being lifted into the air by the giant and tossed onto the huge rock. Pieces of the rock shattered from the impact. Aldrik was up and moving again towards the giant, but just as he was about to reach him, the giant swung out with its massive blade, slicing Aldrik's abdomen open.

Demetri's heart sank as he let out a scream, which sounded more like a gasp. "No!"

Looking over at Demetri, Aldrik smiled, but just as quickly as the smile appeared, it disappeared. He fell to the ground, blood spilling, body exposed. He was looking in the direction of Demetri, but his eyes were vacant, distant, and lifeless.

Enraged, Demetri jumped to his feet, focusing his energy at the beast who had just taken down the love of his life. His thoughts were intense, his body alive with energy. He didn't realize it, but he was floating off the ground, hovering over the spot where he had just been standing. His chest bowed outward, an energy shot forth from his body, speeding at the giant who was now looking his direction.

As the giant stepped forward, the energy hit him on the chest, sending him stumbling backward, but still on his feet. His body tensed as he regained his footing and continued toward Demetri, kicking Aldrik aside as he passed.

Demetri began focusing his energy, conjuring thoughts of magical spells, both old and new. His arms stretched out in front of him, he cupped his hands together and began chanting an ancient spell, one he knew, but should not have known. Within his hands, the air began to spiral, become dense as the displacement was becoming visible. Within seconds, a fireball appeared within his cupped palms. He sent it forth, just as the giant was within a few feet of him, hitting his left shoulder, burning the skin and knocking him onto the ground.

Demetri hovered closer to him, chanting, concentrating on making another ball of fire to hurl at the thing. But he was up and off the ground before Demetri could. Grabbing him by the feet, the giant flung Demetri to the ground, stunning and knocking the breath out of him. The giant was relentless in its attack on him, tossing him around.

Demetri had been up against some strong foes before, but this one seemed to not be fazed at all by the attempts at magic on him, and as for physical contact, well, he wasn't able to get many punches in. This was definitely a supernatural being, made from wickedly strong magic. He was defeating one of the best and all Demetri could think about was finding a way to get the better of him so he could run to Aldrik's side.

He lay on his back looking upward at the undead creature as a foot was brought down towards Demetri's abdomen. Reaching deep within, he summoned all the strength he had left in him and hurled an energy ball at the giant's foot, sending him flying backward off his feet.

Dizzy, confused, bleeding and aching all over, Demetri turned and crawled on the ground towards Aldrik. He had to see if he was still alive. He knew it would take a lot to kill him, but the blade cut deeply, damaging so much on the inside. Almost to Aldrik's side, Demetri cringed as he heard a thud of a foot vibrate from the thing he had just knocked over. He had been so concerned about Aldrik's condition, that he had not finished the fight and destroyed the beast.

As the vibrations intensified, he knew it was running at him. Demetri rolled over on his back with every intention of hitting him with another energy ball, but as he turned over, he was face to face with the beast. The last thing he remembered was a massive fist headed towards his head and then nothing.

Chapter Fifty-Two

Arabel and Athdara had longed for the day when they would be able to walk this earth once again, to bring Urguhart Castle back to its former glory. But that day was not today. The sister witches had risked much to secure this magical being they had in tow. She was the grand prize, one who would help them in their quest to restore the world back to its former glory. The day when witches and warlocks were feared, not respected, but humans knew to stay out of their way for fear of being killed, or even worse, turned into one of their walking dead.

No, today was not the day for them, but it was fast approaching. They would once again be beautiful, powerful and not have to be hidden behind the fallen remnants of their once beautiful castle.

As they made their way back onto the grounds of the castle, a sense of pride and accomplishment took over. Knowing they still had many months ahead of them before the time for their resurfacing to the world was bittersweet. But it was a bitterness they were willing to swallow. After three hundred fifty years, what was another few months?

They had work to do, extremely important work. They would have to prep this undertaking themselves, sending out word to the remaining clan. They were not the massive clan they once were, but with this magical being by their side, they soon would be. They made their way down into the depths of the castle, down into the parts that no one living knew about. It smelled of earth and dampness, of ages long gone. The passages they made their way through weren't on any map, this they had made sure of. To live so long without discovery had taken patience, planning, and complete isolation. It was a maze, a labyrinth of tunnels that led deep within the ground, running alongside the lake, twisting and turning. With each step they took they came to another torch which lit up just from their presence. The sisters exuded energy.

Gina was in tow between the witches, fast asleep, never waking from the moment they swooped her out of the hotel bed. She was under their spell, floating silently and peacefully into the depths of the tunnels which lay under the ruins of the castle.

Both witches were happy and proud to have secured the powerful witch. They delighted in the knowledge that she was young, with little guidance and leadership in her true potential. She would soon learn she had the power within her to raise an army of witches, warlocks, dragons, and many other creatures and beings thought only to be myth. She could raise an army of the undead. One to match any army of this day and age.

Yes, they had planning to do, but their fates had shown them this years ago. The powers of the cards, the looking glass, and the books all foretold of this day. They did not know when it was to happen, but feeling the strength of this one, when she touched foot on their homeland, a surge of power coursed through the land. The sisters picked up on this power and knew it had to be her. It had to be the one the books foretold would come and set them free. But this young witch needed time and grooming. She would need to be put through rigorous tests and trials if she was to tap into the powers she needed.

The thought thrilled them beyond delight, which was an emotion they had not felt for centuries. Not since they had locked themselves away from the world which they had grown weary of. As they made their way towards the end of the tunnel, they could make out the stone wall which held behind it thousands of years of magical knowledge. It was their home, or what had become their home, after they made the decision to withdraw from the world.

As they approached the hidden doorway leading into their self-entombed dwelling, Athdara held out her diamond tipped staff and the rock wall gave way, letting out a waft of musky air as it did. Entering through the door, the witches were relieved to be back in the protective solitude of their safe haven, the only home they had known for hundreds of years.

The witch they had secured was still floating as they entered safely into the room. She was led over to a rock table, ancient and sacrificial looking. Gina was lowered down onto the table which set in the middle of the large room. Arabel then waved her hand quickly and immediately Gina's hands, feet, and neck were secured with a stone looking rope. Still fast asleep, the witches were not concerned with her at the moment and went about their business.

All around the room there were traces of magical instruments. Some of the relics were from age's long past, dating back much older than the sister's years combined. Collectors of these artifacts, but much more important, believers in them, they stand watch over the magical conduits waiting for the time when they would be used again.

Candles were lit everywhere, and they burned bright but didn't melt wax. There was not a comfort to this room as most would have in their homes for it was used for wielding the craft and storage of artifacts. But there was much more to their dwelling space than just the room in which Gina lay sleeping. There were bedrooms for each of the sisters, although they did not require sleep anymore. Once, long ago, they lived and functioned much like any other human being.

But the sisters gave that up long ago, for the powers that flowed through their bodies now.

Further into their dwelling space were other rooms, some for storage, some used many years ago like a kitchen. There was also a dungeon which held many strong magical charms, in which to hold their captives over the years. But the dungeon was empty now. If the sisters have their way, it will once again be filled with magical creatures in which they can draw more strength from.

"When the time is right, we will awaken some of the most terrifying, gruesome beasts this unappreciative world has yet to see. It has gone soft, relying on mechanics and electricity. No one in this day and age can even fathom what a dragon can actually do, let alone what creatures lie just a veil away, a little rip in time. We are so close my dear sister to fulfilling our dreams," Arabel cooed with excitement and longing.

"These fools today think they know what terror is? Well, they don't. There was a time long ago when the darkness was respected and feared. The shadows carried much more than just a silhouette of oneself. The shadows used to reach out and grab you. Eat you up whole," Athdara squealed quickly, thrusting her hands up for emphasis. "A darkness is coming, one that will rain blood down on this world. The moon, from whom we gain much power, will shine red, red like blood. When the moon is full, it will rise a full Blood Moon. That is how we will know, sister. When the moon shines red, it will be a signal to the entire magical world that their empire is rising."

"Yes, sister. We will once again see our world brought back to its darkened splendor. We will once again be free to rebuild our kingdom, feed our thirst, in the light of the red moon," Arabel paced back and forth. "So much blood will spill, so much death, for us to gain our freedom. But it will be worth it to see the true giants, the true wonders of this world running free once again."

266

Walking over to a wall on the far side of the room, Arabel waved her hand and the wall seemed to disappear, leaving the appearance of a window. It was magic at play, but it still showed what she had intended. Beyond the window lay a body of water, Loch Ness, the second largest body of water in Scotland, but the deepest by volume. As she stood looking, she saw what she was looking for, her baby, her pet.

"They call you Nessie my dear, but soon they will know your true name. Soon they will know all of you, for you are not one, but many. You will no longer be bound by the silence we have asked of you. You will be able to be the beautiful creature you were born to be." Arabel spoke to it, as it swam by again, its singing echoing back at her. She smiled as she closed up the magical portal.

"The time is near, we must prepare. We must gather the coven, and awaken the army. We will not fall into the depths of banishment again, we will fight for our freedom and annihilate anyone or anything that tries to stop us."

Chapter Fifty-Three

The tears would not stop flowing down Brandy's face. She lost him, found him, and now had lost him all over again. *I wish I had powers to fight that fucking Bastiquil. I want him gone. I want him dead. I want him to know fucking pain like no other pain has ever been felt.* Frustrated, she laid her head back against the sofa, in Mathias' Tulsa home.

Just beyond, in the other room, she heard them talking. Ethan, Mathias, and the other six werewolves who had helped save her. But not Alex. *I'm so sorry Alex, I'm so sorry. We will find a way, we will get you back.* Brandy knew they needed Gina and Demetri. They needed people with as much power as Bastiquil to be able to save Alex.

Her anger, fear, and frustration were getting the better of her and she could no longer sit on the couch idly pouting, waiting for someone to do something. Getting up from the sofa, she walked into the dining room where all of the men were gathered. When she appeared in the doorway, a hush fell over the room.

"Don't stop on my behalf," Brandy stated. "One of you I hope has an idea of how we are going to stop Bastiquil's army and get Alex back?"

"We are working on it, but we are not even sure what we are up against now that he has rejoined with Alex's body," Mathias stated the obvious concern in the room.

"Well, someone in this room had better tell me that we are not giving up?" Brandy looked around at each of them, one by one, searching their faces for a sign of where their heads might be in this fight.

"No, we are not giving up, but rather regrouping," Ethan offered. "You saw those things, they were ferocious and strong."

"Yes, they were. But aren't you even stronger? Aren't you able to get an entire pack of werewolves here that we can use to attack them," Brandy pleaded.

"It's not that simple," Ethan spoke up. "Rumor on the street is that the last time this demon was in your friend's body, he had control over everything, vampires, humans, and even werewolves. No one but Demetri was able to battle him. Right now, we are thinking that Demetri is all we have and he isn't even in the country."

"So what, you are giving up? You are going to let him get away with this, to start killing and ravaging this city?" Brandy couldn't hide her emotions, especially her anger.

"That is not what we are saying at all." A tall, solid man of obvious Native American decent stood up from the table. "My name is Chief Mitsis Shomecossee, Chief Wise Wolf. My friends call me Basil. I am the leader of the wolf clan on Lake Tenkiller."

"Are we friends, Basil?" Brandy asked, glaring at him. "Because I just met you."

"Come on Brandy, take it easy. Everyone in there was trying their hardest to help get Alex out. It was Alex who made the decision to get you out and to take on the demon himself," Mathias tried to tell her.

"Speaking of which, I saw the look you two exchanged with each other. Did you not think I would see it? Do you think I am some stupid blond bimbo who can't see what transpired in there? You left him there to die."

269

"No one is saying anything of the sort," Mathias blurted. "I can't believe you would think anything like that, especially after everything we have been through together."

"Oh, really? You think that just because you saved me, that I should be grateful it was me who made it out and not my best friend?"

"That is quite enough, young lady," Basil said, in a tone that made Brandy stop and listen. "A lot of people put their life on the line tonight, to save some complete strangers. My son, Ethan, is one of them, and I for one, am glad he made it out alive. I am sorry about your friend, but he broke free and went at the demon, we didn't make him. I understand you are upset, and rightfully so, but your anger needs to be focused on something other than the people who tried to help you."

Brandy's eyes filled with tears as the weight of his words and the realization of what she was saying to these people began to sink in. "I'm so sorry," she said sobbing.

Mathias got up and walked over and put his arm around her shoulders. "Hey, don't cry. We will figure something out."

Turning to him and wrapping her arms around him, she cried, letting it out as the others watched, some looking towards the ground, not knowing what to do. They all stood there in silence for what seemed like an eternity. Brandy collected herself, wiped her eyes and looked at Mathias. The exchange was something neither had expected.

Composed and ready, she turned to the group of men who had indeed saved her life tonight. "I want to apologize to you. I am racked with worry, mourning, and fatigue. You didn't deserve any of what I said to you and I understand if you wish to bow out now. No one, especially me, can blame you if you do."

"No one is going anywhere," Basil said, standing up and speaking to the group. "We are all here for one reason, and one reason only. We owe a debt to Demetri and we will see that debt paid. We will fight for what is right, for what we believe to be a threat to humanity, even though most of humanity imagines us to be barbaric. We will not give up so quickly, and even though we stand here defeated, we still have a war raging and we will rise to the call. We are Lykens, and we are proud people. We are a quiet people, but we will not stand idly by and watch this demon terrorize a city that has fought so long and hard to find peace amongst the various races of supernatural and human beings. So put on your brave face Brandy, for we will find a way."

Brandy was smiling at Basil, so happy that she had not offended him enough that he would have walked out of here. She felt safety with the numbers around her and she felt safe with Mathias. They would have to come up with a plan that didn't include Demetri and Gina. They couldn't guarantee they would be back here anytime soon or at all. So, it was up to them. They would do this or die trying. She had to believe that there was some part of Alex still left inside the demon. She would reason with him, reason with Alex and try to get him to fight from the inside. She had to. There was no other way.

Mathias held his arm around Brandy, helping to steady her as they all committed to sticking together and making an attempt at saving Alex.

The room was quiet, everyone deep in thought. It was Ethan who broke the silence as he stood up from the table, grabbed his empty glass, and started to walk away.

"I'm feeling a bit parched….," was all that came out of his mouth as the glass hit the floor, shattering into pieces. Ethan was next to hit the floor. His body was seizing and contracting.

Basil ran to his side, as did Brandy.

"Don't try and stop him. Just keep him from hurting himself until it stops," Brandy said, as she knelt down beside him.

271

"What the hell is happening to him?" Justin, one of the pack, asked.

"He is having a seizure," Basil said, calmly.

This had taken Brandy by surprise as he seemed too calm, but she had to remind herself, he is the chief of a pack of werewolves and he must see lots of things.

As soon as the seizing stopped, Brandy began looking around his body, looking for any sign of an allergic reaction to a sting or insect bite. Then she unbuttoned his shirt and pulled it back and she gasped at seeing multiple snake bites on his chest, shoulders, and upper arms.

"I remember him being attacked in the store by two men who had snakes coming out of their arms. The snakes were snapping at him, and he yelled out in pain. It must have been the demon's doing," Brandy said, looking at Basil and then back at Mathias. "We have to get him to a hospital."

"A hospital cannot help him now. I have some people who will be able to help. We still have medicine doctors, healers within the tribe who work some amazing marvels. I have to get him home, though. I'm sorry, but that means I will have to leave, but I will leave the others behind, to help you, to keep you safe."

Brandy reached over and hugged him. "I'm so sorry he got hurt helping us."

"Ethan is a good boy, young and impulsive, but he comes by it honestly. We would do it over again if we had to. We must leave you now. I'm sorry. We will be back as soon as we can, but it will take some time for them to work out the demon's magic from his blood," Basil said, looking at Brandy with soft, caring eyes. Then he turned and quickly spoke to the others. "Justin, Nathaniel, grab ahold of your cousin and get him to my truck. I must get him home as quickly as possible."

The boys jumped up and ran to Ethan's side. They picked him up and carried him to the truck. Mathias was once again at Brandy's side as she stood in the doorway, looking at Basil and Ethan as they pulled out of the driveway. Basil looked back at them and raised his hand to bid them farewell. Brandy raised her hand and waved goodbye.

An uneasy feeling began to creep back into her, one that was eating away at her confidence. They were dropping, one by one, and if they didn't figure something out soon, they would all perish at the hands of this demon.

Chapter Fifty-Four

Victor was out of breath by the time he had come to the end of the trail. He prided himself on being one of the best trackers in the world He had tracked the witches the best he could by staying caught up with the fog.

He went with his instincts, his gut, which had never led him astray and it looks like today was no different. When he came to the top of a hill, looking down into the valley, there was a clearing leading right up to Lock Ness. He could see a castle or the ruins of one, and as he scanned it, he caught the end of the fog disappearing into the cliff's edge of the castle. *I got you, evil crones!*

He took off in a run, trying to make it to the cliff's edge before the fog was gone for good. He had never encountered an entity before that left no trail for him other than fog. The fog moved at an incredible speed. These were some powerful witches indeed. He would have to be extra cunning with them, as he was still not fully recovered from his injuries. The pain he could handle. He was used to pain, and pain made him feel alive. It was the injuries and the toll it had taken on him that left his body feeling drained and not up to full strength.

Jumping over rocks and other obstacles, making his way to the cliff's edge, he dove to the ground, leaning over to see where the entrance point for the fog was, but he had missed it. *What the hell am I going to do now? They have*

Gina, who knows where inside these ruins of a castle. Master will not be pleased about this. I will get her back, one way or another and these ole witches will rue the day they messed with Bastiquil's plans.

As he worked himself into a fury over the ambush they had received, he noticed something below. It appeared that the cliff went straight down to the water, but it actually did not, it was a three-dimensional illusion. *Extremely clever witches! I will give you that, but you have to do a hell of a lot better than this to outwit me.*

Victor was on his feet, moving around the edge, looking for a hidden entrance along the cliff's edge. It had to be here, it had to be. *Look, Victor, concentrate. Find the fucking entrance.* He started to panic a little, but it wasn't what other people would call panic. There was so much confidence in his abilities that panic to Victor was like child's play, a game to overcome, to win. It fueled him, the intrigue, the mystery, and the desire to rip the heads right off of these two wenches.

Frustration and anger started to remove what panic he had been feeling. He was getting more pissed by the minute. He was not seeing an entrance point and he would be making a huge leap of faith in his own abilities to just go over the edge and drop down to the trail. He was pretty confident it existed, but it was a high-risk plan of action. He had to be sure. His death was not what he hesitated for, it was Gina who made him heed with caution. Her safety and return to the master was the ultimate goal. The master asked that it be done, and he would deliver her safely. Failure was not an option.

Noises came from the direction behind him and put him on high alert. His instincts and senses were working in overdrive. Ducking behind a fallen wall of the castle, he waited for what was coming. He planned on it being the witches. By all assumptions, they should be where the fog disappeared. But he lay low, waiting, watching, and ready to pounce when the opportunity presented itself.

What came walking over the hill took him by surprise. Not much surprised him, because in his world, anything was possible. But the giant approaching held his complete attention. He had only heard legends of this beast. Durward, doorkeeper, or warder of the gate. He had many names. The witches he was tracking were much more than just your ordinary witches. This was the darkest of magic. To be able to command such power to create the Durward, well, this was not a good sign. It could mean only one thing. Whatever the master recognized in Gina, these witches must have sensed it too. This may be the battle to the death he had always known he would face one day.

As the Durward came closer, he was able to make out that he was carrying something, or rather, someone. The strength in this thing was incredible. He had whatever, or whomever it was, draped over one forearm, carrying it as if it were a shirt flung over its arm. What came next, Victor had not, nor could not have planned. As the Durward was within feet of him, he could make out that it was carrying Demetri, the witch from Tulsa. *Oh, this was a fun twist, a fun one indeed. The Durward had not only fought the witch, but it had defeated him too. If only his master were here to see this.*

Victor watched as the Durward approached the edge of the cliff, a huge blade in tow. The blade with a handle was taller than Victor. *Such a beautiful creature, such poise, and power.*

He held in his breath, trying not make a sound. The last thing he needed at this moment was to attract attention. He had faced many powerful beings before, even the one who had fallen to the Durward, Demetri, but if he could get through this without having to take on that creature he was going to do it. Just the sight of it was impressive. It moved with such self-control and elegance for a dead being. The same is most often said about vampires and their graceful movements, but the Durward wasn't a vampire, it wasn't being controlled by demonic blood. It was a dead being, raised by powerful magic, manipulated, contorted and made into this massive creature walking in front of him.

Victor watched him as he came to a point at the cliff's edge and took a step off the cliff, into the air. But instead of free falling and plunging into the lake below, the Durward began to walk along the cliff, slowly downward as he began to fade and the pointed metal mask disappeared from view.

He immediately jumped up and quickly, but quietly ran to the edge and peered over. A small pebble that moved from the brush of his foot fell over the edge and hit the hidden walkway below. As it made impact with the path, with the slightest of sounds, made the creature stop, turn, and look back in his direction. Of course, Victor had rolled away from the edge, once again holding his breath, not wanting to see the creature alter its current trajectory. He needed to find a way into the witch's chambers and get to Gina. What he didn't want to happen was to distract the creature from his task at hand, which appeared to be disposing of Demetri.

He had decided that he couldn't wait any longer. Like it or not, he had to get on this path or risk not finding the entrance. Placing his foot out on the ledge, he securely planted one foot on the path while balancing the rest of the weight of his body backward, just in case the path did not appear for him. The witches were strong, they could have made a magical path that only they and their chosen ones could walk. Fortunately for him, they had not.

He eased his way down, trying not to make the mistake of unnecessary noise. The path was quite impressive, three dimensional, so it looked as if it were part of the cliff wall but invisible to the naked eye. Magic was strong here. You could almost smell it in the air. As he inched his way downward, he stopped as the creature paused and turned towards the cliff wall. Victor placed his entire body as close to the wall as he could so as not to draw attention from the

Durward. His eyes were cut as much as they could be so he could watch how it planned to enter.

To his amazement, he just walked directly into the wall and disappeared from his view. Relaxing his posture, he turned and made his way down to where the creature had entered. Standing in what he thought was the exact same position, Victor found himself standing in front of a rock wall. *What the hell? He just walked through rock, or maybe it closed up once he was inside.* Either way, unless he figured something out, Gina's fate would be sealed with those witches.

Raising his hands towards the wall, he placed them close to the rock itself and instantly felt a tingling of magic. It has a warming sensation, almost a prickle effect. It warmed his entire body. He had felt it many times over the years, especially in the early years with the Balashon when he was being trained to combat such magical creatures as the ones he encountered today. Moving his hands closer, they began to enter the rock, become one with it. The energy used to make this faux doorway was intense. His body was on fire.

Then he felt hands clasped around his forearms. Enormous and powerful hands. His adrenaline kicked in and his heart began to race. He braced himself for battle with the giant Durward. But, as he was initially pulled forward a bit, he was immediately flung backward and off the cliff plunging towards the lake below.

Chapter Fifty-Five

The men sat quietly waiting, watching, as he paced the room, looking at each one closely and intently. They did not know what he was thinking, but knew he didn't look happy. Among them were five men who they did not know, but what they did know was that they were confused, frightened, and also wearing uniforms from the Tulsa Police Department. As he walked by one of the younger members, a handsome man, he reached out and ran his fingers through the young man's hair and let them run down onto his cheek. The young man looked up at him and smiled hopefully.

"You have failed me," he said to the young man. "You, so beautiful, young and rich, so full of vitality and life, I bet you just get all of the woman and men hot, don't you?" Once again, he ran his fingers through the man's hair, stroking it, making him feel at ease. Then out of nowhere, he snapped the man's neck, letting his chin fall to this chest as if he were sleeping. But an eerie chill swept the room as the other men looked at the young man who sat in his chair, dead, but eyes wide open, as if looking through their soul.

"You have all failed me. I have spent the last three thousand years making you all wealthy men, your ancestor's wealthy men, making you all the most powerful humans on this earth. And what happens? The first instance of problems, you run like mice scattering from a cat on the hunt. You may have technology on your side in this generation, but you lack the integrity of your ancestors. You lack the killer instinct. When the witch attacked, you should have been ready to pounce, to step up and welcome death while trying to defeat him. But you didn't, you cowered and ran. I am disgusted by you. But I am not giving up on you just yet. This young man here, he may be dead, but even he still fuels my fire, quenches my hunger. His soul will fuel me for the battle to come."

The rest of the room, which was but a fraction of the Balashon, was looking intently at their master, afraid to answer, afraid to speak out. They had thought him dead until those who were left in Tulsa had been summoned by his new creations, his new fledglings. Shocked to hear about Bastiquil's quick return, they came as they were told. Unsure of what they would find, they had their own trepidations about seeing him. But when they walked inside and saw him in the vessel's body, healthy and thriving, they were overcome with joy. Then slowly, one by one, he began to stalk them, walk by them individually appraising them until he snapped the young man's neck.

This put each of them on alert. He was aware of their intentions of leaving town; of thinking he was dead and not returning. Had they known, they would have been by his side, they would have been caring to his every need.

"You have shown me weak, spineless, and cowardice behavior. Why should I keep granting you the luxuries you have grown accustomed to? You were willing to go back into those lives, to leave me for dead, to step back into your powerful companies and live out the rest of your days calling this effort a complete failure." He was raising his voice at them as he walked around the library of the mansion. "But you will all have a chance at redemption. Strip off your clothes and leave them where they fall."

The men looked around at each other and decided it best to do what the master was asking. Each stood, stripping off the clothes they had on, letting each article fall to the floor as they were instructed.

Bastiquil was walking around the room, looking at each of them. He stopped at a man who stood six foot, two inches tall, extremely handsome, and looked him up and down. "I said to take your clothes off. That means your underwear too."

The man hooked his thumbs into the band of his underwear and pushed them down from his waist, lifting his feet out of them as they hit the ground.

Bastiquil smiled at him, at his willingness to do as he was commanded. Then he looked down at the man's cock, then back up at the man's eyes. "You are a beautiful man. But you already know that don't you?"

The man looked at him, nervous, but also excited that his master acknowledged him. "I am what I am because of you master. If I am beautiful in your eyes, it is all because of you and the many gifts you have bestowed upon me and my family before me. We would be nothing without you and the fact that we have failed you brings shame to me and my ancestors. Your gifts have been many and we love you master. Please accept my apologies and know that I am grateful for all of your blessings. How can I make it up to you my master? How can I please you and make you know my loyalty lies with you?"

Bastiquil grabbed the man and began to kiss him, pressing his tongue through the man's lips until it touched his tongue. As he kissed him deeply, passionately, the tattoos that adorned Bastiquil's body took life and reached out from his body enwrapping the man and pulling him closer to Bastiquil. The man felt Bastiquil's hardness against his nude body and in turn, his cock began to become erect. He felt the many hands, rubbing and holding his body tightly to his master. He felt the strength, passion, and warmth of the kiss.

Holding him tightly, but turning his head to address the group, he smiled at them. "You will all join me now, not just in allegiance, but you will all carry my blood with you, my mark will be with you, making it impossible for us to ever be seperated. We will become one."

An elderly man stood up to address Bastiquil. "What do you mean my lord?"

"You will carry my blood, tattooed within your skin. My blood will flow within your body. What an honor it will be for you to have me inside you."

"But what can an old man like me do for you, master?"

Bastiquil stopped smiling at the man and just glared at him. *Night Fury, get this maggot out of my sight.*

The group heard something coming but didn't know yet what it was. Then, Night Fury came flying into the room, hovering about the tall vaulted ceiling. In her hand, she carried a sword. She looked at her Master.

Bastiquil nodded and with that, she flung herself down, sword held out until the blade made contact with the old man's face, piercing it until what used to be his nose met the handle of the sword. The other men in the room dared not make a sound or acknowledge what had just happened for fear they would be next.

One man fell to his knees and began chanting, "Hail Bastiquil. Hail Bastiquil."

Every man in the room fell to their knees and joined in the chanting.

The doors opened and a group of men came in carrying tattoo guns, ink, and other supplies needed to make Bastiquil's plan come to life. *These men will soon learn the consequences for their greed and lack of action. I will take them and we shall join Victor and the beautiful witch in Europe and we will be one. Then I will deal with the rest of the Balashon members who fled and left me for dead. As for the police officers, I am going to be putting a lot of faith in them to cleanup and run interference here in Tulsa for anyone getting too close to figuring out what has really been going on. Their tattoos will be special. They will make them powerful and my blood will enhance their intelligence.*

He smiled to himself as he thought of rejoining them in Europe. Things would be different this time around. Things would go according to plan. He would start small and build his army a little at a time. He would use the full resources of the Balashonian empire to start taking over every aspect of the business world. He would lead them into a glorious new age, where evil would once again rule and people would give proper respect to him and his army.

A little bit of him felt a tingle of pleasure as the first tattoo gun fired up and the buzzing sound filled his ears. He didn't know though if it were him feeling it or a part of Alex still in there feeling nostalgic at the sound.

Chapter Fifty-Six

Fear had been a familiar companion over the past few weeks. She had feared for Alex and his dreams, then about Demetri and Gina and what they were plotting against Alex. But even when she was given reason to trust them, the knowledge about the demon came forth and once again she was thrust into fear mode. Being kidnaped had not helped to curb or ease the feeling of fear, but now knowing that Alex had gone up against the demon, she had a new respect for the fear she felt. It fed her, kept her alert and thinking. She had to find a way to help him.

Then there was Ethan, poor Ethan. And she had seemed so unappreciative of their help. That wasn't her intent at all, but she knew it came out that way, and now, even he was fighting for his life. But something told her Basil would take care of him. He had a strong personality. She felt his leadership and his love for his son.

As for Alex, she would find a way. Science has led her down a path where she did not believe in a heaven or hell. She could be more swayed to the fact of a heaven in which people described a calming, peaceful feeling once death was upon them and inevitable. But as for hell, she didn't buy it, not now, not ever. This creature could not be a "demon" from hell. It just couldn't. There had to be an explanation for it.

She sat pondering her thoughts, her beliefs and what had actually transpired over the past few weeks and she had to admit, it sounded almost crazy. If she were telling her peers this, they would laugh her out of the room. It went against everything she knew to be true. The big bang, evolution and the cellular makeup of a person did not involve hell. Hell just did not compute into that equation.

Mathias came up to her and handed her a cup of hot tea and then joined her on the sofa. "What can I do for you? Tell me if there is anything you need."

"You are already doing what you can. Unless we can come up with a way to save Alex, then there is nothing you can do."

"I understand what you are saying about Alex, but I'm talking about you, and what I can do to help ease some of your burdens."

"I will be okay. You have been more than kind to me and have saved me on more than one occasion. It means the world to me, you just being here. Sitting with me is a huge help," Brandy said, blushing a bit. "I honestly don't know what I would do without you."

Catching her blush, he in turn blushed. "I will protect you until my last breath. That I swear to you."

"You are so sweet. Thank you. I hope it doesn't come to that."

Mathias was looking at her, feeling something he had never felt before. Yes, he had lusted after women before, but this was a new feeling for him. They had been through a battle together. She was a strong and powerful woman, and he found that extremely appealing. It didn't hurt that she was a knockout, but it felt more than that.

"So, do you have a boyfriend," he asked, testing the waters, feeling vulnerable and regretting the way he had just phrased it. It made him sound like he was in junior high school.

"Well, um, no, I don't have a boyfriend," Brandy said, smiling and unsure of where he was going with this. "Are you flirting with me, Mathias?"

Blushing, he thought about looking away but dared not break eye contact with her. "Would it be horrible if I were?"

"No, sweetie, it would not be horrible. I am not really sure what to say. I'm flattered."

"Oh, okay, I guess flattered is a start," he said, hanging his head, taking in the humiliation he had just put himself through. *How could you be so stupid to think she would be into you? You idiot!*

But his humiliation turned into something much more, when she leaned over, put her hand on his chin and lifted his head to where he was looking directly into her eyes.

"I said flattered. I didn't say I wasn't interested," she said, as she leaned in and kissed his lips.

He met her kiss and had to keep telling himself to not rush it, keep it cool and calm. But as she kept kissing him, and didn't pull away like he expected her to, he slipped his hand behind her head and his tongue into her mouth. He could feel the growing affection for her in his jeans as she began to suck slightly on his tongue. He was in new territory and wasn't quite sure what to do, or where to go from here.

He didn't have to wait long to figure it out, as she stopped kissing him, stood up and grabbed his hand. "Where is your bedroom?"

"Um, it's down the hallway and to the right."

"Well, I don't want to go alone, so why don't you show me." Brandy smiled at him.

"Oh, right. Yes, sorry. This way." Still holding her hand, he led her down the hall and into the door leading into his room. *Holy shit, is this really happening?* He had expected her to laugh in his face, but she hadn't. He had forgotten about the others in the house, the ones Basil had left behind to help keep watch over her.

Brandy looked down and saw that he was showing quite the bulge in his pants. "Is that for me?" she asked him, as he looked at her with big eyes.

"Anything I have is yours," he said with boyish innocence.

"Can I ask you something? Please, don't be offended by this."

"Sure, you can ask me anything."

"Have you ever been with a woman before? I mean, sexually?"

His awkward silence answered her question before he even spoke. "No, I haven't, but I sure would like for you to be the first."

His gaze came back up to her as he noticed that she was removing the shirt she had on. She wore no bra and her breasts were perfect and round. He wanted to scream from excitement, but he maintained control of himself for fear she would stop what she was doing if he showed too much enthusiasm.

"Okay, now your turn," she said.

Looking at her with confused eyes, he didn't know what she was asking.

"Your shirt, take it off," she said, smiling sweetly at him.

He pulled off his t-shirt and stood before her, his bare chest showing and his hands clasped around the shirt which was hanging between his legs.

Lifting her hand up to his chest, she leaned in and kissed him again, softly moving her hand over his nipples. He gasped softly at the pleasure he felt. It was an entirely different sensation from the times he had done it himself. A foreign hand to his body, moving across his nipples, made him feel as if he were in a dream, one that he had no control over. If this was a dream, he did not want to wake up.

Pulling away from his kiss, Brandy started to unbutton her jeans, never taking her eyes from his. Once she had unbuttoned the last one, she reached over, putting her fingers inside the top of his jeans, pulling them out just a bit. With her other hand, she began to unbutton the top one, then the next. He had already begun to get hard, but when her hand touched the inside of his abs, brushing his pubic hair, he knew he was rock hard.

Smiling to herself, she was inwardly pleased he was so excited. It fed her desire to feel him next to her, to feel him inside her. She had felt a connection with him from the start, but wasn't sure if it was gratitude or a genuine attraction. There was no questioning or denying it. It was a pure attraction. He was not anything she would typically go for, but she felt something for this boy, this man. As she continued to unbutton his jeans, she was taken by surprise that his cock had grown outside the top of his underwear. *This man was packing.*

As his pants were pulled down, along with his underwear, his cock fell out and stood proudly erect. He put his hand behind her head and pulled her into him, her breasts on his chest, kissing her passionately. His tongue pressed through her lips and met hers, lightly touching at first and then furiously kissing her.

Mathias wanted so badly to turn on the music in his head, to combine this new experience with what he was used to. But to find a song that matched this feeling, this longing, he wasn't sure what that song would be. So he continued down this unfamiliar path, hoping he was doing what she wanted, pleasing her the way she deserved to be pleased. He was surrendering to the moment, letting it happen, letting the sensations and the primal instinct guide him.

Wrapping his arm around her waist, he led her over to the bed, sitting her down on the edge and laying her back. He smiled to himself as a song finally hit his head, an appropriate song, but one that still made him chuckle too. He thought, *okay, as the song says, let's get it on.*

He saw the surprised look on her face as she was slid up onto the pillows, not by her own means, or by his helpful hands, but by the song being played in his head.

"No, not like this. No, magic. Just you and me, two human beings who want each other, who need each other. We don't need magic to help us through this. We just need each other."

"I'm sorry," he said, hoping it didn't ruin what was happening. "It was instinct. I didn't mean to…"

"It's okay, really it is. Just turn the music off in your head and come join me."

Shaking and a little taken aback, but still erect, he joined her on the bed, reaching over and grabbing a condom out of the nightstand drawer.

"Never been with a girl before? You are certainly prepared for it," she said, smiling at him and taking the condom out of his hands, opening it up and sliding it onto him.

Just the touch of her hands on him made him swell with pleasure. He couldn't believe this was happening. This beautiful woman, wanted him, wanted him to please her.

Grabbing his arm, she gently guided him to where he was positioned on his back. She straddled him, letting his cock ease inside her, as she took her time, letting it fill her, she moaned with pleasure and her head fell backwards, desire consuming her as she adjusted to his girth.

The feeling of her sliding down onto him, hearing her moans and the pressure surrounding his cock, made him give out his own moan. She smiled to herself as she heard him whimper the word, "yes."

With that, she started to move herself up his cock and then back down again, creating a rhythm, slow at first, but gradually picking up speed. The mattress began squeaking and moving with her, and he began to give little thrusts upward as he became more comfortable and relaxed with the extreme ecstasy he was feeling.

Out of nowhere she was moving at a high speed, moaning, almost bouncing on his cock. They were both sweating now, breathing heavily, and both had their own rhythm of movement and moaning. She knew he was getting close as his body started making little twitching movements, little spasms, as she continued to ride him. She could also feel a sensation taking over her body. It took her quickly, as she screamed out in pleasure.

That was all it took for him, hearing her, his body jerked as his balls contracted and he shot his first orgasm, or the first one that didn't involve himself and an adult magazine or internet porn. He wiggled and squirmed as the contractions of the ejaculation took over. He had never felt anything like it. He didn't know if he would ever feel anything like it again.

She collapsed onto him, his cock still inside her, and rested her head on his heaving chest. The sweat between them was cool and it served to remind him of the intenseness of the interchange they had just experienced. She lifted her head from his chest and looked at him, then gave him a kiss.

"Before you even ask, I will just tell you. It was amazing. You were amazing," she said, knowing this was his first time and also remembering the need to feel he did it right, and made her feel pleasure too.

He beamed with pride, for himself and for this beautiful woman, who lay on top of him.

Chapter Fifty-Seven

The sisters were busy preparing a spell to keep Gina asleep until they had time to figure out a better way of dealing with her. They were still overjoyed to have found her but didn't want to tempt fate too much by allowing her to be awake and possibly develop more skill. It would take a powerful spell to get her to disavow her thoughts of the past and to join them in creating the world they longed for, a world of chaos, evil, and mythical creatures, which were not really so mythical.

They no longer had the luxury of smell, so the animals that had been killed in the name of the great undertaking had no bearing on their nostrils. But the stench of rotting flesh, dried meat, and blood surrounded the room in a pungent, almost unbearable odor.

While one was carving up a goat, trying to get to the needed organ, the other was grinding up herbs needed for the spell. Athdara looked up quickly, sensing something new. Something had invaded their space, their home. She grunted to Arabel, who in turn, looked up from her carving, to find her sister standing vigilant. She too, sensed the intruder, grunted her agreement. Athdara grabbed her staff and proceeded to the doorway.

They sensed them at the same time, the other magical force and their Durward, coming home from the day's hunt. He was such a great pet. Never argued, didn't eat, and never disappointed them. Of course, he had taken twenty-five years off each of their lives, but it had been such a wonderful sacrifice to make. His creation has proven invaluable many times over.

Durward carried with him a beaten and broken Demetri. They sensed him, his power, and the lack of control he had over his magic. They sensed his potential, but knew that he had pulled off a magical spell in which he didn't know the consequences. Not even the sisters have tried such a spell as that one, and they have tried many, many spells. The past life spell was a dangerous one, one in which you could lose yourself and your mind. If not done correctly, you could lose your total identity and be left in limbo. Death was better than stuck in a world in which your magic no longer worked. But, oh, what a great specimen he would make. They could harness his magic and use it to fuel them forward in their goal. He might even be persuaded to join them in their battle to reclaim the world in which they longed for.

"What a good Durward, so thoughtful and kind to bring his mistresses such a powerful being. When we sent you out to protect our journey, we had no idea you would encounter such a witch as this. But I sense more from you. You battled for this one. You also battled another, an undead, an old one, a vampire of considerable strength. I also see that you have eliminated him. That is good Durward," Arabel said, talking to him as if he understood and might possibly speak back to her. But those days were long gone.

"Take him to the dungeon and I will lock him away. We don't need this one waking up and tossing about his manly magic. When they are alive, filled with hormones and as scattered as this one appears to be, he could be more dangerous than a caged lion. No sense taking chances at this stage," Athdara stated, following Durward into the hallway and down to the dungeon.

As Demetri was tossed into the cage, it roused him a little, and as he opened his eyes he caught a blurry view of the two. His head was pounding, foggy, and not recognizing anything he was looking at. He jumped a bit as the metal door slammed shut. He noticed the old witch, who looked like death had knocked on her door many times, wave a staff that lit up, causing the metal door to light up. He crawled on his stomach towards the door, knowing just enough to realize he was in trouble.

Reaching the door, he grabbed the metal, letting out a scream as electricity flowed through his body.

He looked up as he heard the witch laughing. "You think your powers can get you out of this cage? You have come to the wrong place, my friend. There are ancient powers flowing through this cage, holding you here, making you a prisoner to me and my sister. You will not escape and to waste any more efforts on it is pointless. You will spend an eternity here with us, and even when your earthly body dies, your soul will be left here and serve as a source of energy for us."

"Lady, you have no idea who you are messing with…" Demetri started to say.

Athdara just smiled and waved her staff, causing Demetri's mouth to be silenced as stitching looped from lip to lip, rendering him unable to speak. "You think you are the first to spout such words at us. We have lived here for hundreds of years. More powerful witches than you have sat in this cell and threatened us. Their souls are still stuck here, feeding us when we need it. You will learn that fighting is futile."

With that, she turned and walked away, leaving Demetri trying to scream out at her, but unable to do so. He grabbed at his mouth and felt panic overtake him as he ran his fingers over the stitching. His thoughts began to spin out of control. *How am I going to save Gina? What about Aldrik? Is he really dead? Did I see him sliced open and fall dead to the ground? Can he be killed that easily? Who the hell are these people and did she say sister? What the fuck*

293

was that thing with the metal mask? None of his thoughts were helping to calm him down and the more he thought about it, the more panicked he became.

He wanted to scream out so badly, out of anger, fear, and frustration, but the stitching only allowed a murmur. He tried to send an energy ball at the metal door, but he was so weak that it dissipated before it even hit the door. He crawled backward on the floor until his back was up against a stone wall. He knew he had the powers to get out of this cell, but he was still unable to call upon them at will. He had brought all of his past life memories into his body, and all of the powers and spells that came with those lives, but he was still unable to control them. He banged his fist down upon the stone floor and cursed inside his mind.

He had to calm himself down, to not let this overwhelm him to the point that he couldn't reason and rationalize even with himself. If he had any hope of getting out, it would take all of his concentration, no distractions, to call upon the magic needed to break free and battle the two witches and their watchdog. He couldn't allow himself to think about revenge at this moment. That would come for Aldrik when he broke free. He had to keep the goal in mind, and that was finding Gina and getting her home safely.

He stopped what he was doing and just listened, trying to quiet his mind, so he could hear if the witches were close by or if he was further inside whatever lair they had him in. He figured it was still Scotland by the way she had talked, but he couldn't be certain.

Once he made the effort to quiet his mind, he was able to hear some noises in the background, some voices speaking.

"So did you get him in the dungeon," Arabel asked.

"He is in there and very much awake. He tried, just like many before him, to intimidate me, but he soon found he was no match."

"You just love putting men in their place, don't you my dear sister," Arabel laughed.

"We put up with men telling us what to do for too long my sister, far too long. With this lovely specimen of a witch," she said, pointing at Gina, "we will once again rule this country, maybe even the world."

"She is so beautiful, full of life and power. She reminds me of us back when we were her age, so long ago. She has such beautiful auburn hair and such lovely alabaster skin."

"Yes, she is our salvation and we will soon have the power to turn her once we feed upon the male. He has enough magical energy flowing through him to make the spell happen."

Demetri's eyes widen as he listened to the two, faintly, but enough to catch the gist of their conversation. *They have to be talking about Gina. She was here, just down the hallway. All was not lost. I just have to get out of here.*

Chapter Fifty-Eight

Fingers numb, his muscles aching, sweat dripping down his face into his eyes, Victor knew if he didn't act now, this would be his last adventure, his last act of service. If his master were here he could save him, but that was not the case so he must pull from deep within and make this happen himself. When the Durward knocked him backward off the cliff, it was like being hit by a bull. It knocked the breath out of him, stunning him, but if it were not for his training from the Balashon, he might have been laying on the rocks at the bottom of the cliff. He was trained to take blows like the one he had taken, but this thing was like no other. It had strength he had not felt in a very long time. This was the second time today he had the breath knocked out of him.

He felt his grip on the rock starting to slip. Summoning his iron will, the motivation for survival, he used his footing on the side of the cliff to help him push his body upward just enough for his fingertips to snatch hold of a small ledge in the rocks. He could feel the adrenaline rushing throughout his body, but he could also feel the cramping in his muscles as they were beginning to tire out.

Master, please help me, if you are out there, please give me strength. I beg of you, fuel my body.

All he felt was the pain in his muscles. He needed to find some inward inspiration or he would meet his doom when his body crashed onto what lay beneath him.

Come on Victor, fight. Push through this. You have been in worse situations than this. You have fought your way out of dozens of fights where you should have perished. One more time, just one more, you got this.

Another push with his feet and his free hand went upward reaching for anything it could grasp ahold of, but there was nothing to grab onto. When his body swung back from his heave upward, his fingers, wet with sweat, lost the hold it had on the rocks and he started to free fall down the cliff.

He was reaching for anything at this point, anything his hands could latch onto. Shock filled him, then fear, as he felt his hands slam into the hard, cold side of the cliff. The abrupt stop from his free fall had a heavy toll to pay on his shoulders as they felt stretched to their limits. Hanging there, vulnerable and knowing the inevitable was coming, he screamed outward in rage and then began to laugh.

Of all of the harrowing experiences he had been through, this was how he was going to die? *This cannot be happening. It just can't. I don't believe it. Victor Von Helsberg, skilled tracker and assassin for the Balashon, will not meet his doom at the bottom of a cliff. There is no way that is going to happen. No fucking way.*

But even as he thought this, he knew his strength could not hold out. The things he had yet to do flashed before him, as did the things he had done, the good and the bad. In most people's eyes, Victor's bad list would outweigh the good, but it was a matter of perspective. Everything he had done had been for the betterment of the Balashon. Well, almost everything. Even hanging here, on the cliff which would bring his death, Victor had to admit to himself that the sexual side of him, the fetishes, the torturous side of his sexuality, which often led to the death of the recipient, had nothing to do with the Balashon. This was his own doing, his own making. He had become the monster of many people's nightmares. And he had loved it, loved every minute. Even going into his death, he had no regrets.

Master, forgive me. I wanted to fulfill your every desire. I wanted to see your vision made whole. I wanted to see your reign on this earth. I tried with all my might Master, I really did. I go to my grave knowing that I fought for you and alongside you. No regrets, Master. No regrets.

Closing his eyes, he prepared for the inevitable fall. His eyes opened when he heard a whisper in his ear.

"My dear Victor, I have not forsaken you. I am alive and back in the vessel's body. I am coming for you, but you have to make it. You have to hold firm. Don't give up so close to our victorious day. You have been my faithful one, all the way through. You have never once taken your eye off the prize. If I had an army of men and women like you, I would be invincible. But I don't, so I need you, my loyal subject, my friend. I am once again whole, reunited with the vessel and we will show this world what true power is."

The sound of his master's voice and the knowledge he was alive, and in the vessel's body fueled his desire to fight, to live. But he knew he was on borrowed time hanging here on the cliff's edge. His fingers were raw, his muscles aching and spent of energy. His arms were quivering, his body now feeling as if it were dripping cold sweat. What this all meant, he knew all too well. He was going to die here. His master was alive and he was thrilled, but he also knew that he had no more energy to climb up this cliff.

He let his eyes drop to the rocks below and saw the waves crashing up against them. He no more wanted to die than the next person, but he could die knowing he had fulfilled his destiny on this earth. He had helped his master get back into this world where he could rule again and seek the revenge he had been waiting three thousand years for.

He smiled to himself and felt a strange sensation overcome him. A tear welled up in his eyes and had it not been for the feeling that had overtaken him, he would have argued that it was from the wind blowing hard in his eyes. But this strange feeling had him perplexed. He was mourning. Not for his own death, but for not being able to finish what he had always dreamed he and his master would accomplish together. He felt sad, alone. In his final minutes on this earth, he was alone. Not surprising since he was being called one of Tulsa's most ferocious serial killers. *Killers die alone, don't they?*

If he was going to die, it would be on his terms. His back would feel the crushing of the rocks as they smashed him inwardly, crushing every bone in his body, severing veins, arteries, and crushing his skull. The impact of the rock against his skull would likely kill him instantly, but he had one last hope, one last ditch effort before accepting the destruction of his body against the hard stone below.

Pulling his feet up as far as he could without losing his grip on the rocks ledge, he steadied himself. His footing was not perfect, but with the energy he had left it would have to do. *You got this Victor. You can do this. I am a warrior and I will go out like one. They may have thought they had beaten me, but I still have a shot. I just have to make sure I do this right.*

And with that thought, he pulled himself as close as he could to the wall, letting go of the hold his hands had, pushing with all of the strength he had left with his legs, propelling himself outward as he plunged downward, fast, towards the rocks and the water's edge.

In only a few seconds, it felt as if a million thoughts coursed through his mind, but he did not indulge them. He wanted to stay focused. Just before he was to hit the rocks below, he pulled himself into a fetal position, hoping that he would hit water and not rocks. He knew even if he hit the water, the pain would be terrible and he also had to hope that it was deep enough to take the impact of his body, without hitting the bottom below the water.

The force of the water against his body knocked him unconscious. His body floated below the water's surface, drifting downward into the dark waters of Loch Ness.

Chapter Fifty-Nine

Bastiquil sit back in his seat, a smile on his face as the plane was in the air heading towards his rendezvous with fate. He felt proud when he thought back on the accomplishments that his secret society, the Balashon, have been able to pull off. They had more money combined than any other entity or person on the planet.

Bastiquil was not like most demons. His powers allowed him the vision to view this world and to see how it worked. It was about money. Whoever had the money and the political pull was the one who made all of the calls in this realm. So he did what he could from his side to guide them, making sure the line stayed strong, smart, and stealth.

As the 747 airliner, courtesy of one of the larger Balashonian corporations, carried him and his army, he looked around. Yes, he was proud of what they had been able to accomplish over a three-thousand-year time period, but when the shit hit the fan, most had failed him. Some died an honorable death, but most disappointed and let him down. But there was always a way to redeem yourself if you are willing to lay down your life for the greater good. Their redemption lay in absorbing his blood into their skin, the blood he had put into the ink. He had made some fascinating and beautiful creations, creations that could deliver a death blow when fueled by his demonic blood.

He was most proud of Night Fury. She had taken to her new role quite well. She was a force to be reckoned with and his admiration of her grew quickly. She would soon be at his and Victor's side as he ruled the lands, taking them one at a time. He would start with the financial and then move to the physical. He had learned his lesson with the male witch. This world contained some powerful witches, and he had to move and treat them with more discretionary caution. That was why his plan with the female witch was so crucial. Gina would help to bring him power in this world, power like Zamaranum had wielded all those years ago. She was his source of earthly power and that was why it was so important to find her and Victor.

But his last connection with Victor had shown trouble on the horizon. Trouble that he hoped Victor could handle. His faith in him was not misplaced. Victor has shown his devotion to him many times over. His entire existence was to serve and promote Bastiquil's agenda. Oh, how he loved the name Bastiquil. It struck fear in many hearts. He knew that this fear would help feed his flame in this world. But he had to get his plan in place. He had to have time to grow and let his power within the vessel gain momentum. He knew he would be unstoppable in time, but right now was a crucial time, especially with the male witch having tapped into the powers of Zamaranum. This made him an enormous threat. He had to hope that the witch had not learned to control those powers yet.

"Master, they estimate that our arrival into Scotland is about three more hours. Is there anything I can get for you in the meantime," Night Fury said, as she stood over him, waiting patiently for his reply.

He looked up from his thoughts and smiled at her. "No, my dear, I am good."

"Very well, please let me know if you change your mind Master."

He looked at her as she turned to walk away. "On second thought, can you bring me the ten marked with the brand of coward on their hands? I have a task for them," he smiled at the thoughts going through his mind.

"Certainly Master, right away," Night Fury said, marching over to the group of ten men sitting with their heads bowed in shame. "You ten, come with me. The master wishes to see you."

The men stood up, all ten, knowing to whom she was speaking. There was hope and fear on their face. *Would he allow them redemption? Or would he kill them on the spot?* This ran through each of their minds as they followed her to where the master was sitting.

"Here they are Master. Should I stay?"

"No, Night Fury, I will handle this myself. Thank you for your loyalty. It will not go unrewarded." She turned to go as the men lined up in front of him, waiting impatiently to hear what their master had to say.

"You let me down. You let the entire line of the Balashon down. You were cowards when we needed you, when I needed you. This is now why you carry the sacred demonic brand of a coward on your hand. But I am willing to give you all another chance," he said to the group of men, who looked around at each other, smiling at the chance to regain the trust of the master.

Bastiquil stood up and looked at each of them, one by one. Then he reached for his pants and started to unbutton the top button. He looked at the one standing directly in front of him, the pretty blond, blue-eyed one with the gorgeous smile. "Get on your knees and unzip my pants with your teeth."

The look of shock on the man's face was genuine and fearful. He had never been with another man. He swallowed, blinking as he did. "Master, please."

"If I have to ask you a second time, I will slit your throat and drink your blood until your body is dry, then I will feast upon your soul for an eternity."

Bending down on his knees, the man leaned forward, reaching up with his hands to help him with the zipper. He winced in pain as he felt a searing heat from the master's hand as it made contact with the side of his face. The other men jumped as well as they watched the punishment and couldn't help but wonder what was in store for them.

"You are dangerously close to joining your fallen comrades, but I will assure you, your torment will be that of a thousand slaps a second for an eternity. Now when I say use your teeth, I mean use your teeth," Bastiquil said, as he looked up at the others, disgusted.

The man moved in and pressed his forehead against Bastiquil's stomach as he attempted to grab hold of the zipper with his teeth. It took him a few times to get it, but when he did, he held onto it tightly and began to pull downward slowly as the sound of the zipper seemed to be the only thing you could hear on the plane aside from the roar of the engines.

"That's a good boy," Bastiquil laughed, as he looked down at the man. He placed his hands on both sides of the man's face, making him extremely uncomfortable. The man's face was still looking towards Bastiquil's crotch, his pubic hair and skin of his cock showing. He pushed the man's face closer, letting his nose graze the exposed pubic hair. "The men of this world think this piece of male equipment, this cock, is a sign of power, but it is not. It is for pleasure, for taking of the flesh. But true power comes from something much greater as you will all learn to respect. You will know my power and will not disappoint me again, for in doing so you will unleash destruction upon yourself and the line of descendants you have created throughout the years. I will take each one, male and female as my sex slave, taking them as I see fit, before ripping into their flesh, taking their beating heart into my hands as I tear it from their chest, squeezing the very life from it."

The men looked at him with scared, believing eyes. The blond man with his nose still perched into the master's pubic hair had tears running down his face. He knew he had disgraced them all, himself, and his family. And how the master knew he had fled when the witches and vampire attacked during the master's ascension, he had no clue. But he knew and this was his punishment.

Taking his hands and putting them under the man's chin, he lifted his face upwards so that he was looking into his eyes. "I know what each and every one of you have done since the day you were born into the path of my legacy, my demonic clan. I know what your thoughts are now. Once you have been born into this clan or swear your allegiance to me, I can hear you for a lifetime. Upon your death, you become mine forever. I know the thoughts of the thousands that did not come to see me reborn in Tulsa. And I know the thoughts of the ones I knew could not be there, and of the ones who chose to not be there. None of you can hide from me. I am in you all. So you will all do well to remember this and to not think that you can have a voice or opinion when I give you an order. Your only task is to jump and accomplish it or perish trying."

While the men watched, Bastiquil took the blond man there in front of them on the floor of the plane, as he screamed out asking for forgiveness, he found none. He did find the harsh reality of what defiance and cowardliness brought to him. And as the master was thrusting himself inside of him, he chanted to himself while tears rolled down his face, "hail Bastiquil, hail Bastiquil."

Leaning down to his ear, as he thrust inside him the last time, he spoke so only he could hear. "You will bear my demon seed inside you as an honor I bestow upon you. It will fuel the power I had already given you through my blood. You will not doubt me again, will you Peter?"

The man shook his head. "Never Master, never again. Thank you for giving me this wonderful lesson in humility and faith. I will not fail you."

Bastiquil smiled as he stood, zipping his pants, buttoning the top button. He looked at the other nine who stood before him. Turning away, he walked back to his seat where he awaited their arrival into Scotland.

Chapter Sixty

Legs wrapped around his tiny waist, Brandy helped to pull him deeper inside her with each thrust. They were both panting and sweating with labored breath. This was the third time and he showed no sign of fatigue. *Youth and hormones are a gift. This is simply amazing. I can see now why women go for younger men.*

"You are the most beautiful woman I have ever seen."

"You aren't so bad yourself stud."

"I honestly can't believe this is happening."

"Well, you said that the last two times too. So I am pretty sure this is happening unless we are in some time loop."

"Hell, if we are in a time loop, I don't ever want it to stop."

"You are too damn cute," she panted, as she leaned her head up and kissed his lips.

Arching her back, she let out a moan, which Mathias had already learned was a good thing. He kept going as her body shuddered beneath him. It set off a reaction inside him that he could not stop and he shot once again. He did notice that his balls were beginning to ache, and he hoped that was normal.

Falling beside her on the bed, he looked up at the ceiling fan and stared at the rotating blades. They had never felt so good against his sweat-soaked skin.

Leaning towards him, she laid her head on his chest as he wrapped his arm around her, pulling her body close. He liked this feeling. It was new to him, but it felt right and he knew he would do anything he could to protect this woman.

Brandy had not forgotten all that had been going on and what deep trouble they were in. She knew the Balashon were still out there, Bastiquil had once again taken Alex, and that the police still wanted to talk to all of them. But she needed this distraction, just for the time being, to regain some semblance of normalcy even if it was a smoke screen. *But what was normal about this? I am having sex with a much younger boy, well, man. Hell, who cares what people think? I have been through a lot and this man wanted to comfort me, he protected me.*

"What's on your mind, handsome?" she asked.

"I am experiencing pure joy, absolute happiness right now. Does that sound corny?" he grimaced, looking at her.

"Not at all," she smiled, knowing that he must be in heaven. She knew every boy had fantasies about their first time, but he had gone three times in a row and had rocked it. "You were amazing. This was amazing. I can't believe how much I enjoyed it."

"Really, you didn't think you would enjoy it?" his eyes were wide, his mouth open.

"Wait, that didn't come out right. Yes, I enjoyed it, more so than I had expected. Okay, before I dig a deeper hole for myself, let me put it this way. You exceeded my wildest expectations."

The look of shock on his face was replaced with a smile. "So you liked it?"

She smacked him playfully on the chest and they both burst out laughing.

"I wish we could stay like this forever," he said, feeling naïve and stupid for saying it.

"Actually, that doesn't sound like a bad plan to me either. But we both know that can't happen. We have to try

308

and find a way to help the others. We have to find a way to get Alex back."

"We will. I promise you. We will do whatever we can to get him back and to help get the others back too. I know you haven't known me long, but I am a man of my word."

"I can tell that about you," she said, turning her face to where she was looking at him. "You saved me at the expense of your own life. That is huge. That is something I will not forget."

He reached out and kissed her lips again. As their tongues met, their lips pressed against each other, his cock started to react as well.

"Can I tell you something," he said, as he pulled back from her kiss.

"You can tell me anything," she whispered.

"I have to pee so badly."

They both burst out in laughter again, bodies shaking as he pulled his legs up close to his body. "Don't make me laugh. I am seriously going to piss myself."

"Well, you had better get up and take care of that."

Jumping up, he made the decision not to put on his boxers as he made his way from the bed and towards the bathroom door.

Confusion and fear hit Brandy as the glass in the window pane shattered and she saw Mathias' back arch slightly, and then fall to the floor. A scream escaped her lips as she saw him lying there, a dart in his right butt cheek. She scrambled off the bed and crawled on the floor to him. He was unconscious, but alive.

She heard a loud noise at the front door as the wood gave way to the kick from the man's foot. A group of men rushed inside the house, taking out the five Basil had left behind before they made their way to the bedroom. Mathias was knocked out from the tranquilizer dart and Brandy was lying next to him, crying and holding onto him.

One of the men, dressed all in black, rushed at her. As he advanced, Brandy kicked up at his crotch, her foot meeting his balls, sending him to his knees, where she followed up with her fist to his nose. Three more men advanced, grabbing her and throwing her down onto the bed. As they held her down, one of the men reached into his pocket, pulling out a syringe, and quickly jabbed the needle into her neck.

The last thing she remembered was looking back towards Mathias, and a blurry image of him being lifted off the ground, still nude and carried out of the room. Then all went dark.

Chapter Sixty-One

Arabel took the mixture she had blended together with the mortar and pestle and walked over to where Gina rested on the table. Placed all around the table were field flowers, herbs, dead animals, and other offerings. It looked like a sacrificial table with Gina being the sacrifice.

Taking Gina's shirt, she lifted it up and placed it just below her breasts. Using the tip of her athame, she pricked the tip of her own finger letting some blood flow into the pestle. Turning to Athdara, she motioned for her to hold out her finger. She pricked it and let some blood drop into the mixture. Then she took the mortar and mixed the blood into the other ingredients.

Using her hand, Arabel scooped up some of the mixture and proceeded to rub it onto Gina's stomach as she chanted, "as a crone's hand caresses this life within, a taking over of a soul shall begin. As a crone's hand caresses this life within, a taking over of a soul shall begin." Nodding her head to Athdara, her eyes lingered. "Sister please, I need you to join me in this. She is powerful, but not as powerful as we. Here, take my hand and join me." The sisters joined hands and began chanting the spell together. "As a crone's hand caresses this life within, a taking over of a soul shall begin."

The sisters were chanting it over and over with ever increasing speed and intensity. Their hands joined, placed strategically on Gina's abdomen as they said the spell. The energy in the room was heating up and a wind began to move about the room. Even in the dungeon, Demetri could hear them chanting and could feel the change in the atmosphere.

A blue light began to form around the hands of the witches where they had them placed on Gina's abdomen. Then the light shot out, sending a wave of energy shooting in all directions and sending the sisters flying backward as well. Both landed against the wall behind each, hitting hard. Athdara looked at her sister laying across the room as dazed as she herself felt, and then looked down to see that she had landed on a spear, which was protruding out of her chest.

"What the bloody hell was that?" Athdara screamed out to her sister, as she tried to get up but remembered she had a spear protruding from her chest. "Damned spear, I told you to put it away sister." Gaining her footing, she proceeded to lift herself up and off of the spear, and as she did so, her wounds immediately began to heal.

"What are you?"

Both sisters turned to look at where the voice had come from and were startled to find Gina sitting up on the table, looking at them both in disgust.

"What are you doing awake? I had you under a sleeping spell," Arabel said to the perplexed looking Gina.

"Well, I guess that would mean you are witches, but how did you heal yourself like that? I have only seen that from vampires."

Spitting on the ground, Athdara looked at her. "I am no vampire, nor will I ever be. I am a witch far older than you can imagine, one that is more powerful than you can imagine. I am no longer confined to the rules of the living. With my age and power come many luxuries in life and healing is just one of them. You too can have this, my child. You too are part of the sisterhood."

"What do you mean I can have this too? Where am I? Where is Victor?"

312

"You need no man to protect you from us. I told you, you are among the sisterhood of witches. We are not your enemy. You are here with us in our castle, in our sanctuary. You are a powerful witch and are growing more powerful by the day. You can help us take it back. You can help us make it what it used to be before," Athdara passionately explained.

"What is it you think I can help you take back? I don't even know you. I need to get home. I have so many people worried about me."

"Please dear, relax," Arabel said, as she sent a spell to make Gina relax. But when it reached Gina, it bounced off her and shot back at Arabel who was knocked to the ground with a dazed, relaxed look on her face.

"What the hell are you trying to do? Are you forcing me to be here? What was that spell you just cast at me?"

"I think the better question my dear, is how did you repel it? We are extremely powerful witches and were able to take you from the hotel unaware and the man you call Victor, was unable to stop us. So you need to be asking yourself the right questions and you will find your answers," Athdara said, with a smile on her face, her yellow, decaying teeth prominently displayed.

"What did you do to Victor? If you hurt him, you will be sorry."

"Dear please, try and pay attention. You don't need him. You have us. We can take it back, we can have it all. You just need to trust us and let us show you the way."

"You keep going on about taking it back. Take what back? What is it that you want me to help you take back?"

"The world, we can have it all. We can bring back the magical lands. We can unleash the beautiful, powerful beast again. We can make the legends and myths real again. You have that power my dear, with us, that is. We can make it happen. We just need to all channel our powers into making the moon shine red, a Blood Moon and then our powers will be unstoppable. We can rule the world."

"Are you mad? You two are fucking crazy! I can't believe I am hearing this. I have to be dreaming."

"Snap out of it. You are in no dream and we are far from crazy. This world is but a shadow of what it once was. Your man-made machines are but a mere glimpse of the power we can bring back to this world. It was here once and it can be again."

"I am not that powerful of a witch, even if I did believe you about this magical world and mighty beasts and the red moon, which I don't, by the way. I am just a witch, a nature-loving witch. I can cast a few spells here and there, an energy ball and talk with the spirit world. But conjuring up another world that you say is long gone? I don't have that kind of power."

"Not alone you don't my dear, but the baby growing inside you does."

"What did you say?" Gina looked at Athdara in shock.

"You heard me. You have this world's most magical being growing inside you and it shall rule the world and live among the magical royalty that it so deserves. And we will be there to help you obtain this. We will help you to grow your own powers and to nourish your unborn child."

"You will do no such thing. I will not help you. You are crazy to think that I would. And I cannot be pregnant. I would know if I were. I want to leave now. Victor! Victor!" Gina yelled, looking around frantically for him. "Where is Victor?"

"Victor is gone. You need to settle down now," Arabel said, coming out of her dazed state and walking towards Gina.

"Gone? What do you mean he is gone? What did you do to him," Gina said, finding herself getting angry and knowing she shouldn't care about him, but she also knew he would protect her from these two and get her to a safe place.

"I told you earlier, if you have done anything to harm him, I will kill you both."

"Kill us? Oh dearest, we cannot die. We have already faced that many hundreds of years ago and cannot be brought back from it. Your Victor met his fate at the hands of our Durward," Arabel said, laughing. "It's just you and us now dear, and of course Durward."

"Who is Durward and what do you mean he met his fate? Victor? Victor, I need you," Gina screamed.

"Enough of this," Athdara screamed. "We offer the world, a magical world and you scream for a man? A man, by the way, who is not so innocent as he thinks he is. Do you think we don't know what he has done? What he did to you and your friends? He is a killer and he got what was coming to him."

"How dare you, you old bitch? You cannot hold me here. You cannot keep me here." As the words came off her tongue, Gina had no clue of the scathing tone in which they flowed from her mouth. Nor did she notice the energy ball forming in front of her as she spoke to them.

"I said enough of this," Athdara screamed. "Durward, come forth."

Immediately Gina heard heavy footsteps hitting the ground. She turned to see the thing called Durward as it turned the corner and entered the room. She gasped at the sight of it. It was enormous and frightening. The metal mask alone sent chills down Gina's spine.

"We did not want to keep you by force, but if force is what it will take, then we are more than prepared," Athdara said, angrily. "Durward, hold her down while we continue to prepare her."

"Like hell you will," Gina screamed, as the energy ball shot out and hit Durward, knocking him back a few steps, but he kept coming towards her. "Victor, please help me!"

In the waters of Loch Ness, deep down in the darkness, Victor's eyes shot open as he heard the scream of Gina. Startled and not realizing where he was or why he was in water, he struggled to bring himself to the surface. *Did I die? How could I be under the water and not be dead? I had to have drowned. And where was Gina? Why can I hear her calling to me?*

All these thoughts raced through his head and he frantically swam towards life. He realized he must be dead because in the distance, in the depths of the water, he saw a massive thing moving towards him at a rapid pace. *What the hell is that? Where the hell am I?*

He swam faster and harder, fear sweeping over him as he realized he should be drowning, but also, this thing was charging at him in the water.

As the light above him started to get brighter, he knew he was closing in on the surface. He had to get there. He had to get air and get out before this beast got him.

He gasps as he broke the surface, air filling his lungs, as he threw up water that he had taken in. As he coughed, his lungs clear of the water, he realized he had drowned. He had been dead, but for some reason he was alive again. Memories flooded his mind of what had happened to him, of where he was.

As he swam for the rocky shore, he realized what he was swimming from. *Could it be? Was it the legendary beast that so many people feared, yet flocked to every year hoping to catch a glimpse?* Victor felt the water around him starting to displace and knew the beast was upon him. He was only feet from shore, but he had to know. Taking a breath in, he turned and went under and found himself face to face with the beast.

Chapter Sixty-Two

He could not bear to hear what sounded like an attack on Gina in the room down the hall. He was here, so close to her, yet unable to get to her. The witch had sealed his mouth so he was unable to speak, to yell, to let her know he was just feet away. He tried to scream, but it just came out a mumble.

It infuriated him knowing he had so much power inside him, yet he was like a child, unable to control anything. Like a teenager who hit puberty, his hardness, his power comes and goes like the wind. *What am I missing? I am all of these things, these images of the past. I was given them back for a reason. I have to concentrate. I have to gain control. If I do not, then I will die, along with Gina.*

He began by closing his eyes. He pictured stillness, darkness, a place where nonexistence occurs he may stand a chance. If he can get there, he can move into the meditation that helped him before. He saw nothing, felt nothing, but the darkness in which he had placed himself. *Bring my powers. Bring them forth, oh great mystic forces of the past, present, and future. I am your humble servant, calling forth the powers from the four corners, north, east, south, and west. Bring your wisdom, your strength, your insight, and your power to me. Help me to center myself. Help me, oh great ones. Center me. Bathe me in your wisdom so I can walk in your light. Bring my powers. Bring them forth, oh great mystic forces of the past, present, and future. I am your humble servant, calling forth the powers from the four corners, north, east, south, and west.*

He continued to chant this inside his head, feeling the energy within and around him begin to change. It was working and he could feel himself regaining control, feel the power inside him charging up like a battery hooked up to jumper cables. It felt incredible, it felt strong and it felt right. He kept it going, kept the charge happening as he pulled the images of his past together, remembering who he was, what he was, and what he was capable of doing.

Power was in his blood, his being, his soul. He had harnessed some of the greatest power known to mankind and had wielded it less than a week ago, back home in Tulsa. He had fought the demon and expelled him from Alex. He could do so again. He recalled the phone conversation with Brandy about the demon being back.

Stop this Demetri. Stop the chatter. Stop the outside noise, for it will only defeat what you are trying to accomplish. Clear your head. Clear your thoughts. Only think of your powers, your past lives, and how you can tap into each of them.

The sound of Gina's voice brought him back from his thoughts. At first, he figured it was in his head, but then he realized she was awake and talking with the witches. He could hear them, their conversation soft, then loud. *She sounds so confused, so displaced.* He could hear the fear in her voice and could tell she was struggling to not go bat shit crazy on the two.

As their conversation went on, Demetri could not believe what he was hearing. She was asking for Victor, for this killer. She was asking about his safety and wellbeing. She even threatened them if harm had come to him. *What was going on? This isn't my Gina. My Gina wouldn't be concerned about whether these two witches had killed Victor. Something has happened to her, they have done something to her or the demon has gotten to her. Wait a minute. I can't hear them. I can't hear her thoughts.*

As he kept trying to listen, he was being shut out, sometimes painfully, from listening to her. It was as if she had a security system guarding against anyone trying to get inside her head. *What the fuck is going on?*

He kept trying, but each time he was cast away. He got more worried by the minute. His heart rate picked up and he had a feeling that something wicked was happening to her and he had to stop it now, before it took her over completely.

As he kept trying to get to her, to try and break the binds the witch had placed on him, he was being thrown back. First the mind block Gina had, then the spell the witch cast on him. He was getting more and more frustrated, panicked, and angry by the minute. Then he heard her scream out, he heard her scream Victor's name. He became silent, pissed, and unsure of what he was even hearing. He couldn't comprehend it.

A wave of magical energy, magical power came blasting through the air. It hit the bars of the door that held him, rattling them, but when it hit him, he could feel it was Gina, feel her power, it was amplified a thousand times more powerful than he ever remembered feeling. It shattered his shackles, freeing his hands and feet. He stood, hearing her screams and he ran at the bars that caged him. They had not been shattered, but they had been shaken. He was chanting to himself, fueling himself, getting in attack mode. He was pleading with the powers that be, to take him out of here, to take him to where he could help his loved one.

His eyes closed, he was willing it to happen, willing it to take him, to forget about the rules that apply and send him out of there through time and space. He felt that nothing else mattered but this moment, this wish, and this spell. He was powerful. He was from a line of magical beings transcending millennia. He had not even realized that he was floating, he was spinning, the witches spell that had been cast on his mouth was gone. His thoughts became a vocal chanting and did not even realize it. The air around him was moving with him as he spun in place.

Then with a flash of lightning, he was gone from the cell. He opened his eyes to see streaks of light, streaks of space and time flying past him. Then it all slowed, almost to a complete stop, as he prepared himself to do battle with the witches.

Another flash and his feet hit the ground. He turned firing energy balls at the witches, but they were nowhere to be found. He was shooting into the dark, into the night. When he felt a hand wrap around his ankle, an energy ball appeared in his hand and as he looked downward, at the thing he was about to annihilate, he gasped as if being sucker punched. *It couldn't be, could it?* "Aldrik, honey, is that you?"

He could barely make out the mumbling coming from him, but as he fell to his knees, he could see that he was alive, barely. He was not regenerating like he should be. *Maybe it was the witches' hit man? Maybe he had done something to him?* But tears filled his eyes as he watched his love struggling, trying to tell him something.

"Blood!"

Demetri knew exactly what he had to do, and as he was sitting on the ground, he lifted Aldrik up just a bit, so he could get his neck to his mouth. His heart was racing, so he knew that if Aldrik could, he would hear his heart, smell his blood.

He felt the teeth sink into his skin, felt the connection of the teeth into his artery. He could feel Aldrik's tongue on his skin, feel his lips closing the gap between his mouth and the air. He was sucking down his blood, and as he did, Demetri could feel himself becoming dizzy. He had not done this before, as Aldrik had never asked nor needed him to. But as he lay here, being drained, he knew that the one word from Aldrik had been a plea. Blood, so he would not die. Blood, so he could regenerate. Blood, so that the demon inside him could be fueled back to life, bringing his lover back to life with it. Blood was being spilled so his world, his way of life would remain intact. As he lay in the arms of his loved one, his blood being drank, he looked upward and smiled. He knew it couldn't be, but he could swear there was a Blood Moon shining brightly above him.

Chapter Sixty-Three

As soon as Victor was standing on the rocks of the shoreline, he could hear the screams of Gina. He could hear her inside his head. He knew she was in trouble and he had to get to her. He had been around far too long to not know she had saved him. *Somehow, the little witch had pulled something out of her hat and saved me. I should be dead. Actually, I was dead, but she had pulled out some serious magic and saved me. Now she needed me to do the same for her. I am no magical being, but I am a warrior and I can do this for her, for the master.*

He had learned from his brief stint hanging from the cliff's edge that he would not be able to get to her by climbing up, so he would have to go around. So he took off, jumping from rock to rock, trying to get to a safe place and as he ran, he could see the water out on the lake, displaced and moving as if running with him. It must have been the beast he had seen, the thing they call Nessie. He had seen many things over his lifetime, but this one was honestly one he had thought only to be myth. He had said this earlier with the Durward, but now he found himself marveling at the wonder of it all. What a remarkable, magical, mystery driven world they all lived in. So many people lived their lives not getting to experience anything magical and if they did, they would just chalk it up to nerves, or try and debunk what had happened. If only they knew the truth.

He made his way to a rugged, less intense area of the cliff, one he felt he could manage to navigate safely. Grabbing onto the rocks he began to pull himself upward, one rock at a time. Gina needed him and he had to get to her. She fueled his determination. Those crones would rue the day they got between the master and Gina. Making his way onto the hidden path along the cliff, he eased his way down towards the entrance to the witch's chambers. He was on guard for the Durward because he, quite frankly, didn't know if he could tangle another round with him on this tiny ledge. If he was going to have to do battle with the Durward, it would have to be in the open or, at the very least, a room where he could gain some vantage on him.

Listening carefully at the entrance, he did not hear anything that made him think it was being guarded. Peeking his head around, he saw a tunnel, one that was long, with dark patches in between the torched lit areas. He began to carefully head into the tunnel, senses alert, body ready for anything that might jump out at him. It was usually him doing the stalking, but in this instance, he knew that he was the prey. He was the one in the lion's den, body drenched in blood, just begging to be devoured.

As he walked the length of the tunnel, he found that it curved and went further, deeper into the cliff. It was well hidden beneath the castle remains. How long these two had been here was anyone's guess. After what seemed like a long time, he was just about to give up, thinking he had missed a door or corridor that would have taken him to the witch's lair, then he heard her. It was Gina, she was yelling for him.

Taking off into a full run, he quickly made his way towards her voice. She was panicked, he could tell by her tone. When he reached the entrance, he slowed so he could take inventory of what he was actually dealing with. It would do no one any good if he were to go in there outnumbered and get himself killed. What he saw next was an amazing site to behold.

The Durward advanced at Gina, but she was somehow holding him at bay with her hand outstretched towards him. The two other witches were using their staffs to shoot the same bolts of energy in which they had used on him back at the hotel. But as it came at her, there seemed to be an invisible energy field protecting her as the lightning bolts were repelled. *How in the world is she doing this?*

"You can't defeat us? Why are you trying? We are not going to let you out of here, not with it."

"I'll be damned if you think you are going to keep me here against my will. I am leaving, and as you can see, you won't be able to stop me."

"We can't allow you to leave, we can't. Our entire existence has been built around this day, this time in question, and that baby you are carrying inside you."

Victor's eyes widen in shock and bewilderment. *This had to be the master's plan. This had to be it. When Gina was beside him at the mansion in Tulsa, he must have sensed it inside her. He knew that the vessel has impregnated the witch and she was carrying his offspring. That's it. That is the plan.* Victor smiled widely, happy to know what was happening. He was brought back to the here and now by the crackling of the lightning-like energy bolts and the talking taking place in the room next to him.

He had to do something, he had to help. Stepping inside, he quickly made his way over to where the Durward was stuck in limbo, as if he had hit a brick wall and was still trying to walk through it. Running up behind it, he raised his leg in the air and brought it heavily down onto the back of the knee, as the Durward buckled, falling down onto the floor, his head, hitting the wall of energy, the metal mask making a noise of a braking freight train. Gina swung her hand that she had been holding out at the thing to one side, sending it flying across the room.

"Victor! You are alive!"

"That I am, thanks to you," he said, as she looked at him briefly with a confused look on her face.

"Now, for you two," she said, turning back to the sisters, her face with a look her friends would say they had never seen before. There was a determination in her eyes, a mother's protective spark kicking in.

Behind them, the Durward had gotten to his feet, grabbed his blade and was coming at Victor, the blade already swinging in the air.

Victor had no time to react, but Gina without turning waved her hand and sent the Durward flying backward against the wall. "Now sit," she said angrily. The Durward, was on the floor, unable to move or pick himself up off the ground. Victor looked on at her in awe.

Athdara had been trying to make her way to the door which led to the cell that held Demetri. She needed to feed off of him. She needed his power to be able to defeat this hormone, enraged witch.

But Gina was having none of it. Raising both hands outward toward the sisters, she squeezed her hands shut, stopping them in their tracks. "You will not harm me or my baby. How dare you think you can do this? You live in the past. You dwell on things long gone. How sad and pathetic. We have a new day coming, a new magical era, one that doesn't involve relics like you."

"You can't kill us, we are already dead."

"I don't need to kill you because you can't stop me from walking out of here. You will stand where you are, or I will bring this cliff down on you both, burying you alive. So you decide, you wicked fucking bitches, do you want to spend eternity laying under a mountain, or are you going to chalk it up to a bad day and let me walk out of here."

"You know we will come for you. We have to. Your baby is the power that brings our reality back into this world. Your baby is the salvation for magical beings," Arabel pleaded with her.

"Well, you do what you have to, but you are warned. I am done playing fucking games with you. If I see your faces again, I will know you made the wrong decision and I will find a way to wipe you both off the face of this planet. I feel the power flowing through me and it is amazing. I wouldn't tempt fate if I were you," Gina said, as she walked over to Victor, who did not quite believe what he was hearing or seeing. Grabbing his hand, she walked out of the witch's lair and into the tunnel.

"A baby?" Victor asked of her.

"So it seems. I am going to need you more than ever. It seems my baby is going to be an attraction for all things evil. You can't let anything happen to me or it. I mean it Victor. I am afraid. I am afraid of what even the good ones will do if they find out about this baby. I don't know yet if this is a good or bad thing, but I just know I have to find out."

"Nothing is going to happen to you, either of you. I won't allow it. If I can't handle it, I think you can."

Making their way out of the tunnel and into the night sky, they headed away from the castle ruins and the two witches. But Gina and Victor both knew the witches would not stop trying to get to the baby growing inside her. They would use everything in their arsenal to get it. They also knew that the witches were not the only ones that would be coming for this baby. The entire supernatural world will feel its presence.

Chapter Sixty-Four

Athdara and Arabel were still reeling from what had happened. Durward was just able to move and pick himself up from the ground. They knew it meant that Gina must be far away by now. Her magic and its strength were now fading in her absence.

Athdara knew she would need the male witch's strength if she were going to take on Gina and win the baby. She headed in a fury back to the dungeon where she had him waiting. She would drain him until there was nothing left of him.

"How dare she think she can thwart our plans? I will take your powers and show her what a real witch is made of," Athdara said, as she headed to the door of Demetri's cell. When she arrived, she was dumbstruck.

"Impossible. It cannot be. No one has ever escaped our dungeon. Arabel! Arabel!" she yelled, screaming for her sister to come help her. But she did not. She didn't even answer her back.

Frustrated and angry, she headed back into the main chambers where she had left her. "Arabel, what the…" Her voice trailed off as she was standing there looking at her sister and a beautiful creature of a man.

"Who are you to dare come into our home without permission?"

"Silence witch or it will be your last."

"Awe, I see you now, I see you for what is behind the human mask."

"Then you know very well what I am capable of," Bastiquil said, as he looked on with curiosity and a bit of impatience. "Where is the female witch, Gina? I can smell her, sense her presence here."

"You are too late. She is gone. You have created quite a powerful little witch in her. It is giving her power beyond power, feeding her, and it feeding off of her. She will have everything evil in this world stalking her for that baby."

"And it will find the army of hell, my army, defending them both. Anyone who even tries will meet a fate they will never forget."

"Oh please. You think you scare us. We know what you are. We know what you claim to the world to be. You try and frighten with stories of hell, of a devil, of being a demon. But we know where you truly come from and it isn't a place these humans have come to fear from a two-thousand-year-old written text with promises of fire and brimstone. We know what realm you come from, what you are capable of, and most importantly, what your limitations are. Who do you think we are," Athdara spat at him.

Bastiquil smiled at her, a big, bright smile. "I'm impressed by you. But you seem to think you know something about me that simply isn't true. Try my patience again witch and it will be your last. I smell the death on you, but you forget death is what I deal in. I can make your death a much more miserable existence than it is right now. So you would do well to bite your tongue off than say another cross word to me. You are brave, powerful, and wise witches, but if you think for one second that you will lay hands on this baby, then you are mad, completely mad. It will not happen."

"We all want the same things, for magic to rule once again, for evil to live freely, without constraint. We all want those beautiful creatures to be restored back to this world, the ones who are either in hiding or in banishment. They deserve to live once again among us. They deserve for their story to be told. These humans think that they know large creatures, with their museums of large bones, of large reptiles, but these creatures are larger than their towering buildings."

"Silence witch! I care not for what you want, or what this haggard thing of a sister wants. You will not rule this land. It will have one ruler and that is me, Bastiquil."

"So you put us at odds then. Such a pity, our powers together would have rivaled any on earth. But if this is your decision, then leave our home, leave this place. When we meet again, it will be as enemies," Athdara said.

"You make the mistake of thinking we were ever friends," Bastiquil smiled at them both.

"Just know, we have dealt with your kind before, and can again."

"You can try witch, you can try," Bastiquil said, and turned to walk away. Walking toward the open air of night, he could feel them. His beloved Victor and the witch were not far ahead. He could feel the baby growing inside her. A part of him grew inside her. His heir to the world he is going to create, his empire.

With each step he took, his thoughts went to visions of things to come. And with it, came destruction, a world on its knees, begging for mercy. It will take time, but he had nothing   other   than   time,   time   to   kill.

Made in the USA
Columbia, SC
24 June 2023